Lost Innocence

Susan Lewis is the bestselling author of twenty-two novels. She is also the author of *Just One More Day*, a moving memoir of her childhood in Bristol. She lives in France. Her website address is www.susanlewis.com

Acclaim for Susan Lewis

'Spellbinding! . . . you just keep turning the pages, with the atmosphere growing more and more intense as the story leads to its dramatic climax'
Daily Mail

'A multi-faceted tear jerker' *heat*

'Deliciously dramatic and positively oozing with tension, this is another wonderfully absorbing novel from the *Sunday Times* bestseller Susan Lewis . . . Expertly written to brew an atmosphere of foreboding, this story is an irresistible blend of intrigue and passion, and the consequences of secrets and betrayal' *Woman*

'One of the best around' *Independent on Sunday*

'Sad, happy, sensual and intriguing' *Woman's Own*

'Mystery and romance *par excellence*' *Sun*

'We use the phrase honest truth too lightly: it should be reserved for books – deeply moving books – like this' Alan Coren

Also by Susan Lewis

A Class Apart
Dance While You Can
Stolen Beginnings
Darkest Longings
Obsession
Vengeance
Summer Madness
Last Resort
Wildfire
Chasing Dreams
Taking Chances
Cruel Venus
Strange Allure
Silent Truths
Wicked Beauty
Intimate Strangers
The Hornbeam Tree
The Mill House
A French Affair
Missing
Out of the Shadows

Just One More Day, A Memoir

Susan Lewis

Lost Innocence

arrow books

Published by Arrow Books 2010

2 4 6 8 10 9 7 5 3 1

First published in Great Britain in 2009 by
Arrow Books
Random House, 20 Vauxhall Bridge Road,
London SW1V 2SA

www.rbooks.co.uk

Addresses for companies within The Random House Group Limited can be found at: www.randomhouse.co.uk/offices.htm

The Random House Group Limited Reg. No. 954009

A CIP catalogue record for this book
is available from the British Library

ISBN 9780099525660

The Random House Group Limited makes every effort to ensure that the papers used in its books are made from trees that have been legally sourced from well-managed and credibly certified forests. Our paper procurement policy can be found at:
www.rbooks.co.uk/environment

Typeset in Palatino by Palimpsest Book Production Ltd,
Grangemouth, Stirlingshire
Printed and bound in Great Britain by
CPI Cox & Wyman, Reading RG1 8EX

To James, with love

Acknowledgements

Having received so much advice and support during the research for this book it's hard to know where to begin with the thank yous when everyone's input was so enthusiastic and invaluable. However, I think my biggest debt of gratitude must go to Ian Kelcey of Kelcey and Hall, who not only provided the inspiration for Jolyon Crane, but who so patiently guided me through the process of bringing a rape case to trial. If I have made any errors, please know they are entirely mine. PC Carl Gadd of the Avon and Somerset Constabulary is my hero – thank you so much, Carl, for your incredible support and all the vital information you provided regarding arrest and interrogation procedures. Also from the Avon and Somerset Constabulary I'd like to thank PC Liz Cole of the Sexual Abuse Investigation Team for so much detailed information on the role of a SAIT officer. From the Crown Prosecution Service I would like to thank Mark Barton for helping me to understand the rudiments of the CPS role at the outset of a prosecution. And last but not least for this section, a big thank you to Melissa Cullum at Corporate Communications of the Avon & Somerset Constabulary.

My love and thanks go once again to my dear friend Lesley Gittings, who gave so generously of her time and her wide knowledge of Somerset to help me situate the book. More love and thanks to an exceptionally talented sculptor Clare Tupman, whose strikingly beautiful art provided the inspiration for Alicia's sculptures. Please go to www.claretupmansculpture.co.uk to see for yourselves. Also to Jake Tupman for his highly entertaining and energetic tour of Bruton, plus the invaluable flashes of insight into the minds of young men his age. A huge thank you to Lisa Trowbridge, a dear friend and wonderful vet who provided such helpful advice. And to David Anderson, the Bridge Master of the Clifton Suspension Bridge for sharing his expert knowledge of this exceptional landmark.

Once again I want to thank my wonderful editor Susan Sandon for all her amazing support and insightful advice. Also Georgina Hawtrey-Woore, Kate Elton, Rob Waddington, Trish Slattery, Louisa Gibbs, Louise Campbell, David Parrish and everyone else on the Arrow team. And of course my dear friend and agent, Toby Eady.

Lastly, a very special thank you to Rachel Herrington whose generous donation to Autism Speaks resulted in her name being used for Alicia's dearest friend in the book.

Chapter One

Nothing ever happened in Holly Wood. Buried like a plum in a pudding, in the heart of the Somerset countryside, it was no more than a sleepy backwater, looped on three sides by a meandering river, and connected to its neighbouring villages by sweeping grassy glades, and a tangle of country lanes that flowed through the hedgerows like a loose ramble of veins. It could boast no more than a few hundred dwellings, some dating back to the sixteenth century, several to Victorian times, and others, such as the avenue of bungalows that curved like a jaunty tail around the southern outskirts of the village, to the sixties. Lately a uniformed arrangement of new builds had sprouted up in what used to be the Bluebell Field, next to the Bruton Road. This estate stood huddled like a batch of new boys at the gates of an old school, still too gauche to be accepted into the fold, but eagerly and shyly waiting its turn.

Holly Wood's high street was both quaint and banal, starting on one side with a terrace of four picture-book cottages, followed by Tom Sebastian's car-repair shop and taxi service, then came the Friary with its mock-Tudor frontage and swinging neon sign that lit up the letters O P and N when the fish and chip bar was serving. Next to it was the old Midland Bank which had long since closed its doors, then came Neeve's, the village shop, that used to double as a post office until recent cuts. Now the locals had to drive four miles into Bruton for their stamps, pensions and parcels, while those who didn't have cars either gladly accepted lifts or rode the number eighty-five bus along a circuitous, scenic route into the medieval city of Wells. After the shop was the turning into Holly Way where the village's most exclusive residences backed on to the river, then came St Gregory's, the crumbling old Norman church that sat snugly amongst its clutter of tilted and faded gravestones, like a crusty grandfather watching over his sleeping brood. The main street was sliced down the middle by a narrow stretch of green where Holly Wood's obelisk of a war memorial and a couple of benches with shiny brass plaques were like sentries at each end of a lovingly tended bed of impatiens, or marigolds, or cyclamen, depending on the time of year – and what Mimi the florist had in stock.

Opposite the church was a long swathe of garden that belonged to the Traveller's Rest, while the pub itself, whose cosy interior was dominated by a large stone fireplace and an abundance of crooked black timber beams, was on the corner of The Close – a narrow, leafy street that ran down to the riverbank, then curved round to offer an alternative road out of the village. On the opposite corner was a high brick wall surrounding a piece of wasteland, next to which was a boarded-up charity shop with the soaring steeple of an old clock tower rising above it like an oversized magician's hat, then came Mimi's flower emporium with its colourful hanging baskets and highly prized Interflora franchise. After that there were a few more flat-fronted cottages and a small rank of empty shops that used to belong to Stan the butcher, Goldie the greengrocer and Felicity the seamstress. Now, Felicity ran up curtains and designed the odd wedding dress at home, while Stan presided over the meat counter at the local Tesco and Goldie laboured for a landscape gardener.

While Holly Wood was definitely a pleasant village with its enticing cobbled enclaves and a claim to having once given refuge to a fleeing King Charles – the hiding place itself was so secret that even the locals didn't seem to know where it actually was – it wasn't appealing enough to tempt many tourists from the county's more exotic offerings, such as those at Glastonbury, Wells and Cheddar. However, the village sign, about a mile outside the village itself, was often photographed by venturesome ramblers and holidaymakers, who seemed to enjoy the idea of stumbling upon such a quaint little signpost with lofty and glamorous pretensions in the heart of the English countryside.

Though the Holly Wood residents were, on the whole, a friendly bunch, they generally preferred tourists to take their snapshots and be on their way, because they didn't much welcome being stared at, or asked which films they'd starred in, or where George Clooney lived, followed by snorts of laughter, as if the joke had never been made before. In fact, they didn't much care for being fussed about by outsiders at all, especially those who tried to change things, or tell them how to run their lives. Some interference they couldn't avoid, such as bossy county councillors with their befuddling recycling rules and even more bizarre pots of yellow paint to prevent parking in the high street – an imposition that was universally and rigorously ignored. The residents of Holly Wood prided themselves on being a successful self-regulating community with a vigilant Neighbourhood Watch scheme; a highly efficient chauffeur service for the elderly and infirm – paid for by weekly door-to-door collections carried out by the Guides and Brownies – and an environmental awareness (once the confusion about bins was resolved) that had earned them some very high praise in *Fosse Way Magazine* and *The Buzz*, two oracles of great local standing.

On the day Alicia Carlyle drove towards the village, a lone car weaving through the lush green flow of the countryside, with a small suitcase and laptop computer on the back seat of her second-hand Renault, and a rawness in her heart too tender to touch, there were no indications of what was to come. The summery stillness was as smooth and unshakable as a painting, and she was only focused on trying to empty her mind of what she'd left behind. What awaited her, after a prolonged absence – not of her choosing – could be worse, but she wasn't going to think about that either. She was simply going to continue her journey, keeping her eyes on the road and her thoughts skimming over easy issues such as the need to pick up some milk when she reached the village, and how wonderfully familiar and welcoming everything looked in the generous sparkle of the sunlight.

Alicia was tall, very slim, with long, crinkly fair hair that flowed down her back in a tangle of bouncy coils. Her eyes were pale blue – as clear and inviting, Craig used to say, as a tropical sea before it reached the shore. 'They make me want to wade in so I can get even closer to you and maybe find out what's hidden in the darkest depths.' She smiled as she recalled the words, then her lips shook and tightened as grief threw its black cloak over the memory. She hadn't had any secrets back then, and as far as she knew nor had he.

Alicia's large, ruby red mouth formed a vital part of her beautiful smile, as infectious as the ring of her girlish laugh. Though she'd turned thirty-nine a week ago, thanks to the events of the past two years – the last six months in particular – she felt closer to fifty. She'd acquired several lines in recent weeks, and plenty of shadows, both inside and out. Today she was dressed in her usual get-up of skinny jeans with rips in the knees, a long white shirt girdled by a low-slung belt, and a hand-embroidered waistcoat, plus her trademark man's cap, to top it off – a look highly approved of by Darcie, her fashionista of a twelve-year-old daughter.

Alicia had grown up in Holly Wood. After leaving to take up her place at Oxford Brookes to study the history of art, she'd always visited regularly, spending long weekends with her mother, as well as summer holidays and every Christmas. This hadn't changed when she'd met Craig and they'd married. The only Christmas they'd missed was the year Darcie was born, when

Monica had come to London, to help take care of five-year-old Nathan.

Alicia would never have got through the first eighteen months of Darcie's life without her mother's support, and nor would Craig. The terror that they might lose their precious baby girl at any moment had made it impossible for them to carry on functioning as a normal family until the mysterious virus attacking her tiny heart was diagnosed and treated, or gave up of its own accord. Monica had been there throughout, calm and steady, throwing reins around rampant fears, and always keeping their hopes alive even in the darkest hours. And, just as importantly, Monica had been wonderful with Nat, making him feel special and the centre of her world while his mummy and daddy were at the hospital, willing his little sister to stay with them.

The mystery virus never had been identified, but these days no one would ever guess at Darcie's difficult start in life. She was the picture of health, as lively and gregarious as any girl her age could be, with a properly pounding heart and an overly developed sense of her own importance. Merely thinking of her was enough to warm Alicia all the way through and when she added her handsome young son, now seventeen, to the mix she was reminded of how very much she had to be grateful for.

Now, as she turned from the main A37 road, away from the distant view of Glastonbury Tor, to start winding towards Holly Wood, Alicia's insides were unbearably tense. She wondered how much the village might have changed since the last time she'd seen it, while knowing it almost certainly wouldn't have, because it never did. It was one of the things she loved most about it, and also what she was dreading.

She'd never have stopped coming if her mother hadn't insisted. She'd have found the courage to brave out the mess they were all in, but Monica couldn't bear the rift that had developed between Alicia and her older brother, Robert, who still lived in the village with his wife, Sabrina, and her flighty, exquisitely lovely young daughter, Annabelle. Though neither Robert nor Alicia was to blame for what had caused the rift in their family, whenever Alicia was around Monica felt forced to choose sides, without ever doing so. When she became ill with cancer Alicia had given up arguing. The stress would only worsen her mother's condition, and loving her as much as she did she wanted her around for many more years to come, even if she wasn't allowed to visit her.

Monica had died a year ago. By then she was in a hospice about ten miles from Holly Wood, so Alicia had been able to visit without upsetting her. She'd stayed with her right to the end, holding her hands, smoothing her face and swearing on her children's lives that she forgave her for pushing her away.

'I didn't mean to exclude you,' Monica croaked, tears rolling from her jaundiced eyes. 'You know I love you with all my heart, don't you?'

'Of course I do,' Alicia assured her. 'It was an impossible situation. You were right in the middle . . .'

'But it wasn't your fault. I should have been there for you.'

'It doesn't matter, Mum. I survived and it was important for you to be able to go on living in the house.'

Monica didn't argue with that. She couldn't, when Holly Wood was the only home she'd known for the past forty-two years – the nineteen before that had been spent growing up in a neighbouring village.

During the final days, at her mother's request, Alicia had brought Nat and Darcie to say their goodbyes. It had been heart-rending to watch Darcie, barely eleven at the time, sobbing as she clung to her grandmother's bony hand begging her not to go, but harder still was the way fifteen-year-old Nat, who'd always adored his grandmother, had refused to come any closer than the end of the bed. His pale, handsome face had shown his grief, but the fact that Monica hadn't wanted to include his father in her final goodbyes was a slight he couldn't forgive.

Craig hadn't come to the funeral, either. He and Alicia had agreed it would be for the best if he stayed away. Alicia knew that Nat was still baffled by the decisions his parents had taken, but to explain them would have hurt and confused him even further, and no one, least of all Alicia, wanted to do that.

So this was the first time since her mother's funeral that she was going to set foot in the village where she and Robert had grown up, her mother had organised all the charity events and her father, and grandfather before him, had been the local GP. As children they'd been devoted to their father, who'd had the magical knack of making everything all right when the end of the world was closing in fast, and turning small achievements into the greatest triumphs with his booming laughter and ready praise. Losing him when they were still in their teens had opened Robert's and Alicia's eyes to how randomly cruel life could be. Robert's realisation of this was particularly acute, as their father had drowned trying to save his son from a freak riptide on holiday in Spain. Though more than twenty years had passed since that terrible time, still hardly a day went by when Alicia didn't think about her father, and she knew Robert did too. During the past couple of years she'd often found herself wondering how he might have reacted to the events that had torn his family apart. How different their world might be now if he were still with them.

The strangeness inside her began sharpening and softening as the lazy sprawl of the village came into view. It was painful to see, yet wonderful too. Beside it the new estate sat basking in the sunshine, seeming too gaudy and polished next to the crumbling old cluster of buildings, like a hopeful tart on the doorstep of a stately pile, as Craig had once described it.

The high street was deserted as she drove in, no sign of anyone even in the pub garden, as far as she could make out. News of her return would spread soon enough though, since her decision to call into the shop to pick up the milk she'd forgotten to get at Sainsbury's on her way out of London would be bound to speed things along.

The quaint little store hadn't changed much – the same tinkling bell over the door, the familiar smell of liquorice and tobacco, and shelves crammed full of jars, boxes and cans dating back to the 1970s. The cold counter was in its usual place, stuffed with Wiltshire hams, sides of country-cured bacon, pressed loaves of locally made corned beef, and succulent rounds of cheese from Cheddar. The till had clearly been updated, but the newspapers were still displayed on a rack in front of the ice-cream freezer, and an oval island in the middle of the shop remained home to everything from Tetley's tea bags, to tubes of Germolene, to disposable barbecues in silver-foil trays. What used to be the post office was now a large cold store offering freshly made baps, Cornish pasties, quiches, Scotch eggs and an impressive selection of soft drinks. There was even, Alicia noticed, a separate fridge for wine, and two bistro tables sporting tea menus chalked on little blackboards propped up between the sugar bowl and the condiments: Holly Wood's answer to café society.

As Mrs Neeve came bustling through from the back, Alicia helped herself to a half-litre carton of milk and took out her purse to pay.

'That'll be sixty p,' Mrs Neeve announced, clearly not recognising her right away.

Alicia handed over the money and smiled as Mrs Neeve's expression turned from bland to curious to outright astonishment and pleasure. 'Alicia?' she said, tilting her head to one side. 'Yes, it is. Well, I'll be damned. There's a surprise.

Never knew you was coming. How are you, my dear?'

'I'm fine,' Alicia assured her. 'How are you?'

'Oh, you know, mustn't grumble, but it's been that hot these last few days . . . On a visit, are you? How long are you staying?' Her voice darkened. 'I'm really sorry about your loss. I know how close you were, so it must have been hard for you these past . . .'

'Thank you,' Alicia said softly. 'I see the post office is gone. I expect you miss running it.'

'Oh, I do, that's true, but there was nothing we could do. Not that we didn't fight to hang on to it, mind you. You might even have seen us on the news. You know what Sabrina's like when she starts up one of her campaigns. She nearly always wins, God bless her, whether she's sorting out something for the old folk, or protecting the wildlife, or trying to save our little-biddy old post office. She kept us going a lot longer than some, though, because this was the second battle we fought. You might remember how we won the first one a few years ago. There was no winning this one, though. Their minds was made up, they had to make cuts and we was for the chop no matter what. I think Sabrina took it hard. She doesn't like losing, and what with her not really being herself at the time . . . She seems a lot better now, I'm glad to say. Or she did the last time I saw her, but you know what it's like, one day up, the next down. I don't think they ever found out what was wrong with her, did they? I was only saying to Mimi the other day, she takes on too much in one go, that's her trouble. She should pace herself a bit more. Mind you, I don't know where half of us would be without her. We got in a right pickle when we was left to organise the summer fete ourselves thanks to her problem, and the harvest festival, and she still wasn't up to much come Christmas.'

Alicia was smiling politely, knowing she'd have to get used to hearing Sabrina's name, but wanting only to think of a suitable exit line without seeming rude.

'Listen to me rambling on,' Mrs Neeve clucked, 'and I haven't even asked about the children. They here too, are they? Be lovely to see them. I expect they've really grown up since the last time I saw them.'

'Probably too much,' Alicia told her wryly. 'I'll be sure to send them in when they arrive. I'd better go now, thanks for the milk,' and before the gossipy old soul could draw breath to lavish any more praise on the redoubtable Sabrina, or ask again how long she, Alicia, was staying, she beat a hasty retreat. She knew that by the time she reached her mother's house news of the surprise visit would be buzzing through the Holly Wood phone lines like currents of electricity, perking up everyone's interest. They'd probably all have an idea as to why she'd turned up now, some would even speak with the kind of authority that suggested they had inside info, but they didn't, because she hadn't contacted anyone before coming. For a while she'd toyed with the idea of getting in touch with her oldest and dearest friend, Rachel Herrington, but had decided in the end to wait until she was installed before letting Rachel know she was back. Rachel would feel obliged to take time off to greet her, and as the only vet for miles around, it was time her friend could ill afford.

Alicia steered the car around the village green, as the locals called it, in spite of its narrowness and lack of grass, and felt a lump starting to form in her throat. Would she be able to face driving into The Close, then going into her mother's house without her mother being there? She had done this once, after the funeral, but the place had been so crowded with mourners that the emptiness had had no real chance to register.

Now, after avoiding it for a year, she was dreading what she might find; broken windows, mice, mould, a hopelessly overgrown garden? She wondered how she could have allowed her mother's pride and joy to go to rack and ruin. She felt so much shame that she almost braked to stop herself going any further.

A few minutes later she was still sitting in the car outside the Old Coach House, staring at the recently mown lawn and baskets of fresh flowers hanging either side of the black front door. In days gone by this was where the carriages of travellers used to be stored while their gentrified owners rested at the local hostelry. Her great-grandparents had turned it into a home which had undergone several internal changes down the years, but the outside, being listed, had never been altered, only restored. Now, its honey-coloured Hamstone walls, arched leaded windows and black slate roof were glistening wetly after a summer downpour a few minutes ago. It made the place look slick and new. The ornamental carriage wheel beside the door, appeared as polished as the brass knocker, and the yellow flowering clematis roaming its way over the climbing trellis was as healthily abundant as it had ever been in her mother's day.

It was as though someone was living there, or expecting her, but that couldn't be. The only explanation she could think of was that Robert had decided to take care of the place, or perhaps paid someone else to do it.

Feeling more tension building inside her, she reached for her bag and got out of the car. In the warmth of the July day the scent of damp earth mingling with roses immediately assailed her. Some of it was coming from the hybrid teas that lined the garden path, the rest was wafting over from next door, where Jerry Bright's prize blooms were as exquisite as any rose could be. He'd installed a new pergola over his front gate, Alicia noticed, which was covered in a vivid pink climber, and next to it was a fancy little free-standing mailbox that his sister, Emily, who lived in one of the waterfront bungalows, had no doubt chosen for him, and probably came to buff up every day.

Alicia walked around the car and went to push open her own gate. Though its hinges creaked, it wasn't in need of a lick of paint, nor did the paving stones of the path seem particularly troubled by weeds. She gazed up at the old cedar tree that dominated one side of the garden and immediately caught flashes of long-ago picnics in its mighty shade, and daredevil climbs into its lofty limbs.

She could hear echoes of her and Robert laughing as she approached the front door, and her father calling out for them to take care.

She rummaged in her bag for the key. She didn't really think her mother was inside, but her heart was thumping so hard that her hands were shaking, and in spite of coming this far she still wasn't entirely sure she had the courage to go in.

'Alicia! Is that you?'

Starting, she turned round. Across the road, where the stables used to be, was a gaily painted terrace of Victorian cottages, rose pink, sea-foam green, sky blue, primrose yellow, with a row of garages further along towards the river, each one coloured to match the house it belonged to. Coming out of the rose-pink cottage was a plump, curly-haired woman of Alicia's age, with a cheery smile and noticeable limp.

'It is you,' she cried happily. 'How lovely to see you.'

Alicia started back down the path to greet her. 'Cathy,' she said affectionately. 'It's lovely to see you too.'

'I wondered if you might come,' Cathy said, taking Alicia's hands and gazing directly into her eyes. 'When I heard about Craig . . . I'm so sorry.'

'Thank you,' Alicia whispered. Six months on and it still felt like yesterday. She swallowed and tried to sound bright as she said, 'How are you?'

Cathy's dark eyes remained mournful pools of compassion. 'More to the point, how are you?' she insisted. 'It must have been a terrible shock. In your shoes, I don't know what I'd have done.'

Alicia shook her head.

'How have the children taken it?'

'Hard, but we're getting there.'

'Are they with you? How long are you staying? You know, if there's anything I can do . . . Dad's always at home these days, and I'm only a couple of miles away.'

'Thank you,' Alicia said again.

'Alicia!' This time the voice was coming from up the street. It was Maggie Cox, landlady of the Traveller's Rest, and one of her mother's oldest friends. 'As soon as I heard you were here,' Maggie said, enveloping Alicia in an affectionate hug, 'I said to Andy, I have to go and see how she is. You know we're all here for you, don't you, sweetie? It's how your mum would want it, so it's how it'll be.'

Alicia's defences were starting to fold. They didn't know the real truth, they couldn't, and because they were so kind and loyal she wished she didn't have to deceive them. 'How is Andy?' she asked. 'The last I heard you two were going to open up a bar in Spain.'

'Oh, it'll happen one of these days,' Maggie assured her, 'when we have time to get round to it. Cathy, is that your Matthew I can hear crying?'

Cathy cocked an ear. 'Blimey, it is and all,' she replied, 'I'm getting as deaf as our dad,' and with a hasty squeeze of Alicia's hands and a reminder of where to find her, she took off back to her father's rose-pink cottage.

Chuckling, Maggie said, 'She's a good girl, that one. Too many kids by half, but her heart's in the right place.'

'How many does she have now?' Alicia asked.

'Little Matthew's her fourth. But what about your two? How are they? Bet your Nathan's turning into a handsome young fellow. How old is he now?'

'Seventeen.' The mention of her son softened her, seeming to remove the barbs from her tension.

Putting a hand to Alicia's cheek, Maggie said, 'It must have been terrible for you, coming out of the blue like that. When I heard, I said to Andy right then, I wonder if Alicia might come back here. I'm glad you did, my love. We can take care of you, the way your mother would want. I pop over to her grave, you know, every second Sunday, with flowers. Robert does too, when he's here, but I expect you know that. I said to Andy, they're probably from all of you, but Robert's here more, so it makes sense for him to take them on your behalf.'

Realising Maggie was making excuses for her failure to visit her mother's grave, Alicia felt her cheeks start to burn. 'I'll go myself in the next couple of days,' she assured her.

'Of course you will. I'll come with you if you like.'

'Thank you,' Alicia said, wondering how many times she had said this since she'd arrived.

At the sound of a car turning into the street they both looked round, and realising who it was, Alicia's heart gave a beat of pure joy.

Maggie's eyes were playful. 'Should have known she'd be here any second,' she commented. 'Always were inseparable, you two. Where one was, the other was sure to be found.'

Alicia's emotions were close to spilling over as

a racy-looking Honda pulled up behind her battered Renault. 'What on earth are you doing here?' she chided, as Rachel came round the car to embrace her, all flushed cheeks, dark shiny bob and crystalline green eyes. 'How did you know . . . ?'

'I know everything,' Rachel informed her, 'no thanks to you. I'd have been here sooner, but I'm afraid I had to resuscitate a hamster.'

'Sooner?' Alicia laughed. 'Your practice is at least twenty minutes away, and I haven't been here more than ten. Even the Holly Wood grapevine's not that good.'

'Don't you believe it. I had no fewer than five calls on my way here letting me know you'd hit town, but they weren't even close to stealing a lead on the one I got an hour ago telling me you were on your way.'

Alicia's expression turned knowing. 'Unless Holly Wood has installed its own watchtower,' she said, 'I'm guessing you were tipped off by one of my offspring.'

'Correct,' Rachel grinned. 'Hi Mags, sorry to ignore you . . .'

'Oh, don't mind me,' Maggie interrupted. 'I'm on my way now. Pop in later, the two of you. Drinks on me.'

'So why didn't you tell me yourself you were coming?' Rachel demanded, treating Alicia to a frank once-over as Maggie trotted back to the pub. 'You've lost weight,' she told her, 'and you're looking a bit peaky, but I guess that's hardly surprising. I'm sorry I haven't made it up to London since . . .'

'It's OK. I know how busy you are and I've coped.'

Rachel's eyes were showing her concern. 'You always do,' she said, 'but this time . . .'

'This time has been harder, it's true. There's more that I haven't told you about yet. The house . . .' As her voice faltered she pressed a hand to her mouth, and Rachel slipped an arm around her.

'Come on, let's go inside,' Rachel said softly. 'I guess you still have a key.'

Taking a breath, Alicia forced a smile and held it up. 'I think Robert must have been coming in,' she said, as they started along the path. 'The garden's in such good shape that someone must have been tending it. I feel terrible now that I haven't been for so long.'

Taking the key from her, Rachel inserted it in the lock and pushed the door wide. 'Welcome home,' she said gently.

Swallowing hard on more rising emotion, Alicia braced herself and stepped over the threshold into the spacious, flagstoned hall, where a wide wooden staircase with an intricately carved banister and rails mounted one exposed stone wall, and a large gilt-framed mirror covered the other. The coat rail, telephone table and shoe rack were exactly where they'd always been, as was the burgundy velveteen armchair, the hand-painted oriental vase with long stems of fake bamboo, and the small Victorian chest where the family had always deposited their keys when they came in. What hit her most forcefully, however, was the scent of sandalwood mingled with polish and something citrusy that was indefinably her mother. As the sense of loss welled up in her she closed her eyes and bit down hard on her lip. She knew very well that her mother wasn't going to rush out of the sitting room to greet her, but she longed for it so much she could almost believe it might happen.

'Someone's obviously been coming to clean the place,' she finally commented.

'And air it,' Rachel added.

Alicia continued to look around the hall, hearing echoes of voices, feet thundering on the stairs, music blaring from a bedroom, her mother banging about in the kitchen. All three doors opening off the hall were closed, and she wasn't entirely sure she wanted to go through any of them. The one at the foot of the stairs led into the small waiting room that used to serve her father's surgery beyond. After his death it had remained that way for several years until her mother had finally found the heart to turn the wing into a small study for herself, and a large playroom for the grandchildren.

The door at the end of the hall led into the kitchen, but it was the one to the right that Rachel was already opening. Alicia followed her into the sitting room where the low oak beams, inglenook fireplace with wood-burner, window seats, capacious dusky pink sofas and mismatched armchairs were like ghosts from the past simply biding their time, awaiting her return. It felt like a dream, a bizarrely timeless illusion. If she shut her eyes and opened them again she might see her mother kneeling at the hearth polishing her brasses, or plumping up a cushion, or standing at the window tidying the fold of a curtain. The unexpectedness of finding it like this was almost too much to bear. It was as though no time had passed since the awful day she and Robert had taken their mother to the hospice, but it had, and so much else had changed that it was hard to make sense of anything right now.

Rachel moved to stand in front of her, peering curiously into her eyes. Her comical concern brought a smile to Alicia's pale lips. This was something else that hadn't changed over the years, thank God, their friendship, and the understanding of one another that often required no words.

Alicia looked around again, taking in the amateurish watercolours she'd painted years ago of the village high street and war memorial; of Glastonbury Tor; the Somerset Levels; Bath Abbey; there was even one of the station at Castle Cary. What on earth had induced her to paint that, she wondered now. And why had her mother kept it? All the paintings she'd produced before leaving home, though, were here somewhere. Monica used to change them around from time to time, but pride of place, over the mantel, had always gone to her favourite, the humpback bridge that crossed the river into Holly Copse. As Alicia looked at it a faraway smile curved her lips. She was drifting back to a time when she'd hardly ever put her paints away. She didn't even own any now, unless there were some hidden in the attic. Her artistic efforts were focused on sculpture these days, witty or poignant pieces made of bronze and steel.

Coming to stand beside her, Rachel gazed at the painting too. It was twenty years or more since Alicia had last gone into the Copse, which was actually large enough to qualify as a wood. As young children it was where their father used to take them blackberrying in spring, or picnicking in summer, hunting for conkers in autumn, or collecting pine cones to decorate for Christmas. By night, in their vivid imaginations, it came alive with witches, fairies, hobgoblins, all kinds of terrifying monsters. It was the venue for school nature trails, and later, for teenage rites of passage. Many were the parties they'd attended there, while in the sixth form. Too much booze was regularly consumed, pot was smoked and both she and Rachel had experienced their first grown-up kisses in the nook below the tump known as Lovers' Dip. A couple of their friends had even lost their virginities there, or so they claimed.

'Do your children ever go there?' Alicia asked as Rachel gave a dreamy sigh.

'Less now than they used to,' Rachel answered. 'They're too old to see it as an adventure any more, and too young for the raves.'

Alicia smiled. Since Rachel and David had waited to start a family their eldest, Una, was the same age as Darcie, and Todd had only recently turned nine. 'So there are still parties?' she said, moving on across the room.

'From what I hear they've become one of the must-do events of the region. Apparently kids come from miles around these days. They've all got cars or motorbikes or some kind of transport; they even hightail it down from London by train, I'm told.'

With so many public and private schools within a twenty-mile radius of Holly Wood, there would never be a shortage of young people, Alicia was thinking, as she wandered into the dining area and pushed open the door to the kitchen. 'Shall we have some tea?' she suggested. 'Or wine, if you don't have to go back to work.'

Rachel grimaced. 'Great idea, but I'm afraid I didn't bring anything with me.'

'No problem. I've come prepared. It's all in the car.'

Rachel was suitably impressed. 'Then what are we waiting for?' she smiled. 'Let's go get the vino. I've taken the rest of the day . . .' She broke off as the telephone in the hall started to ring. Her eyes met Alicia's.

'You answer,' Alicia said. 'If it's Robert tell him . . .' *Tell him I'll never speak to him again as long as he's got that bitch living under his roof.* 'Tell him I'm not here.'

As Rachel started along the hall Alicia turned away. Her eyes were large and glassy and no longer focusing on her surroundings. They were eyes that wanted to forget what they'd seen, to erase the images that haunted them, but never could.

'Craig! Have you seen the time?' Alicia shouted. 'Come on, or we're all going to be late.'

'On my way,' he shouted back.

Alicia quickly returned to their smart, newly installed black granite and bleached-oak kitchen, where Darcie was perched on a stool at the centre island scoffing down Coco Pops while watching

GMTV on the flatscreen, and the kettle was whistling on the Aga, desperate to be taken off. Obliging, Alicia scalded some fresh mint leaves in a cup for herself, then doused a breakfast tea bag for Craig, while whisking freshly crisped slices of granary from the toaster, and swinging round to take some jam from the fridge.

It wasn't often they overslept, but this morning they had and now it was touch and go whether they'd get the children to school on time.

'What time's Daddy due in court, do you know?' Alicia asked Darcie.

Slurping on a generous spoonful of her favourite cereal, Darcie shook her head. Her wide, chocolate-brown eyes remained glued to the screen. Apparently whatever Andrew Castle had to say this morning was even more fascinating than the latest copy of *heat* that lay open, but discarded, next to her bowl. Knowing Craig wouldn't be impressed by the magazine, Alicia grabbed it and stuffed it into her capacious handbag. Rows were something they didn't need this morning.

'Hey!' Darcie protested. 'That's mine.'

'I'll give it back to you this evening,' Alicia told her, 'but you know what Dad thinks of it.'

'He's sooo old-fashioned,' Darcie grumbled.

'Go and put your hair up,' Alicia said.

'Can you do it? I brought the brush down.'

'There should be a please in there somewhere,' Alicia informed her, starting to shake out Darcie's silky blonde spirals, so like her own.

'A French plait, please,' Darcie said, passing her the brush.

'Do you have drama class after school today?'

'No, it's been cancelled, but Mrs Jay is going to give us a dance lesson in its place, so I'll still be finishing at five. Are you coming to pick me up?'

'No, Verity's mother is doing the afternoon runs this week. Which reminds me, you'd better call Verity and tell her we're running late.'

As Darcie went to unplug her mobile, Alicia stayed with her, still braiding her hair. At last Craig and Nathan were on their way down, their footsteps thundering on the stairs, their voices overlapping one another's as they kept up some kind of banter. By the time they reached the kitchen Craig was saying, '. . . so it was a no go because she didn't have enough currants in her cake.'

Nat was grinning. 'What does that mean?' he asked.

'That she wasn't fruity enough,' Craig answered, and Nat burst out laughing.

'Oliver said that?' he cried, referring to Craig's partner in chambers, who was better known for his stuffiness than any kind of risqué humour.

'I promise you, it's what he said,' Craig answered, laughing too, as he scooped the tea bag out of his cup. With his thick, jet-black hair, intense dark eyes and finely chiselled features, he was a strikingly handsome man whose height, at six feet two, could, at times, make him appear even more intimidating than the air of the highly successful QC that he was. This morning, in his dark Armani suit, with a crisp white shirt and a slate grey tie hanging loosely round the collar, he looked as rakish as a playboy who'd been on the tiles all night, since he'd clearly not yet had time to shave.

'That is such a brilliant line,' Nat, a virtual carbon

copy of his father, apart from the eyes, was saying, as he began spooning down the Weetabix his mother had already prepared. 'I've got to remember that. Not enough currants in her cake.'

'You're so sexist, you two,' Darcie informed them, as Alicia finished securing the plait. 'Is it still raining? If it is, we won't have games.'

'You'll need to take the bag anyway,' Alicia told her.

'Where is it?'

'In the hall, ready to go.'

'Great. Dad, you haven't forgotten that you're giving a talk to Upper Sixth tomorrow, have you?' she wanted to know.

'Of course not,' he assured her, taking his mobile from the charger. 'It's in my diary.'

'Only I don't want you embarrassing me by forgetting, or suddenly cancelling because some big case has come up.'

'I won't let you down,' he told her, pressing a kiss to her forehead. 'Will you be there?'

'*Duh*, I'm twelve, still in year eight,' she reminded him, 'but everyone will know you're my dad, so don't make life difficult for me by turning into a no-show. And don't tell too many jokes either, OK, because, I'm sorry, Dad, but you're soooo not funny.'

Alicia gave a splutter of laughter at Craig's comically hurt expression and after removing the cup from his hand, she replaced it with his briefcase, saying, 'You have to go, or Nat will be late. Shave in the car. What time are you due in court?'

Craig glanced at his watch. 'Just over an hour,' he grimaced. 'Come on son, let's move it.'

'Take your coats,' Alicia called after them, 'it's

freezing out there this morning. And watch out for ice on the roads.'

'Hang on, Dad,' Nat said, starting up the stairs, 'I have to get my laptop.'

Coming back to press a kiss to Alicia's lips, Craig said, 'I'll probably be late again tonight, so don't wait up.'

'Again?' she groaned. 'It was gone one when you came to bed.'

'It should be earlier than that tonight,' he assured her. 'I'll call and let you know.'

As he made to turn away she pulled him back and looked directly up into his eyes. She didn't have to tell him what was bothering her, he'd know without her having to voice her suspicions.

'I swear it's not what you think,' he said softly, 'and you have to stop doing this. It's over, and I don't want to have to keep telling you.'

'Do I look like a fool?' she murmured.

'Alicia, stop,' he growled. 'We don't have time for this now, and you know what a difficult case I'm on . . .'

'Fine, I'm sorry. It's just . . . I can't make myself . . .'

'I know, but you're wrong,' and sensing Darcie's eyes on them he pressed another kiss to Alicia's lips, gave his daughter a wink and disappeared along the hall.

'Nat,' he shouted, as he grabbed his overcoat. 'I'm parked right outside, so get a move on.'

'Right there,' Nat shouted back. 'Can I drive?'

'In your dreams.'

'You let me last week.'

Craig had already gone, closing the front door behind him to keep in the warmth, the sound of his footsteps on the short tiled front path coming to an abrupt halt as he reached the S class Mercedes.

He was right, Alicia was thinking, as she started packing Darcie's school bag. She had to make herself get over it. He wasn't the only married man in the world who'd ever had an affair – so many did and marriages survived. Theirs could too – no, it already was – but if she carried on like this, never trusting him, always questioning where he was and who he was with, she was going to make herself impossible to live with, and then she really would lose him.

The mere thought of that dug such a deep well of dread into her heart that she could feel herself starting to fall, down and down to a place where she could see no light and might never be found. She'd change, she told herself firmly. Starting today. She wasn't going to check his mobile phone any more, or his emails, and she'd never mention the other woman again. It was their nineteenth wedding anniversary on Saturday, so she'd make sure the children were elsewhere and prepare a candlelit supper, just the two of them, the way she used to before . . . She'd put candles around the bathroom too, and in the bedroom. He loved romance, they both did, and they'd shared so little of it lately.

'Are you going to the studio today?' Darcie asked, putting her bowl in the sink.

'If I get time,' Alicia answered, scooping her purse and mobile phone into her bag. 'I might get a new commission, did I tell you? Blast, I forgot to tell Dad. Nat, are these your keys?' she shouted, as Nat came bounding down the stairs.

'Yeah, I think so,' he answered, and dashing along the hall, his laptop and school bag both crushed under one arm, he gave her a loud kiss on the cheek, grabbed the keys, and after dropping another kiss on Darcie's forehead he said, 'See you later. Don't forget Summer's coming back with me tonight.'

'I wish he meant the season and not his girlfriend,' Darcie muttered. 'I hate it when it's so cold out.'

'Come on,' Alicia said, 'we have to get a move on. Did you call Verity?'

'I sent a text.'

'Mum, did you put those empty CDs in my bag?' Nat shouted from the door.

'Yes.'

'OK. Thanks. I'm gone.' He tugged open the door and Alicia had just picked up the remote to turn off the TV when she heard him shout. The tone in the single word 'Dad!' turned her blood cold. Then suddenly she was running, Darcie hard on her heels. By the time she tore open the door Nat was at the car, stooping over his father who was slumped half in and half out of the driver's seat.

'Craig,' Alicia gasped, and dashing along the path she threw herself down with them. 'What is it? What's happened?' she cried, shaking so hard it was unhinging her mind.

'I don't know,' Nat answered. 'Dad,' he said urgently, shaking Craig by the arm. Craig's body was lifeless, his face was grey, his mouth had turned a purplish blue. 'What's happened to him?' Nat said hoarsely as Alicia, barely knowing what she was doing, laid a cheek on his chest.

'Call an ambulance,' she croaked.

Ashen-faced, Nat fumbled for his mobile.

'Mum!' Darcie wailed, her hands bunched to her mouth.

'Craig. Oh God, please Craig,' Alicia cried, starting to bang her hands on his chest.

'No, Mum, no!' Darcie shrieked.

'Ambulance please,' Nat said into his phone.

'Go and see if Dr Cramer's at home,' Alicia shouted at Darcie.

Darcie took off along the street and swung in through the gate four doors down.

Nat was staring in horror at his father as he told an operator their address. At the end of the square traffic roared and swished along the King's Road. A siren, too soon to be coming for them, wailed and hooted like a fairground horn. Alicia grabbed Craig's lapels and shook him, as though her anger and panic might inject some life back into him. His head lolled to one side, his eyes were half open, as though peering at her in a tired, playful sort of way.

'You're going to be late,' she raged through a sob.

'He's coming,' Darcie said, racing back to them.

Minutes later Dr Cramer dropped down next to Alicia, his knees in the same puddle. She cleared the way, allowing him to get to Craig, but she knew, even before he turned to shake his head, that it was already too late.

She clasped a hand to her mouth as an hysterical sob tore from her heart. 'Craig!' she cried desperately. 'Craig, *no*!' and throwing herself on to him she clung to him tightly, and she was still lying with him, sobbing his name, when the ambulance crew came and gently pulled her away.

Chapter Two

Rachel was searching for a corkscrew and glasses as Alicia unloaded the shopping she'd brought in from the car. The fridge was switched on now, as were the other appliances, though she hadn't yet checked to see if they were all working.

The kitchen was large and wonderfully homey, with a nearly new range in an arched niche in one wall where copper pots and pans hung from steel hooks, and a collection of miniature teapots adorned a thick wooden mantel. Shiny beechwood surfaces over white lattice-front cupboards was a countrified style that was so typical of her mother, with a big square butler's sink in front of a deep bay window where Monica used to grow an assortment of herbs. There was an old-fashioned dresser too, where the best Royal Doulton was displayed, and double French doors led on to the back patio and garden. The table at the centre of the room was made from old pine, while the six spindle-back chairs were an odd mix of beech and oak.

'Shall we go outside?' Rachel said, filling two glasses with a very pale Pinot Grigio.

'Why not?' Alicia responded. 'I'll find some nibbles to take out, and there might be a parasol in the shed.' She'd taken her cap off now and shaken out her hair. The fluffiness of it made her seem younger, more vulnerable somehow.

The phone call, fifteen minutes ago, had been from Mimi, the florist, who was also Rachel's aunt. She'd wanted to pass on her condolences and let Alicia know that if there was anything she needed she only had to pick up the phone.

'Pete's happy to come and help in any way he can,' Mimi had reminded Rachel, referring to her wry-humoured and long-suffering husband, whose services were regularly and randomly offered for anything Mimi could find for him to do. She'd even once put his name forward to deliver the sermon when Canon Jeffries had been laid low with flu, blithely ignoring the fact that Pete was neither ordained, nor a good public speaker, nor even a particularly devout Christian.

So the first breathless moment of dread was over. It hadn't been Robert on the phone, for which Alicia could only feel thankful, since she really didn't feel up to tackling that particular hurdle just yet. In her worst moments she wondered if she had the energy to face anything at all, for losing her husband and her mother in such a short space of time had torn her apart at the seams. Nothing ever felt right now, she didn't seem to fit inside her own skin, or even to be the person thinking her thoughts. Sometimes it was as though the entire world was slipping beyond her reach and she was only hanging on by the merest thread. One enormous gasp and she might find her footing again, or maybe the weight of the air would be too much and she'd plunge helplessly into the void.

Leaving Rachel to carry out the drinks and a dish of pretzels, she went to prise open the shed door, and immediately found herself whirling back to her own and her children's childhoods. The pungent mix of creosote, earth and turps was evoking so many scenes from the past that she almost put up her hands to stop them crowding in. She couldn't allow her memories to hijack the present as though to make it their own. She must keep them buried, carefully tucked away in a place where they were safe and treasured, only to be taken out one at a time, not en masse when they swept her away in a tide of longing and despair.

Quickly she began rummaging through all the old gardening tools, wheelie toys, deckchairs and paint pots in search of the parasol she felt sure must be there somewhere. Eventually finding it propped behind an old treadle sewing machine that had belonged to her gran, she yanked it free, brushed off the cobwebs and carried it over to the table, where Rachel was already absorbing the wonderful summery day.

The back garden, like the front, had a lush green lawn with a stone bird bath in the middle, and a heavily laden apple tree drooping over the colourful shrubbery in one corner. Many moons ago there had been a swing and slide on the grass, and on hot summer days Monica used to fill a paddling pool for the children to cool off and splash about in. Most of Alicia's contemporaries would have fond memories of this garden, either playing dress-up in the clothes from Monica's charity shop, or doctors and nurses with a well-stocked first-aid box and an old stethoscope of her father's, or staging plays directed by Mimi and Monica. Some of the best games, though, had been devised by Robert, who'd had a knack, even then, for inventing outlandish and fascinating devices that might fly, or speak, or walk, or anything they weren't supposed to do. It was no surprise to anyone that he'd gone on to become a scientist, and he now ran the Ministry of Defence research labs in Wiltshire with a team of two hundred other scientists working under him. Though all his projects were top secret, even if he'd been free to discuss them the details would have been sure to go straight over most of their heads.

After slotting the parasol into a cast-iron base and opening it out to provide some shade, Alicia let the feel of the garden settle around her as she pulled out a chair and sat down with a sigh. The sky was a perfect deep blue, the air was hot and humid with only the occasional twitter of a chaffinch and a few skimming butterflies to break its stillness. It felt right to be here, comforting and safe, and yet, at the same time, completely wrong.

Catching Rachel watching her, Alicia picked up her drink to toast her. 'Here's to you,' she said. 'Thanks for being here. I'd probably have gone to pieces if I'd come into the house on my own.'

Not doubting it for a minute, Rachel said, 'I'm glad Darcie had the good sense to ring me.'

'Ah, so that's who grassed me up. I thought it might have been Nat. Did she tell you she was in France when she called?'

Rachel looked surprised. 'No, what's she doing there?'

'One of her friends' parents have a house in Brittany, so she's staying with them until the second week of August. She needed a holiday – and a break from me, if the truth be told.'

Rachel regarded her steadily. 'She's worried about you,' she said softly.

Alicia nodded. 'We're all worried about one another.'

'Of course.'

They sat quietly for a moment, sipping their drinks and absorbing the easy and familiar pleasure of simply being together.

'I should have come back here after Mum died,' Alicia said eventually. 'I wanted to. I always hated to think of the place empty and uncared for, all her things . . . But I just couldn't make myself face it. Actually, face *her*.' She gave a harsh, humourless laugh. 'My husband and my sister-in-law. What a joke. What a sad, sordid little cliché.'

Having no fondness for Sabrina herself, Rachel wasn't going to disagree.

'Craig offered, more than once, to come with me,' Alicia went on, 'but I didn't want him anywhere near her. I kept imagining him standing here, in this garden, or inside the house, thinking of her and wondering what she was doing, if she might be able to sense he was close. Maybe he'd find a way of letting her know he was coming, so they could try to sneak off together. I conjured up all sorts of telepathic communication between them that would bring them together in the high street, or the pub, making it look like a coincidence when all the time it was a bond they shared that transmitted messages like a phone, or email, or text.' Her smile was becoming heavy with a bitter sadness. 'So when Robert rang to ask if he should start clearing the place, I let him carry on without me. He said it was only Mum's clothes and some books that he'd give away, he'd wait until I felt ready to deal with things myself before making decisions about furniture and the house itself. I just hope to God his wife didn't lay a finger on my mother's belongings. I don't think he'd have let her, knowing how I'd feel about it. If he did, I'd rather not know.' She turned to look at Rachel, and her expression softened as she pictured her brother's kind and serious face. 'These past two years must have been really hard for him,' she said, 'his wife having an affair, losing Mum, having no real relationship with me when we used to be so close. I'd like to try to make that up to him, but it's hard to see how I can while he's still married to her.'

Always having considered it remarkable that both marriages had managed to survive the affair, Rachel said, 'Do you know how they're getting along these days?'

Alicia shook her head. 'On the few occasions Robert and I have spoken he never mentions her, and I never ask.'

'What have you told the children? He was always such a fantastic uncle, and they were pretty close with young Annabelle, before everything blew up.'

'I've always kept it quite vague, just saying that Sabrina and I don't get along and we've decided it's best we don't see much of one another. They missed coming here though, but at least Mum used to get up to London quite often, before the dreaded cancer really took hold.' She sighed and swallowed a knot of tears. 'Quite a catalogue really, isn't it?' she said. 'First my husband has an affair that creates a rift between me and my brother, a year later my mother dies, six months after that my husband drops dead of a pulmonary embolism; I can only begin to imagine what might be next.'

'Whatever it is, it can't get any worse,' Rachel assured her meaningfully.

Alicia's eyes shot her a warning. 'Please don't tempt fate,' she urged soberly. 'I used to think that way, and I was always wrong, so now my reserves of optimism have run dry. It's best just to take things one day at a time, and thank God for how wonderful and supportive the children are being. Especially Nat.' She attempted a smile. 'He's so stoic, and capable and grown-up, and everything I can feel proud of, but he still won't talk about his father. I don't think he's even cried yet.' Her eyes came up, and in spite of the courage she was trying to summon there was a hint of her inner desolation as she whispered shakily, 'Craig was his hero. You know how he idolised him. Nothing Craig did could ever be wrong.'

Rachel's expression showed her sympathy. 'You've obviously never told him about the affair.'

'Of course not, and now Craig's dead there's no need for him to know. There wasn't anyway.' She took a deep, faltering breath. 'He's always believed his father was totally loyal to us, the absolute mainstay of our family, which he was, so there's no reason for Nat to think otherwise.' Her smile was weak as she glanced at Rachel.

'Who'd ever have thought he'd die so young?' she said bleakly. 'It never seemed possible, did it? It still doesn't.'

Already knowing the details of how the dynamic and dashingly charismatic Craig Carlyle had been seized from his family in the prime of his life, Rachel put a hand on Alicia's arm in a hopeless gesture of comfort. Craig and Alicia had certainly had their difficulties in recent years, but Rachel had never been in any doubt of how much Alicia had loved him. So to lose him like that, and so soon after Monica's death, with no warning at all, and when things were just starting to come good again, had been totally devastating for Alicia, and the children. Six months down the line it was no wonder all three of them were still reeling from the shock.

'Where's Nat now?' Rachel asked.

Alicia swallowed some wine. 'Still in London. He's on work experience this week with Henry Taverston.'

Recognising the name, Rachel looked surprised. 'Why not with someone at Craig's chambers?' she asked.

'He and Nat decided between them that Nat should spread his wings a little, and not become too protected by his father, so Craig set it up for him to spend this week with Henry, and another with Jolyon Crane in Bristol at the end of Aug—' Her eyes went down as her voice was swallowed into a gulf of grief.

Holding her hand as she struggled with her emotions, Rachel waited patiently, wishing there was something she could say or do to ease the loss.

They'd spent many hours on the phone these past months, going over and over the happy times, as well as the betrayal, the final moments of Craig's life, and then the nightmare that had followed. Coming to terms with the sudden death of a partner, and a father, was probably one of the most difficult tests life delivered.

'How long are you planning to stay?' Rachel asked, as Alicia reached for her wine.

Alicia's eyes stayed down as she said, 'This is my home now. The house in London has been sold.'

Rachel only just stopped her mouth dropping open. 'I didn't even know you'd put it on the market,' she said cautiously.

'The cars have gone too,' Alicia continued. 'Actually, the garage took both the Mercedes as settlement of the outstanding payments.'

Rachel's shock was mounting. 'But those cars were worth a fortune . . .'

'So was the house. Almost two million, would you believe? I sold it with the contents and after paying off the mortgage I was left with the princely sum of two thousand five hundred and forty pounds, plus the little bit of money I still have in my personal account.'

Rachel was looking more alarmed and perplexed than ever. 'I don't understand,' she protested.

'There was no insurance on the mortgage,' Alicia explained, 'and with prices going down the way they have . . . I had to sell it for virtually what we paid for it.'

'But how could someone like Craig have overlooked . . . I'm sorry, that's not helpful. I'm just surprised . . .'

'Of course you are. So was I. We remortgaged about a year ago to release some of the capital, and apparently Craig was still negotiating the insurance part of the deal when he died.'

'So the insurance wasn't in place?' Rachel didn't want to believe what she was saying.

Alicia shook her head.

Rachel searched for words, but none would come. In the end she said, 'So what happened to the capital you released?'

Alicia's eyes came to hers, then went down again. 'He gave it away,' she answered.

Rachel was sure she hadn't heard right.

'It's a long story,' Alicia began, 'but there's a family . . . They lost both their children in a fire and Craig felt if he hadn't got the arsonist off a previous charge he'd have been behind bars, and the children would still be alive. He wanted to try to help the parents, to do something to make the future more bearable, so he gave them enough to buy another house. It was a lot better than the one they'd lost, which – and how's this for an irony – hadn't been insured, so they'd lost their home and their children. Craig did what he could to fill one of the gaps, and then, as though to go on making amends, he took on a lot more pro bono cases than he used to, which was some comfort to his conscience, even though our income started to fall. He kept telling me it would be OK, we'd get through it, and I'm sure we would have, given the chance, but alas we weren't.'

Thinking that her friend had already been through too much, Rachel could only look at her in stark pity and frustration. She wanted to help, she needed desperately to make this added burden go away, but it was already too late. The house was sold, and Alicia was here. 'I can't believe you haven't told me this before,' she said finally.

Alicia shook her head, seeming not to understand it either. 'I suppose I didn't want it to be real, losing our home, having to change our lives . . . I kept thinking it would all go away, or something would crop up to sort it all out . . .'

Rachel sat back in her chair, still too stunned by the news to fully take it in. She turned to look across the garden, as though out there somewhere she might find a rational explanation for this additional blow Alicia had received. 'I don't know what to say,' she murmured, turning back again.

Alicia's smile was weak. She was watching a couple of warblers splashing about in the bird bath, and thinking of how much pleasure her mother used to get from watching the birds. She wouldn't allow herself to long for her mother to come and sit down with them now; instead she would tell herself that Monica was there, in her own dimension, watching, listening and caring.

'Are you in debt at all now?' Rachel asked.

'No, thank goodness, but it was a close thing. Anyway, even if we had been insured, I still wouldn't have been able to run the house or pay the school fees without Craig's income, so selling and moving out of London was inevitable, I guess.'

Rachel was watching her with tender eyes, wondering how she was managing to look and sound so gentle and normal when inside she must be in a thousand pieces.

'I keep thinking of how he was over the last few

months,' Alicia said shakily. 'He was much more stressed than he was letting on to us all, I know that. He was worried about me, and how upset I was over losing Mum, and how afraid I was that he was still seeing *her*. He swore he wasn't, but I was never brave enough – or stupid enough – to believe it. He was working such long hours. I know that's not unusual for a lawyer, but . . .'

'Don't do this,' Rachel interrupted. 'You have to put those thoughts out of your head, because they won't help you at all.'

Alicia took another mouthful of wine and felt its acid burn on her tongue, a moment's distraction from the much fiercer burn in her heart. 'At least he used some of the capital we released to pay off the inheritance tax on this house,' she said, the words seeming to come from a detached and distant part of herself, 'or the children and I would be homeless now. I wonder if he did it to make sure I had somewhere to live before he abandoned us all and went off with her.'

Rachel swallowed hard. Though she couldn't accept that was the case, she understood perfectly why Alicia would think it. 'Do you have any evidence to say he was seeing her again?' she asked.

Feeling claws of denial digging into her heart, Alicia found it hard to keep her voice steady as she said, 'I haven't found anything, and believe me, I've looked.' Her gaze returned to Rachel, then drifted again. 'He always said that it had been a terrible mistake, and he'd never do anything like it again. According to the evidence so far he was telling the truth, but there have been so many lies, and he was so good at covering his ground the first time. That's presuming it *was* the first time. For all I know there have been others before and since . . . I don't know. I shared my life with him for the past twenty years, and now I'm beginning to think that I never really knew him at all.'

Hearing the strain cracking her voice, Rachel covered her hand. 'No one ever knows anyone as well as they think they do,' she said gently, 'but underneath it all he was a good man and a great father.'

Alicia turned away, having to swallow hard before she could speak. 'The ridiculous thing is,' she said angrily, 'that I'm sitting here grieving because I loved him so much that I almost wish I'd died with him. How foolish is that? The man has an affair, he lies and cheats, and I still . . .' She gasped raggedly. 'I'm so furious with him for dying,' she cried. 'Even more furious than I am about the affair, or the insurance. But where's that getting me? Precisely nowhere. And anyway, it's not about me, or him, any more, is it? It's about the children. Darcie will manage, changing schools, she's still young enough for it not to make too much of a difference, but it could be a disaster for Nat. He's about to start Upper Sixth, and he's been doing so well, in spite of losing his dad. He desperately wanted to make Craig proud. He's due to sit his interview for Oxford in December, and now he's . . . Now he's . . .' As she started to break down Rachel came quickly round the table to hug her.

'Ssh, it'll be all right,' she soothed. 'Nat's an intelligent boy, he won't let this make a difference, because he understands that sometimes life isn't as fair as we'd like it to be.'

'You're right, he does, and he's trying to convince me that he's happy to finish sixth form in one of the local schools here. "It'll really round out my education," he insists.' She sobbed again. 'Isn't that just like him? Saying what he thinks I want to hear because he doesn't want me to be worried or upset, when all the time his whole life is falling apart.'

'Of course it isn't. He's got his mother's resilience, remember, and his father's intellect coupled with the go-getting charm, so he'll do every bit as well at Stanbrooks or Bruton as he would have at Westminster.'

Alicia laughed through her tears. 'It won't be Bruton, we can't afford that,' she replied, 'and if I didn't know better I'd swear you two were in cahoots, because that's exactly what he says.' She gave a tremulous sigh. 'I know I'm his mother so I would say this, but he's growing into such a wonderful young man. He's so considerate and supportive, as well as intelligent, ambitious . . . I'm sorry, I . . .'

'He's also highly entertaining when he wants to be,' Rachel continued, 'extremely generous, a great brother, the best son in the world and let's not forget drop-dead gorgeous while we're at it.'

Alicia spluttered with laughter. 'He's also maddeningly stubborn, full of teenage arrogance, impatient, hotheaded and too damned big these days to feel at all intimidated by his mother.'

Rachel was smiling. 'If I know Nathan Carlyle,

he'll be seeing it as his role now to take care of you,' she said.

'Which is what I'm afraid of. He's my responsibility, not the other way round, but I keep reminding myself that it's still early days. Hopefully, once he's engrossed in his A levels and making plans for his gap year . . . I haven't told him yet that we won't be able to afford it, but . . .'

'What are you talking about?' Rachel cut in. 'Kids these days finance those trips themselves and I'm absolutely sure Nat won't have a problem with that.'

'Probably not, but my son has big plans for his future . . .'

'All of which will happen, so stop tearing yourself apart now. He's going to be fine. They both are.'

Alicia tried to smile. 'Mainly thanks to my mother,' she said. 'If she hadn't left me this house and the shop I don't know what we'd do.'

'She always did come up trumps in a crisis.' Rachel's eyes were filled with fond memories.

Alicia nodded and wondered if her mother could hear them now. If she could then maybe she'd be able to hear Alicia's thoughts too, the unspoken words of love and gratitude and a longing that would never be fulfilled.

'Has Robert ever mentioned anything about your inheritance?' Rachel asked, picking up a pretzel.

Feeling a pang of guilt for the way her brother had been left out of that part of her mother's will, Alicia shook her head. 'Not to me, but I think he knows Mum was trying to make up for the way she stopped me coming here.'

'And he's so well off these days, he wouldn't need the money. There again, nor did you when she drew up her will. When was the last time you spoke to him?'

Alicia let go of a troubled sigh. 'It was at Craig's funeral,' she replied. 'I really didn't think he'd come, but I'm glad he did.'

'Of course he'd be there for you,' Rachel said.

Alicia smiled weakly. 'Just thank God he left that evil witch of a wife at home. If she'd turned up I swear I wouldn't have been responsible for my actions.'

'That makes two of us, but luckily she either didn't have the nerve to show her face, or she discovered a stray shred of decency that persuaded her to do the right thing.'

Alicia shuddered. 'I dread to think how she's going to take it once she knows I'm back.'

'Under the circumstances I don't think you should be the one doing the worrying. Anyway, from what I hear she's got her hands pretty full these days with that daughter of hers.'

'You mean Annabelle? She was always such a sweet little girl, in spite of having Sabrina for a mother.'

'Mm,' Rachel murmured darkly, 'I think you'll find she's morphed out of the little angel you used to know. Not that I run into her often, but you know how people talk. It's always amazed me how word never got out about Craig and Sabrina.'

Hating hearing their names coupled together, Alicia forced herself past it, saying, 'I'd like to think it was a big secret, but everyone knows how close we are, so if they do know they probably wouldn't mention it to you.'

'You could be right. So did you tell Robert you were coming today?'

'No, but if he's around, I'm sure he'll know by now that I'm here.'

'I wouldn't doubt that,' Rachel agreed, 'which means he's probably off on one of his trips, because I'm sure he'll be in touch the instant he finds out. How could he not be? You're his sister, and though the closeness you two always shared might be buried under the fallout of that invidious affair right now, I know in my heart that it's still there and even, probably, very much intact.'

Chapter Three

It was just after nine in the morning when Sam Ellery, the local postman, cycled into the village to begin his rounds. Having little in his bag for the residents and tradespeople of the high street, he was soon on Holly Way, the smart, maple-lined road that curved away from the main street like the splay of a fan, to end in a leafy puff of a cul de sac with a small turning island at its centre to circle back those who were lost. Now the schools had broken up for summer there were only birds to greet him this morning, chirping and flitting about the richly dense branches, and the odd cat languishing on the bonnet of an expensive car, or waiting patiently outside a porticoed front door to be allowed in for breakfast. The air was warm and scented by a pleasing mix of jasmine, honeysuckle and the lingering tinge of someone's burnt toast. He could hear the river in the distance, bubbling over rocks on its way to the lock, and the sound of Radio Two coming from an open window.

After dropping off a small package at number eight, and a handful of birthday cards at number ten, Sam wheeled his bicycle past the next four houses who had no deliveries this morning, to the magnificent Queen Anne manor at the end. It was the only residence on Holly Way to be fronted by electric gates and a CCTV camera that registered all the comings and goings outside. Sam knew the security was because of Robert Paige's job, but exactly what Robert Paige did he couldn't rightly say, except it was something scientific. He received a lot of special deliveries, and if he wasn't around to sign for them then Sam had to take them away and leave a note to let Robert know on his return that something was waiting. Apparently not even Mrs Paige could accept his mail, though Sam had never asked why. He simply went along with the system as he'd been told to, minding his own business and feeling secretly glad that he didn't have the same kind of pressures in his job that Robert Paige probably had in his.

Propping his bike against the impenetrable laurels, he was about to ring on the entryphone when he heard a car coming into the street. Turning round he squinted against the morning sun, trying to work out who it was. He knew everyone, and liked to wave out to his customers, but as yet he couldn't make out who the car belonged to. It definitely wasn't one he recognised, but then he wouldn't, because he could see now that it was a taxi and it seemed to be coming right down to the end of the road.

Next thing the solid black gates behind him began sliding open. The taxi slowed up, waiting to gain entry, and as it came to a stop the back window went down.

'Morning, Sam,' Robert Paige called out. 'Have you got something for me?'

Sam held up the large brown envelope he was on the point of delivering. 'Something from Florida,' he said, bringing it over. 'Needs a signature, so our timing's good today. How are you? Out and about early for a Saturday morning.' He'd known Robert Paige since the day Donald and Monica had brought their squalling bundle home from Yeovil hospital, which was going on forty-one years ago now, and right from then he'd had a soft spot for the lad.

'I've just come down from Heathrow,' Robert told him, deciding to get out of the car there, instead of inside the gates. 'Took the red-eye back from Washington.'

'Been hobnobbing at the White House again?' Sam teased as he passed over his book for Robert to sign.

Robert laughed. 'I was too busy to fit them in this time,' he quipped. 'I'll give them your best next time I'm there.' He was a fine-looking man, in Sam's opinion, maybe a little thick around the middle these days, and starting to lose his fair hair in recent years, but there was a genuine warmth to his blue eyes that never failed to remind Sam of Donald, his father, and an infectious cheeriness to his smile that both he and Alicia had inherited from their gentle beauty of a mother.

Chuckling as he took his book back, Sam watched Robert haul his briefcase from inside the car, and pay the driver. 'Right, best be getting along,' he said, as the taxi started to reverse. 'Oh by the way, good news about your Alicia paying us a visit, eh? Haven't seen her yet, but my Missus had a little chat with her last night at the pub. Bloody shame about her husband, wunnit? Must have been a terrible shock for her, being that sudden and all. And the kids still so young. Made me think of how you lost your dad when you was about the same age.' Belatedly remembering how his old school chum, Donald Paige, had met his end, he felt an uneasy heat spread up from his collar. 'Yeah, well, it's good to see you, as always, my boy,' he mumbled, reaching for his bike. 'Forecast's for more sun today, and we could do with it after all the rain we've been having.'

As Sam pedalled away Robert stood watching him, aware that he'd failed to reassure the old man that he hadn't caused any offence with the remark about his father, but he was still in the grip of surprise at hearing Alicia was in Holly Wood. He should feel pleased, and somewhere, at a distance, he knew he was, but before that was the realisation of what it was going to mean to his wife. Already he could feel a horrible sinking dismay, and fighting a near overwhelming urge to turn tail and go right back to Washington, he waited for the gates to close and started towards the house.

Sabrina Paige was already in the process of preparing her husband's welcome-home breakfast when she heard the gates open at the end of the short drive and a taxi pulling up. She'd known, more or less, when to expect him, because he'd rung from the airport to let her know his plane had landed on time, at which point she'd promptly rolled out of bed, showered and dressed in a pair of bright white capri pants that showed off her long legs to perfection, and a copper-coloured silk vest that generously revealed her well-toned shoulders and arms and added a lustrous burnish to her naturally olive skin. Her rich, glossy dark hair was carelessly scrunched into a clip at the back of her head, and her exotically slanted deep brown eyes and sensuous mouth were subtly enhanced by an expert use of kohl and colour. At forty, she was still an exceptionally beautiful woman. However, over recent times her famously sultry looks had become faintly ravaged by excesses of emotion and perhaps a little too much wine.

As Robert let himself in through the door of their spacious farmhouse-style kitchen she turned to him with a smile of affection and went to embrace him. Since he'd taken an overnight flight he'd probably want to sleep off some jet lag after breakfast, and though she wasn't really in the mood to go back to bed, if he wanted her to join him she wouldn't let him down.

'You look tired,' she murmured, peering into his face. 'Did you sleep at all on the plane?'

'A little,' he replied, and dropping his briefcase on the table he loosened his tie and began tearing open the envelope he'd just signed for.

'Hungry?' she asked, going back to the Aga where she was heating butter ready to scramble eggs. She knew better than to express interest in what had arrived in the mail, particularly when it was something he'd signed for. His work was always classified, which was something she'd always found irresistibly attractive about him. She loved the air of importance and exclusivity that surrounded his research, and how highly regarded he was in his field. And the fact that he was a senior enough government official to be invited to social functions at some of the most prestigious addresses in the world was as great an aphrodisiac to her as the envy of all her friends.

'Mm,' Robert murmured, quickly scanning the documents he'd taken from the envelope. Clicking open his briefcase he dropped them inside and unfolded a copy of the *Financial Times*. 'Everything OK here?' he asked, shrugging off his jacket. 'Where's Annabelle?'

Breaking eggs into a bowl, Sabrina said, 'Still in bed, of course. I've no idea what time she came in last night. She'd like me to think it was eleven, but when I checked at one o'clock this morning her room was empty, so she'd obviously sneaked out again.'

Robert was nodding, the way he often did when not paying full attention. Then, apparently registering what had been said, his eyes came up. 'She's here now,' he said, not making it a question.

'She is, but not alone. Georgia's in the other bed, and I think someone's on the floor in a sleeping bag. The room's such a mess it's hard to make out what's breathing and what's not.'

Relaxing, Robert came to stand behind her and kissed the back of her neck. 'You smell good,' he murmured, tightening his embrace.

'And you need a shave. Would you like me to cut up the smoked salmon and put it in with the eggs, or would you prefer it on the side?'

'On the side,' he answered, and giving her a playful slap on the rump he went to pour himself a coffee.

After taking a sip, he turned and leaned against the unit behind him. For several minutes he watched her whisking the eggs and grinding in salt and black pepper. When she stooped to take warm plates from the oven, he noticed the outline of the thong she was wearing, and because he'd seen her naked so many times he was easily able to conjure an image of her gently rounded buttocks and their silky flesh. He knew already that she wasn't wearing a bra, because her nipples were evident through the flimsy copper top, and the warmth of her greeting had told him that he wouldn't be rebuffed if he wanted to take her to bed. What he also knew was why she was being so wifely and welcoming, and it injured him far more than he'd show to feel the ghost of her past love intruding on them again.

As she set the plates down on a work surface next to a pack of smoked salmon, he took another sip of his coffee and said, quite casually, 'I hear Alicia's here.'

Sabrina continued laying out slices of salmon, then returned to the Aga, apparently pretending she hadn't heard.

'Did you know?' he asked.

'Of course,' she replied. Then with a sigh, 'I suppose that old busybody of a postman told you.'

'His name's Sam. So why didn't you tell me when we spoke last night?'

'Because,' she answered, picking up the pan to

start sharing out the eggs, 'I didn't want it playing on your mind during the flight home.'

He assessed that for a moment, and decided it could be the truth, because in spite of her feelings for Craig, and the dreadful depths she'd sunk to after the break-up, he'd never really doubted how much she cared for him.

'Are you going to see her?' she asked, putting the pan back on the warming plate.

'She's my sister, why wouldn't I?'

She turned round to face him. 'I know who she is,' she said tartly, 'and I could give you several reasons why you shouldn't see her, the first being out of loyalty to me.'

At that his eyebrows gave a flicker of surprise that made her flush, but his only response was to take another sip of coffee as he walked to the table and opened the paper.

Remembering how important it was to keep him on her side, Sabrina forced down her frustration and finished preparing his breakfast.

'I don't suppose she told you she was coming,' she said, when their plates were in front of them and they were both sitting down.

'If she had, I'd have passed the information on,' he replied, starting to eat.

Sabrina cut a sliver of salmon, but finding she had no appetite she put down her fork and picked up her coffee. 'I don't know how you can sit there so calmly,' she said, 'when you know . . .'

'Sabrina, let's drop the subject before we start saying things we'll both end up regretting.'

'You're the one who brought it up.'

He couldn't deny that, but now, knowing how

she was taking it, he wished he'd left it to be swept up with the leaves outside and burned to ash that might disappear in the wind.

'I just don't understand what she's doing here,' she went on angrily. 'She's got that enormous house in London, God only knows how much in the bank. She could go anywhere, so why . . .'

'I don't understand why you're making it your concern?' he interrupted irritably. 'Considering the fact that she's so recently lost her husband, it might be a little more charitable of you to start trying to mend fences.'

While her heart jarred on the words, her eyes rounded with disbelief before she gave a scornful laugh. 'Even if I wanted to, which I *do not*, do you seriously think she'd listen? She's so full of hate towards me she'd never even let me through the door.'

'Then try calling her up.'

'Don't be cute, it doesn't suit you. A door,' she persisted, 'which happens to be every bit as much yours as hers . . .'

'Don't let's get into that again. My mother left the house to Alicia for a very good reason . . .'

'You're her son, the eldest child. You were entitled . . .'

'If the circumstances had been different I'm sure we'd have both inherited, but you're getting into some very dangerous territory now so let's drop it and finish our breakfasts. I'll have some more eggs if there are any.'

Getting up from the table she snatched up the pan and came to ladle the last two spoonfuls on to his plate.

'When you do talk to her,' she said tersely, 'I think you should make it plain that it's a bad idea for her to stay.'

'Who says she's going to?'

'That's what I've heard, but she's got to be rolling in it now, so she could live anywhere. It doesn't have to be here.'

'Holly Wood is her home.'

'No! It's *our* home. She hasn't lived here for at least twenty years, and she's hardly set foot in the place these past two years.'

'And we know why.'

Though the muscles in her jaw knotted, and she felt herself yearning for Craig's support, she chose to ignore the reminder as she said, 'Does she have any idea how upset you were when your mother cut you out of her will? Have you ever told her?'

'She wouldn't need telling, and it was you who suffered most over that, not me. As far as I'm concerned Alicia deserves the Coach House.'

At that Sabrina's eyes flashed with temper. 'Do you know what I think?' she snapped angrily. 'I think you're afraid of her.'

He blinked in astonishment.

'You never confront her over anything,' she accused him heatedly. 'You let her get away with treating me as though I'm some kind of pariah, and now she's back here and about to make my life intolerable, you're simply going to sit back and let her.'

'You're making a lot of assumptions . . .'

'Because I know you, Robert Paige. You'll bury yourself in your work, the way you always do, and pretend nothing's going on. Well, let me tell you this . . .'

'Enough!' he barked. 'I don't know why you're getting yourself into such a state over this. Much less can I fathom why you're behaving as though you're the injured party, when we both know that's very far from the case.'

Flushing darkly, she said, 'Well, thank you for your support. I should have known you still blame me for what happened . . .'

'Because you're the one who did it, Sabrina. You and Craig. If you hadn't had an affair my family wouldn't have been torn apart the way it was, and my mother wouldn't have had to live in dread of you and Alicia fighting in front of her again the way you did when it all came out. That's why she stopped Alicia coming here, you know that as well as I do. She couldn't bear the thought of a repeat performance, or of other people finding out, not because of what it would do to her, but because of how shaming it would be for me if the whole world knew that my wife had cheated on me with my own brother-in-law. That's why Alicia hardly saw my mother until she was in the hospice, to spare her the fear of another showdown, and that's why my mother left the house to her, to try to make up for the way she'd shut her out. So yes, Sabrina, you carry the blame for what happened, along with Craig, but he's dead now, so you're on your own with it, and though I might have forgiven you, I don't imagine for one minute that Alicia has, or ever will.'

Annabelle didn't hang around to hear her mother's response to Robert's diatribe, she was too afraid she'd come storming out of the kitchen and bump right into her. So turning silently on her bare feet she ran quickly back along the hall and up the carpeted staircase to her own personal domain at the far end of the first landing. She was wearing only a flimsy pair of pyjama shorts and the same skin-tight white T-shirt she'd worn to the party she'd crept out to last night. The bra she'd started out in had vanished somewhere along the way, probably mixed up in the sheets on Melody Gillman's parents' bed. She'd better remember to call Melody to ask her to check before it fell into the wrong hands.

'So what happened to the smoothies?' Georgia queried, blinking bleary-eyed from the guest bed as Annabelle let herself back into the room.

Raking her copious dark hair from her mascara-smeared face, Annabelle stood with her back to the door, one hand gripping the round brass knob, the other coming to rest across her ripe young breasts. Her bronze eyes were glittering, her plump, heart-shaped lips were curved in a wickedly satisfied smile.

Surfacing from a sleeping bag covered in discarded clothes, Catrina yawned and groaned. 'Why are you looking like that?' she said croakily. 'God, my head hurts. Tell me, did I really do what I think I did last night? I've been lying here thinking about it . . .' Her voice faded in a hangover cringe.

Annabelle arched her immaculately plucked eyebrows, turning herself, did she but know it, into a younger, slighter version of her mother. 'Depends what you think you did,' she replied, leaving the door and going to her dressing table which was a sweeping corner unit of drawers, cupboards and mirrors covered in make-up, hair paraphernalia, books, magazines, and enough junk jewellery to deck out a dozen fashion shoots.

'Shit, will you look at the state of me,' Georgie grumbled, checking herself out in a hand mirror.

'Me too,' Annabelle moaned, wincing at her reflection. 'Just as well I didn't run into the she-devil and Dr Freak while I was down there.'

'Where are the smoothies?' Georgie repeated, her throat raspingly dry. She swung her long legs off the bed and tried to stand up, but only got so far before staggering back and collapsing in a groaning, giggling heap.

'You are so stoned,' Annabelle informed her, starting to rub her face with a cleansing wipe.

'Where's my mobile?' Catrina asked. 'I'd better text my mother to let her know where I am, or she'll end up doing something insane like calling the police, or ringing my dad to tell him she can't cope any more. Stupid bag.'

'So how did it go with Marty last night?' Annabelle asked Georgia. 'You were so wasted when you came back to the party I thought you were going to throw up.'

'I think I did while we were outside,' Georgia confessed. 'I can't really remember now. What about you?'

Annabelle grinned, and held up three fingers.

Georgia's eyes rounded. 'You're kidding.'

'What? What's happened?' Catrina wanted to know.

'She had three last night,' Georgia told her.

Catrina looked at Annabelle, dead impressed. The youngest was turning into the hottest. 'Still haven't broken the record,' she said, referring to the target of four she'd set herself a few weeks ago 'but still amazing. Who was it? I know one of them had to be Carl's mate, what was his name again?'

'Tom,' Georgia provided.

'That's right. So was it really his first time?'

Annabelle nodded and carried on inspecting her reflection. 'That's why I said I'd do it,' she reminded them. 'He's kind of cute and I was feeling generous, but I don't think I'll go there again. Carl was all bump and grind the way he usually is, but then someone else came in the room and started to join in. I can't remember his name now . . . Jason, I think, or Justin. Actually, it might have been James. Anyway, I wasn't going to let him, but then Carl said he was a good mate, so I thought, hell why not? I've never done three in the same night before, unlike *some*,' she added, eyeing Catrina. 'Anyway, that's nothing to what Melody did. Did you see her in the kitchen?'

'Oh my God, yeah, yeah, I did,' Georgie squealed excitedly. 'She was only using Rudi to show Katie Bridge how to give a blow job, then she started heaving and had to dash to the loo. It was so disgusting. Someone said she passed out after, and she might have because I don't remember seeing her before we left.'

'That's because you couldn't see *anything*,' Annabelle reminded her. 'What about Archie?' she asked Catrina. 'Did he turn up in the end?'

'I told you on the way home,' Catrina replied

glumly, 'he came, but he brought the F-F-Felicity with him, didn't he? He's such a bastard. When I saw him in the afternoon he promised he'd get rid of her and come on his own, but she was stuck to him like frigging Velcro.'

'You still got off with him though,' Georgie reminded her.

'Only for a quick snog behind the guest house. I'm supposed to be seeing him this afternoon, actually. He said he'd pick me up in his car outside the station. I have to work out how to get there yet. Annabelle, we need liquids, girl, I'm gasping.'

'All right, I'll go back down,' Annabelle replied, tugging a brush through her hair. 'I couldn't go in the kitchen just now because the She-Dee and Freak were having some kind of set-to about my aunt Alicia. Apparently she's back in Holly Wood and the mother person is not happy. They absolutely detest one another.'

'Why?' Catrina asked, not really interested, but making an effort to be polite.

Annabelle got up from the boudoir chair. 'No idea,' she answered airily. 'All I know is that if Alicia stays chances are my cousin Nathan will be coming to visit, maybe even to live.'

'Oh, no, not the famous Nathan,' Georgie teased, making Catrina laugh.

'So we might get to meet him at last,' Catrina said.

A momentary concern peeped through a crack in the shell of Annabelle's grown-up demeanour. 'If you do, just keep your hands off. He's mine,' she informed them hotly.

'He's your *cousin*,' Georgie piped up. 'That is so gross.'

'We're not blood-related.'

'It's still not right though.'

'Who says? Anyway, I'm going back down to see what I can find to drink – and eat. If my mobile rings and it's Carl tell him I liked his friend Jason, or whatever his name was, so he should bring him to Ed's tonight.'

Taking a wrap from the back of the door, she pulled it on and ran silently back down the stairs. There were no voices coming from the kitchen now, and when she cautiously pushed open the door, to her relief, there was no sign of anyone inside. The last thing she wanted was a showdown with her mother when Robert was around to offer husbandly support, particularly when it was likely to end up with her being grounded for sneaking out last night. Still, even if she was it wouldn't stop her going to Ed's party tonight. Everyone was going to be there, and according to Ed he had a new supplier for E, so she definitely wasn't going to miss out on that.

Going to the fridge she helped herself to a double punnet of strawberries, another of blackberries and a dish of chopped mango which she dumped next to the blender before peeling a couple of bananas. She was thinking now about the row she'd overheard earlier, and feeling weird little frissons eddying through her. The she-devil and Craig. Amazing. Gross, but still amazing. Actually, it explained quite a lot, except, maybe, why Robert hadn't chucked her mother out. Perhaps he hadn't wanted to come over as a hypocrite, seeing as he'd been sleeping with her mother while she was still married to her first husband, Annabelle's drippy dad. Come to think of it, her mother was a bit of a serial cheater, because Annabelle was sure she'd had other flings before Robert came along. It was probably where she got her own overactive libido from, she decided, and giggled. She loved the way Carl and his friends described her like that.

Anyway, whatever, she could only feel relieved that Robert hadn't chucked them out, because living in this house, in Holly Wood, was amazingly, seriously cool, and the last place she wanted to end up was in some downgrade semi or flat in Bath, or Bristol, or worse, London, with no money, because there was no way her mother could earn anything like the megabucks Robert got paid. Worse still would be finding herself being shipped off to her father, not only because he lived on another planet now, or it might as well be, Australia was so far away, but because he had another family these days who looked a right bunch of mingers from the photos he sent her.

It wasn't until she'd turned the blender off that she realised her mother was standing behind her, hands on hips, apparently about to go mental.

'Get over it, Mum,' she said, before her mother could weigh in first.

'Where were you last night?' Sabrina demanded.

'Out.'

'I'm aware of that. You're fifteen years old, young lady, and the rules of this house are that you have to be home by eleven and stay here.'

'Yeah, yeah, blah, blah.'

'So where were you?'
'I just told you, out.'
'Annabelle, look at me.'
'What for?'
'I said look at me.'
'I'm busy, aren't I?'
'So help me, I'll send you to your father if you don't start showing me more respect.'
'Oh, that's a new one. Haven't heard that before. Can you excuse me please, I need to get some glasses out of the cupboard.'
'Who's upstairs?' Sabrina demanded, standing aside, and thinking, not for the first time, how rarely Annabelle ever looked her in the eye.
'None of your business.'
Sabrina's face clenched with anger. 'If there are boys in your room . . .'
Annabelle sighed and rolled her eyes. 'If you must know it's Georgie and Catrina. OK? Satisfied?'
Sabrina's expression was still tight. 'I wish you had friends your own age,' she stated. 'OK, I know you've always known them, but they're in the sixth form now and you're . . .'
'Are there any biscuits or anything?' Annabelle interrupted. 'We're starving.'
'It's called the munchies,' Sabrina told her, yanking open a cupboard. 'It's what happens when you've had too much to drink, and let me remind you yet again, you're underage . . .'
Annabelle suddenly burped, which made her laugh. 'Sorry, that wasn't meant to come out,' she said, pressing her fingers to her lips.
Sabrina shook her head in disgust. 'Were there

any drugs involved wherever you went last night?' she asked bluntly.

'Oh Mum, unravel yourself, will you?'

'I want an answer.'

'Well you're not getting one, because if I say no you won't believe me, and if I say yes you'll just go off on one.'

Feeling the intolerable bite of frustration, Sabrina said, 'Your attitude is going to get you into a lot of trouble one of these days, young lady.'

Annabelle didn't bother to reply. She simply put the drinks on the tray, took the biscuits and started towards the door.

'There used to be a time when I was proud to call you my daughter,' Sabrina told her, her voice shaking with anger and despair. 'Now I just feel ashamed, and do you know why? Because you look like a tart, and I wouldn't be at all surprised to find out you behave like one.'

'You know what,' Annabelle said nastily, 'Alicia's not the only one around here who can't stand you, because there's always me,' and leaving her mother with tears of helplessness and fury stinging her eyes, she went off to feed her friends.

Turning back towards the sink, Sabrina put her hands on the edge and held on tightly. She dared not let go of her emotions for fear of how fast and furiously they might tear through her if she did. Robert wouldn't tolerate it if he thought she was still grieving, God knew he'd found it hard enough when he'd first broken the news of Craig's death. Typically, he'd been patient and kind at first, understanding, in spite of how much it was hurting him, that she'd needed some time and space to come to terms with the loss. It would be too much to expect him to carry on considering her feelings when to his mind she had no right to them anyway, but how could she just put them aside as though they didn't exist, when most of the time they were the only part of her that seemed real?

While Robert was at the funeral, which he'd forbidden her to attend, she'd gone to the church, here in Holly Wood, and sat alone at the back, whispering to Craig in her mind, feeling the words in her heart. She'd told him how much she still loved him and always would. She'd pictured them together during the times they'd laughed and made love, forgetting the pain and wretchedness that had all but destroyed her after their break-up. She'd never believed then, and she still didn't now, that he'd stopped loving her. No matter what he told Alicia, or himself, she'd always known that deep in his heart he remained hers. It was why she'd found their parting impossible to accept, and the news of his death had come as such a terrible blow. The dreams, the certainty, that one day they would be together could never now come true.

And if they couldn't she had to wonder if there was any point to going on.

Were it not for Robert and Annabelle there really wouldn't be, and she'd caused so much damage in her relationships with them that she often felt afraid that they might actually be better off without her. She asked herself, if there was a door she could open that would lead her to Craig, would she go through? Would she really turn her back on two people she loved so much, whom she felt as bonded to as her own heart, to be with another who was no longer in this world, and yet meant more to her than life?

The answer was, she didn't know, but a part of her was breathless with relief that there was no such door, so the choice didn't have to be made.

Chapter Four

'Hey Mum, sorry did I wake you?'

'No, not at all,' Alicia lied, struggling to come to. 'Is everything OK?' Not, what time is it? How are you, darling? Or, what have you forgotten? Already an ocean of dread was closing around her heart, drowning the beat. Was this how it was going to be from now on, always living in fear that another sudden disaster had struck?

'I'm cool,' Darcie told her chirpily. 'It's just that my mobile might not work where we're going today, so I didn't want you to worry if you couldn't get hold of me.'

'Where are you going?' Alicia asked, glancing at the clock. Still only seven thirty, making it eight thirty in France.

'Oh, just on a hike, but it's pretty remote in places, apparently.'

'Don't forget to wear a hat and cover yourself in factor thirty,' Alicia cautioned, thinking of her daughter's tender fair skin.

'Yeah, yeah. So how are you? Sorry I missed you last night, Verity and I went into the local village with her sister where they were having some kind of fete. It was really cool. Did you go over to Rachel's for a barbecue in the end?'

'I did,' Alicia confirmed. 'They all send their love. Una's dying to see you.'

'Tell her, me too,' Darcie trilled, not adding *she's the only good thing about moving there*, but Alicia heard it anyway. 'So what are you doing today?'

Alicia thought, then remembering, a swell of pleasure made her smile. 'Nat's arriving this afternoon,' she reminded her. 'I'm picking him up from the station at three.'

'Oh yeah, of course. Is Summer coming with him?'

'Yes. She's staying until Wednesday, apparently.'

'Mm.'

'What?'

'Nothing.'

'Come on.'

'It's just that I'm not really sure about her,' Darcie confessed.

Knowing it was unlikely Darcie would feel sure about anyone who threatened to steal her place in Nat's affections, Alicia said, 'Nat likes her, and that's what's important.'

'Do you? Be honest now.'

'She's OK.' Alicia wouldn't confide any more than that, since Darcie was likely to blurt it out to Nat. Not that she had anything against Summer, who'd certainly been there for Nat these last few months, it was simply that, like Craig, she could have wished Nat wasn't involved in such a serious relationship when he was still so young.

'Are you going to let them sleep together?' Darcie asked.

Stifling a laugh, Alicia said, 'He hasn't asked if they can, so I'm going to make up my old room for Summer and Uncle Robert's for Nat.'

'So that means you're sleeping in Gran's?'

Alicia's smile faltered as she looked around the familiar room, burnished now in a rich golden glow from the morning sunlight trying to blaze its way through the coppery curtains. It had made sense for her to start using it right away, but even after two nights in her mother's sumptuous sleigh bed she was still finding it hard to accept that this was all hers now, or that her mother wasn't going to come through the door at any moment and be startled to find her there. 'Yes, I am,' she confirmed. 'It feels a bit odd, but we'll soon settle in, all of us.'

'Yeah, I guess so,' Darcie said, not sounding at all convinced.

'You used to love this house when you were younger,' Alicia reminded her. 'You'd plead with me to bring you here.'

'I know, but we didn't have to live there then. Not that I mind,' she added hastily, 'because it's a really cool place, it's just that it's going to be a bit different to living in London, and I'll miss all my friends.'

'I know, sweetheart,' Alicia said softly, 'but you'll make others, and Verity, or whoever you like, can always come to stay. You can visit them too during the holidays.'

'Yeah,' Darcie responded flatly.

She wasn't stupid, Alicia was thinking, she knew life would move on in London without her, and she'd soon be forgotten, but hopefully, considering her naturally high spirits and easy-going nature, once she was established in her new school she'd be every bit as popular, and happy, as she'd been at St Paul's.

'So have you seen Uncle Robert yet?' Darcie asked, changing the subject.

'No. He left a message last night saying he'd like to come over today, if I'm free, but it was too late to call him back.'

'Will Sabrina and Annabelle come with him?'

'He didn't mention it,' Alicia replied. Though Darcie was aware that her mother and Sabrina didn't get along she had no idea why, and Alicia hoped to keep it that way.

'I'd like to see Annabelle when I come,' Darcie said. 'She always used to be really nice to me, and she is my cousin, after all. Or kind of, anyway.'

Realising how important it was to Darcie to make connections, Alicia said, 'I'm sure she'll be happy to see you.' Even if that were true, Alicia knew Sabrina would probably do her utmost to talk Annabelle out of it, but that thorny little issue was for another day; there was no point troubling herself with it now. 'Have you spoken to Nat this weekend?' she asked.

'Yeah, yesterday afternoon. It sounds as though his work experience went really well. He says he's looking forward to spending some time with Jolyon next month too, and apparently Summer's been on his case to go to Italy with her and her family next . . . Oh, sorry, Mum, I think I have to go. Verity's dad's just come back with all the stuff we need for our picnic so I have to help prepare it. Stay cool, OK? I'm really missing you.'

'I'm missing you too,' Alicia said, experiencing a powerful urge to wrap her daughter tightly in her arms and never let her go.

'I'll call tonight if it's not too late when we get back. Give my love to Nat – and Summer, if you feel you have to. Definitely to Rachel and Una, and to Uncle Robert. Love you, Mum. Love you, love you, love you.'

'Same here,' Alicia whispered, and after waiting for Darcie to ring off she replaced her mobile on the low oak chest that served as a nightstand, and lay back against the pillows.

Her heart felt so full that it was making her breathing shallow, and her muscles were tense as though to keep the building emotions from breaking through her control. The mornings were always the worst, when she woke up with only the vestiges of a disappearing dream on her mind, until the unbearable realisation that her world had fallen apart tore through her heart. Craig had gone. He wasn't a part of her life any more, and he never would be again. The reality of it was so harsh that she was still struggling to accept it. As each day passed she seemed to miss him more, not less. Not even the mess he'd left her in, or the betrayal, was freeing her from the grip of her longing. She wanted him back so badly that sometimes the effort of forcing herself into the day was almost beyond her. It was how she'd felt during the days and weeks after she'd found out about his affair, only worse, because this time there really was no going back.

Putting her hands over her face she tried to stop the memories of that time, but they were already flooding in, filling up her heart, crowding her mind, coming together with a clearer and more insistent reality than the one she was in.

'So where's the birthday boy?' Rachel cried, pressing a path along the hall to where Alicia was instructing the caterers in the kitchen. The house and its small garden were crammed to overflowing with their friends and families, all gathered to celebrate Craig's fortieth birthday.

'He must be outside somewhere,' Alicia answered, wrapping Rachel, and then her husband Dave, in a welcoming hug. 'I was starting to give up on you.'

'Not my fault this time,' Rachel jumped in, before Dave could blame her. 'I might have had a sick cat on my hands, but his lordship here had to sort out a dispute with one of his tenants. Don't ask, too boring for words. Just give me a drink, someone, please. I'm gasping.'

As one of the caterers put a glass of champagne into her hand, Nat came into the kitchen with Annabelle, asking if they could change the music.

'Feel free,' Alicia told him, 'but you'll have to answer to Dad. He created this mix specially for today.'

'Where is he?' Dave asked. 'We have to toast him. We've left his present in the hall with the others.'

'Great,' Alicia replied, nodding to a waiter to start taking round another tray of canapés. 'Could you open more bottles,' she said to someone else. 'Oh yes, and you wanted extra glasses. They're in a box over there. Nat, darling, could you pass . . . Excellent, thank you,' she said, as Nat hefted the box on to the table.

'Do I get a glass now?' Nat pleaded. 'Dad said I could today.'

'For the toast,' Alicia reminded him.

'I'm nearly *fifteen*, for God's sake,' Nat protested.

'No way,' Rachel cried. 'Let me get a look at you behind all that hair.'

Laughing, Nat backed away, he didn't allow anyone to touch his fringe, and gesturing to Annabelle, his adoring slave, he made good his escape into the sitting room.

'Teenage spots on the forehead,' Alicia muttered when he was out of earshot.

'Oh,' Rachel responded knowingly.

'So did you bring in your bags?' Alicia wanted to know. 'You're in the guest room. Mum's in with Darcie, on the futon, and Robert and Sabrina are going to sleep on the sofa bed in the den.'

'We'll bring them in later,' Rachel answered, 'there are so many people we haven't seen for ages and I'm dying to say hello. How many did you invite in the end?'

'Eighty, would you believe? Go on through. You'll find Craig out there somewhere. I'll come and find you in a minute.'

After Rachel and Dave had melded into the throng, Alicia turned towards the downstairs loo, so desperate to go she was starting to dance. To her dismay there was a queue, so after setting yet another waiter on his way with a tray of brimming glasses, she quickly dashed upstairs to use the guest en suite, since it was the closest.

As she pushed open the door to the guest room she was already starting to hike up her dress, until, seeing someone was there, she came to an abrupt and embarrassed stop and let it fall again. She was making a discreet departure when she realised it was Sabrina lying on her back on the bed, her legs wrapped around someone who was pumping her so hard that neither of them had noticed they were no longer alone. The man's trousers were around his knees, his shirt was open, and Alicia's first thought was, *Why is that man wearing Craig's shirt?* Then as the truth struck its terrible blow she took a step back.

For interminable, dead seconds she continued to stand where she was, unable to move, or to believe what she was seeing. They were thrusting and panting, grunting, urging each other on, oblivious to everything beyond the storm of an approaching eruption. Something wasn't connecting in Alicia's head. Her mind was distorting what she was seeing, playing her tricks, pushing her to wrong conclusions, making her see things that weren't there. Craig wouldn't do this, he just wouldn't.

Then she realised Sabrina was watching her, and to her horror, instead of behaving like any other guilty woman, throwing Craig aside and scrambling for her clothes, Sabrina only smiled. There was a chilling gleam of triumph in her eyes and as she clung more tightly to Craig she urged him to go faster and harder.

The instant Craig began to ejaculate Alicia turned and left the room. She felt sick in ways she'd never known it was possible to feel sick. Every part of her needed to expel the treachery she'd left behind, her mind, her stomach, her heart, her very soul, wanted rid of it.

She walked to the top of the stairs and stood there

shaking. She wasn't sure how much time passed before Craig came out of the room, it could have been seconds, or minutes, she only knew that as his arms went round her the urge to push him down the stairs overwhelmed her. He grabbed the banister in time, righting himself before he plunged to the bottom.

'Alicia, listen,' he whispered urgently. 'I've had too much to drink. I wasn't thinking . . .'

'Don't speak to me,' she hissed. She tried to break free, but he held her firm.

'You can't go back down there like this,' he said.

'How long has it been going on?' she asked shakily.

'It just happened . . . I . . .'

'Tell her the truth, Craig,' Sabrina said from the door.

He spun round. 'Sabrina, just go . . .'

'It started,' Sabrina said to Alicia, 'when we were all in Italy last summer.'

Alicia reeled. They'd been screwing like that for over a year? All the times she'd thought Craig was working late, or away, or taking phone calls from colleagues and clients . . . Why hadn't she realised it was a sham? How could she not have suspected? She looked at him and it terrified her to see how pale and unsure of himself he seemed. This affair was serious, she thought. It really meant something to him.

'Does Robert know?' she heard herself ask, in a voice that came from the bottom of a void.

'He's too busy, and hardly ever here,' Sabrina drawled.

Alicia turned to look at her. This wasn't mattering

to her. She didn't care that she'd just been caught screwing her sister-in-law's husband, or that she'd betrayed a good man who loved her. If anything, she seemed almost pleased with herself.

'Get her out of here,' Alicia said.

Craig baulked. 'Alicia, Robert and your mother are downstairs . . .'

'I'm aware of that, so you can go and explain why *she* has to go, and then the party's over,' and wrenching herself away from his grip she started up the second flight of stairs to her own room.

'Alicia,' Craig called after her. 'Think about the children. What am I going to tell them if you . . .'

Alicia rounded on him in fury. 'You should have thought about that before you dropped your trousers for that whore,' she raged.

'How dare you!' Sabrina shouted.

'Keep your voices down,' Craig implored. He was deathly white now and more agitated than Alicia had ever seen him. 'Sabrina, whatever excuse you use, you have to leave,' he told her.

Sabrina was staring at him hard. 'Why don't we just tell the truth?' she replied. 'You're always saying you want to leave her, so isn't this the perfect opportunity?'

Alicia reeled again and stared at Craig with such bemusement and hurt that no words would come, no thoughts, no anything beyond the shock and pain.

'Don't listen to her,' he said. 'It's not true. I don't want to leave you.'

'But you have been screwing her for over a year?'

He shook his head. 'No, I mean, yes, but . . .'

'Mum! Are you up there?' Darcie yelled from the

bottom of the stairs. 'Nat's changing the music and Dad'll go ballistic. Do you know where Dad is?'

'I'm here,' Craig answered, keeping his eyes on Alicia. 'It's OK if Nat . . .'

'Get out of my way,' Alicia seethed under her breath. 'And don't bring your whore back to the party or I swear I'll tell everyone right away exactly how you've been celebrating your fortieth birthday.'

Swinging her legs off the bed, as though to escape the sheer awfulness of that day, Alicia pushed back her hair and tried to block it out. But it was persisting, coming over her in wave after wave of torturous memory, reminding her of how, in the days and weeks that followed, Craig had continued to swear that Sabrina meant nothing to him. Nothing had happened in Italy, he told her. Sabrina had lied, and he had no idea why. No, of course he wasn't planning to see her again. He swore on the children's lives that he still loved Alicia, and that nothing in the world mattered more to him than keeping his family together. He was as convincing as any trained barrister could be, and Alicia even believed him for a while, but then she found herself doing something she'd never done before, checking his mobile phone records and credit-card statements. To her horror, it soon became evident not only that he'd been lying about how long the affair had been going on, but also that it was still far from over.

'I don't understand it,' she raged when she confronted him. 'What is it about her? Do you love her? Is that what's happening? Do you want to leave us, break up our home and go to be with her?'

'No, of course not,' he cried. 'You and the children mean everything to me, you know that . . .'

'Then *why* are you doing this? It's not as though we don't have a sex life, or is it only me who finds it satisfying? It must be, because it's only you who's looking elsewhere. Does she give you more? Is she doing things . . .'

'Alicia, stop,' he pleaded, his handsome face haggard. 'Nothing's wrong between us. I love you as much now as I ever have, probably more.'

'Then *why*?' she repeated desperately. 'Explain it to me. Make me understand why you're doing this.'

His head went down as he shook it. 'I wish I could,' he replied hoarsely. 'I don't want to blame her, or to pretend I'm innocent . . . I just . . . It's something . . .'

'It's *what*?' she shouted, wanting to punch and slap him as though to make him feel her pain.

Still he was shaking his head. Craig Carlyle, the great orator, the brilliant barrister who'd found words to defend some of the lowest forms of human life, paedophiles, gangsters, serial killers, could find no words to defend himself.

Alicia knew she should have made him leave then, or left herself, but she hadn't, mainly because she hadn't been able to bring herself to tell the children what was happening. They adored their father, to them he was everything, and the pathetic truth was that as much as she hated him for what he was doing, she couldn't stop loving him either. He wasn't only someone who'd betrayed her, he was the man whose love of his children made her heart trip, whose smile could still melt her all the way through, whose very presence in their world held it all together and made every day worthwhile. She'd watched him cry over the tragedy of a case he was working on, she knew about the kindness he showed to victims and their families. There was so much more to him than this madness with Sabrina, so she couldn't throw it all away. In the end, they'd agreed that provided he ended it with Sabrina once and for all, she'd give him another chance.

How he broke it to Sabrina Alicia guessed she'd never know now, but whatever he'd told her, it soon became evident that Sabrina herself wasn't ready to let go. She kept calling, morning noon and night, often drunk and half demented with grief and rage as she threatened Alicia, or begged Craig to see her. She swore she'd end her marriage to Robert if Craig would do as he'd promised and leave Alicia. Craig fiercely denied ever making such a promise.

'I've never had any intention of leaving you for her, or anyone else,' he insisted one night, after Sabrina had woken them with yet another of her drunken calls in the early hours.

'So why is she saying you did?'

'I don't know. She's making it up, telling herself what she wants to hear, but it's nonsense. All I want from her is for her to leave me alone.'

So Alicia drove down to Holly Wood to confront Sabrina. By then Robert knew about the affair, and was as devastated as Alicia, but he had no idea Alicia was coming so was completely unaware of his mother's crazy decision to play mediator. He only found out after the terrible scene that erupted between the two women was over and Sabrina returned home bleeding from the nose and with huge handfuls of hair torn from her scalp.

Robert had immediately marched over to his mother's where he'd found Alicia in no better shape, but his main concern had been for Monica.

'How could you do this?' he shouted at Alicia. 'Look at her. She's your mother, for God's sake. What were you thinking, when you know how sick she is?'

'I'm sorry,' Alicia cried. 'I didn't mean it to happen . . .'

'Robert, calm down,' Monica pleaded. 'I'm OK, just a bit bruised from where I tried to break it up. I'll heal.'

'It's not good enough,' Robert growled, still glaring at Alicia. 'I want you to leave here right now . . .'

'Robert, no,' Monica protested. 'She's hurting every bit as much as you are, and I'm sorry to say this, but Sabrina's much more to blame than your sister.'

Having to concede that, Robert turned stiffly away, but not before Alicia saw how shattered he was inside. She went to put a hand on his shoulder, and as he turned to look at her they gazed deeply into one another's eyes. Then his arms went round her and they held one another tightly. Had their mother not been there Alicia was sure they'd have both broken down and tried to seek some comfort from each other, but Monica had been through enough for one day. She was tired, she needed to lie down, and Robert had to get back to Sabrina.

It was a week later, when Alicia called to tell her

mother she was coming for a few days, that Monica asked her not to. It would probably be best if she stayed away from Holly Wood for a while, Monica said as gently as she could, and because she'd sounded so weak and weary Alicia hadn't argued. Instead, she'd allowed herself to be banished from the home she'd grown up in, the village she felt so much a part of, and the mother she adored, all because Sabrina couldn't let go of Craig.

Later, Alicia learned from her mother that Robert had threatened to divorce Sabrina if she didn't pull herself together and stop pestering Craig with phone calls and emails. Apparently, afraid of ending up with no one, Sabrina had finally given up her persecution, but the damage that had been done to both marriages was already incalculable, and, to Alicia, often felt irreparable. In spite of remaining committed to one another, and trying hard to recapture what had been lost, it was never the same between her and Craig again. Like a priceless vase, her trust had been shattered, and no matter how carefully she attempted to put it back together the cracks always showed.

Whether Craig had taken on more work after that to fill the void Sabrina had left, was impossible to say now. She wanted to believe it was to try to straighten out their financial affairs, because if she blamed Sabrina for how stressed and tired he'd become it would mean he must have really loved her to have felt the loss so deeply. This wasn't a possibility Alicia could begin to tolerate, because the hate and jealousy Sabrina inspired in her wouldn't help at all as she tried to make a new life for herself and the children. She could only hope that Sabrina decided to stay away from them now, because Alicia had not a shred of desire to be on any kind of terms with her ever again.

By midday Alicia was up, dressed and ironing freshly laundered sheets ready to make up the beds in her and Robert's old rooms. All their childhood possessions had been carted up to the attic years ago, or donated to jumble sales and her mother's charity shop, or simply thrown away. Now the decor in both rooms owed more to Laura Ashley than to a plastering of pop posters. However, the beds were still singles and an impressive collection of board games and children's books were still stacked on the shelves, and inside cupboards, left over from the days when Nat and Darcie used to come to stay.

For a while, earlier, she'd considered going to the eleven o'clock service, not because she was particularly religious, or in need of communicating with God, it was simply that the thought of being close to her parents who'd married in the church, and used to attend most Sundays, and were now laid to rest in the graveyard outside, was a comforting one. In the end, however, she'd decided to delay her visit until fewer people were around. Being as fragile as she was at the moment, she didn't want to risk going to pieces when someone might see her.

Now, as she folded one sheet and laid it on top of another, then took a pillowcase from the basket to begin pressing out its creases, she was wondering, not for the first time, where her ashes might be buried when the time came. Since Craig's were in Berkshire, along with his mother's and uncle's, something his overbearing father had insisted on, should she go there too? Or would it be acceptable for her to be with her parents in a place she knew and loved? It was a maudlin dilemma, and one she didn't have to resolve now, but if she and Craig had taken time to discuss the matter, he might be here in Holly Wood too, where she felt he belonged. However, the mere thought of Sabrina taking flowers to the grave and sitting over it like a tragic widow was enough to make her thankful he wasn't, and was what, in the end, had made her give in to her father-in-law's demands.

Turning to pick up her mobile as it bleeped, she opened the text and felt a pleasing warmth run over the chill of her thoughts. It was from Nat, letting her know that the train was on time so he'd be with her in just under two hours. She quickly sent a message back assuring him she'd be waiting at the station, and after clicking off she looked up as she heard the front gate open. Seeing Robert coming down the path, her insides gave a jolt of nerves and guilt. She should have called him back by now but hadn't, because she'd been unable to get through on the mobile number she had for him, and she hadn't wanted to run the risk of Sabrina picking up the phone if she tried the house.

Putting down the iron, she unplugged it and went to open the front door just as he was raising a hand to knock.

'Hello,' he said, with a sardonic smile, his hand still in the air. 'Is it OK to drop in unannounced?'

'Of course,' she assured him, feeling an unsteadying sense of relief wash over her. Whatever had happened between their spouses, it hadn't changed how much she loved and cared about him. 'It's good to see you,' she said, and to prove it she stepped forward to give him a hug.

His embrace felt as warm and safe as it always had, and when he held on to her a little longer than she expected, as if to let her know that his affections were every bit as constant as they'd always been, she felt tears prick her eyes. 'Don't be nice to me,' she warned, 'you know you don't like it when women cry.'

He chuckled. 'Did I say that?' he replied, following her inside.

'You used to, when we were younger, especially after you'd done your level best to get me bawling.'

He grimaced. 'What a brute I must have been.'

'And don't you ever doubt it,' she teased.

He laughed. 'Did you get the message I left last night?' he asked, as they went into the kitchen.

'Yes, but I couldn't get through on your mobile and I wasn't keen to call the house.'

He gave a sigh of self-exasperation. 'I changed my mobile number about a month ago. I should have told you. Anyway, how are you?'

She shrugged. 'Surviving, I guess. I take it you're responsible for keeping the house up together.'

'Not me personally,' he replied. 'I paid Mrs Jessop to carry on coming after we moved Mum to the hospice, and her husband took over the garden.'

'Thank you,' she said quietly. She wasn't sure

whether to mention the fact that he hadn't inherited with her, or to ask how he felt about it. If he minded she knew it wouldn't be about the money, it would be for sentimental reasons, and she could hardly blame him for that.

'I know what you're thinking,' he told her, 'and it's all right. It should be yours.'

She swallowed and tried to smile. 'You know you're always welcome here.'

'I should hope so,' he retorted. 'Now, do I get a cup of tea?'

Her eyes sparked playfully. 'I have blackcurrant juice,' she told him.

Since it had been a favourite of theirs as children, his smile was quick in coming. 'How about tea with a blackcurrant chaser?' he suggested.

Liking the idea she turned to fill up the kettle, feeling even more pleased than she'd expected to see him here, but as a silence settled between them awkwardness began stealing in like a shadow. It dismayed her, though she guessed it was only to be expected when this was the first time they'd been alone together since the day he'd ordered her out of this house. After that, all discussions about their mother had taken place on the phone, and the only times they'd actually seen one another was at Monica's bedside, or at her funeral. He'd come to Craig's too, which she loved and admired him for, but there had been so many people around, and she'd still been in such a daze, that even when they had managed to speak she'd hardly registered what either of them said.

'Still no milk or sugar?' she asked, taking two mugs from the cupboard.

Seeming pleased she'd remembered, he nodded. 'Same for you?'

She smiled, and nodded too. She was starting to feel more relaxed now, and wanted to give him another hug.

'So how are the children?' he asked, folding his arms as he leaned against a counter top.

'Bearing up,' she replied, 'but you know how close they were to their father, especially Nat.'

'This won't have been easy for him,' he agreed.

Knowing that he, more than anyone, would understand what Nat was going through now, losing his father while still in his teens, she said, 'He'll probably appreciate having an uncle again, if you think it's possible.'

Robert's eyes were kind. 'I don't imagine I can ever replace Craig,' he said, 'but I'll do my best to be there for him in any way I can.'

She smiled. *I don't imagine I can ever replace Craig.* She couldn't help wondering if he'd ever spoken those words to Sabrina. If he had, she didn't want to know. 'He's on his way here,' she said, opening a box of Earl Grey and dropping two bags into the mugs. 'I'm picking him up from the station at three.'

Robert glanced at his watch. It was still only twelve thirty, plenty of time before she had to leave. 'What about Darcie?' he asked.

'She's on holiday with a friend in France, due back in the middle of August. It feels strange without her, but I have to admit, it's a bit of a relief to have some time alone. These past few months have been quite a challenge on several fronts.'

'I'm sure.' He was about to say more when her mobile started to ring.

It was Rachel checking to make sure Alicia was still up for getting together tonight.

'Absolutely,' Alicia confirmed. 'I'm doing a barbecue for Nat and Summer about five, so shall we see you at the pub at seven?'

'Perfect. Any other news?'

'Robert's here,' Alicia replied, glancing at him.

'Ah ha.' Rachel's tone was dark with understanding. 'Then I'll let you go. Say hi from me, and you can tell me everything tonight.'

'Rachel,' Alicia told Robert as she rang off. 'She says hi.'

Acknowledging the greeting with a raise of his eyebrows, he picked up the kettle as it boiled and filled both mugs. 'Shall we sit in here, or outside?' he asked.

'Do you mind if we stay inside? I need to finish some ironing, but open the doors to let in some air, and I'll bring everything through from the sitting room.'

After she'd set up the board, and they'd spun out the niceties as long as they could, he finally said, 'I guess there's no point me going on pretending that the gossip mill hasn't got round to me, so time to come to the point. Is it true you're intending to stay here in Holly Wood?'

Keeping her eyes on the path the iron was smoothing over the folds of a pillowcase, she nodded. 'Yes, we are,' she confirmed. Her insides were starting to tighten. Was he going to object, and ask her to leave? It wasn't a showdown she'd welcome, but she could hardly blame him for feeling worried about having her and Sabrina in the same vicinity.

'Do you think that's wise?' he asked.

Putting the iron down, she raised her head and fixed him with steady eyes. 'This is my home, Robert . . .'

'I'm talking about changing the children's schools,' he interrupted, apparently realising where she was going. 'Surely losing their father is a big enough disruption. Why have you sold the house? Is it even true that you have?'

'Yes, it is,' she answered stiffly. Then deciding to get it over with, she said, 'There's no money left. The mortgage wasn't insured and we'd run up some debts . . . If it weren't for Mum leaving me this place, we'd have had nowhere to go.'

Robert sat quietly for several seconds, digesting the unexpected bombshell, and knowing, as did she, that this was the very reason Monica had given her the house. After Craig's betrayal she'd wanted to make sure Alicia was taken care of, should he ever let her down again. How perspicacious their mother had been, though he doubted she'd ever imagined something like this.

'I know you're going to say I could have sold this house and the shop,' Alicia went on, 'but it wouldn't have been enough, and I've lost so much lately. I'm sorry, but I couldn't bear to let go of this place too.'

'I wasn't going to say that,' he assured her. 'Of all people I understand how much this house means to you, and though Sabrina might not forgive me for it, I think you did the right thing coming here. It's a place you know, Rachel's close by, and so am I. But what are you doing about schooling? Is there enough left to carry on sending them privately?'

'No, but Stanbrooks did very well for us, especially you, so I'm sure it'll do the same for Darcie and Nat.'

He nodded gravely. 'Would you prefer them to be weekly boarders?' he asked. 'It would free you up . . .'

'I can't afford the fees for one of them, never mind . . .'

'They're my niece and nephew, and in the circumstances it's the least I can do.'

Thrown by the unexpected generosity, and deeply touched, it took her a moment to answer. 'Thank you,' she said quietly. 'It's very kind of you, but I can't accept.'

'Maybe you should think it over.'

She regarded him frankly. 'Have you thought about what your wife would say if she found out?' she countered. 'No Robert, please listen. I haven't come here to make trouble. I just want to get on with my life the best I can, and give my children some semblance of security after what they've been through. If the circumstances were different I'd be more than happy to let you see Nat through sixth form, but I don't want to be responsible for causing you any more problems at home, and we both know it would if you do anything to help me.'

Sighing, he sat back in his chair. 'So what are you going to do?' he asked, letting the offer drop for now. 'How do you intend to make a living?'

'Actually,' she said, taking a sheet from the basket, 'I'm going to open up the shop again.'

He seemed confused. 'But there's no money to be made in that . . .'

'I'm going to turn it into a kind of gallery to sell my sculptures,' she told him. 'There's space at the back I can use as a studio, and I thought I'd promote other local artists and artisans as well, and charge a commission. I can learn how to make jewellery, and there's nothing to stop me buying in various things to sell at a profit. It would be a kind of arty gift shop, if you like.'

'I see,' he said, in a way that managed to sound both doubtful and encouraging. 'You seem to have given it some thought, so I wish you every success. Have you sold any of your sculptures to date?'

'As a matter of fact I have, through a gallery on Primrose Hill. One of them went for fifteen hundred pounds, and two others for seven apiece. After the owner had deducted her commission and VAT I went away with just over a thousand.'

His eyes boggled.

She smiled. 'Surprised they went for so much?'

'No, shocked by the owner's percentage. If it's that high you definitely ought to be selling them yourself. How much do you need to get started?'

'I have enough,' she assured him, hoping it was true. 'And I have six finished pieces ready to put on display. Seven if I count the one I'm working on now.'

'Where are they?'

'Still in London. A removal van is coming tomorrow with all our personal belongings. I sold everything else with the house.' How easy it was to say those words, *I sold everything else with the house*. How devastating the reality was, letting go of everything she and Craig had collected and built together. It was as though someone else was moving into their skin, taking over their dreams and living their lives in strange and different ways. Would she ever be able to think of that house as belonging to anyone but them?

Clearly still trying to get his head around how she'd lost it all, Robert said, 'Is the sale actually complete yet?'

'It should be by the end of next week. I have to admit, I'm dreading it, but I'll probably be able to sleep a lot better once it has gone through. The buyer's got himself a great bargain and no one's anticipating any delays or disasters.'

He still wasn't looking especially impressed. 'Why didn't you tell me what was going on?' he demanded. 'There might have been something I could do.'

Deciding to speak honestly again, she said, 'Your wife wouldn't have appreciated it if you had, and frankly, Robert, she was the last person I needed to deal with when the truth began hitting me like a ton of bricks.'

'Nevertheless . . .'

'It's done now,' she said, cutting him off. 'We're debt-free and here in Holly Wood, ready to make a fresh start. I'm only sorry you and I won't be able to see one another as much as I'd like, but you'll always be welcome here on your own, you know that. Or with Annabelle, if she'd like to come. Darcie's very keen to see her . . .' Noticing the mask that dropped over his face, she said, 'But no pressure. As I said before, I don't want to cause you any difficulties at home.'

'It's not that,' he said, 'it's that Annabelle might not be such a great influence on Darcie these days. She's going through a bit of a . . . what's the word? Challenging? Yes, challenging phase.'

Alicia's eyebrows rose.

He was about to enlarge when loyalty staged a discreet interruption.

'It's OK,' Alicia assured him, 'I know what teenagers can be like, though I count myself lucky that Nat hasn't put me through anything like the kind of nightmares I've seen some of my friends go through. He has his moments, of course, and he's still only seventeen so we're not out of the danger zone yet. However, so far, so good.'

Robert smiled fondly. 'I take it he's still planning to follow in his father's footsteps.'

Alicia looked down as she nodded. 'Absolutely. I don't think anything could dissuade him from that. He and Craig had it all planned out, the GCSEs and A levels to start him on his way, the universities, Oxford being his first choice, naturally, Craig's alma mater; the firms and chambers he'd apply to for work experience, the bar exams, the dinners, right through to the time he could join his father as a junior.'

'I hope Craig realised how lucky he was,' Robert murmured, a note of bitterness clinging to the edges of his tone.

Alicia looked at him. It would be foolish to think he had any more fondness for Craig than she had for Sabrina, and knowing how much the affair had hurt her brother made her hate Sabrina all the more for not treating Robert with the love and respect he deserved. 'I think he did,' she said softly. 'He always adored the children.'

Robert looked as though would have liked to say more, but whatever it was, it didn't materialise, and she wondered if alongside his resentment of Craig he was feeling his old sadness at not having any children of his own. A long time ago he and Sabrina had been through the tumultuous hope and despair of fertility treatment, but it hadn't worked and in the end he'd declared himself perfectly happy to be a devoted stepdad and uncle. Though he was wonderful in both roles, Alicia and her mother had always known how deeply disappointed he was in himself for not being able to father his own child.

'I have no problem at all imagining Nat as a leading QC one of these days,' he said, the gentleness of his tone conveying only affection for his nephew, and no jealousy or anger towards Craig. 'You'll be very proud of him.'

Loving him for caring about Nat, Alicia said, 'I already am, which is why I'm praying hard that losing his father, and making this change, right in the middle of sixth form, doesn't send him off the rails. I don't think I could bear it if it did.'

'He's always had his head screwed on the right way,' Robert reminded her reassuringly. 'I don't think you've got anything to worry about there.'

She smiled. 'Thank you for that. Now, before I go any further into the insufferably boastful mother routine, am I allowed to ask how things are going in the world of rocket science?'

His eyes lit with humour. 'Alicia, I've seen your expression glaze far too many times in the past to be tempted down that road now. It's still all very dry, and highly confidential, and as frustrating as ever when there are so many governments involved. I can tell you this much though, provided you repeat it to no one, my latest project has developed a very interesting side effect that could, I stress *could*, provide a new kind of energy source that would kick most other oil alternatives out of the arena. However, it has a long way to go before it reaches a viable stage, and for the moment we don't want the press getting hold of it, because it's bound to be misunderstood, or blown out of all proportion.'

Her head tilted playfully to one side as she regarded him. 'I always knew we'd be able to rely on my brother to solve the world's problems,' she teased.

He laughed. 'Right now I'd settle for solving a few of my sister's, but she's proving even harder to deal with than the current US regime, and that's saying something.'

'I'm sure it is, but honestly, I can manage. And stop trying to return the subject to me, because I haven't finished with you yet. Are you still travelling as much as you used to?'

'More,' he sighed. 'I only got back from Washington yesterday, I'm off to Helsinki on Tuesday. Then comes Dubai, followed by Rome. After that, I shall be with my team for a month at the labs.'

'Hectic,' she agreed. 'Are the labs still in No Man's Land?' It was the phrase they'd always used for Wiltshire, because the actual location of his research facility was as classified as the projects themselves.

He nodded. 'At least when I'm there I get to come home at night.'

'Which must be a great comfort to your wife,' she commented, hoping there wasn't too much of an edge to her voice. 'Does she ever accompany you on your trips?'

'Less now than she used to. She's afraid to leave Annabelle for long, even though Annabelle insists she's perfectly capable of taking care of herself.'

Alicia smiled. 'I can almost hear her,' she said. 'How old is she now? Fifteen, sixteen?'

'Going on twenty-five. Luckily she gives me an easier time than she does her mother, which isn't saying much considering how often I'm away.'

Unable to summon any sympathy for Sabrina, Alicia said, 'You were always quite close, you two.'

'I like to think so, but these days I think she sees me less as a father than as a brainless moron who's become disconnected from the real world.'

'Charming.'

'She can be that too, when it suits her, which is usually when she wants something, but I guess that's the same with most children.'

Alicia rolled her eyes in agreement. 'Darcie's got it down to a fine art already,' she confessed. 'She could twist Craig around her little finger in ten seconds flat.'

He smiled. 'She must be missing him,' he said, his tone managing to convey more sympathy for Darcie than antipathy for Craig.

Alicia's eyes went down as she nodded.

After a while he glanced at his watch. 'I guess I should be getting home,' he said. 'Sabrina's taken herself off on some sponsored walk for the day, and Annabelle's staying with a friend, so I can shut myself in my study without being accused of neglect. And you have to get to the station.'

'There's still plenty of time,' she reminded him, 'but I do need to make up the beds. No, don't worry, I'm not about to rope you in for assistance, but if you're on your own today, why don't you come and join our barbecue at five? I know Nat would love to see you.'

His expression was more eloquent than his words as he said, 'There's nothing I'd like better, but I think I'd better take a rain check for today. Coming here now has already created a . . .' he searched for the word, 'situation, so I don't want to make things worse.'

'Of course not. I understand. Just as long as you know this is still your home any time you want to come.'

Getting to his feet he drew her into a brotherly embrace. 'Thank you,' he said, clearly meaning it.

As she pulled away she looked into his wonderfully gentle eyes. 'Tell me,' she said, her voice a little shaky, 'did we do the right thing in forgiving them?'

He took a breath and expelled it slowly. 'I've often asked myself the same question,' he admitted, 'and the only answer I can come up with is that love can make you as weak as it can strong, and when you're afraid of losing someone you start holding on even tighter, even though it might be better for you to let them go.'

Knowing exactly what he meant, she said, 'Do you think you really have forgiven her? In your heart of hearts?'

Again he gave it some thought. 'Probably as much as you forgave Craig,' he replied. 'It's forgetting that's the bigger problem.'

'Isn't it?' she sighed. 'But you do understand that I can't forgive her?'

He looked at her sadly and pressed a kiss to her forehead. 'Maybe one day this will all be behind us and forgiving and forgetting will no longer be an issue,' he said. 'For now, I think we're all still stumbling our way there.'

Feeling certain he was some way ahead of her in forgiving Craig, she linked his arm and walked with him to the door.

'Say hi to Nat for me,' he said as he stepped outside.

'Of course. And don't forget to text me your new mobile number.'

'Consider it done.'

As he walked down the path she stood watching him, no longer seeing the man he'd grown into, but remembering the boy he'd once been, and a time when life had seemed so innocent and uncomplicated – and untarnished by the selfishness of two lovers who'd caused them both so much heartache and pain.

Chapter Five

Sabrina was walking, walking and walking. Her feet were covering the miles, her heart was beating the pace. There had been a rain shower just now, but neither she nor her fellow walkers had paused. This was for charity. They, who had so much, were raising money to help those who had nothing at all.

Though her legs ached, and her trainers pinched, she kept on going, hardly feeling the pain, or registering anything around her. She was cushioned by memories, propelled by her now impossible love, drawn to the finish by futile and childish promises that when she crossed the line Craig would be waiting to catch her. She was doing this for him, to prove that she'd never given up on him, and to show herself that she never would.

They'd been in Italy for over a week by now, and the heat was relentless. The olive trees in the terraced groves covering the hillsides around their villa glistened like silver in the afternoon sun, the ground was dusty, cracked and parched. Up here, on this hill, where the villa sat like a small fortress overlooking the gentle sweep and rise of the valley, there was a perfect, crystalline pool to cool off in, and shady pergolas to wander through or lie under, thick with the scents of jasmine and colourful roses.

About an hour ago Alicia and Monica had set out for Siena, taking Annabelle and Darcie with them. The men hadn't shown any interest in accompanying them, and Sabrina had cried off at the last minute, saying it was too hot to go mingling with crowds of tourists, and she really couldn't bear all those endless queues to see a few crumbling churches and a bunch of tortured old saints. She'd prefer just to relax by the pool with a good book, she'd said, but later, when it cooled down a little, she'd drive into the village to shop for dinner. It was her turn to cook tonight, and she was planning an assortment of antipasti that she intended to pick up at Luigi's, along with some fresh pasta and all the other deliciously fresh ingredients she needed for the sauce.

Now, as she strolled from the shadows of the sitting room where Nat and Robert were playing chess in front of the vast empty fireplace, the sudden glare of the sun caused her to squint. She lowered her glasses from the top of her head to shield her eyes, then sauntered on across the terrace and down the steps, where plumbago tumbled like powdery blue stars over the gnarled and crumbling stone, to the pool.

She wondered why she always felt so aroused in the sun. Maybe it was the heat forcing her to take off her clothes, or the sensation of air on her almost naked skin. Or maybe it was the looks she and Craig had been exchanging over the last few days. She knew he wanted her as much as she wanted him, she could see it in his eyes, and feel it in the tension that sparked between them like the flashes of heat lightning that daggered the night sky.

As she walked towards him now, sharp and exquisite sensations were shooting like darts between her legs. They were making her want to touch herself, or tear off the two small shimmering pieces of bikini she was wearing, in order to abandon herself to the power of an exhilarating desire.

Though his eyes were closed as he lay in the shade of a parasol, she guessed he was only dozing, if he was asleep at all. She gazed hungrily at his body. It was long and hard, and still wet from the pool. She'd spent many hours lately wishing she could remove his shorts in order to make the picture complete. In her mind's eye she had no trouble conjuring images of his cock, swollen with lust, throbbing just for her, or of his tapering fingers sliding over her breasts. In her imagination they'd already fucked a hundred times, savagely, sweatily, insatiably – today, she felt sure, it was going to become a reality.

'Hi,' he murmured, opening his eyes as her shadow fell over him.

She smiled and stretched her arms lazily over her head. She was enjoying the tautness of her stomach, and the sensation of her skimpy bikini bottom riding down to where there should be pubic hair, but wasn't. Her skin was a deep golden brown; her legs were long and bare and close enough for him to reach out and touch.

'It must be near to forty degrees,' he commented, glancing towards the sun.

'Mm,' she responded, and shaking loose her hair she lay down on the bed parallel to his.

For a long time they simply soaked up the stillness, hearing only the buzz of cicadas, and the droning of the pump that cleared the pool. She wondered if he'd raised one knee to hide his erection, and smiled secretly to herself. She wanted him more than she'd ever wanted a man in her life, and she sensed it was the same for him. The only difference between them was that he was still trying to resist it.

She sensed him turn to look at her, and waited for him to speak, but it was a while before he said, huskily, 'You look sensational in that bikini.'

She smiled. 'I'm glad you think so, because I had you in mind when I bought it.'

The sexual charge in the air sharpened and was suddenly burning hotter than the sun.

He said nothing.

Her eyes remained closed behind the dark lenses, her heart was thudding quietly beneath the hardened bud of her nipple. 'No one will know,' she said softly.

When he didn't respond she turned to look at him and found him staring past her to the house.

'We can't,' he said. 'There's too much at stake.'

'Only if they find out, and if we're careful, there's no reason why they should.' She wouldn't tell him yet that the risk would drive her wild, he'd find out soon enough.

He looked away and more breathless, expectant minutes ticked by.

In the end, accepting that to do anything here, at the villa, for the first time would be too hard for him, she swung her feet to the ground, and said, 'Come with me to buy something for dinner.'

His eyes rose to hers and as she brushed the back of one hand over her breasts she saw him swallow.

'Where's Nat?' he asked.

'Still playing chess with Robert.'

He nodded, and a note of irony came into his tone as he said, 'For once he's not playing draughts with Annabelle.'

Amused, she said, 'Do you think that's what they're doing when they shut themselves up in her room?'

'At their age, I hope so.'

Teasing him, she said, 'At their age, is that what you would have done? Play draughts?'

He laughed. 'I doubt it.' Then getting to his feet he said, 'I'll go and see if either if them want to come with us.'

Hiding her dismay she watched him pick up his towel and book. 'I'll meet you at the car in ten minutes,' she told him as he walked away.

His hand went up to let her know he'd heard, and presumably to say he'd be there. Hopefully alone.

Taking a side entrance into the villa, she went up to her room, tied a sarong over her bikini to form a dress, then rolled her hair into a clip before picking up her purse. She'd remove the sarong when she reached the car – maybe she'd remove the bikini as well, provided Nat and Robert weren't there.

She found them still intent on their game when she wandered back through the sitting room. There was no sign of Craig. 'Are either of you coming to the village?' she asked, stifling a yawn.

Robert shook his head. 'Craig's already asked, and I'm about to be beaten so we're staying here.'

She feigned a moment's interest in the board, then feeling Nat's eyes on her she looked at him and smiled. He didn't smile back, and she could sense his antipathy. She'd known for a long time that he didn't like her, mainly because he wasn't sophisticated enough to hide it, and the feeling was mutual. She had no time for boys who considered themselves men long before their time, and who watched her with eyes that seemed to see too much. He couldn't know about her and his father, because, as yet, there was nothing to know, but smug little bastard that he was, he always made her feel that he knew she wasn't to be trusted.

Putting more sweetness into her smile, she dropped a kiss on Robert's head, and sauntered off to the car.

It was parked in a clearing at the end of the drive, out of view of the house, but in full sight of the road that snaked past outside. As usual there was no sign of traffic, just a couple of geckos scuttling across the track to the shade of a cactus on the other side.

Craig was already in the driver's seat with the engine running.

Untying her sarong, she slipped into the passenger seat next to him, and as their eyes met she knew with certainty that, at last, they had reached the point of no return.

Alicia was waiting close to the exit gate when Nat's train pulled into Castle Cary station, bang on time. A clutch of anxious and excited butterflies were on a merry spree inside her, reminding her of how she used to feel when she was first dating Craig (and later, after the affair, but in an awful way then, when even to think of him would cause her insides to clench with dread). Today she was experiencing only joyful anticipation, knowing her son was on this train and for the first time in three days she'd be able to wrap him in her arms and know he was safe.

As the doors began to swing open and people to clamber down, she glanced searchingly along the platform, ready to wave as soon as she saw him. She could picture his face already, lighting up when he spotted her, and Summer, with her autumn-coloured hair and prettily freckled cheeks bobbing along beside him.

Minutes ticked by. The platform started to empty, and with each passing second the sparkles of her anticipation were turning to dust. He'd texted to say he was on this train, so he had to be here. Maybe he'd had to get off early for some reason, but if he had he'd have called to let her know. She must have missed him. Somehow he'd been masked by the crowd, and he was already outside, looking for her. But there hadn't been a crowd, no more than a dozen people had got off, and she was right by the gate.

Panic welled up inside her as the guard began closing the doors. She had to stop him. She couldn't let the train go until Nat was off.

'Excuse me,' she said, her voice sounding shaky and shrill. What was she going to say? 'Have you seen . . . ? My son was supposed to be on this . . .'

'Hey, Mum!'

She looked up and relief unravelled so fast

inside her that she almost sobbed. He was here. Nothing bad had happened to him. Her precious boy was safe and swaggering towards her in his cool, teenage way, a heavy bag slung across one shoulder, his dark jeans and T-shirt tight enough to his body to show how close he was now to becoming a man. He was already almost as tall as his father had been, and shaving had lately become a daily event. Luckily his voice had long since shed all the lingering squawks of puberty and his complexion was, more or less, free of the spots that made some of his less fortunate friends' faces look like the inside of a kiwi fruit, as Craig had once put it, making her cry with laughter.

As he reached her, his aquamarine eyes, a replica of her own, were shining with humour, while his dazzling white smile, so like Craig's, turned her heart inside out. Carelessly dropping his bag he scooped her up in his arms. 'We fell asleep,' he told her, 'and only just woke up in time.'

'Typical,' she chided, holding his face between her hands and gazing at him with motherly adoration. His dark hair was tumbling into his eyes and snaking down his neck, but she wouldn't tell him he needed to get it cut, she'd given up on that a long time ago.

After hugging him again she turned to greet Summer, who at five foot three was much shorter than Nat, though the four-inch wedges she was balanced on brought her closer to Alicia's height. 'Hi sweetheart, how are you?' Alicia said, embracing her fondly. 'I'm so glad you were able to come.'

'Thanks for letting me,' Summer smiled. 'I'm

really looking forward to it. Nat says it's a really cute house and the village is pretty cool too. It's a great name, isn't it? It was a real trip telling my friends I was going to Nat's mother's place in Holly Wood. They were like, no way.'

Laughing, Alicia said, 'I'm afraid there are no walks of fame or avenues of the stars here, but we've got a nice pub on the high street and the Holly Wood Players have been known to put on the odd good show once in a while.'

'Oh, yeah, like that travesty of *A Midsummer Night's Dream*,' Nat scoffed as they started towards the exit. 'Do you remember when they performed it next to Holly Copse and Puck's tail got stuck on a branch and he couldn't get free?'

Alicia burst out laughing. 'And Titania fell out of a tree in the middle of someone else's scene.'

'Oh God, I'd forgotten that,' he cried. 'We had to creep away in the end because we were laughing so much.'

Loving that he remembered it so well, in spite of only being twelve at the time, Alicia tucked an arm through Summer's, saying, 'We'll overlook the fact that Brenda Lovejoy, who was playing Titania, fractured a rib when she hit the ground. My family were a disgrace to me that night . . .'

'What! You were the one laughing the hardest,' Nat protested. 'Dad had to put his hand over your mouth to try and stop you . . .'

'And then completely lost it himself when someone's dog ran on to the set and stole the show. Gran was no better, sniggering away like a schoolgirl. I'm still not sure if Darcie really knew what she was laughing at, but she got so loud that it was mainly thanks to her that we had to go.'

Summer was clearly enjoying the moment. 'Sounds like a really cool time,' she commented.

'We used to love coming here as kids,' Nat told her, as they crossed the car park. 'Gran had everything in her house, all the toys and stuff we wanted, and she'd take us places like Wookey Hole and Cheddar, and Glastonbury. I told you, didn't I, that Dad and I went to the festival last year, and the year before, which was awesome, both times.'

Surprised, and heartened to hear him talking about his father when he'd barely mentioned him these past few months, Alicia began rummaging in her bag for the car keys.

'Oh,' Summer said, clearly startled when they stopped next to the Renault. 'What happened to the Mercedes?'

Alicia's eyes shot to Nat. He looked uncomfortable, but he was the one to say, 'It wasn't practical for down here in the country, and Mum needs an estate to transport her sculptures.'

'Oh, I see,' Summer replied, blushing slightly. 'This one's really cool,' she added. 'I love the colour.'

Since it was beige Alicia knew she was trying to make-up for the faux pas, and gave her a grateful smile. 'Come on, let's get you home,' she said, opening up the back, and after dumping their luggage inside, she found herself spilling over with happiness as she closed down the hatch and Nat gave her another quick hug. Her life felt almost complete now he was here, and Darcie's arrival would be a further source of joy

– and over time, once they got used to Craig not being around, the awful, aching emptiness he'd left behind would, please God, finally start to fade.

Forty minutes later they were back at the Coach House and while Nat and Summer went upstairs to unpack, Alicia got the barbecue under way – chicken and home-made sausages for her and Nat, soy-marinated tuna for Summer who'd decided to become a vegetarian. The salads were already prepared, a crunchy Waldorf, one of Nat's favourites; a creamy goat's cheese with cherry tomatoes; and a tasty mix of crushed new potatoes, fennel and chives.

After lighting the gas in the cylindrical pod she and Craig had bought for her mother several years ago, she pushed the crowding memories to the back of her mind, and began setting the table. From the delicious aromas wafting over the high stone walls surrounding the back garden it was clear that one, or more, of her neighbours was cooking up a late afternoon feast of their own. She could hear the low murmur of their voices, peppered with laughter and the clinking of glasses, and somewhere in the distance someone was mowing the lawn. It was a perfect sleepy Sunday afternoon, with red admirals and painted ladies flitting around the aubretia and lavender, and the melodious trill of a song thrush coming from next door's pear tree.

'This place is so sweet,' Summer declared, stepping out of the back door in more sensible flip-flops and knee-length denim shorts. She had good legs considering her lack of height, and sumptuously youthful creamy skin, a lot of which was exposed thanks to a skimpy red polka-dot bikini top and no covering shirt. 'It's like the ones you see on post-cards and old paintings of the countryside,' she added.

Alicia smiled. She knew Summer didn't mean to be condescending, so she wouldn't take offence. 'It was a lovely place to grow up,' she told her, 'and to bring the children for holidays when they were younger.'

'Nat was just telling me on the train how it was absolutely the best, coming here for Christmas when his gran used to let him roast chestnuts in the fire and his dad used to keep pretending they didn't have any presents.'

'Yes, he was quite a tease,' Alicia agreed. Then, unable to stop herself, 'Does Nat talk about him much to you these days?'

Summer shrugged. 'Not really,' she answered, 'but I think he should, because it's no good bottling things up.'

'Is that what you think he's doing?' Silly question, of course he was.

Summer coloured slightly, seeming embarrassed about being invited on to forbidden territory. 'I asked him the other day if he'd cried at all since his dad died,' she confided, 'and he said it wouldn't bring him back so what was the point?'

Alicia's heart tightened. Though it was the answer Nat had given her when she'd asked, so was no surprise, it still disturbed her to hear it.

'I don't think you really need to worry about him though,' Summer assured her, apparently feeling the need to brighten things. 'He's a pretty together sort of person, so I'm sure he'll be fine.'

Alicia nodded and smiled. 'I'm sure he will too,' she murmured, wanting to believe it, but unable to. 'Now, what will you have to drink? There's plenty of fruit juice, or Coke. Or you can have wine if you prefer.'

'Oh, let me,' Summer offered. 'If you just tell me where to find the glasses.'

'They're already on the table,' Alicia pointed out, 'but the drinks are in the fridge.'

'I expect Nat will have a beer,' Summer said, turning back into the kitchen. 'He usually does at barbecues.'

Wishing the proprietorial air hadn't grated, Alicia let her go and went to check on the barbecue. She'd have to get used to sharing him one day, so perhaps she should try viewing this relationship as a rehearsal rather than an intrusion, especially when she quite liked the girl. Which was just as well, she remarked to herself a few minutes later, when she turned round to find them smooching in the kitchen. Nat was pretty smitten, she'd never been in any doubt about that, and the fact that they'd been sleeping together for at least six months – Alicia only knew because Nat had confided in his father – didn't seem to have got it out of his system. If anything it had brought them closer together, which would have been fine with Alicia if he was ten years older.

Still, what mattered for now was that Summer made him happy, and though he might be a minefield of emotions on the inside, at least she wasn't making the situation any worse. Nor, considering their brief conversation just now, was Summer insensitive to what he was going through.

'Hey Mum, are you going to have some wine?' he shouted.

'Lovely,' she shouted back. 'And can you bring the meat out now? This thing's about hot enough.'

When he brought the tray and set it on the table next to her she could smell the beer on his breath, and turned to look at him. She wanted to touch his face and hold him, but knew it would be the wrong thing to do.

'Mum, you're too intense,' he told her under his breath. 'I'm fine, OK?'

'Of course you are,' she responded, affecting a laugh. Had Summer told him about their little chat? Or was she really overdoing the concern? It was the latter, of course, so she needed to ease up.

'Please tell me I didn't just hurt your feelings,' he said, half irritably, half jokingly.

'You didn't,' she assured him. 'And you're right, I am a bit strung out. I guess I'm still trying to get used to thinking of this as our home. Anyway, Uncle Robert was here earlier, he says hi.'

'Here's your wine, Alicia,' Summer said, coming up behind them with a large glass of Chardonnay. 'I poured one for myself too, I hope that's OK.'

'Of course,' Alicia assured her warmly. 'You must help yourself to whatever you like.'

Summer smiled and rested her head against Nat as he slipped an arm around her. 'It sounds like mine?' he said, as a phone started to ring inside the house. 'It might be Simon Forsey, I sent him a text to let him know I was coming.'

Pleased to hear that he was already getting in touch with friends in the area, Alicia clinked her glass against Summer's and gave her an impulsive hug. It was going to be all right, she told herself firmly. They'd get through these next few days just fine and that was as far ahead as she could dare to look right now.

'Oh, so you decided to come home,' Sabrina remarked crisply as Annabelle sailed in through the door, all jangling beads and a flouncy miniskirt that showed off most of her long bare legs.

'Yeah, I thought I would,' Annabelle chirped, going to yank open the fridge. 'Have we got any Babybels? I'm starving.'

'They're in the second drawer, with the other cheeses, but don't overdo it, we're going to the pub for dinner.'

'Cool. Georgie's on her way over, can she come too?'

'I don't see why not. Is she staying the night?'

''Spect so. So, how did your sponsored walk go? Did you finish?'

Sabrina's heart caught on a wave of unhappiness. Yes, she'd finished, but she'd felt no sense of achievement when crossing the line, only a return to the way her world was now, empty and sad on one side, full of guilt and confusion on the other.

'Hello! Did you finish?' Annabelle prompted.

Quickly assuming a playful twinkle, Sabrina said, 'Provided everyone coughs up I have just raised one and a half thousand pounds for Shelter. Isn't that amazing?'

Annabelle looked impressed. 'Mega,' she agreed, peeling the thick red skin from a mini cheese and biting into it. 'Wish you could raise that much for me. So where's Robert?'

'In his study of course. Actually, buzz through and tell him I'm about to pour us a drink. It's high time he came up for air.'

Using the intercom linked to Robert's study which was in a lavish sort of bunker at the far end of the garden, Annabelle said, 'Earth to Planet Robert, earth to Planet Robert, come in for vodka tonic please, come in for vodka tonic,' and letting the button go she flopped down at the table and opened that morning's *Style* magazine.

'Didn't you bring a bag home with you?' Sabrina asked, dispensing ice into two tall glasses.

'Georgie's mum's bringing it in the car.'

'So how did you get here?'

'Someone gave me a lift.'

'Oh? Who?'

Annabelle turned a page. 'A friend. OMG, look at these shoes. They'd go really well with the purple dress I bought when we were in Bath last week, and they're only four hundred and sixty quid.'

Sabrina slanted her a look, not entirely sure whether she was joking. 'So, who brought you home?' she repeated.

'I just told you, a friend.' She turned another page and bit into a second cheese.

'Male or female?'

'Um, let me think. Yep, I guess he must have been male, but before you start freaking out, no we didn't stop on the way to have sex in the back seat.' She popped the rest of the cheese into her mouth. 'We did that last night.'

As images of the times she and Craig had made love in a car flashed in her mind, Sabrina cast Annabelle another look. She was being baited, she decided, and choosing not to rise to it, she poured two generous measures of vodka over the ice before returning to the fridge for the tonic. 'So what's his name?' she asked, trying to keep it casual.

'Who?'

'The boy who brought you home?'

Annabelle shrugged. 'Dunno. I didn't ask.'

Sabrina sighed with exasperation. She was trying so hard to engage, but was receiving nothing in return. 'Annabelle, why does everything have to be so difficult with you?' she asked, trying not to sound as though she was nagging.

Annabelle threw out her hands. 'You're asking the questions, I'm answering, so what's difficult about that?' she cried.

'We used to have lovely conversations about all sorts of things,' Sabrina reminded her. 'Now I barely get a sensible word out of you.'

Annabelle put back her head. 'Um, let me see, and that would be because . . . Oh yes, I'm stupid, don't have a brain in my head and am a total waste of space.'

Sabrina looked at her aghast. 'What on earth . . . ?'

'It was a joke!' Annabelle cut in.

'Did anyone ever say those things?' Sabrina asked, horrified in case she had.

'Duh! I just told you, it was a joke.'

As Annabelle went back to her magazine Sabrina stood staring at her, wanting to say more, but unable to put the words together for fear of where they might lead. 'Ah, darling, there you are,' she said, as Robert came in through the back door. 'I thought I should drag you out now or you'll be in there all night.'

'Good thing you did,' he responded, going to wash his hands at the sink. 'I was starting to fall asleep. Still a bit jet-lagged, I guess. Hi Annabelle. How's tricks?'

'Everything's cool,' she replied, still scanning the magazine as she gave him a wave.

'I got your text,' he told Sabrina. 'So, I owe you five hundred pounds. Well done. How many miles again?'

'Twenty,' she replied, handing him a towel. 'A cheque will do, I know you're good for it.'

He smiled and leaned forward to kiss her briefly as he dried his hands.

'I thought we'd go to the pub for dinner,' Sabrina said, rehanging the towel and passing him a drink. 'Annabelle and Georgie are going to join us.'

Robert immediately looked uneasy. 'Uh, I was thinking I might light the barbecue,' he said. 'It's a nice evening, and we haven't used it yet this year.'

Sabrina frowned. 'I've already booked a table,' she informed him.

'It's easy enough to cancel.'

She was staring at him hard. Then, realising what the real issue was, the colour started to fade from her cheeks. 'Maybe I don't want to cancel,' she said stubbornly.

'Maybe you do,' he said pleasantly.

Sensing the tension Annabelle looked up. 'It's just the pub,' she told them, 'what's the big deal?'

Ignoring her, Sabrina said to Robert, 'Could we have a word, please? In private?'

'Oh, don't mind me,' Annabelle said, closing the magazine, 'I'm going up to my room anyway. Send Georgie up when she arrives.'

As the door closed behind her, Sabrina waited to hear footsteps disappearing down the hall before turning back to Robert. 'I take it your sister's going to the pub tonight,' she said tightly.

He nodded and sipped his drink. 'She's meeting Rachel,' he said, 'and unless I'm gravely mistaken, I thought you'd prefer not to be under the same roof as her – or in the same garden, given the weather.'

Sabrina's face was becoming more pinched by the second. 'I don't see why we should change our plans because of *her*,' she said bitingly.

'Then go,' he replied, 'but if it's all the same to you, I'll stay here.'

Her drink hit the worktop with a clang. 'This village is our home,' she fumed, 'it's where I live and I have every right to go to the pub whenever I choose.'

'I'm not arguing, I'm just saying I'm not going to spend the evening ignoring my own sister, which is what you'll want me to do, and nor do I want to bear witness to some embarrassing confrontation between the two of you. There are other pubs . . .'

'Then let her find one. We're going to the Traveller's.'

'I just told you, I'm staying here.'

Since he knew full well she wouldn't go without him, her frustration almost hit boiling point. 'So what happened when you went round there today?' she demanded, making a valiant effort to hold back her temper.

'Nothing *happened*. We had a cup of tea and chatted for a while, then I left.'

'Did you find out what her plans are?'

'Yes. She's staying here in Holly Wood and sending the children to Stanbrooks.'

Sabrina's jaw dropped as her eyes rounded with horror. 'But she can't,' she protested. 'Nathan's at Westminster. Craig would never have wanted him to leave.'

'At risk of pointing out the obvious, Craig no longer has a say in it. The London house has been sold and all their personal belongings are due to arrive tomorrow.'

Sabrina looked as though she'd been slapped.

'Let's go to the Wheatsheaf,' he suggested. 'I'm in the mood for a good steak and theirs rarely fail to hit the spot.'

'So what's she going to do here?' Sabrina demanded. 'Become one of the idle rich, I suppose?'

'Actually, she's going to open the shop and sell her sculptures,' he answered, not enjoying this very much, in spite of how relaxed he was managing to sound.

Sabrina was staring at him in mute disbelief.

'She's hoping to champion some local talent too,' he continued, deciding to get it all out. 'She's describing it as an arty kind of gift shop.'

Sabrina's eyes blazed. 'We don't have *gift* shops in Holly Wood,' she spat scathingly.

He almost smiled, but managed not to.

'Next thing she'll be trying to bring in tourists and that's not what this village is about. We don't want outsiders tramping all over our streets, staring in our windows and taking our parking places.'

'She needs to make a living,' he said quietly.

Sabrina glared at him incredulously. 'Are you seriously asking me to believe . . .'

'She's had to sell the London house,' he interrupted, 'but I'm not going into any more detail than that, because it wouldn't be right when you feel the way you do about her.'

So thrown by the fact that Craig hadn't left his family as comfortably off as she'd expected, it was a while before Sabrina could say, 'Funny how you never have a problem being loyal to her, but when it comes to me you seem to forget the meaning of the word.'

He kept his eyes on hers until she realised how inappropriate her comment was, particularly considering how he'd stood by her when she'd got herself into such an appalling state after being forced to break up with Craig.

'I'm sorry,' she mumbled, 'I shouldn't have said that.'

'Why don't you start giving some thought to apologising to her?' he dared to suggest. 'Since you're going to be living in the same village, you're bound to run into one another . . .'

'I have nothing to apologise for,' she cut in angrily. 'Not to her.'

'How can you say that when Craig was her husband . . .'

'So it was for him to apologise to her, as I did to you.'

Sighing, he picked up his drink and took another sip. 'I don't know why you've always had such a down on her,' he said. 'You took against her right from the start . . .'

'Excuse me!' she cut in savagely. 'She's always considered herself better than everyone else . . .'

'If you'd ever bothered to get to know her properly you'd know how wrong you are.'

'What about her getting to know me? She could barely bring herself to speak to me when we first got together.'

'I surely don't need to remind you how sick Darcie was at the time.'

'Other people who have sick children bother to be polite. She didn't even come to our wedding. And in case you've forgotten, I was always a very generous hostess whenever they came here, which is a lot more than I can say for her when we were in London.'

He blinked in amazement. 'You clearly have a very different view of hospitality to mine,' he told her, 'but this is a fatuous argument that's getting us nowhere. The problem today, as I see it, is that you can't face up to your own guilt, and unless you do, you're the one who's likely to suffer the most.'

'Really?' she snapped nastily. 'We'll see about that. She might have been born in this village, but I'm the one who's lived here for the past twelve years, and I'm the one who's on the parish council. So that tacky gift shop of hers? It'll happen over my dead body.'

As the door closed quietly behind him Sabrina sank down at the table and buried her face in her hands. She wanted to cry and scream and tear out her hair, she felt so wretched and ignored. No one was sparing a thought for how Craig's death might have affected her, and the struggle to keep her grief hidden was getting harder all the time. Now, with Alicia showing up and planning to stay, it was as though someone up there was trying to punish Sabrina by making her seem more insignificant than ever. God, how she detested Alicia for being the wife everyone sympathised with, as though she was the only woman who'd ever mattered to Craig. If it weren't for his children he'd have left her two years ago, and how desperately Sabrina wished he had, because there was no doubt in her mind that he'd still be alive now if he'd found the courage to leave and make a new life with her.

Chapter Six

Alicia was standing at the back of her mother's charity shop, in the space she was intending to use as a studio. To anyone else it probably wouldn't have appeared at all inspiring, but with her artistic eye she was able to see past all the cobwebs and mice droppings, rotting boxes and books, cracked windowpanes, grimy sink, rusty pipes and peeling paint to a large, bright room with French doors opening to a small back patio with its bedraggled flower pots and the outside loo (as yet unexplored). Though the space was smaller than she remembered, it was definitely big enough for her to work in, while the shop itself offered plenty of room for display stands and cases, and a deep bay window where prize pieces could be exhibited to the passing world.

Since Holly Wood didn't attract many visitors, she'd have to be imaginative and highly motivated when it came to marketing herself, but she had friends in London who she was sure would advise, and perhaps even send the odd client or ten her way. Locally she could advertise in parish magazines and West Country newspapers – when she could afford it. To get started it might be a good idea to design a flyer to put up in the county's main tourist offices, as well as various village halls and gastropubs.

Meanwhile, she needed to make some room here for the removal men to deliver her work table, welding equipment, and finished sculptures. Since the only brush to hand was all woodworm and no bristles, she'd have to run back to the Coach House to get one. At the same time she'd pick up some bin bags, a bucket, scouring pads, Cif and some rubber gloves.

Letting herself out of the shop, she locked the door with its old-fashioned key, gathered up an abandoned bag of old shoes that someone had left heaven only knew when, and turned towards the pub. She was still a little bleary-eyed after one too many last night, but it had been fun sitting in the Traveller's garden with Nat and Summer, and Rachel and her family, feeling able to relax for a few hours before the real challenge started today. Just thank goodness Sabrina and Robert hadn't shown up. Maggie had told her they'd booked, but had cancelled last-minute, which was no problem for Maggie, since there were plenty waiting to take their place. For Alicia it was a dizzyingly narrow escape, though obviously the dreaded encounter would have to happen sooner or later. When it did it would be the first time they'd come face to face since the day they'd laid into one another in front of her mother – apart from at Monica's funeral when they'd studiously ignored one another – and right now the only feeling Alicia could muster for the woman was that she'd like to punch her all over again.

As she rounded the corner into The Close her spirits rose to see Rachel's car parked behind the removal van. 'What are you doing here?' she called out, as Rachel emerged from the front door with Nat.

'I had a house call on Sheep Lane,' Rachel answered, coming to give her a hug, 'so I thought I'd drop in to find out how it's all going. How's the shop?'

'In need of much elbow grease and TLC, but nothing seems to be leaking, so it shouldn't take too long to turn around. My able-bodied son here has offered to paint it for me, haven't you darling?'

'I have?' he blinked.

She smiled.

'I have,' he confirmed.

Rachel laughed. 'I've got a whole surgery that needs doing,' she told him, 'if you want to earn some cash.'

'That's more like it,' he responded, rubbing his hands together. 'It's only slave labour around here, and I've got an expensive girlfriend to support.'

'What are you saying about me?' Summer demanded, tripping out of the house in a tight little mini dress and clumpy basketweave wedges.

'Mrs Carlyle? Are you down there?' a removal man shouted from the top of the stairs. 'Do you want us to put this desk together for you? We've got time.'

'You're an angel,' Alicia called back. 'Thank you.'

'Most of your stuff's in now,' Nat told her. 'They're in Darcie's room at the moment. Mine's done, so it won't be long before they're ready to come to the shop.'

'In which case I need to get myself back up there pronto to make some room,' Alicia replied, starting in through the door.

'Wrong direction,' he pointed out.

'Brushes, brooms, buckets,' she informed him.

Glancing at her watch Rachel said, 'I've got half an hour to spare before I'm due back at the surgery, I'll come and lend a hand.'

Ten minutes later she and Alicia were hauling and sweeping rubbish out of the back room into the shop, where Nat and Summer were bagging it ready to take to the tip. There was no clear route through to the soon-to-be-studio yet, but at the rate they were going there would be by the time the removal men turned up.

'Need any more hands?' a voice shouted from the front door. It was Rachel's Aunt Mimi, popping in from her flower shop next door. 'Pete's free if you want anything doing.'

'I think we're OK for the moment,' Alicia laughed, going to embrace her.

'Unless Pete's up for sorting out a grungy old loo,' Rachel shouted.

Mimi's devilish eyes twinkled. 'I'll give him a call and get him down here pronto,' she said, 'then I'll bring in some coffee for you all.'

'You're a sweetheart,' Alicia told her.

Mimi had barely left before Alicia heard more voices out at the front and, looking up, she felt her insides give an uneasy lurch when she saw who it was.

'Oh blimey,' Rachel murmured.

Annabelle, looking breathtakingly grown-up, was blatantly checking Nat out, while the friend with her was treating Summer to an outrageous once-over. However, Summer wasn't the daughter of an earl for nothing, because her look back was so witheringly disdainful that the other girl blushed and turned away.

'Annabelle,' Alicia said warmly, breezing into the shop. 'What a lovely surprise.'

'Hey,' Annabelle responded, tearing her eyes from Nat. 'I heard you were here so we came over to say hi. It's been ages since we last saw you. I thought you'd forgotten about us. Oh yeah, and I'm sorry about Uncle Craig. That was terrible.'

Alicia kept her smile in place as she embraced her stepniece. She probably hadn't meant her condolence to come out as such a crude afterthought. 'Thank you,' she said. 'It's good to see you. You've grown into a very striking young lady.'

Annabelle preened and glanced at Nat. 'So how long are you staying?' she asked.

'We live here now,' Alicia answered, still shaken by how adult and apparently full of herself Annabelle seemed. 'We're just sorting out the shop ready to turn it into a kind of workshop-cum-gallery.'

'Cool.' Annabelle cast another look in Nat's direction, but he'd turned away to carry on filling bags.

'Hello, I'm Alicia,' Alicia said to the other girl.

'Oh, sorry,' Annabelle said, 'this is my friend Georgie.'

'Hey,' Georgie said, fanning her fingers.

Annabelle turned her attention to Summer. 'And you would be?' she prompted rudely.

'This is Summer, Nat's girlfriend,' Alicia informed her.

Annabelle looked Summer up and down. 'Nice to meet you too, Nat's girlfriend,' she drawled. 'Cool dress. D&G?'

Summer nodded. Her pale freckled face was showing how confused she was by the undercurrent.

'Mm, thought so.' Turning back to Nat, Annabelle said, 'We'll have to catch up sometime. Maybe we can have a game of draughts.'

From the way Nat reddened and Georgie sniggered, Alicia guessed the comment was a sexual euphemism that probably only teenagers understood.

'We need to go,' Georgie muttered. 'They'll be here any minute.'

Annabelle turned back to Alicia. 'It's great you're here,' she said. 'You'll have to come over to the house sometime, I know Mum would love to see you,' and with a sweet little smile she started towards the door. 'Oh, in case you're interested,' she said to Nat, 'there's going to be a rave in the Copse in a couple of weeks. Everyone's going.'

'Yes, Simon Forsey mentioned it,' he told her.

Her eyebrows went up. 'Then maybe you'll both come,' she murmured, and with an outrageously suggestive sweep of her eyes, she followed Georgie out into the street.

'Who on earth was that?' Summer demanded as soon as Annabelle was out of earshot.

'A kind of cousin, but not,' Nat answered. 'Her mother's married to Mum's brother. Anyway, forget her, she's no one.'

Alicia blinked at the sharp dismissal of someone he'd once been very close to, but actually she was rather glad of it, considering how awkward it might be if they were to become friends again. Returning to the studio, her eyebrows lifted as she met Rachel's eyes.

'Talk about jailbait,' Rachel murmured.

'She's terrifying,' Alicia agreed. 'If her mother was anyone but Sabrina I'd feel sorry for the poor woman.'

'As it is, we won't waste the time. What was that about draughts?'

'I've no idea. You probably have to be their age to understand it.'

Rachel was shaking her head, and watching as a BMW convertible pulled up across the road for Annabelle and Georgie to get in. 'We weren't like that at her age, were we?' she said. 'I know we were into boys by then, but I can't imagine we were ever so upfront about it.'

'Are you kidding? I was eighteen before I could even look a boy in the eye.'

Rachel laughed. 'Yeah, really,' she said. 'More like fourteen, but that was about all we did, and a bit of snogging, I suppose. As for her, if that girl's still a virgin then I'm a talking horse.'

Alicia laughed, then yelped as Nat came up behind her and dug her in the ribs. 'Removal men just called, they're on their way up,' he told her. 'I'm going back to the house to carry on sorting stuff there. Call if you need me.' He put his mouth to her ear. 'And when we're done there's something I want to ask you.'

* * *

'So what was that about draughts?' Summer wanted to know as she and Nat walked back to the Coach House.

His expression tightened slightly. 'Oh, she was just being puerile,' he replied irritably. 'Take no notice. She's not someone we have to bother about.'

'But if she's your cousin . . .'

'She's not really, and anyway, it makes no difference. We never see them. I mean, Mum sees her brother, or she did yesterday, but that was the first time in I don't know how long. Apart from at Dad's funeral.'

'Really? Did they have a falling-out or something?'

'Not them, it's Mum and his wife, Sabrina, who don't speak. Something happened a couple of years ago, but don't ask me what, it's not something I've ever gone into.'

Summer shrugged and stood aside at the gate for two removal men to traipse past on their way out.

'Mum's about ready up there,' Nat told them. 'The sculptures are basically unbreakable, but they weigh a ton, and her welding stuff's more precious than jewels, so good luck.'

'That's an impressive computer you've got in your room,' one of them commented. 'Wouldn't mind something like that for my lad.'

Nat's eyes flickered to one side. 'It was my dad's,' he told him.

The removal man gave Summer a friendly wink and carried on out to the truck.

'Are you going to talk to your mum about us

sharing a room?' Summer murmured, once she and Nat were inside and locked in an embrace.

'Mm, when the time's right. I'll take you over and show you the Copse later, it'll give us a chance to be on our own for a while.'

As he kissed her he found himself thinking about the first time he'd kissed Annabelle, in her room over at Uncle Robert's house. She'd been twelve at the time, and he was fourteen.

'I thought we were supposed to be playing draughts,' she teased, as they sat together on the edge of her bed, holding hands and their lips barely inches apart after their first brief touch.

'Didn't you like that?' he asked, feeling hot and self-conscious and rigid with terror at the thought of someone coming in.

Her eyes went down as she thought about it, then came up to him in a childishly flirtatious way. 'Why don't we do it again, and then I'll be able to tell you,' she said.

Overcome by her response, he put his lips against hers again, feeling his own trembling slightly as he moved them around a little, then opened them up. Her lips were soft and yielding and came apart with his in a way that made him feel drunk and afraid, it was so good. He took a peep and saw that her eyes were closed. He was trying to ignore what was happening to him down below, but it was becoming bigger and more urgent by the second. He put a hand on her neck and smoothed the skin, still kissing her and wondering if he dared use his tongue. He had with other girls, but they were the same age as him so that was all right. Annabelle was still young and he didn't want to scare her. Then he felt her tongue touching his lips and suddenly he was so hard that it made him dizzy with lust and excruciating embarrassment.

'Oh my God,' she giggled when she realised what was happening.

'I'm sorry,' he mumbled, trying to get away from her.

'No, don't be,' she said. 'It's good that it happened. It means you really like me.'

'Of course I like you,' he said, needing to get to the bathroom.

'I really like you too,' she said. 'You kiss much better than anyone else I know.'

He stared at her in amazement.

'Don't look like that,' she laughed. 'I've had lots of boyfriends. Well, two, anyway, that I've kissed. Actually, I was practising on them for when I kissed you, because I always thought we would. Did you?'

Flustered, he said, 'Yeah, I suppose so. Look, wait there, OK? I'll be back.'

'Shall I set up the draughts board, in case anyone comes in?' she asked.

'Uh, yeah, do that,' he told her, and closing the bathroom door behind him, he leaned against it, taking a deep shuddering breath. She really, really turned him on, and she was so up for it, he wasn't sure what to do next. In some weirdly unbalanced part of his head he wanted to go and ask his dad, but that was a definite no go, and anyway, it wasn't as if he'd never felt a girl up before. Thinking of doing it to Annabelle his eyes closed and he almost whimpered at the renewed tightening in his groin.

The best thing for him to do now, he decided, was to go back downstairs where everyone else was watching a DVD. If she wanted to do something again next time he came here, or when she was at his place in London, he would, but they'd been up here long enough now. The last thing he wanted was anyone suspecting, when even the thought of it burned him up inside and out with total, all-out, toe-curling, brain-numbing embarrassment.

It was late afternoon by the time Alicia finally left the shop to return to the Coach House, tired, dirty and in sore need of a long soak in the bath. She'd had so many visitors during the day, locals offering sympathy for her loss, or advice for her future, or wanting to find out what she was up to, or in some cases to help with the hard work, that she hadn't achieved quite as much as she'd hoped. However, the place had now mostly been cleared of rubbish, the sink and loo were more or less approachable, and her precious sculptures, though still temporarily stored in their packing cases, were at least in the right venue.

As she let herself into the house the sound of Radiohead blaring from Nat's iPod speakers caused her to groan and want to retreat. However, instead of going upstairs to ask him to turn it down, she wove a path through the boxes in the hall to the kitchen, tugged open the fridge and took out a bottle of cold beer. After pouring it into a glass, she played back two messages on the answerphone, both from friends in London asking how she was settling in and telling her to give them a call when she had time, then wandered outside to sit down in the garden. She still had a mountain of unpacking to get through, but she had all summer for that and right now she just wanted to close her eyes, enjoy her drink, and try not to think of why she was here. For a while she drifted dreamily, seeming to float in an open, empty world, where nothing was pushing her on or holding her back. She was free of her own thoughts, unleashed from the pain, detached from the memories. Everything was light and white, unspoiled and perfect in a way that had no substance or meaning, or weight to pull her down. How long was it before she landed? Seconds, minutes? She had no idea. She only knew she was back in London and feeling excited and happy as she heard Craig's key in the door.

Saying a quick goodbye to her mother on the phone she hung up and dashed across the kitchen. 'I've got it!' she cried, as he stepped into the hall. 'I passed. I'm now a fully qualified welder.'

Dropping his briefcase he laughed delightedly as he swung her round with pride. 'My wife, the blowtorch babe,' he teased. 'All that hard work and now you can repair the car, put our pipes back together and solder cheese graters to brass knockers to make modern art.'

She gurgled with laughter and threw back her head for him to kiss her hard.

Now, sitting in her mother's garden, she was smiling through her tears as she recalled those moments, long before the affair, when she'd become so used to their happiness and so sure of his love that it had never even crossed her mind that anything would happen to spoil it.

They'd celebrated at home that night, with Nat and Darcie, aged seven and twelve, who didn't really understand why their mother wanted to be a welder, or even, in Darcie's case, what a welder actually did. To them it only mattered that their parents were in playful moods and that their mother, according to their father, was going to become a world-famous artist, making sculptures out of stainless steel.

'I thought you made them in bronze,' Nat said, confused.

'No, plasticine,' Darcie corrected.

'I make the moulds in plasticine,' Alicia explained, 'that are then cast in bronze. But now I can make sculptures in steel as well.'

'Why do you want to do that?' Nat asked, pulling a face.

Alicia glanced helplessly at Craig and threw out her hands. 'Because it's how the mood takes me,' she answered with a laugh.

'Your mother's an artist who follows her whims,' Craig informed them, putting a steaming hot bowl of noodles on the table. 'And a good thing too, because they're as beautiful as she is.'

'Did you meet any murderers today?' Darcie asked, dismissing all this nonsense talk and returning to the macabre interest she'd recently developed in her father's world.

'No, but I had lunch with Father Christmas who told me what he's bringing you this year,' Craig answered.

'But I haven't sent a note yet,' Darcie protested.

'That's what he said, so I think you'd better get round to it.'

'We can get Mum a welder's helmet,' Nat suggested.

'I already have all the gear,' she told him. 'It's a place to work I need now I've finished college. A little studio all of my own would be lovely, if you can manage it.'

'Whooosh, went the genie,' Craig responded, 'your wish is my command. We'll find you somewhere by the end of the week.'

He had as well, a small workshop in Fulham with a vast rent, that she'd had to give up long before she'd let go of the house. Anyway, after Craig died she'd lost the heart to create.

Taking a sip of her beer, she wrested her mind away from her memories, finding them too difficult to deal with when she was so tired and feeling anxious about ever being able to create anything again. Her thoughts returned to the new studio she was trying to set up, and then she was thinking about Annabelle's impromptu visit earlier. Seeing the child looking so grown-up and flirting so brazenly had been an unsettling experience. Not that Annabelle hadn't always had a knowing sort of way with her, seeming to understand how powerful her looks made her, but there had been a sweetness and innocence to her before which had been totally absent today. And if the way she'd carried on with Nat was typical of how she behaved with the opposite sex then Robert was right, it wouldn't be a good idea for an impressionable young Darcie to spend much time with her.

In fact, all things considered, Alicia would rather Darcie didn't see her at all.

'Hey, you're back,' Nat said, appearing in the kitchen doorway. 'I didn't hear you come in.'

'I wonder why,' she smiled, realising the music had been turned down. 'Where's Summer?'

'Taking a bath. Like another?' he offered, nodding towards her glass.

'Yes, why not?' She was trying not to be annoyed that Summer was where she wanted to be, reminding herself that this was how it was going to be from now on, with only one bathroom in the house, so she'd better start getting used to it.

After fetching two more bottles, Nat topped up her glass and pulled up a chair for himself. 'So is everything OK at the shop?' he asked. 'I was about to come and find out how you were getting on.'

'There's still a lot to do, but we'll get round to it. How's your unpacking coming along?'

'Not bad. My desk is a bit small for the computer, but it's no big deal.'

'We'll have to get someone in to mount the TVs on the walls in your and Darcie's rooms,' she said, feeling suddenly very weary at the thought of how much needed doing that she'd have to pay for. 'And we should order a new satellite dish for the Sky boxes.'

'I'll do it,' he said, 'but there's no rush. There's never anything on worth watching at this time of year anyway. Apart from cricket.'

Smiling at the way he was trying to make her feel better, she put a hand on his arm and squeezed.

'You've got dirt on your face and a cobweb in your hair,' he told her.

'Does it suit me?'

He laughed, and tilted his beer to drink.

A few minutes ticked quietly by. The music had finished altogether now, so all they could hear was the faraway drone of a plane going over, and the pleasing squawk of crickets. A dog began barking somewhere nearby, followed by a voice calling it in. Then a car started up across the street, and whoever it was drove away.

She was so enjoying sitting there, just the two of them, that she almost didn't hear when Nat said, very quietly, 'Do you miss him?'

As his words wrenched at her heart she could feel his loss tugging at her as though it were her own. What she wouldn't give to be able to turn his world back into the safe and happy place it used to be. 'Yes, I miss him a lot,' she answered.

He nodded. His face was paling, and his mouth showed his tension.

'Do you?' she asked.

He looked down at his beer. 'I try not to think about it,' he said.

Wanting desperately to put her hand on his, but sensing he wouldn't welcome it, she said, 'There's nothing wrong in missing him.'

'I know, I'm just saying . . .' He shifted uncomfortably, and put the bottle to his mouth to drink. 'We went over to the Copse this afternoon,' he said gruffly. 'It hasn't changed.'

Saddened by the change of subject, but daring to hope it might be a roundabout route back to something he wanted to say, she waited for him to go on.

'I've been meaning to ask you,' he said, after a

while, 'I mean, if it's OK with you . . . Would it be all right if Summer and I shared a room?'

Smiling past the ache inside her, for she knew this was a question he'd have found far easier to ask Craig, she said, 'It's fine, but you only have a single bed. It won't be very comfortable.'

'We'll manage.' He looked at her quickly. A moment later his eyes came back to her, and as he started to smile she did too. 'Thanks,' he said.

She sipped her drink, then let her head fall forward.

'Are you OK?' he asked.

'Just tired. We need to think about what we're going to eat tonight. The Friary's closed on Mondays, or we could have had fish and chips. Are you hungry?'

'Famished. I could drive over to Bruton and pick up some pizzas.'

He'd passed his test a week before Craig died, but had hardly driven since, so she wasn't sure about letting him take a car he didn't know without her being next to him, at least for the first trip out. 'We could go together,' she suggested.

'I can do it,' he insisted. Then, 'Mum, you have to stop worrying about me all the time. I drove Dad's Mercedes . . .'

'Once, and he was with you – and my Renault has a long way to go before it can make that class.'

To her surprise he laughed. 'You're right about that,' he told her. 'It's a heap, but if I did any damage at least it wouldn't cost as much as if I pranged the Merc.'

'It's you I'm concerned about, not the car, but OK, to demonstrate my faith in you, you can take it. I'll have a bath while you're gone. Presumably Summer will go with you.'

'Yeah. We want to make the most of our time together, before she leaves on Wednesday.' He took another sip of his drink. 'Did I tell you her parents have invited me to join them in Italy?'

Alicia's insides churned. 'Darcie mentioned something about it,' she said, having to push aside a sudden urge to cling on to him. 'That's very kind of them.' Then, forcing the next words out, 'Do you want to go? It's fine with me, if you do. It wouldn't be fair if only Darcie had a holiday. You need one too.'

'No, I'm good,' he said.

'If you're thinking about me, then don't. I've got so much to be getting on with the time'll just fly.'

'It's OK, I'm happy to stay here. I'm going to paint the shop and help design a flyer for you, and I can catch up with some friends before I start the new school.'

'Nat, you don't have to take care of me,' she told him softly. 'I want you to do whatever makes you happy, and if going to Italy is what you want . . .'

'It's not, honest. I shouldn't have brought it up. It was just that Summer didn't want you to think that they hadn't invited me.'

Alicia smiled. 'That's sweet of her.' Then, remembering his parting words when he'd left the shop earlier, 'Is that what you wanted to talk to me about? Or no, I guess it was the sleeping arrangements.'

He took a breath and stared out across the garden.

'Actually, it was neither,' he replied. 'I mean, it was, because obviously I wanted to . . . Well, what I wanted to ask you, actually, was why you and Sabrina don't speak? I mean, it makes no odds to me,' he went on hurriedly, 'I've never really liked her anyway, but if it causes a problem between you and Uncle Robert, that's not good, especially now we're living here.'

Touched by his concern for her, and obvious desire to understand a situation that had probably never made any sense to him, she managed to sidestep the question, saying, 'Uncle Robert and I can work things out, don't you worry about that. He knows Sabrina and I have never really got along, and rather than pretend to like one another, we've decided it's probably best if we don't actually see one another.'

Nat nodded, and seeming more or less satisfied with that, he got up from the table. 'Half each of a Four Seasons and a Chorizo?' he said.

Alicia looked up at him. 'Summer might want to swap and share,' she reminded him tactfully.

He coloured slightly. 'Of course. Hell, we can all swap and share,' he declared. 'I'll go and find her. And try to clean yourself up by the time I get back, there's a good girl. The witchy look really doesn't do it for me.'

Chapter Seven

'Catrina, you are so outrageous,' Annabelle squealed, falling back on her bed and kicking her legs in the air with excitement.

'What?' Catrina replied, looking at Georgie, all innocence. 'I reckon it's a great idea.'

'Who's going?' Georgie wanted to know.

'Everyone. Theo, Kennedy, Melody, Carl, all the usual gang and anyone else we want to invite. It'll be a scream. Theo's getting some E from his cousin, who might come too, and Petra says she can probably get some weed from her uncle, you know, the one in East Lydford, who grows it. We have to go. We can't not.'

'Too right,' Annabelle agreed, sitting up and raking back her hair. 'And do you know what's really great about it,' she added mischievously, 'we won't have a problem deciding what to wear.'

As they burst out laughing there was a knock on the door, silencing them abruptly.

'Who is it?' Annabelle demanded frostily.

'Who do you think?' Sabrina replied from the landing. 'I'm off now. Robert's in his study, but he'll be going out in about an hour if you want a lift into Wells.'

'Cool,' Annabelle shouted back. Then under her breath, 'Get lost now. We don't need any more of you.'

When she didn't hear her mother walking away Annabelle crept over to the door, turned the key and peered out on to the landing. Finding no eavesdroppers she stepped back inside, and signalled to Georgie to put on some music as she relocked the door.

'OK, so where were we?' she said, sinking cross-legged on to a downy floor cushion next to Catrina. 'OMG, a topless pool party. It is going to be soooo wild.'

'So you're definitely up for it?' Catrina said. 'Good, cos I've already told Theo we'll be there.'

'Actually, I reckon he should make it a nudie party,' Annabelle stated recklessly. 'Once we've all had a drink and some E and start swimming it'll all come off anyway.'

'Is that your phone?' Georgie said to Catrina, recognising the ringtone.

Reaching behind her to where she'd left it on the bed, Catrina saw who was calling and clicked on straight away. 'Hey Archie,' she said, beaming at the others, 'how're things?'

Georgie looked at Annabelle. 'Bet you she agrees to see him,' she murmured.

Not appearing particularly interested, Annabelle said, 'Of course she will, she always does.'

Georgie shrugged. 'I wouldn't let anyone mess me around like that,' she commented.

'That's because you're not in love.'

'I so am, well kind of, anyway. I was thinking,

why don't you invite your cousin to the party? It would be amazing if he came, wouldn't it?'

Annabelle's eyes narrowed, and catching the wickedest of wicked gleams, Georgie started to grin.

'I have to meet him outside the Shell garage at three,' Catrina stated, dropping her phone on the floor.

'You know he's just going to shag you and take you home again,' Georgie told her.

'You're just jealous,' Catrina retorted. 'So what's going on?' she asked Annabelle.

'Georgie has had the most brilliant idea,' Annabelle informed her. 'We're going to ask my cousin, Nat, to the party.'

Catrina looked distinctly unimpressed. 'Big deal,' she said, rummaging through her make-up. 'Do you think he'll come?'

'We won't know unless we ask.'

'If he does, then he's mine first,' Georgie piped up.

Annabelle's eyes flashed. 'You know what you can do,' she told her hotly.

Georgie laughed, showing she'd been teasing. 'Question is, how do we get rid of the ginger one?' she said. 'We don't want her dragging along, and I, for one, definitely don't want to see her in the nud, snooty bitch.'

'Oh, yuk, rusty pubes,' Catrina commented, applying mascara.

Annabelle giggled. 'Who cares about her? All we've got to do is find out his mobile number so we can invite him.'

* * *

June Downey-Marsh could feel the intensity of Sabrina's gaze even before she looked up from the computer screen in front of her. With a sleek cap of dark blonde hair, caramel-coloured eyes and a girlish tilt to the corners of her mouth, June didn't look her entire forty-six years. However, despite her attractive appearance, since her divorce she still hadn't been able to find a wealthy man to replace the one she'd so foolishly let slip. So she was currently living in a modest apartment on the second floor of a grand stately home, halfway between Shepton Mallet and Holly Wood. This was where she and Sabrina were now, not in the apartment, but behind the grand house in one of the offices that they leased from the National Trust. It was from here, with its eye-catching views of a water garden, a magnificent sweep of lawn and several Renaissance-style statues, that they ran the bi-monthly freesheet they'd devised and largely financed to serve the surrounding area.

'Do you really want to do this?' June asked seriously.

Sabrina's expression hardened. 'That shop only has a licence for retail,' she stated tightly, 'which means she will be operating illegally if she starts up a manufacturing enterprise.'

'Does sculpting qualify as . . . ?'

'What's more, she has it in her mind to start bringing tourism to Holly Wood, and the people of Holly Wood don't want it.'

'Have you asked them?'

'I don't have to. I live amongst them, so I know how they feel about the village being invaded by coachloads of Japanese and check-trousered Americans.'

'Sabrina, get real, one little art shop isn't going to put Holly Wood on anyone's tourist map, and even if it did, no one would come, because Holly Wood doesn't have anything else to offer.'

'I thought you were supporting me over this,' Sabrina said crossly.

'I am, I'm just trying to point out the holes in your argument. And this letter,' June added, indicating the one on the screen, 'is too emotional. You need to tone it down and put forward a rational case for why the shop should not be used as a . . . *manufacturing* unit.'

Sabrina looked at her own copy of the letter she'd drafted before coming here.

'The point is,' June went on, 'even if you manage to stop her turning it into a workshop, she's still entitled to sell her sculptures, and anything else she might choose.'

'Not if the rest of the village don't want her to reopen the shop. I could get up a petition.'

'Sabrina, save yourself the embarrassment. She's from that village. They've all known her since she was knee-high to a grasshopper, and everyone loved her mother. I'm telling you, for your own good, they won't take your side against her, not over something like this.'

Sabrina's eyes closed in frustration. 'June, I have to do something to get rid of her,' she groaned. 'We can't exist in the same village, you know that as well as I do, so help me out here, come up with a plan.'

Sitting back in her chair, June folded her arms

and regarded her sadly. 'You won't want to hear this,' she said, 'but I'm afraid I agree with Robert. You should try to make peace with her. No, hear me out,' she said, as Sabrina looked about to erupt. 'The chances are she won't want to have anything to do with you . . .'

'Save your breath, June,' Sabrina broke in. 'There's no way in the world I'm going to speak to her. Would you, if you were me, after everything that's happened? Craig and I *loved* one another. If it weren't for her . . .'

As her eyes filled with tears, June gave a murmur of sympathy. More than anyone, with the exception of Robert, she knew how Sabrina had suffered after her break-up with Craig. The heartbreak had consumed her as voraciously as the affair itself, though whether Craig had been equally distraught, or obsessed, June had never been sure. It had obviously meant something to him while it was happening, though, because they'd spent every available minute together, travelling back and forth across the country, meeting halfway in fancy hotels or cheap motels, in one another's houses, sometimes even in the car. Secretly June had always been afraid of how it would end, because relationships of such intensity were almost always doomed to disaster, and when the dreaded explosion did finally come, she had rarely seen displays of emotion like it. Many and long were the days and nights she'd sat with Sabrina, watching her tearing herself to pieces, so desperate to see Craig, or even hear him, while swearing the worst imaginable revenge on Alicia, that June had been afraid to leave her alone.

* * *

'I have to speak to him,' Sabrina choked, slopping her wine as she reached for the phone. 'I can't go on like this. I need to tell him how I feel.'

'He already knows,' June said kindly, 'and it's gone one o'clock in the morning.'

They were in Sabrina's bedroom, Robert was next door in the guest room, where he'd been sleeping since the day Craig had told Sabrina it was over. Three months banished from his own bed was more than most men would take, but Robert was hiding his own heartache while trying to be patient and understanding, and asking for June's help when he needed it, because, when drunk, Sabrina couldn't stand to have him near her.

'It doesn't matter what time it is,' Sabrina slurred. 'I know he'll be lying awake thinking of me.' Her face crumpled as more tears spilled on to her ravaged cheeks. 'I can't bear to think of him hurting too,' she wailed. 'We have to be together. It's wrong for us to be apart like this.' She poured more wine into her glass. 'You know she blackmailed him into going back to her, don't you?' she ranted. 'She threatened to tell the children about us and turn them against him, and he couldn't have stood that. Nat and Darcie mean everything to him.' She drank some wine and hiccuped. 'We used to talk about how wonderful it would be if they could come to live with us,' she ran on, 'how we'd be a family, all of us. Annabelle used to get along so well with his two. They were like brother and sisters already, but that bitch wouldn't let him go.' She was swaying badly and as her head went down she started to cry again. 'He never really loved her,' she sobbed, 'but it wasn't until he met me that he realised how shallow their marriage actually was. What we had together . . . It was like nothing I've ever experienced before. Nor had he. We just couldn't get enough of one another.' Seeming to register the phone in her hand again, she looked down at it blearily, and suddenly remembering why it was there she opened it up.

As she dialled the number she was hardly able to see, she'd cried and drunk so much, and June could only watch helplessly, knowing she'd turn violent if she tried to stop her.

'It's me,' Sabrina slurred into the phone when he answered. 'I know it's late . . .'

June heard him say, 'I can't speak to you now. You have to stop ringing here.'

'Craig, please listen to me. I'll do anything . . .'

'I don't want you to do anything. I'm sorry . . .'

'Please, let's just talk,' she begged. 'That's all I'm asking.'

'There's no more to say.'

'I know you still love me. It's only because *she's* there that you can't say it.'

'I have to go.'

'No! Don't hang up. Craig, *please*. I'll drive up to London . . .'

Alicia's voice came down the line saying, 'If you call here again I'll report you for harassment,' and the line went dead.

'Oh God, I can't bear it,' Sabrina seethed, rolling on the bed and clutching her knees to her chest as she sobbed. 'She won't let him speak to me. She knows how much I mean to him and she's afraid he'll leave her. If he doesn't, June, I swear I'm going to kill myself. I mean it, I can't go on like this. There's no point to anything without him.'

Hoping Robert wasn't able to hear, June went to try and comfort her.

'Mum? What's the matter?'

Startled, June turned round and her heart burned with pity to see poor young Annabelle standing in the doorway. Though it wasn't the first time she'd witnessed her mother in this state, it was plain to anyone how much it was scaring her.

'It's OK,' June said, going to her. 'She'll be fine.'

'No I won't,' Sabrina choked. 'Nothing will ever be fine until I'm back with him.'

Annabelle turned her bemused eyes to June. 'Who's she talking about?' she asked.

'No one,' June answered, trying to usher her out.

'I'm dying,' Sabrina gasped from the bed. 'My heart is breaking and no one in this house cares.'

'Sabrina,' June said sharply, hoping to make her stop.

'I care, Mum,' Annabelle said shakily.

'Just go away,' Sabrina cried. 'I don't want you here.'

'She's had too much to drink,' June whispered, as Annabelle started to cry. 'Come on, I'll take you back to bed.'

'She's really stupid, the way she carries on like that,' Annabelle wept, as June tucked her in. 'She shouldn't drink, because she says horrible things and hurts people's feelings.'

'I know,' June whispered, 'just as long as you understand she doesn't mean them.'

'Anyway, I don't care if she does, because I've got my friends and everyone.'

'And Robert,' June reminded her.

'Yes, and him.'

After pressing a kiss to her forehead, June returned to Sabrina's room to find her on the phone to Craig again. 'If you won't see me I swear I'm going to kill myself,' she was crying.

June didn't hear his reply, so could only imagine how angry, or afraid, or guilty he was feeling.

'I *will*,' Sabrina shouted. 'OK, then tell me you love me. Yes you can. I don't care if she's there. No! It's not over, Craig. It never will be and you know it, because it's not what either of us wants.'

Since June had never discussed anything about the relationship or the break-up with Craig, she had no idea how he'd really felt about it all. She only knew that until the day he'd died Sabrina had never allowed herself to stop believing that somehow they'd be together again.

'The last words he said to me,' Sabrina murmured, as June went to pour them both a coffee, 'were "I love you." I never spoke to him again after that, but it was still as though we were soulmates, two halves of the same person. I know he didn't share any of that with her.'

Yet he stayed with her, June was thinking, *and if you believe it was because of the children, I'm sorry, but you're deluding yourself, because children survive divorce and if two people love one another as much as you seem to think you and Craig did, then nothing would keep them apart.* 'You're happy with Robert though,' she said, aloud, making it a statement rather than a question.

Sabrina sighed. 'I suppose so. I mean, yes, of course, but it's not the same as the feelings I had for Craig. Not even close.'

'Maybe it's . . . healthier, the way things are with Robert?'

Sabrina nodded, but she didn't seem to be listening. Then her eyes focused again on the letter she'd drafted about Alicia's workshop. 'I have to get her out of Holly Wood,' she said forcefully. 'The place isn't big enough for both of us, and as far as I'm concerned she has to learn that she can't have everything.' She looked up as June passed her a coffee. 'She might have taken Craig away from me,' she said brokenly, 'but I swear I'll kill her before I let her do the same with my home.'

Alicia was about to leave the house when her mobile rang on the hall table, providing a timely reminder to take it with her. Grabbing it, she tucked it under her chin as she riffled through the mail Sam had just sent cascading through the front door.

'Hi, is that Alicia?' a voice came cheerily down the line.

Recognising Annabelle's voice, and wondering what happened to the 'Aunt', Alicia said, 'Yes, it is. How lovely to hear you. You're up early this morning.'

'Oh yeah, well, I'm staying with a friend, you met her, Georgie, and we kind of haven't really been to sleep yet. Anyway, that's not why I'm ringing. I was hoping you'd be able to give me Nat's mobile. There's this party that loads of his friends are going to, and we thought he might like to come too.'

'You mean the one in the Copse, because I think he's already going to . . .'

'Oh, no, that's not for another couple of weeks. This one's on Saturday. Everyone's going to be there, and I thought, if he's going to be living here now, that it would be a good chance for him to catch up with everyone. They all want him to come, and they've made me promise to make him, so if you could let me have his number . . .'

Suspecting Nat might prefer her not to have it, especially while Summer was around, Alicia said, 'I could probably take my phone up to him now. I think I heard him moving around a few minutes ago.'

'Oh no, it's OK,' Annabelle responded. 'I don't have the actual address yet, so if you can just give me his number, I'll ring later to give him the details once I have them.'

Sensing herself being outmanoeuvred, and not liking it too much, Alicia said, 'Actually, it's in the phone I'm speaking on, so I'll have to ring off and call you back.'

'That's cool,' Annabelle chirped. 'I'll wait to hear from you. Oh, and by the way, I think what you're doing in the shop is fantastic. It's just what Holly Wood needs, something upscale and arty. Let me know if there's anything I can do to help.'

After thanking her smoothly Alicia rang off, sensing the offer was more about irritating her mother than about actually lending a hand, which was fine just as long as Alicia herself didn't get dragged into the fray.

It wasn't until she reached the end of the street that the blindingly obvious way to put Annabelle off finally occurred to her, and with a smile that would have made Nat laugh if he'd seen it, she took out her mobile again.

At her end Annabelle was sprawled out on Georgie's bed in a skimpy vest and boy boxers, admiring her legs as Georgie prattled on about whether she should ask for a membership for the Cowshed gym at Babington for her seventeenth birthday, when it came round next March.

'This'll be her,' Annabelle interrupted, clicking on her phone as it bleeped with a text.

Her smile was smug and sleepy until she read Alicia's message: *Have passed your number to Nat so he can call you. Ax*

Annabelle's eyes sparked with frustration as her pretty mouth tightened. 'Shit!' she muttered.

'What?' Georgie prompted.

'She's only getting him to call me, and we both know the ginger's bound to stop him.'

Georgie smirked. 'It's really bugging you, isn't it, that he didn't seem interested?'

'You are so wrong about that, because I know he is. I've told you about the things we used to do when our parents thought we were playing draughts in the bedroom. He was practically my first.'

'Yeah right, when you were eleven.'

'Twelve and fourteen, actually. We felt each other up and snogged and I even went down on him a couple of times.'

'Yeah, really. In your dreams.'

'No, not in my dreams. And he's definitely interested, he just didn't want to let it show in front of the ginge – and if you ask me, his stupid mother's trying to keep us apart because of her feud with the she-devil.'

'Yeah, what's that all about?' Georgie asked, holding up her nails for inspection.

Annabelle's eyes narrowed as she recalled what she'd overheard on Saturday morning. Wild. However, she didn't want to get into it now, so she simply said, 'Who knows? Who cares? I'm only interested in getting Nat to Theo's party on Saturday night.'

Georgie yawned and rolled on to her front as Annabelle went to open a window. 'Are you going to tell him what kind of party it is?' she asked. 'I mean, if you ever get to speak to him.'

Annabelle shrugged and stood looking down the morning-misted valley in the direction of Holly Wood. 'Dunno. I'll decide that when I put plan B into action.'

'What's plan B?'

When Annabelle turned round she had the kind of danger in her eyes that invariably made Georgie's heart trip with excitement. 'You'll find out soon enough,' Annabelle murmured, and returning to the bed she flopped down on her back, revelling in the thought of what was to come.

Alicia was so engrossed in scraping and washing down walls ready for Nat to paint that she didn't hear anyone entering the shop. She only knew Robert was there when she turned to go and refill her bucket and found him in the doorway, gazing around the old place.

'Gosh, you made me jump,' she scolded. 'How long have you been there?'

'A minute or less.'

As she watched him taking in the cracked and bubbled paint, bare light bulbs, dusty counter and empty racks, she knew what he was thinking even before he said, 'God, this place takes me back.' He was shaking his head in wonder. 'Funny how it makes me think of us as kids, even though Mum was still running it right up to the time she fell ill.'

Alicia smiled. 'I like to think she's still here,' she said, hoping he wouldn't be embarrassed by the fancifulness.

He was still drifting in nostalgia. 'It certainly feels as though she is,' he stated. 'She used to love this place, all the comings and goings, bags piled up so you could hardly move, waiting to be emptied, the treasures we used to find.'

'Until we were teenagers when we wouldn't be caught dead in the stuff,' Alicia laughed.

He smiled, and for several minutes they wandered off down memory lane, recalling the games they used to invent with their friends, who were always invited around when a new donation came in. They'd played cowboys and Indians with moth-eaten headdresses and dented bowlers; devils and ghosts thanks to old black jackets and voluminous white shirts, or big fat people when huge knickers and underpants turned up. Once in a while something magical would fallout of a pocket, or reveal itself at the bottom of a handbag, like a chipped crystal necklace or a fob watch with no hands which Robert had used to power a very realistic toy rat, providing endless hours of fun. Or, on one dazzling occasion, a real diamond ring, which their mother had returned to the owner, who'd been so relieved to find it after believing it lost for so many years that she'd donated fifty pounds to the shop, and given a ten-shilling note each to Robert and Alicia.

'I'd forgotten that,' Alicia laughed, 'and Mum was too polite to explain that the notes weren't in use any more.'

'So Dad gave us fifty pence to make up for it.'

As they sighed and smiled, Alicia went to give him a hug. 'So what are you doing here?' she asked, carrying her bucket through to the sink. 'Aren't you off to Finland today?'

'I'm leaving in half an hour, so I thought I'd pop over to find out how you're doing. I've just left the Coach House, actually, where I had a little chat with Nat and his girlfriend.'

'Really?' she said, pleased. 'So you found them up.'

'Only just, by the look of them.'

'How did he seem to you?'

'Fine, but it wasn't a good time to try to draw him out on anything. I've suggested we get together when I'm back, maybe go for a hike, or over to the county ground for the day. He seemed up for it.'

'He would be if cricket's involved.'

He smiled and watched her wringing out a sponge to start again. 'Mum would be pleased to know you're opening the place up,' he told her.

Her eyes came to his. 'Thank you for that,' she said softly.

'My offer still stands, if there's anything I can do . . . I know, you don't want to cause any problems, but if you find yourself running into difficulties . . .'

'I'll be sure to let you know,' she said, certain she wouldn't. Then, starting to rub down a wall she'd already scraped, 'So, does Sabrina know you're here?'

'I told her I was going to drop in before I left,' he replied. 'Her magazine goes to print today, so she left the house about an hour ago.'

Surprised, Alicia said, 'What magazine?'

'Actually, it's more of a newsletter, but you didn't hear that from me. She and June Downey-Marsh started it up a year or so ago to serve the local communities. You know the kind of thing, updates from council meetings; neighbours in the news; what's on; who's doing what to whom. They get a bit of advertising from local businesses to help cover their costs. Sometimes they even make a profit.'

Alicia rinsed out her sponge. 'How wonderful that she's found an outlet for her journalistic talents,' she muttered, trying not to sound sarcastic, and failing.

Robert slanted her a look.

She smiled sweetly. They both knew how Sabrina had always exaggerated the short time she'd spent working at the *Daily Mail* at least two decades ago, when, to hear her tell it, she'd been a star reporter about to be given her own column until she'd made the grandiose mistake of getting married. In reality she'd been a glorified secretary working for the sub-editors, and as far as anyone knew had never actually had anything in print, or certainly not under her own name. 'So, remind me again how long you're going to be away,' she said, deciding to get off the subject of his wife.

'Ten days, and I'd like your promise that war won't have broken out by the time I get back.'

'Ah,' she said knowingly, 'so that's why you're here.'

'Only in part. I'm genuinely interested in what you're doing with the shop, and I wanted to make contact with Nat before I left. How long do you think before you're ready for business?'

'I'm hoping it'll be soon so I can try to entice in some summer traffic, but I'm probably being a tad ambitious.'

He didn't disagree. 'Once again, if you need any money . . .'

'Once again, thank you.'

He regarded her closely, raising his eyebrows as though waiting for more.

Reading his mind, she said, 'Ah, the promise – no war for the next ten days.'

'I'd rather there was no war, full stop.'

'Well, we're on the same page there, so if it'll give you peace of mind while you're away, I promise that if anything happens, I won't be the one to start it.'

A wry smile crept across his lips. 'That's more or less what Sabrina said,' he told her, 'so I'm going to hope that you both keep to your word and remember there's absolutely nothing to be gained from carrying on this vendetta.'

Craig was standing with his back against the hotel-room door, his arms folded as he gazed at Sabrina. There was a look of amusement, coupled with naked desire, shining in his inky dark eyes. She was stripping like a professional, peeling away her dress, her stockings, then her black lacy bra, rotating her hips, peeking at him over one shoulder, and wrapping herself around the bedpost, as abandoned and provocative as any genuine pole dancer.

When finally the music on the iPod – *Voulez-vous coucher avec moi* – came to an end, she turned to blow him a playful Monroe sort of kiss, then gazed wantonly into his eyes.

'I've never met anyone like you,' he told her as the final beats died.

She smiled. 'I told you I had a surprise for you,' she said, sauntering towards him. 'Did you like it?' She put a hand between his legs. 'Mm, yes, you liked it,' she murmured, and pressing her mouth to his she pushed her tongue deep inside.

Catching her around the waist, he brought her hard up against him, then bending her back he showered her breasts with urgent, hungry kisses. His hands moved to her buttocks, splaying over the silky flesh, but as he made to lower her panties she stopped him.

'Surprise number two,' she whispered, and returning to the bed she lay down on her back and opened her legs wide. The panties were crotchless.

'Oh Jesus,' he murmured, and quickly undressing he went to lie over her, plunging straight into the throbbing heat of her.

They made love wildly, and cruelly, as she urged him to spank and bite her. He wouldn't allow her to do the same to him, but the way she responded to the slaps on her breasts and buttocks sent him soaring all too quickly to the point of climax, and beyond.

She needed to orgasm too, and because he knew

it turned her on so much, he stood her in front of the window where any new arrivals at the hotel might see her. Then he dropped to his knees and used his tongue and fingers to take her, gasping and sobbing, to the throes of a magnificent release.

Later, as they lay together on the bed, still naked and drinking champagne, she gazed adoringly into his eyes as she said, 'Did I ever tell you that sex with you is the best I've ever had?'

He smiled and touched his lips to hers. 'Once or twice,' he replied.

'Is it the same for you?' she prompted.

He swallowed some champagne and turned to put his glass down. 'I can't get enough of you,' he told her, gathering her into his arms. 'I keep thinking it has to end, but then you call, and as soon as I hear your voice I know I have to see you.'

Happy with the answer, she snuggled more tightly against him. 'Do you love me?' she murmured, after a while.

'Yes,' he said.

'More than her?'

'Don't ask that. This time is for us, so let's not spoil it.'

Raising her head she pressed a kiss to his lips. 'How long is the trial likely to last?' she asked, referring to the arson case he was defending at Bristol Crown Court.

'A couple of days.'

She smiled. 'So does that mean you're staying here for a couple of nights?'

He nodded and laughed as she gave a growl of joy. 'I take it that means you'll be staying with me,' he teased.

Rolling on to her back she gazed up at the silvery silk canopy overhead, and moaned softly as he began stroking her legs. 'Of all the hotels we've stayed at, I think this is my favourite,' she decided. 'I love everything about it, from the deer park as you drive in, to the lovely courtyard where we had cocktails the first time we came, do you remember?'

'Of course,' he answered, watching her nipples pucker and harden as he touched them.

'To the stuffy old dining room, to this wonderful suite, because this is where we were when you first told me you loved me. Did you know that?'

He nodded, and brushed a hand over her cheek into her hair.

'Don't you wish we could be together for ever?' she said, pressing her lips to his palm.

'In another life it might be possible,' he replied, trailing his fingers back to the join of her legs.

Opening herself up to him, she said, 'We can always make another life. You, me and the children. Wouldn't you like that?'

'Sounds idyllic,' he murmured.

They made love again, more languorously and tenderly than before, then after dinner they walked in the grounds, wrapped up against the cold, and beckoned to the deer who watched them with unblinking eyes from the twilit woods at the edge of the park. These stolen, precious moments, when the rest of the world seemed so far away, would always stay with her.

As they wandered back along the drive they stopped to look up at the window of their room.

'Are you thinking of me standing there, naked?' she asked.

'Yes,' he replied, tightening his arm around her. 'I think of you all the time,' he said, and tilting her mouth to his, he kissed her with a tenderness that seared straight to her heart.

Sitting alone in the office, Sabrina put a hand to her chest as though to stem the pain of her loss. June had popped over to her flat a while ago to search for a missing press release, and from the minute she'd stepped out Sabrina had done nothing but think of Craig. She knew it wasn't wise to dwell on happy memories, because of how wretched they made her feel afterwards, but while she was reliving them the joy and love were so real that it was as though time had turned back and it was happening all over again.

Now the past had faded, and she was here, in this office, and starting to feel the way she had when they'd first broken up, so desperate to see him that it was as though she couldn't go on if she didn't.

With a sob of anguish she thought of how hard she'd tried to get over him, and of the progress she'd finally started to make. Now, since his death and with Alicia turning up, it was as though she was being sucked right back into that terrible time when her grief had been so agonising that she'd virtually lost her mind.

It was the middle of the afternoon when Alicia left Nat and Summer sanding paintwork in the shop while she went off to B&Q to pick up a hundred and one DIY supplies. The temperature was rising towards ninety by now, making her feel drowsy as she walked back to the Coach House, but she barely had time for the luxury of a yawn, never mind a siesta, if she was going to make her self-imposed deadline of August 1st.

As she drove out of the village she happened to check her rear-view mirror and spotted Annabelle and her friend sauntering across the high street towards the shop. There was no telling if they were intending to go in, but Alicia felt certain they were, and was half tempted to go back, if only to add an adult presence to the mix. Suspecting Nat wouldn't appreciate his mother rushing to his assistance, she sent him and Summer a silent message of moral support instead and drove on. Luckily she'd told him about Annabelle's phone call this morning, so at least he'd be prepared if she brought it up – what else she might spring on him Alicia guessed she'd find out later.

Back at the shop, Summer was in the studio foraging for a new piece of sandpaper when she heard voices at the front, and turned to find Nat's tarty cousin and her equally tarty friend coming in through the door. Summer immediately stiffened, as much with nerves as with dislike, especially of the cousin who'd made no secret yesterday of the fact that she fancied Nat. Not that Summer considered her serious competition: as attractive as she might be, Summer knew that Nat didn't go for girls who were as obvious as her, or who behaved like slappers, which Annabelle definitely did.

Wishing she'd put on at least a layer of mascara before coming here, she went to stand in the arch, wanting Annabelle to know she was there. Annabelle, however, was in mid flow talking to Nat, while her friend seemed to be sending someone a text, so for the moment Summer was invisible.

'... so when you didn't call I thought I'd come over in person,' Annabelle was saying, twirling a finger round a loose strand of hair, 'because I know what mothers are like. They always forget to pass on messages.'

'No, Mum told me you rang,' Nat informed her, 'but we've been busy today.'

Annabelle swept an admiring look over his bare chest and shoulders. 'Mm, I can see,' she commented, apparently unfazed by the put-down. 'You're really working up a sweat.'

Clearly not appreciating her crass attempt at flirtation, but polite to the end, he said, 'So how are you?'

'Oh, I'm cool,' she answered, shifting her weight on to her other leg and tossing back her hair. 'This heat is getting to me a bit though, which is why Theo's party at the weekend will be so good. Did your mum mention it?'

'She said there was something, but not what, exactly.'

Annabelle smiled and Summer's throat turned dry. It was like watching a Venus flytrap preparing to clinch its prey.

'No, well, I couldn't tell her the details,' Annabelle murmured, 'because it's like a really special kind of party, and I just know you're going to want to come.'

Summer's eyes were boring into Nat's face, and

as he looked at her, both Annabelle and Georgie turned round.

'Oh,' Annabelle said, as though a bad smell had just turned up, 'I didn't realise you were there.' Her eyes travelled up and down Summer in a way that brought a rush of colour to Summer's cheeks.

'Thanks for the invite, Annabelle,' Nat said, 'but we won't be able to make it. We're doing something else on Saturday.'

Annabelle turned back again. 'But you haven't heard what kind of party it is yet,' she reminded him, 'and I honestly don't think you'll want to miss out when you do.'

'Whatever it is, like I just said, we're doing something else that night.'

Annabelle stole a quick glance back at Summer. 'You can bring your girlfriend, if you like,' she said. 'I'm sure Theo won't mind.'

Nat's eyes returned to Summer. She was praying he wouldn't admit that she wasn't going to be here, because as soon as he did she knew the Venus jaws would snap shut.

'Once again,' he said to Annabelle, 'we're not free.'

'It's a topless party around the pool,' she informed him, delivering a smouldering look straight into his eyes. 'It could be like when we used to play draughts, only better.'

As Nat flushed, and Georgie giggled, Summer said, 'I don't mean to be rude, Annabelle, but I think Nat's given you an answer, and we've a lot to do here, so if you don't mind . . .'

Annabelle slanted her the kind of look that

was meant to make Summer feel small, and irrelevant, and it worked. Then, turning back to Nat as though Summer had vanished in a dust cloud, she said, 'You do remember when we used to play draughts, don't you? Whoever lost a piece had to take something off, until neither of us had anything on and then . . .'

'That was a long time ago,' he cut in abruptly. 'We were kids. It was just a game.'

She shrugged. 'We used to play it a lot though, didn't we? You'd get hold of my hand and put it on your thing . . .'

'Annabelle, will you just leave,' Summer interrupted. 'We're not going to the party, Nat's grown up now, and you need to do the same.'

Annabelle's nostrils flared. No one ever spoke to her like that and got away with it, least of all some smutty-faced, vertically-challenged ginger with white eyelashes and freckles. 'What was your name again?' she sneered.

Summer's eyes flicked to Nat. 'Summer,' she answered, already tensing for the tongue-lashing of her life, and hoping Nat would step in to stop it.

However, for all her eye-blazing and pumped-up fury, Annabelle wasn't sufficiently seasoned to deliver the knock-out blow when it was needed. So all she managed was a tart, 'OK, Georgie, we're done here,' and turning on an expensive wooden heel, she swept back her hair and stalked out of the shop.

'Phew!' Nat sighed as soon as they'd gone. 'She is such a piece of work.'

'If she actually had a brain she'd be lethal,'

Summer snorted. 'What were you thinking, ever getting involved with her?'

'I said, we were kids. It was just a bit of fun and we weren't *involved*.'

'Well that's not how she made it sound, stripping off together . . .'

'Summer, don't do this,' he interrupted. 'It's what she wanted, to try and cause trouble, so don't give her the satisfaction.'

Still angry, but seeing the sense of what he was saying, she turned back into the studio.

Following her in, he put his arms around her and looked into her eyes. 'You don't have anything to worry about as far as she's concerned,' he told her softly. 'She didn't mean anything me to then, and she sure as hell doesn't now.'

'But what's she going to be like once I've gone?' she protested. 'That's what's worrying me.'

'It doesn't matter what she's like. I won't be having anything to do with her, so it's not an issue.' He kissed her gently. 'I swear, by the time we see one another again, we probably won't even remember her name,' he said.

'That's not fair,' Annabelle grumbled. 'You always win. Are you sure you didn't cheat?'

Nat grinned. 'Totally,' he replied, pushing the draught board aside. 'So, you know what happens now.'

She giggled, and yelped as his fingers closed around her wrist.

'Ssh,' he warned. 'You locked the door, didn't you?'

'Of course.' She was starting to look anxious.

'You don't have to be afraid,' he told her. 'I won't hurt you.'

She giggled again, then moved along as he came to sit next to her.

'Here,' he said, taking her hand.

Letting him guide her fingers, she wrapped them around him and held her breath.

'Can I touch you now?' he whispered raggedly.

She nodded, then gasped as his fingers grazed over her breasts.

'Is that OK?' he asked.

'Yeah.' She swallowed. 'It feels really good.' Then, 'You can touch me down there if you like,' she said shyly.

Nat knew that he'd never forget how much he'd wanted to cover Annabelle's body with his and push himself into her. He'd never gone that far before, but he sensed she'd let him if he wanted to. Maybe he would have, had they not heard someone coming up the stairs.

'The bitch,' Annabelle was fuming, as she and Georgie crossed back to Holly Way, 'who the hell does she think she is, telling me I ought to grow up? I should have smacked her one, or told her there was no way she was invited to the party, because no one wants to see her nasty gingey pubes and flat white tits. Ugh, she's such a minger, I don't know how Nat can stand to look at her, never mind go with her.'

'Whatever,' Georgie shrugged, 'he's definitely not coming to the party, so so much for plan B.'

'She's not getting away with that,' Annabelle

muttered, barely listening. 'I'm telling you, even if he doesn't come on Saturday, I know he wants to go with me, and when he does she's going to know *all* about it.'

Chapter Eight

Over the next few days, apart from taking Summer to the station, where Alicia said her goodbyes at the car, allowing the young ones some privacy for their own difficult parting, she and Nat barely left the shop. Thanks to Mimi's long-suffering husband Pete, and his trusty pickup truck, the remaining junk had been shunted off to the tip, and brand-new display cases made from recycled materials were starting to take shape out on the patio. While Pete sawed, hammered, drilled and planed on his Workmate, Nat whitewashed walls, Alicia painted woodwork and window frames, and Mimi kept up an endless supply of refreshments.

In the evenings, after a quick salad or fish and chips from the Friary if she was too tired to whip something up, Alicia worked at the computer in her bedroom, designing stationery, business cards, promotional flyers and a logo, while Nat concentrated on creating a website. Sorting out the practical elements of running a business was her biggest headache, but Maggie at the pub rode in to the rescue by sitting her down one afternoon and going through everything she'd need to get started, from an accountant, to insurance, to a trusted shipper in the event she needed to send her sculptures or other products to distant destinations.

By Friday, thanks to a slew of recommendations, she had a shortlist for all categories, and when Sam the postman showed up at two o'clock with a special delivery containing a credit-card machine and notification that she'd be able to receive payments from the following Wednesday, Alicia declared it time to celebrate. No matter that the phone still wasn't on, and the electricity was coming through like Morse code, they'd achieved so much in less than a week that they royally deserved a night off.

'At last,' Rachel laughed, when Alicia and Nat joined her and Dave at their local pub near Ditcheat. 'We were beginning to wonder if we'd ever see you again.'

Though Alicia would have preferred to go to the Traveller's, having narrowly avoided running into Sabrina once, she wasn't prepared to chance it again, especially while Robert wasn't around. 'Where are the kids?' she asked, surveying the garden to try and spot them.

'Both on sleepovers,' Dave answered, his merry blue eyes showing how pleased he was to have his wife to himself for the night. 'They're back in the morning, and they both want to know if they can come over to help with the shop.'

'Too right,' Nat piped up. 'I don't see why I should be her only slave, so bring 'em on.'

Laughing as she hugged him, Rachel said, 'You've got paint in your eyebrows and no tan. She's definitely working you too hard.'

Alicia smiled fondly as Nat glanced at her and winked. 'So what are we all going to have to drink?' she demanded. 'Nat's driving, so . . .'

'It's all taken care of,' Dave interrupted. 'It's not every day a girl gets her first credit-card machine, so we reckoned it had to be champagne.'

Alicia's eyes widened as she burst out laughing. 'But I'm buying,' she insisted. 'It was my idea to celebrate, and . . .'

'Will you sit down and behave,' Dave told her. 'This is our treat, and dinner's on us too.'

'Oh no,' she said seriously. 'I'm fully aware of what's happening in the property market, so . . .'

'I have a rich wife,' Dave reminded her. 'She's raking it in at that surgery, which is something else to celebrate, she's finally taken on a partner who's due to start in September, so I might actually get to see something of her.'

'That's great,' Alicia cried, giving Rachel a hug. 'I'd forgotten you were looking for someone.'

'Hardly surprising when the search started almost a year ago, we've all got bored with it by now, but tonight's not about me, it's about you two and new beginnings. Just a shame Darcie's not here to join in.'

'I don't think she'd necessarily agree with that,' Nat told her. 'She's having such a great time in France she's hardly got time to talk to us when we call. Unless she wants my brotherly advice on how to let a boy know she likes him.'

'To which Nat replied,' Alicia butted in, 'if he's French tell him to *tire-toi,* which basically means bugger off, and if he's English she has to give him Nat's number so he can deal with it in person.'

Laughing, Rachel said, 'How very helpful of you. I'm sure she was extremely appreciative.'

'That's one way of putting it,' he retorted, stepping into the picnic bench next to his mother.

'Ah, here's the champagne,' Dave announced, spotting a barmaid toting an ice bucket and four glasses across the grass.

Minutes later they were toasting each other and taking the first welcome mouthfuls of a deliciously chilled Laurent Perrier.

'OK, menus,' Dave declared. 'She forgot to bring them.'

'I'll go in,' Nat said, getting up. 'Anyone want crisps or nuts?'

'Bring a few bags,' Alicia told him.

As he walked away she closed her eyes and let the sheer pleasure of relaxing with her closest friends rise above her grief to warm her. 'God, what a week,' she murmured, stretching out her back. 'Provided I don't think about anything else I'm starting to get quite excited.'

With a quick look at Dave, Rachel reached into her bag and handed over a bulletin sheet with green print on a creamy yellow background. As soon as she saw it Alicia realised what it was and felt her heart sink. '*The Buzz*,' she said, reading the title. 'That's original.'

'I brought it,' Rachel said, 'because I guessed you hadn't seen it yet or you'd have mentioned it on the phone. Dave thought we should wait to show you, but I think you'd rather read it while we're here. There's an article on the inside page that's obviously directed at you.'

Throwing it down, Alicia said, 'I don't want to

read anything she has to say. Just give me the gist of it.'

'Basically she's stating all the reasons why Holly Wood doesn't want tourism, or businesses that might invite it. She goes on about litter and parking and people staring in windows, and how it could increase everyone's council tax if there's more rubbish to collect, and streets to clean and general maintenance required.'

'The bitch,' Alicia muttered.

'I know. She's obviously trying to spook your neighbours into thinking twice about supporting your shop. She doesn't name you, of course, she's too smart for that, but the message is pretty clear. She finishes up with a paragraph about certain permits that are necessary for retail premises to be used as a manufacturing unit, and how important it is for the residents of Holly Wood to make sure that everyone sticks to the law.'

Alicia was looking worried. 'What permits?' she demanded. 'Is she right? Do I need one?'

'Possibly,' Dave answered regretfully. 'I haven't had time yet to go through all the sections, subsections and sorry-ass clauses in the council regulations, but judging by this I'd say she has looked into it, so you probably should too.'

Alicia's face was taut with anger. 'What difference does it make to her if I'm producing sculptures and a few items of jewellery at the back of the shop?' she cried. 'But it's not about that, is it? This is her way of trying to make me leave. Well, she can forget it. Half the village has already been in to lend a hand, or show their support, and I just know the other half will be on my side if it's put to the test. For God's sake, it's only a tinpot gallery. It's not as if people are going to be flocking to Holly Wood in their droves to see my obscure little works. I wish.'

'I'll do some investigating for you on Monday,' Dave told her. 'It shouldn't be too difficult to track down the right information, and if you do need a permit, we'll get it. So problem solved.'

'Depending on how long it takes. I need to open as soon as possible.'

'You're all looking very serious,' Nat commented, dropping an assortment of pretzels and peanuts on the table along with the menus.

Alicia explained about the trading permit, omitting Sabrina's involvement in bringing it to her attention.

Nat immediately looked as concerned as she did. 'We don't want any delays,' he stated. 'It'll really screw things up for the summer. Hang on, though, if the problem's only about you making stuff at the shop, you can always set up at home in the old playroom until the permit comes through. I know it's not perfect, because you really need to be on site, but I can run the shop during August and by the time I go back to school, hopefully the necessary papers will be through.'

Alicia beamed at him. 'That's what I love about you,' she told him, treating him to a resounding kiss on the head, 'you've always got a good answer.'

'Bit of a no-brainer, really,' he mumbled, clearly pleased with himself, and taking out his mobile as it rang, he barked into it, 'Hey! Oh hi, yeah, I'm good, how are you?'

As he got up from the table Alicia watched him walk to the edge of the garden to be more private. 'That didn't sound as though it was Summer,' she remarked, 'which'll make a change. They must speak at least five times a day.'

'How was it having her to stay?' Rachel asked.

'Fine. She's pretty easy-going, and she didn't have a problem mucking in. Oh, I haven't had a chance to tell you this yet, they had a run-in with Annabelle the other day. From what I can gather Summer gave her a bit of a put-down.'

'Good for her,' Rachel cheered. 'Someone needs to. I saw the girl yesterday in Bath. Honestly, you'd think she was Britain's next supermodel the way she struts about the place. Then she laughs and this awful raucous noise comes out of her that makes you want to cringe, or slap her, or both, and her friends are as bad. They've got more flesh on show than a butcher's shop, and why do young girls have to open their mouths so wide when they laugh? It's horrible.'

Alicia rolled her eyes and looked up at Nat as he came back. 'OK?' she asked.

'Yeah, that was Jolyon Crane,' he told her.

Alicia's face lit up. 'About your work experience? Is everything still going ahead?'

'Yeah. Definitely. He was ringing to invite us to dinner next Friday.'

'How lovely. Where?'

'Apparently he's booked a table at somewhere called Hunting Street House?'

Alicia's smile fled as her heart contracted. 'Huntstrete House?' she said, thinking of the credit-card statements of Craig's she'd gone through, and how many times that hotel had featured.

'That's the one. Why, is there a problem?'

'No, no,' she lied, attempting to brighten again. She wasn't going to tell him it was one of the love nests his father and Sabrina had used to carry on their affair. 'Is Marianne coming too?'

'You mean his wife? Dunno, I didn't ask.'

'Well, I guess we'll find out when we get there,' she said, opening her menu. 'Now, what are we going to have to eat?'

As they read through the generous list of local dishes Alicia was barely seeing the words. Though she'd yet to clap eyes on Sabrina, it seemed everywhere she turned the damned woman was there, like a nemesis waiting to torment her. She'd stolen into her marriage and all but wrecked it. She'd created a distance between her and Robert, and made it virtually impossible for her to see her mother. Now she was trying to prevent her from opening the shop. She was even haunting innocent conversations, appearing like a shadow behind the words, darkening their innocence and drawing Alicia back to one of the most painful times of her life.

She had to do something to break free of the woman, to create an existence that could no longer be touched by her, or her future was going to end up as blighted by Sabrina as her past.

'Is that enough?' Robert was asking Annabelle, as they dropped a sackful of straw into the boot of his car.

'Yeah, I think so. It should be,' she told him. 'I just wish it was green, that's all.'

Having no ready suggestions for how she could change the colour, he loaded in a large box of fresh vegetables, careful not to crush her precious straw, and closing down the boot he waved a thanks to Margie, who ran the farm shop, and got into the car.

'So, am I still not allowed to ask what it's for?' he prompted, as they pulled out on to the main road.

'Not yet,' she replied. 'I want to make sure it works first, but thanks for bringing me – and for paying.'

He cast her a glance. 'Are you short of money at the moment?' he asked, carefully.

She shrugged. 'A bit, yes. It just doesn't go anywhere these days. Everything's so expensive.'

Since she had a healthy monthly allowance, which had been transferred into her account only a week ago, he was more than a little concerned about what she might be spending it on. However, broaching the subject wouldn't be easy, given how spiky she was these days, but if she was squandering it on alcohol, or worse, illegal substances, which he and Sabrina had begun to suspect, then they needed to know. 'How much do you have left?' he asked cautiously.

She pulled a face. 'I dunno. About twenty, I think.' She turned to look at him, suddenly all pretty smiles and batting eyelids. 'I don't suppose there's any chance of an advance on next month's, is there?' she asked.

He was about to say no, when he swerved away from the absolute and said, 'There might be if I knew what you spent your money on.'

A scowl descended over her features and she turned to look out of the window.

He threw her another quick glance, then pulled out to overtake a hay cart. 'If you only have twenty left, you must have bought something quite expensive,' he pointed out. 'Was it a dress? Shoes? Make-up?'

She gave a short sigh and said, 'Why is it everyone hates me having what I want?'

Raising his eyebrows, he said, 'I wasn't aware anyone ever criticised your choices, or tried to prevent you from making them. I'm simply wondering where such a large sum of money might have gone in less than a week.'

'What is this, some kind of inquisition or something?' she snapped defensively.

'No, it's me trying to find out if you're buying things you shouldn't be. Such as drugs, or alcohol.'

Her attitude immediately prickled with hostility. 'No, I am not spending it on drugs or alcohol,' she retorted angrily, and tossing back her hair, she turned to stare out of the window again, apparently sending him to Coventry.

Guessing from the tone of her response that he'd hit a tender, if not totally raw nerve, he felt a swell of dismay move through him. If he didn't have to fly off again as soon as he'd dropped her at home, he'd be inclined to pursue the matter, if only to try to drum it into her how dangerous it was even to dabble in those sorts of bad habits. Better still would be if he could persuade her to mix with a different set of friends, girls her own age, instead of Georgie and the others, who were at least a year or two older. The trouble was, she and Georgie went back a long way, so he knew already that he stood almost no chance at all of convincing her that she could be running with the wrong crowd.

'Do any of your friends take drugs?' he ventured, deciding to come straight to the point.

Treating him to one of her superior, long-suffering sighs, she said, *'No-oo!'*

'What about alcohol?'

'Oh for heaven's sake, everyone has a drink now and again. There's nothing wrong with it. It's perfectly legal.'

'Not for you.'

'Oh, Robert, please don't go on. You're starting to sound like Mum, and I always thought you were more open-minded than that.'

Wondering if that was supposed to be a compliment, he said, 'Mum only goes on because she worries about you.'

'Wrong. Mum only worries about herself and what the rest of the world thinks of her.'

He gave a sad shake of his head. 'She might give that impression at times,' he conceded, 'but I can assure you, no one means more to her than you.'

To his surprise she didn't argue with that, only returned to her perusal of the passing countryside, while fiddling idly with the mobile phone in her hand. 'If you're right,' she said suddenly, 'then how come she'd never let me anywhere near her when she was supposed to be ill all that time? She was a real cow to me then, and I haven't forgotten some of the things she said.'

Wishing he could stop the car to take her hands

in his as he answered, but knowing she'd withdraw instantly if he did, because it was the way she always reacted when this subject came up, he said, 'As I've explained to you before, she was going through a very bad depression . . .'

'Yeah, yeah, poor Mum, let's all feel sorry for her. Actually, I know what it was all about . . .'

Experiencing a beat of alarm, he said, 'What do you mean?'

She shrugged in a way that seemed to sharpen her hostility and bring up more barriers than ever.

'There were a lot of things going on at the time,' he said carefully.

'Yeah, fine, I know. Anyway, I've got to ring Georgie. I said I would at twelve o'clock and it's already ten past.'

As she pressed in the number, Robert fixed his eyes on the road ahead, aware of the old bitterness and hurt travelling along in their wake. That damned affair was like a ghost, sometimes disappearing, but then returning often as clear and cruel as if it was still going on. At the time it had all but crushed him – worse still had been watching his wife suffering so wretchedly over another man. These days he was more able to detach from his emotions when the spectre raised its head, but not always. The pain was still there, along with the deep sense of betrayal, buried but certainly not dead.

He wondered if Annabelle really had found out about Craig and her mother, or if she'd been playing her usual trick of sounding more knowledgeable than she actually was. Since she'd become more attitude than personality, it was often hard to tell what was going on in her mind, but he was never in any doubt of how much pain and damage Sabrina's erratic swings from hysteria to melancholy had caused her.

Annabelle was still chatting on the phone when they pulled in through the gates, and after grabbing her bag of straw from the boot she disappeared inside without even a backward glance. It saddened Robert right to his core to realise how they were all drifting apart. He used to tell himself, during those terrible dark months after the affair, that once the worst was over they'd be able to pick up the pieces and somehow carry on as they had before. He realised now how naive and self-delusional that was. The betrayal and breakdown had changed them all, and in ways they still barely recognised or understood. It was as though the memories were continuing the destruction, eroding their bond and resisting his attempts to try and keep them together.

'Are you going straight away?' Annabelle asked as he carried the vegetables into the kitchen.

'I'm afraid I have to,' he answered, glancing at the clock. 'I'm already in danger of missing the flight.'

'Remind me where you're going,' she said, helping herself to a carrot.

'Rome. I'll be back at the weekend. Do you know where Mum is?'

She shook her head. 'No note, but I expect she's somewhere with June. She usually is.'

'OK, I'll give her a call from the car. Will you be all right?'

She looked at him in surprise. 'Of course,' she answered. 'Why wouldn't I be?'

He smiled. 'No idea,' he said, and after hugging her warmly, which to his great joy she returned, he took himself back to the car.

An hour later Sabrina came to an abrupt halt in the kitchen doorway, hardly able to believe her eyes. 'Well, that's a sight I never expected to see,' she commented, dumping her supermarket bags on a counter top. 'What on earth are you doing?'

'If you must know, I'm trying to make a grass skirt,' Annabelle answered, brushing glue on to the back of a white leather belt.

'You could have fooled me,' Sabrina told her. 'Where did you get the straw?'

'From a farm shop, where do you think? And if you're going to stand there making rude comments you can just get lost.'

Sabrina's eyebrows rose. 'Actually, I might offer to help if I knew what it was for,' she said, starting to load up the fridge.

'It's a fancy dress party, OK? I'm going as a Hawaiian girl, hence the grass skirt.'

Sabrina looked impressed by the choice. 'You'll need a lei,' she told her.

Annabelle looked up.

'As in garland,' Sabrina said, with a roll of her eyes. 'Whose party is it?'

'A friend's.'

'Does the friend have a name?'

'*Shit*, it's not sticking. This is driving me mental. You do it.'

'Since you ask so charmingly, no.'

'Oh, Mum, please. I don't have anything else to wear, so it has to be this.'

Going over to the table, Sabrina looked down at the mess and sighed. 'You'd do better to stick the straw to paper, then sew it into some fabric,' she told her.

'That is a brilliant idea,' Annabelle cried. 'I'll get the sewing machine.' She was on her feet before she said, 'Have we got one?'

Sabrina shook her head.

'Why not?' Annabelle demanded furiously. 'Everyone has a sewing machine, except you, of course, because you're not like normal mothers. You have to buy everything, or get someone else to make it. You never do anything yourself.'

'This is absolutely not the way to enlist my help,' Sabrina told her. 'So unless you calm down and start speaking with a civil tongue in your head you can clear up that mess and go to the ball in rags.'

'Very funny,' but Annabelle was too entranced by her idea of wearing a grass skirt to the party to let her frustration get in the way, so assuming her best sweet-girl smile, she said, 'Please Mummy, will you help?'

Sabrina slanted her a look. 'I might, when I've finished this,' she replied, 'but only if you wash the salad before it goes in the fridge.'

Annabelle gave an impatient sigh, but managed to bite back the ripe response that had sprung to her lips. 'OK, it's a deal,' she said. 'Now, where are we going to get the fabric?'

'We can probably use an old sheet, then you can cover it with the belt. What are you wearing on the top?'

Annabelle swallowed. 'I dunno. One of my

bikinis, I expect. And a lei. Can you make one of those?'

'Possibly. You'll have to go and get some flowers from Mimi, and some wire to string them together.'

'Will she have the wire too?'

'She should.'

'OK, I'll go now and do the salad when I get back. Shall I put the flowers on your account?'

Sabrina sighed. 'I suppose so,' and standing aside for Annabelle to get past, she went to make a closer inspection of the debacle so far. It was such a hopeless effort that a six-year-old could have made a better job, and shaking her head in dismay she went upstairs to find an old sheet, collecting her sewing box from the escritoire in the hall on her way back.

By the time Annabelle returned the skirt was virtually made.

'Where have you been?' Sabrina demanded as she came in the door with a bouquet of chrysanths, moon daises, various coloured dahlias and a handful of clarkia.

'I ran into a couple of friends,' she answered.

'You haven't been mixing with those people on the new estate again, have you?'

'So what if I have? You're such a snob, and they go to my school, so I'm hardly going to ignore them, am I? Anyway, is this OK? Did I get enough?'

Sabrina's expression was sour as she nodded. 'I think so,' she responded. 'Here, try this,' and biting off the cotton, she swung the skirt up for Annabelle to see.

'Oh my God, you are a genius,' Annabelle gushed, grabbing it and holding it against herself. 'Do you reckon we could dye the straw green?'

'No,' Sabrina answered firmly. 'It's fine like that. The flowers will brighten it up.'

'So are you going to do that now?'

'Looks like I'll have to. I want you to help, though. I'd also like to know whose party it is, and where it's being held.'

Annabelle gave a long-suffering sigh. 'It's at Theo McAllister's, OK? You know his mother, Jemima.'

'You're right, I do, so I also know that Theo's nineteen. Don't you think you're a little young to be going . . .'

'Oh for God's sake, you are so ageist. No one cares about that sort of stuff any more. We're all friends, that's what matters.'

'But how does someone your age get to be friends with someone who's already at uni? It's not as though you're seeing one another at school.'

'We just know people in common, OK?'

'Which people?'

'Oh, Mum, give it a rest.'

'These are reasonable questions. I don't understand why you're being so defensive.'

With another impatient sigh, Annabelle said, 'Georgie's cousin Hugh is at Manchester with him, OK? And Cat's sister used to go out with him. Satisfied now?'

She was, and wasn't, but as this was showing all the signs of deteriorating into yet another flaming row she decided to let it go. 'Where's the wire?' she asked.

'In the bag. Shall I start cutting the heads off the flowers?'

'I think you'd better let me do that. You can get

on with the salad, but put the sewing box away first.'

'Where does it belong?'

'If you ever did anything for yourself you'd know it lives in the bottom drawer of the escritoire.'

Annabelle wrinkled her nose. 'What's that when it's at home?'

'Oh, for heaven's sake, just leave it and get on with the lettuce.'

Annabelle grinned. 'Just joking,' she said. 'I know what an escritoire is,' and scooping up the sewing box she carried it off to the hall. By the time she came back Sabrina was starting to snip at the dahlias.

'So what are you doing tonight?' Annabelle asked, searching for the salad spinner.

'June and I are going to the gym for an hour,' Sabrina answered, 'and we'll probably stay on for dinner.'

'Sounds cool. Actually, I wouldn't mind a membership of Babington for my sixteenth.'

'If I thought you'd use it you might be in with a chance. It's something we could do together.'

'Yeah, well, on second thoughts . . .'

Trying not to be hurt by the reply, Sabrina let it slide and worked on in silence for a while, mulling over the chat she'd had with Robert on the phone about Annabelle and where her money was going.

For her part Annabelle was thinking about how she was going to blow everyone's minds when she turned up as a Hawaiian girl tonight.

In the end, when Annabelle had finished washing

the lettuce and came to sit at the table, Sabrina said, 'There's something I'd like to ask you.'

'What's that?' Annabelle responded distractedly. She was inspecting Sabrina's handiwork so far and liking what she saw. 'Oh my God, you're not about to do the drug thing are you,' she said, suddenly connecting. 'I already told Robert, it's not an issue.'

'I hope that's the truth,' Sabrina said, trying to meet her eyes, but Annabelle was still focused on the flowers.

'No, it's a lie,' Annabelle retorted sarcastically, 'because as we all know everything I say . . .'

'All right, all right,' Sabrina interrupted. 'Actually, it wasn't only about that,' she went on, and in spite of knowing this wasn't likely to have a good outcome, she braced herself and said, 'I'd like to know if you're still a virgin?'

There was a beat before Annabelle's head came up. Her expression was pure outrage. 'That is so none of your business,' she told her.

'Actually, everything you do is my business,' Sabrina corrected, 'and that wasn't an answer. So are you?'

'I'm sorry, but I don't have these conversations with anyone but my closest friends.'

'I'm going to take it from that, that you're not,' Sabrina said, feeling a horrible sense of failure creeping over her.

'Take it how you want, it's up to you.'

Going back to what she was doing in an effort to hide the tears that had sprung to her eyes, Sabrina said, 'I hope you're using contraception.'

'Oh, puhlease, can we just drop this now?'

'I'm just saying, if you are sexually active, you need to be using condoms. And that's not me giving my permission for you to be intimate with boys, I simply want you to be safe if you are.'

'Mum, everything's sorted, OK? Put it out of your head and stop embarrassing us both.'

Sabrina took a breath. 'Of course, if you are still a virgin . . .'

'Oh, for Christ's sake,' Annabelle shouted, springing to her feet, 'you are driving me mental here. I do what I want to do, OK?'

'No, it's very far from OK, and if you're going to take that attitude we can stop what we're doing right now and you can stay home this evening.'

Annabelle gritted her teeth as she seethed with frustration. 'You are so infuriating,' she growled. 'Here we are, sitting having a nice time, and you have to go and spoil it all with this stupid conversation.'

'I'm sorry, I'm just trying to . . .'

'Upset me, like you always do. Well you've succeeded, happy now?'

'That wasn't my intention. I simply want to . . .'

'If you don't shut up, *right now*, I'm walking out of here.'

'Don't speak to me like that. I'm your mother, you'll show me some respect or you really will be grounded.'

'I'm going to that party tonight, and if you try to stop me you'll be sorry.'

Sabrina's face paled as she looked at her. 'Are you threatening me?' she asked.

'I'm just telling you, get out of my hair.'

Sabrina dropped the wire and flowers. 'Go to

your room,' she said, 'and you can put all thoughts of going to that party out of your head, because it's not going to happen.'

'You can't stop me.'

Sabrina rose to her feet, and grabbing hold of Annabelle's arm she began hauling her towards the door.

'Get your hands off me,' Annabelle snapped, twisting herself free. 'You can't tell me what to do.'

Sabrina's face was white with anger. 'Oh yes I can, and you're grounded for the rest of the summer.'

'No fucking way,' Annabelle sneered and made to push past her.

Catching her by the shoulders Sabrina tried to turn her back, but Annabelle chopped her hands away and shoved her against the wall.

'Annabelle!' Sabrina cried as Annabelle grabbed her bag and the grass skirt and started for the door. 'Come back here.'

Ignoring her, Annabelle stormed out of the kitchen and down to the gate. Sabrina went after her, but by the time she ran into the cul de sac Annabelle was already rounding the corner into the high street. Since she had no transport she'd no doubt go straight to Tom Sebastian's for a taxi, so going back indoors Sabrina picked up the phone.

Luckily, both drivers were out on jobs, which meant Annabelle would either have to wait for a car to come back, or take the bus. Even if she was still in the village, Sabrina had no intention of risking a showdown for all to see, so she tried Annabelle's mobile. Finding herself diverted to voicemail, she was about to leave a message when the landline rang. Snatching it up she drew breath to snap angrily at Annabelle, but then noticed the caller ID just in time. Her tone changed completely as she said, 'Jennifer, what a lovely surprise. Robert and I were only talking about you the other night, wondering how you are.'

'Oh, we're fine,' came the reply in an unmistakably American accent. 'How are you?'

'Never better,' Sabrina assured her, and with all thoughts of Annabelle eclipsed by the possibility of receiving a highly prized invitation to the Bingleigh family villa on the Cap d'Antibes sometime in August, she settled down to give her full attention to the call.

'Annabelle? Is that you?' Alicia said, coming in from the patio and spotting the girl standing in the shop window staring out into the street.

Annabelle spun round and waved. She was talking to someone on her mobile, but rang off as Alicia came through to the front. 'Hi,' she said, 'I'm waiting for a taxi to pick me up, so I thought I'd drop in to see how you're getting on.'

Knowing instinctively it was a lie, or at least not the entire truth, Alicia said, 'As you can see, it's coming together. We might, I stress might, be ready to open in a couple of weeks.' *Tell that to your mother,* she thought angrily.

'Cool. Are you going to have some kind of party?'

Since she wasn't about to admit to Annabelle that she couldn't afford one, she said, 'I've been thinking about it, but I'm not sure yet.'

Annabelle glanced back out to the street, then looked around again, taking in the newly painted walls and empty space where the counter used to be. Then her eyes came to Alicia's and for a startling moment Alicia thought they were misted with tears.

'I used to love it when Grandma had this shop,' Annabelle said croakily, gazing round again. 'I'd come over here all the time, and she'd let me sort through the stuff that came in.' She gave a wavery sort of smile. 'Do you remember how me and Darcie dressed up that year, for Christmas?' she said. 'We had all those beads and things, and Nat made a top hat out of cardboard and decorated it with tinsel.'

Alicia was watching her closely, and realising, with a deep sense of sorrow, that she'd given little thought to how her mother's death might have affected Annabelle. 'Yes, I remember,' she said gently. 'You made us all laugh so much that Grandma got the hiccups and we couldn't get rid of them.'

Annabelle giggled. 'Then Uncle Craig jumped out on her from behind the sofa and frightened her half to death. She was really cross with him, wasn't she, but it cured her hiccups.'

'It did,' Alicia answered. Then, daring to go a step further, 'I expect you miss her, don't you?'

Annabelle's eyes drifted across the shop as she nodded. 'So does Robert,' she said. 'We get out photo albums sometimes to look at her and talk about all the things she used to say and do. Mum misses her too, but she doesn't really join in, she just listens, or goes off to make a cup of tea.' She looked at Alicia again, then seeming to make a sudden break from her reverie she started to strain to see into the back room. 'Nat not here?' she said, clicking straight back into her Miss Cool persona.

'No, he's gone to the cricket with Simon today.'

Annabelle immediately looked interested. 'Really? What about his girlfriend?'

'She's with her parents in Italy.'

The way Annabelle's eyes dilated told Alicia right away that she'd almost certainly made a mistake, but it was too late now. 'Well, you're welcome to wait for your taxi here . . .'

'Actually, I'll wait outside,' Annabelle interrupted. 'He should be here any minute. They said he was on this side of Bruton when I went over there,' and rearranging an odd bundle of straw across her arm she left the shop.

As soon as she was out of earshot Annabelle pressed Georgie's number into her mobile phone. 'Hi, it's me again,' she hissed. 'Is Melody with you yet?'

'Yeah, she's in the shower.'

'Go and tell her she's got to invite Simon Forsey tonight.'

'Hang on, she's just come out.' Annabelle listened as Georgie relayed the message. Coming back on the line, Georgie said, 'She wants to know why you can't do it yourself?'

'Because *she's* the one he's got the hots for, and he's with Nat at the cricket, so if he comes, Nat might too.'

Georgie passed it on, then came back with, 'She says she'll do it, but only if you back off Theo tonight.'

'It's a deal. Tell her to do it now, and call me back when she knows what's happening. My taxi's here, so I should be there in less than ten minutes. I don't have any money though, so you'll have to lend me some until Robert gets back. The she-devil's not in a very good mood with me at the moment.'

Chapter Nine

'I just don't know what to do with her,' Sabrina was saying to June later that evening. 'She didn't exactly hit me, but the way she's behaving lately, I wouldn't put it past her.'

June smiled at the waiter as he refilled their glasses. 'I'm so glad I had boys,' she remarked unhelpfully, 'everyone knows girls are always the worst.'

Sabrina's lips tightened. 'Tell that to Brenda Loveday whose sixteen-year-old is dossing in doorways, saying it's better than living at home,' she retorted.

'Mm, point taken,' June conceded. 'So where's Annabelle now?'

'I don't know. At this party, I suppose. She's not answering her phone, at least not to me. Honestly, I've never felt so angry, or helpless. She does exactly what she wants, speaks to me like I'm an idiot, or dirt, and seems to have given up altogether on even trying to be pleasant. I'm getting to the point where I don't actually like her very much, which is a horrible thing to say about your own daughter.'

'Believe me, you're not alone,' June assured her,

wondering if Sabrina really didn't know why Annabelle was turning out the way she was, or if she was simply blocking it, not wanting to accept that she might be responsible. 'So what was the row about?' she asked.

Sabrina sighed and picked up her wine. 'It started when I asked her if she was still a virgin.'

June's eyebrows rose. 'Yes, that would do it,' she remarked. 'And is she?'

'God knows, apparently it's none of my business.'

'Which means she probably isn't?'

Sabrina shook her head glumly. 'I've seen the way she looks at boys, at men even. She's like someone twice her age the way she turns it on.' With a brief spark of humour she added, 'I can't think where she gets it from.'

June laughed. 'Having the world's most accomplished flirt as a mother is bound to rub off,' she teased.

Sabrina grimaced. 'That's not how I feel at the moment,' she sighed. 'Far from it, in fact. She takes it out of me, and lately I just can't stop thinking about Craig, which is really bringing me down . . .' Her eyes fell to her glass as the flutterings of heartache began again. 'Anyway, if Annabelle was just flirting it wouldn't be a problem, but if she is going all the way I need to know that she's at least using some sort of protection.'

Not, 'I should put a stop to it,' June was thinking, because Sabrina wasn't really engaging with the problem. She was simply going through the motions of what she felt ought to be said, and because she was so distracted by Craig, and Alicia, she wasn't really getting it right.

'It's the diseases that worry me more than the pregnancies,' Sabrina went on, 'but I just can't seem to get through to her.'

No, I don't suppose you can, June thought with an inward sigh. 'Well, that's teenagers for you,' she said. 'How's Robert getting on with her these days? They always used to have a pretty good relationship. Maybe he can do something to haul her back on track.'

Sabrina was shaking her head. 'He tries, but he's away such a lot that they hardly see one another, and when they do, I don't want to destroy what little connection they still have by asking him to come in with a heavy hand. He's not her father and she'd probably wouldn't think twice about throwing that in his face if he tried laying down the law.'

June wasn't without sympathy for how Sabrina was feeling, she just knew it was better not expressed too readily, or Sabrina would be likely to fall into yet another decline over Craig. 'It's a shame you didn't let Robert adopt her when he offered to,' she commented.

Sabrina's smile was weak. 'Maybe,' she said, 'but at the time I was still thinking, hoping, that Craig and I . . .' She waved a hand as though to dismiss the next words. 'If Robert had been Annabelle's legal father it might have made a divorce more difficult. And if I asked him to take her on now he'd probably think it was because Craig's death had done what nothing else could, made me accept at last that we'll never be together.'

'Mm,' June murmured, understanding the

dilemma, and wondering if Sabrina had actually accepted the finality of the situation yet.

'I know it's crazy,' Sabrina said shakily, 'but I still keep thinking he's going to call, or even walk into the room. I just can't seem to make myself believe that he's really gone.'

'It's often like that when you first lose someone you love,' June assured her gently.

'We used to talk all the time about the house we were going to buy in Italy,' Sabrina rambled on, 'somewhere close to the one we were all staying at when we first realised how we felt about one another. It would be like going back to the beginning, he used to say, and doing it all the way we wanted, without the complications of Robert and Alicia forcing us to hide how we felt.'

Having heard all this before, June simply smiled and carried on listening like the dutiful friend she was, having no idea how much of it was a fantasy and how much truth. She only knew how capable everyone was of conjuring an idealised picture, and airbrushing out all the imperfections that would spoil the memory. In the end, she said, 'I'm sorry you're feeling so low tonight. I wish there was something I could say, or do, to make you feel better.'

Sabrina sighed unhappily. 'I'm OK,' she insisted. 'It's the business with Annabelle that really dragged me down, and having my sister-in-law in the vicinity is making everything ten times worse, but actually, I did receive some good news today. Jennifer Bingleigh called to invite us to her villa on the Cap again this year. Robert was thrilled when I told him. He needs a holiday. We both do.'

Fighting back her envy, June said, 'Lucky you. Will Annabelle go too?'

'Of course. I can't leave her here, and who knows, maybe spending some time together away from all her friends, and in that lovely setting, will help us to get over this bad patch.' She took a sip of wine. 'How about you?' she said. 'Do you have any plans for a holiday yet?'

'Nothing so glam, because sadly, singles like me don't get invitations to luxury villas on the Cap d'Antibes, so I'll probably go and spend a week with my sister in Ireland again.'

Sabrina shook her head in despair. 'We really do have to do something about finding you a man,' she said decisively. 'You can't go on the way you are, it's intolerable. Maybe we should start running a lonely hearts column in *The Buzz,* that way you can have first pick.'

June smiled. 'I think you'll find Mr Right or Sir Perfect in Every Way don't need to advertise for women, and even if they do, they don't want someone my age. Speaking of *The Buzz,* however, I take it there's been no reaction to your piece about tourism in Holly Wood.'

Sabrina shook her head. 'Not from *her*, but a couple of people have approached me expressing concern about the possibility of strangers with video cameras and take-out coffees turning up on their doorsteps. There's a parish council meeting next Tuesday. If I can get my fellow members to sign a petition saying we don't want the shop, then we can send it to the district council before they make a decision about issuing a permit, because she's sure to have applied for one by now.'

June was about to respond when a voice beside them said, 'Sabrina? I'm sorry, I hope we're not interrupting.'

Sabrina looked up, and her spirits sank even lower when she saw Clarissa Booth, who lived in one of the larger houses on the new estate, smiling down at her.

'It's such good fortune running into you like this,' Clarissa told her, while her nasty-looking spouse nodded and ogled Sabrina in a way that made her want to wipe her skin clean. 'We're having a little get-together next Saturday, just a select few, if you know what I mean, and we'd absolutely love it if you could come.'

Sabrina's eyes turned so chill that the woman's smile started to fade. 'I'm afraid I'm not free next Saturday,' Sabrina lied. 'Or any other Saturday, actually,' she added meaningfully.

Clarissa drew back. 'Oh, I see,' she said, reddening to the roots of her dark wavy hair. 'I'm sorry to have bothered you,' and taking her husband's arm she quickly bustled him away.

'That was a bit harsh,' June commented, watching them go.

'They're swingers,' Sabrina hissed. 'They wanted me to go and throw my keys in the pot and very possibly spend the night with that disgusting specimen of humanity she was with. Ugh,' she shuddered, as her skin crawled again. 'Of all the damned nerve. How dare she think I'd be interested in her little parties?'

'Ah, but the question is,' June said thoughtfully, 'is either of them on the parish council?'

Sabrina's eyes widened with horror, then for

the first time that evening she found herself starting to laugh. 'Thank God no,' she said, and summoning the waiter she ordered a second bottle of wine.

'Give me some of that,' Annabelle cried, grabbing a bottle of cider as it sailed past on its way from Georgie to Catrina.

'Don't drink it all,' Catrina protested, as Annabelle swigged it back.

'OMG, this is so amazing,' Annabelle gasped excitedly. 'I can't believe we're doing this. Are there any girls out there yet?'

Georgie peered round the curtains to check. Though Theo and his friends numbered at least fifteen milling about the pool in shorts and flip-flops, so far there was no sign of any girls.

'You don't think we're the only ones invited, do you?' Catrina wondered anxiously, 'because there's only, one, two three, four . . . Eight of us, and look how many there are of them.'

'By my reckoning that gives us about two each,' Melody quipped. 'I'm having Theo tonight,' she fired at Annabelle. 'Remember?'

'Simon Forsey just better turn up,' Annabelle warned. 'With Nat.'

'Katie, will you hurry up with that joint,' Georgie pressed. 'We're gasping over here.'

'Does anyone know if Theo got those Es?' Catrina said seriously. 'We need them right now. Someone should go out there and get them.'

'I don't know what we're all getting so worked up about,' Melody stated. 'It's not like we don't know them, or they haven't seen our boobs before.

So come on, let's stop hanging around in here like a bunch of virgins, when we all know none of us are, and act like grown-ups.'

'Great, then you go first,' Georgie told her.

'No way,' Melody retorted, shrinking back.

'Well, someone has to.'

'We can all go together,' Catrina piped up.

'No, I reckon Annabelle should go first,' Melody decided.

Annabelle looked startled, and a little uncertain.

'Go on. You're not scared,' Melody told her.

'Of course she isn't,' Georgie confirmed. 'Go on, Annabelle.'

'Yeah, you definitely should be first,' Catrina agreed. 'You look fantastic in that skirt. That was such a neat idea. Wish I'd thought of it.'

'You're fine in those shorts,' Annabelle reassured her. 'It's what everyone else is wearing, except Georgie in her naughty little ra-ra skirt. What have you got under there, Georgie?' she teased, trying to pull it up.

'That's for me to know and someone else to find out,' Georgie countered, slapping her away, 'so keep your hands to yourself.'

'Oh God, I love this song,' Katie moaned, as Adele's 'Chasing Pavements' started to play. 'Come on, let's go dance. Annabelle, lead the way.'

'OK, this is it,' Annabelle announced, and once the others were crowded like a faithful retinue behind her she stepped out on to the twilit terrace, her young, naked breasts with their large dark nipples peeking mischievously through the silky veil of her long hair. She was Cleopatra presenting herself to Mark Antony; the Queen of

Sheba bearing gifts to Solomon; Kate Moss on a catwalk with the whole world drooling over her magnificence.

It took only a moment for the boys to realise the female contingent had finally arrived, and as they turned to watch the sensational spectacle of eight topless babes approaching they started to whistle and cheer and slap one another on the back as though congratulating themselves for such a great idea. Loving the attention, Annabelle sauntered on ahead, tossing one side of her hair back over one shoulder, and then the rest over the other, so her breasts were completely revealed. The next minute she was in the middle of the throng having drinks and Es thrust at her, while some of the girls leapt into the pool, quickly followed by a handful of boys, and others giggled and squealed as they struck poses for the cameras Carl and Kennedy had brought with them.

'How about I mow your lawn?' Theo murmured in Annabelle's ear.

Treating him to a sultry look she said, 'The skirt stays on.'

'We'll see about that,' he smiled, and closing in on her he pushed his tongue deep into her mouth.

'Ahem,' Melody coughed, behind them.

Annabelle turned round, and smiling sweetly said, 'Maybe later, Theo.' Drifting away she left Melody to it, and went to find more E.

An hour later, as the sun vanished over the distant hills and the garden lights came on, Annabelle was sprawled out on a swinging hammock chair loving the world, her friends, this party, her life, even her mother. Everything was so wonderful and gorgeous and perfect that she wanted to pour endless amounts of love over everyone and make them all feel as happy and chilled as she did. Her smile was beatific, her eyes dreamy and blurred; she wanted to go on lying here for ever, wearing her grass skirt and nothing else, letting the fronds part around her thighs, trickling a hand lightly over her bare breasts unless someone was there to do it for her.

Carl had been lying with her, but he'd gone to get more drinks a while ago and hadn't come back yet. She could hear someone splashing about in the pool, and a couple nearby making out on the grass. The music was like light pouring itself into her, filling her with sounds that made her want to dance like an angel. She could fly around the garden, up over the trees and away into heaven.

She turned her head to one side and saw Georgie, her best friend in the entire universe, swaying towards her. Georgie's skirt had gone, she was wearing only a bikini bottom now, and carrying an alcopop and a fat, half-smoked spliff.

'Hey,' Georgie slurred, rolling around the bars of the hammock and almost staggering into it. 'You'll never guess who's just turned up.'

'Tell me,' Annabelle murmured, holding out a hand to take the drink.

'Simon Forsey,' Georgie announced, hiccuping as she passed it over. 'And guess who's with him?'

'OMG,' Annabelle drawled, 'are you serious? Where is he? Tell him he has to come here because I love him.'

Georgie drew deeply on the joint, then held it out for Annabelle to take. Annabelle put it between her lips, but then her hand fell away and flopped to the ground.

Dropping to her knees Georgie retrieved the spliff, staggered back to her feet and began weaving her way across the lawn towards the vegetable garden.

Annabelle remained adrift on another plain, inhaling deeply and moaning with pleasure as she let the air go. Nat was here, gorgeous, wonderful Nat whom she'd been mad about for ever and wanted to love and love and love and then love some more.

At the other side of the pool where the drinks were set up, Nat and Simon were holding beers and surveying the improbable scene around them. The moonlight was making it seem even more surreal, as though it were a painting of a lewd bacchanal, occasionally stirring into life. Clearly everyone was stoned, or wasted, or both. A couple close by were smooching drowsily to a techno beat, a naked girl was floating like a starfish in the middle of the pool, others were lying around on loungers, or spread out on the grass.

'Hey,' a semi-naked Melody purred, coming up to them, 'this is a topless party. You're not supposed to be wearing shirts.'

Simon grinned and gazed into her eyes, not quite having the courage yet to look where he really wanted to. He was as tall and athletic as Nat, but much fairer, and not quite as good-looking. 'I think that can be remedied,' he replied, and putting down his beer he hiked his T-shirt over his head.

'Mm,' she murmured approvingly. 'You too,' she said to Nat.

'I'm good,' he said, raising his bottle as though she'd offered him a drink.

Unperturbed, she turned back to Simon. 'So you came,' she said.

'Looks like it,' he replied. His eyes stayed on hers as he took a sip of his drink. 'You've got great tits,' he told her.

Nat gave a splutter of laughter, and turned aside.

'Thank you,' she said playfully, and taking Simon's hand she started to lead him away. 'Come on, let's get to know one another a little better,' she murmured.

Glancing back over his shoulder, Simon shrugged and grinned as though to say, 'What's a guy to do?'

Nat saluted him with his beer, telling him to enjoy.

Left alone, Nat continued to drink and look around. It seemed everyone was in couples, or even threes, and since he really didn't want to get involved in an orgy, he stayed where he was. As soon as he'd finished this beer he'd be on his way, not because he was a prude, each to their own as far as he was concerned, but because he was driving and the last thing he wanted was to lose his licence when he'd only just got it. Added to which he'd told Summer there was no way he'd show up at this party, so if he hung around for a few minutes just to be sociable, he could tell her, in all honesty, that he'd only dropped in to keep Simon company until he got into the flow.

Come to think of it, Simon was already in the flow and since there was no one to be sociable with, in the conventional sense, he might just as well disappear. So, downing the rest of his beer, he was about to make good his escape when he noticed a girl swinging indolently back and forth in a hammock at the far end of the pool. Until then he'd assumed Annabelle was inside somewhere getting it on with one or two of the crowd, but to his surprise she seemed to be on her own.

Not entirely sure why he was doing this when he might so easily have got away without seeing her, he picked up a can of Coke and wandered over to say hi. He didn't want to think that his motive was merely to get a look at her breasts, but if he was being honest with himself, he'd have to admit that it was playing a part. She'd always been seriously attractive, and now she had this amazing figure that no red-blooded man could ignore, he was finding himself as drawn to her as he'd been all those years ago when they'd used draughts as a cover for their childish fumblings.

'Hey,' he said, as he reached her.

Her eyes fluttered open and as he came into focus she gave a sigh of pure pleasure. 'Hey,' she murmured back. 'Look who's here. So where's the ginger one?'

'Her name's Summer,' he retorted. 'She's in Italy.'

'Oh yes.' Her lips curved in a deliciously satisfied smile and she inhaled deeply as she closed her eyes. 'Lovely,' she whispered with a sigh.

He lowered his gaze to her breasts and felt a surge of lust tighten his groin. Her nipples were dark, fully erect peaks on firm mounds of perfectly tanned skin. He knew if he stooped to touch her she'd do nothing to stop him, but as irresistible as she was he forced himself to look away.

'I knew you'd come,' she said softly.

'Really?' His voice sounded gruff and grating in this soporific setting. 'That's funny, because I didn't.'

She smiled dreamily. 'I love you,' she sighed, lifting her hands behind her head.

He took a slug of Coke and heard himself say, 'So how come you're alone?'

Fanning out her arms, she said, 'Who knows? Anyway, I'm not now, because you're here and I'm so happy I could float away, but if I did you'd still be here and I love you, so I want to stay with you.'

'How much have you had?' he asked, feeling ludicrously square.

She smiled and giggled. 'Why don't you come and sit down? There's plenty of room.'

'I'm cool,' he said, taking a step back as she reached for him.

Stretching languorously she arched her back, pushing her breasts tantalisingly towards him. 'Do you think they've grown?' she said. 'You can touch them if you like.'

Turning away he kicked off his shoes and went to sit on the edge of the pool, dangling his feet in the water. Though he was rock hard, he wasn't going to let himself do this. Sure, he might want to, but he wasn't in the business of screwing girls who put it out there the way she did. Besides, he loved Summer.

'Don't tell me you're shy,' she teased. 'You never used to be.'

'That was a long time ago.'

'You haven't forgotten though, have you, I can tell.'

Not bothering to answer, he took another sip of his drink and brought a foot out of the water to rest an elbow on his knee.

'You look like your dad,' she told him. 'I expect everyone says that.'

He didn't respond. There was nothing he could say, and he sure as hell wasn't going to get into a conversation with her about his father, especially not here.

'It must have been horrible for you . . .'

'Let's just leave it,' he cut in.

She rolled her head to one side and back again. 'I'm sorry, I didn't mean to upset you.'

'You haven't.'

A few minutes ticked idly by. He was aware of a girl wandering like a sylph through the trees close by, and the low burble of voices now the music had stopped. Theo, the host, climbed out of the pool at the opposite end and padded naked across the terrace into the house. A moment or two later the haunting sound of Take That began drifting around the garden, as ephemeral and intoxicating as the perfumed smoke.

'Your mum's still really cut up about it, isn't she?' Annabelle said.

Nat tensed. Why wouldn't she let it go?

'Mine is too.'

He frowned and half glanced back in her direction. What the hell did her mother have to do with anything? He couldn't give a flying fuck how Sabrina felt about his father's death, or anything else come to that. Why would he, when the woman was a first-class bitch and actively hated his mother? So if this was Annabelle's half-cocked way of letting him know that his father had been special to everyone, she'd do a lot better to leave her mother out of it. In fact, his time here was over, he decided, and got to his feet. There was no point hanging around when he had no intention of getting off his face, had zero interest in pulling, and even less in continuing a futile conversation with a doped-up Annabelle.

'See you,' he said shortly, and scooping up his shoes he walked back to the bar, dumped his can in a plastic sack and left through a side gate. Simon would easily find a ride home if he wanted one, but chances were it wouldn't be until after dawn.

By the time Nat drew up outside the Coach House it was almost two in the morning, so seeing the lights still on in the sitting room caused a tremor of fear to shoot through him. His immediate thought was that something had happened to Darcie, and leaping out of the car he ran up the path to let himself in the front door.

'Mum!' he called, pushing open the sitting-room door. He was about to shout again when he saw her curled up in one of the armchairs, fast asleep.

Dizzied by relief, he picked his way through the boxes she'd evidently been unpacking, and was about to wake her when he saw the wedding album in her lap. Kneeling down next to her, he gazed at the photograph she'd been looking at before dropping off. It was one of her favourites, he realised, of her looking radiant in her lovely shimmering dress, with his father standing beside her, tall and striking in his dark grey tails and lemon cravat, and watching her in his typically sardonic way as she laughed uproariously at something he'd just said. Nat couldn't remember what it was now, but his father had told him once and it had made him laugh too.

It brought a lump to his throat to think of her sitting here alone going through her memories, and having no one to share them with. She'd loved his father so deeply that his death must have left a terrible gap in her life. They'd been so happy together, always laughing, or touching, or sharing little snippets from their days, mainly about him and Darcie, but often about other things too, like the cases his father was working on, or the new ideas his mother was developing for her art. They always took the time to listen to him and Darcie and all their childish nonsense, making them feel the most important people in the world even when they were still very small.

There had been dark times too, nights when they'd argued a lot, and he'd heard his mother crying and shouting, but Nat had always buried his head under the covers, not wanting to hear. By then he'd been old enough to know that all married couples rowed, but he hated to hear his parents raising their voices to one another, so he'd deliberately shut it out.

He wondered now what had happened to make his mother unhappy before his father had died. He supposed he could guess, if he wanted to, but he'd rather not. Or he could ask, but he didn't want to do that either. Something had got to his father one night though. It was a night he would never forget.

'Nathan, will you please sit at the table now,' his mother snapped irritably. 'Your food's ready and you can send that text later.'

'I've almost finished,' he argued, carrying on with what he was doing.

'Where's Dad?' Darcie said, bouncing into the kitchen. 'He was here when I came home.'

'He went out for a run,' Alicia told her. 'He'll be back any minute. Now you sit at the table too, please. Nathan, I won't tell you again, and why are you wearing that shirt? You're supposed to be keeping it clean for my show on Friday.'

'I've got a date, remember,' he protested. 'She's finally agreed to go out with me.'

'Who?' Darcie demanded.

'Who do you think? Summer Corby.'

'That's a nice name,' Darcie commented. 'Summer. Much better than mine. Why did you have to call me *Darcie*?' she asked her mother.

'Dad chose it, and it's a beautiful name. OK, Nat, hold up your plate. How much sauce do you want?'

'Loads if it's carbonara . . . Oh for God's sake!' he cried, leaping up as Alicia spooned tomato sauce on to his pasta and it splashed on to the front of his shirt. 'Look what you've done, you *stupid* woman. What's the matter with you? I can't wear this . . .'

'Nathan!' Craig barked.

Nathan turned in horror to see his father glaring at him thunderously from the doorway. 'But look what she . . .'

'Go into the sitting room *now*,' Craig growled, his dark eyes showing real anger.

Ashen-faced, Nat left the table and skulked past his father into the hall. His father smelled of sweat and cold air and a faint hint of booze.

Once the sitting-room door had closed, Craig tugged the towel from round his neck and slammed it into the arm of the sofa. 'Don't you *ever* let me hear you speak to your mother like that again, do you hear me?' he roared.

Nat's head was hanging as he nodded.

'Answer me.'

'Yes, I hear you,' Nat said.

'Sit down there,' Craig said, pointing to the sofa.

Knowing better than to cross his father when he was in this kind of mood, Nat slumped into the sumptuous cream leather cushions.

'Your mother is the most important person in your life,' Craig told him harshly. 'I hope you realise that.'

'Yes, of course,' Nat mumbled.

'She loves you, and I know you love her, but love isn't always enough, son. It has to come with respect, and what I heard just now showed no respect at all. Is that how you feel about her, that she's unworthy of your respect?'

'No, of course not.'

'Do you ever hear me speak to her like that?'

'No, never.'

'Then why did you?'

'I don't know. I mean, I was angry, because . . . Look at my shirt.'

'I don't care about your damned shirt, it's your attitude that's the problem. You've got a date tonight, with a girl who matters to you, yes? But what good are you to her if you don't know how to treat her right?'

'Dad, I'm sorry. I didn't mean what I said . . .'

'It's too late. The words are out. This is a lesson in thinking before you speak.'

'Yes, Dad.'

'You'll apologise to your mother before you go a step further tonight.'

'Of course.'

'And you'll launder the shirt yourself as a punishment.'

Nat nodded, relieved that he was getting off so lightly. Then came the killer blow.

'Now you'll call your new girlfriend and tell her you're sorry, but you can't make it tonight after all, then you'll go to your room and write an essay on respect.'

Nat was staring at him in horrified protest. 'Dad, no. Please . . . I swear I didn't mean to be rude. I'll apologise to Mum, I'll do anything you say, but please don't stop me going out tonight.'

Craig was adamant. 'One day, when you've qualified as a lawyer,' he said, 'and you're dealing most of the time with men who physically and verbally abuse their wives, mothers, girlfriends, you'll remember this day, and you'll understand that their monstrous behaviour starts in the home. They're almost always carbon copies of their fathers, and that's not who I am, Nat. I despise those men, and I won't tolerate you behaving anything like them. I respect your mother. I love her more than I'm capable of putting into words. That's how I want you to be with the girls you meet, always respectful and one day, when the right one comes along, loving and loyal too. Does that sound like good advice?'

'Yes,' Nat nodded.

'Is that who you're going to be? Someone who's respectful, loving and loyal?'

'Yes,' Nat promised.

'Craig, that's enough now,' Alicia said, coming into the room. 'He's sorry and you shouldn't be taking your frustrations out on him.'

Realising his mother had come awake and was watching him, Nat looked at her and smiled.

'What are you thinking about?' she whispered, touching his face.

He grimaced and slanted his eyes away. 'Actually, it was the time Dad told me off for not respecting you,' he answered. 'Do you remember how ballistic he went?'

'I do,' she said, sitting a little straighter. 'He was going through a difficult time.'

Nat's interest perked. 'What do you mean?' he asked carefully.

Alicia wiped her hands over her face and stifled a yawn. She wasn't going to tell him that it was guilt and self-loathing for betraying her that had made his father so angry that night, but she could tell him what else had been on Craig's mind.

After sending Nat into the kitchen, Alicia closed the sitting-room door behind him and said, 'They're good lessons, Craig, because he should respect women, but we both know that outburst was more about you and how you're feeling than it was about what he said.'

Craig didn't even try to deny it. 'I'm sorry,' he said, pushing his hands through his hair. 'I know I over-reacted, but it's tearing me apart the way we're not as close as we used to be. I wish to God I could turn back the clock, or do something to prove to you that every time I'm out late, or working away from home, or even taking a phone call, there's nothing to worry about. You mean everything to me . . .' He rubbed a fist into his eyes, then to her alarm she realised he was crying.

'I'm sorry,' he gulped, as she came to comfort him. 'It's not just us . . . I had some news today . . .' His eyes closed as the awfulness of it swept over him again. 'You remember the arsonist case in Bristol?' he said.

She frowned. 'That was months ago,' she replied, 'and wasn't it thrown out?'

He nodded. 'I got it dismissed on a technicality. The arresting officer hadn't followed proper procedure . . .' He took a breath. 'The slimeball of an arsonist has struck again,' he said. 'A young mother lost both her children in a fire last night.' His final words were choked with remorse and as he buried his face in Alicia's shoulder she held him close. 'Why the hell didn't that damned police officer do her job properly?' he growled. 'All she had to do was make sure he understood his godamned rights . . . But I blame myself. I knew he was likely to reoffend, but I stuck to the law and made her look a fool in court. My pathetic victory has cost an innocent woman everything that matters in the world. Jesus Christ, what's the matter with me, Alicia? Why am I getting everything so wrong?'

* * *

When she had finished telling the story Alicia gazed into Nat's eyes, and felt her heart turn over to see how troubled he was for his father. Nat's conscience had the same integrity, which was too much, some would say, for a lawyer, but they were the cynics who hadn't had the privilege of dealing with someone like Craig Carlyle.

'So that's why he was so upset with me that night,' Nat said. 'He had all that going on in his head?'

And more, she was thinking.

'It wasn't his fault though, was it?' Nat said.

She shook her head. 'The blame lay squarely with the arsonist, but Dad felt responsible, even though he was only doing his job.'

Nat went on thinking about it for a moment. 'Is this bloke in prison now?' he asked.

'Yes. He went down for life, but Dad didn't play a part in his trial.' *He just gave all his money to the victims' family, which is why we're in the financial mess we are now*, she didn't add. But at least she had her children, and no amount of money could ever make up for losing them.

Nat nodded. A small light started to shine in his eyes as he said, 'You got him to back down about my date with Summer, remember?'

Alicia smiled. 'You still had to write the essay though.'

He rolled his eyes. 'Tell me about it. It took me a whole week to come up with two thousand words on respect. *And* I had to launder the shirt.'

She laughed.

He looked down at his hands, resting in hers. 'He was pretty special, wasn't he?' he said quietly.

She thought of the betrayal, but then she thought of his kindness and love, the joy and pride he'd taken in his children, and the integrity that had been so much more a part of him than the weaknesses. 'Yes,' she whispered, still not used to speaking about him in the past tense, 'yes, he was.'

Chapter Ten

'Apparently things have changed since our day,' Rachel commented drily over lunch the following Tuesday. 'Sounds to me more like an orgy than a party. I bet Jemima and Bob McAllister didn't know anything about it.'

'I'm sure you're right,' Alicia agreed, tearing off a piece of bread. 'I'm told they're in Greece for a month.'

'Lucky them. So did Nat get involved, do you know?'

Alicia shook her head as she ate. 'I guess he wouldn't tell me if he did, but according to him he only had one beer and a brief chat with Annabelle before he left. Apparently she was high as a kite.'

'Now why doesn't that surprise me?'

'According to Simon that particular set is well known for the kind of things they get up to, so I definitely don't want Annabelle anywhere near Darcie. I think Robert will understand, because he's already suggested that it might not be a good idea.'

'Are you going to tell him about the party?'

Alicia sighed. 'I don't know. I feel I should, but Nat doesn't want me to. He says everyone will know it's come from him, and that's not going to make a great start for him, even though he's not particularly interested in becoming part of that set.'

'Mm, a difficult one,' Rachel murmured, and smiled up at the waitress who came to deliver their plates of fresh gambas.

They were in the garden of the Traveller's under a large blue parasol that sheltered their picnic table completely from the sweltering sun, and overlooked the quiet high street the other side of the wall.

'Anyway, I'm glad you dropped in,' Alicia said, shaking out her napkin. 'I was in need of a break – and actually, I have some news.'

'Oh?' Rachel responded, all ears.

Alicia grimaced, as her heart contracted. 'I had a call from my solicitor in London this morning. The house sale is now complete. So,' she went on, picking up her wine, 'shall we drink to my new life?'

Looking as concerned as she felt as she reached for her Coke, Rachel said, 'How well are you really taking it?'

Alicia thought of all their lovely furniture, the paintings and rugs she and Craig had chosen together, the tables, sofas, beds, the beautiful bathrooms and state-of-the-art kitchen, and felt as though something deep inside her was being taken apart. 'Badly,' she admitted, 'but thankful it's happening at a distance. It would feel a lot harder if I was still there.'

'Of course. You did the right thing leaving before it all went through. This way the real break's already happened. How did Nat take it?'

'I haven't told him yet. He knows the completion's imminent, but I don't want to make a big thing of it. If he asks I'll tell him, otherwise I'll just let him assume it's done.'

'Where is he today?'

'Gone to the cricket again. I can't make him spend his whole holiday cooped up in the shop, so I'm doing the ceiling myself, as you can see by my hair.'

Rachel smiled at the random white blobs that speckled Alicia's fringe and ponytail. 'Staying with the shop and your new life,' she said, breaking open a prawn, 'Dave's been doing some ringing around for you regarding permits, et cetera. He's printed out what he's found so far . . .' Wiping her hands on a paper napkin, she reached into her bag and pulled out a small buff envelope. 'Basically, if you're going to do it legally, and you won't want to do it any other way, then I'm afraid there's no chance of opening for at least six weeks, and even then you might still have to wait before you can actually work in the studio.'

Alicia's appetite died as despair folded around it. 'Why can't anything ever be easy?' she murmured in frustration.

'From what I can tell,' Rachel went on, 'you have to start with a change-of-use application to register the place as an arts and crafts shop. The fee is £335, which you send together with details of how many square metres will be used for retail, and how many for workshop. You need to list the kind of equipment you'll be using to make your sculptures, which is where the big delay could kick in, because, as we know, you do a lot of welding, and to get that cleared you have to contact the environmental protection people and building control. Possibly the fire brigade too. It's all there, most of it as time-wasting and farcical as you might expect when dealing with the local authorities.'

Alicia's face was paling with strain.

'However, the good news is,' Rachel continued in an upbeat tone, 'Dave has a contact at the planning office who's going to try to fast-track things for you, and we'll come round later with the kids to help you measure the place up.'

As Alicia looked at her, she was barely registering what Rachel was saying. 'How could I have been so stupid?' she said. 'Why didn't I realise I'd have all these official channels to go through? I'm like some idiot airhead who thinks everything's possible just because it feels like a good idea.'

'You're new to this, so how could you know?' Rachel said defensively. 'And besides, no one can be expected to think straight when they're going through as much as you are.'

Alicia still looked annoyed with herself.

'It's going to work out, I promise,' Rachel told her firmly. 'It'll just take a little longer than you'd hoped.'

'But I don't have time on my side. I have to start earning soon or God knows what we'll do.'

'OK, Dave and I have talked about this . . . I know you're probably going to say no, but hear me out . . .'

'I'm not taking a loan. It's the quickest way to lose friends, and losing you isn't an option.'

'I'm not offering a loan. I'm offering to buy into

your business. I can be a sleeping partner, or a shareholder if you like, and take a percentage cut of the profits when they come. Meanwhile, you'll have a little capital to tide you over.'

Alicia was shaking her head. 'It's a wonderful offer, but I know what a terrible mess the property market's in, so with Dave's income being reduced . . .'

'He has six rental properties on the outskirts of Frome,' Rachel reminded her. 'If anything, they're in greater demand than ever, so we're a long way from having to exist on my income alone.'

'I'm glad to hear that, but all the same, I can't take your money.'

'What else are you going to do? OK, there are banks, but there's no way of knowing how much joy you'd get from them these days, plus you have to think about the interest they'll charge, and how long it might take for the application to go through. You just said yourself, time isn't on your side.'

'I'll think of something,' Alicia said. 'I'll get a job of some sort. Do you need a receptionist? Maybe Maggie wants help here, in the pub.'

'You should to be building up inventory for the shop,' Rachel reminded her. 'At the moment you've only got six sculptures and with the best will in the world, you know they don't exactly fly off the shelves.'

'I'll bring the prices down.'

'Even if you do that, you still need more stock, and for that you have to be creating and finding other artists to promote.' She looked up as someone behind Alicia caught her attention.

'Who is it?' Alicia asked, glancing over her shoulder.

'I'm not sure,' Rachel said, smiling and waving politely at a well-groomed man who'd just come into the garden. 'I know I've seen him . . . Oh, that's right, he brought his dog in with an injured paw last week. He probably doesn't know who the heck I am out of context. Anyway,' she went on, picking up where they'd left off, 'there is one other alternative.'

Alicia swallowed. 'If you're thinking of Robert, he's already offered and I turned him down too.'

'But why?'

'Because I don't even want to think about how that whore would react if she found out he'd loaned me money, especially for a shop that she's trying to stop me from opening. Not that I'd mind one bit sending her off into orbit, you understand, but I certainly don't want my brother's life turned into a living hell.'

Taking her point, Rachel picked up her drink and took a sip. 'Then it's me or the poorhouse,' she declared.

Alicia still wasn't going for it. 'I told you just now, I'll think of something,' she said. 'Meanwhile, I still have a bit left in the bank, and a five grand overdraft facility which they haven't had any reason to cancel yet, thank God. It should feed us for a while, and buy what Nat and Darcie need for school. It might even stretch to some supplies so I can start making jewellery, because I won't be able to do any welding in the old playroom.' She sighed heavily, and shook her head as she stared down at her drink. 'You know, I was actually starting to think I might make my own deadline to open at the beginning of August.' Her laugh was bitter. 'I know Sabrina doesn't make the rules, but I still can't help blaming her for this.'

'It's true, round one does seem to have gone to her,' Rachel conceded, 'but this is only the beginning, and I know you, Alicia Carlyle. It'll take a lot more than a bit of paperwork and a scheming bitch with more venom than brains to fell you.'

Alicia's eyes came up. 'It's not going to be pleasant, though,' she said.

'No, because that's not an adjective one ever uses where your sister-in-law's concerned.'

Alicia's smile was weak. 'Actually, I spotted her coming out of the village shop yesterday morning. The way she stalked back to Holly Way was like a one-woman victory parade. It was so obvious she was hoping I was watching that it might have been comical, if it weren't so pathetic.'

'You're going to come face to face with her sooner or later,' Rachel said. 'Have you thought about how you're going to handle it when you do?'

'I guess it depends on where and how it happens. I have to admit though, the longer it's dragging on the more anxious it's making me. I just hope it doesn't turn into some all-out slanging match, or worse, because if it does . . .' She took a breath and shook her head slowly. 'I just hope to God it doesn't,' she said, and left it at that.

After accompanying Rachel to her car, which she'd left outside the church, Alicia walked back along the high street, her spirits weighted by the small brown envelope she was carrying. No matter how fast a track Dave's contact could find for her application, common sense was telling her that she had to abandon all thoughts of opening in August, because it simply wasn't going to happen. Instead, she'd have to spend the time driving back and forth to local government offices taking them every last tedious piece of information they'd forgotten to ask for the last time she was there, adapting her application in ways to suit someone who probably knew nothing about her line of work, or waiting hour upon hour outside some planning officer's inner sanctum while he or she enjoyed the little power they had over lesser mortals.

With all these gloomy thoughts going round in her head, their edges sharpened by what she'd like to do to Sabrina, it took her a moment to register the fact that a man was outside the shop, peering in through the window. Annoyance tightened the band around her head. Surely some official bod from the district council wasn't dropping by uninvited already? It would be just like Sabrina, with all her contacts, to put them up to it, and being in no mood to deal with the stranger politely, she was sorely tempted to take an about turn towards home. However, on closer inspection, the expensive-looking white polo shirt and khaki shorts, combined with the shock of silvery hair that lent him a decidedly distinguished air, sat somewhat at odds with her image of a local council snoop.

Shielding her eyes from the sun as she approached him, she said, 'Can I help you?'

As he turned round she noticed the striking contrast of his black eyebrows against his much lighter-coloured hair. His face was tanned, making his teeth appear whiter as he smiled in a way that transformed an otherwise serious face.

'Hello,' he said. 'I'm looking for Alicia Carlyle. I was told I might find her here, but the place seems to be all locked up.'

Suddenly realising he was the man Rachel had recognised at the pub, and feeling, oddly, as though she too had seen him somewhere before, she said, 'I'm Alicia Carlyle. Please don't tell me we had an appointment and I've forgotten.'

His smile deepened the creases around his navy blue eyes, and she wondered if he wasn't much closer to forty than the fifty she'd first assumed. 'Cameron Mitchell,' he said, holding out a hand to shake.

She swallowed, and tried not to do a double take as she put her hand in his. She was having no trouble recognising him now, because anyone in her world knew exactly who he was. As a highly respected art dealer and critic he'd launched several stellar talents. He'd also stopped others dead in their tracks, which was why he was viewed with some trepidation by fringe hopefuls like her, who still dreamt of discovery. So what on earth was he doing here? Which bottle had she rubbed for this kind of genie to pop out on the very day her dreams had been sold by an estate agent in London, and throttled by red tape in Somerset?

'It seems we have a mutual friend in Antonia Bassingham,' he explained. 'She asked me to say hi if I managed to catch up with you.'

Alicia's jaw almost dropped. She'd lost count of the times she'd all but begged Antonia for an introduction to this man, but Antonia, one of London's glittering hostesses and a very successful social networker, had never come through. Now, suddenly, here he was on her doorstep in, of all places, Holly Wood. 'Hi,' she said, as though Antonia were there, and they both smiled.

'It's good to meet you.'

'Likewise.' She gestured awkwardly towards the shop. 'Did Antonia tell you . . . ? As you can see, we're not open . . .'

'Don't worry,' he said, 'she warned me you probably wouldn't be up and running yet, but I'm not actually here in a professional capacity. That's not to say I wouldn't be interested in taking a look at your work,' he added politely, 'it's just that I'm thinking about buying somewhere in the area, and Antonia informs me that you're from this neck of the woods so you might be able to give me some pointers.'

Thrown by the unexpectedness of it, but instantly grateful for the opportunity to help someone who could, should he choose, do so much for her, she said, 'As it happens I've just discovered that I'm going to have more time on my hands than I'd expected in the next few weeks, so I'd be happy to help. Do you have anywhere particular in mind? Where are you staying?'

'Some friends have kindly lent me their house for the summer. It's in Wyke Champflower, do you know it?'

'Yes, of course. It's very pretty around there.'

He nodded. 'What there is of it. A random bunch

of houses and a cheese-making dairy farm, as far as I can tell, but that's what I'm after, some English-style country living.'

She laughed. 'Are you American?' She couldn't remember registering an accent whenever she'd heard him on radio or TV, but she was picking up on one now.

'Half, thanks to my mother,' he replied. 'My father's a Scot and I was born in France, but only because I couldn't wait to get into the world. In other words, I brought an idyllic holiday to an abrupt end by showing up five weeks ahead of time.'

With no little irony she said, 'So now you make a habit of impromptu appearances?'

His eyes lit with humour. 'Seems like it,' he confessed. 'I'm sorry, I guess I should have called first, but it's such a lovely day that I decided to venture out for a spot of exploring, and when I found myself round this way I remembered Antonia telling me about you. She said you've only recently moved back here, is that right?'

Alicia nodded and felt the warmth fade from her smile. 'My husband died a few months ago,' she told him, 'and we couldn't carry on . . .' She stopped. He didn't need her life history. 'Would you like to come in?' she suggested, taking out her keys. 'I can offer you some tea, or there might still be some fresh lemonade in the fridge if you'd prefer something cold. One of the locals makes it and sells it in the village shop. It's very good.'

'Then I'll give it a try,' he replied, following her inside.

'As you can see, it's not quite finished yet,' she

apologised as he looked around, and she almost winced as she thought of the glossy, high-end gallery he owned in London. She'd actually been to a preview there a couple of years ago, but she wouldn't mention it now because she couldn't for the life of her remember the name of the artist he'd been promoting.

'When are you planning to open?' he asked, as she walked through to the studio which was still cluttered with boxes, brooms, cleaning paraphernalia and her unceremoniously dumped equipment.

'If you'd asked me that yesterday,' she said over her shoulder, 'I'd have given you a very different answer. As it is, any time this decade would be good.'

He came to stand in the arch. 'What's the hold-up?'

'I think local authority regulations should probably cover it,' she answered, rinsing out a couple of glasses.

He grimaced.

'This used to be my mother's charity shop,' she explained, 'now I'm turning it into something else, and like a fool I didn't think about environmental protection, building regulations, health and safety, trading standards, or the whole nine thousand yards of red tape that has to be got around. Anyway, you didn't come here to listen to me whingeing on about bureaucracy, which is a pity because I really feel like letting rip right now. However, I'll spare you, if you promise to come to the opening when it does finally happen. Only if you're in the area, obviously,' she added hastily, embarrassed by her temerity. 'I wouldn't expect you to come all the way from London . . .'

'It's not that far, and I don't see why not,' he said. 'If I've found a place by then it might be a good way of getting to know some neighbours.'

'Do you really not know anyone?' she asked, passing him a glass of semi-flat lemonade.

He smiled and gave her a salute before taking a sip. 'Mm, very good,' he agreed.

Her eyes twinkled in a way that made him laugh.

'OK, time to be truthful,' he said. 'I've been coming to these parts for the last five or six years, usually staying with friends who have a place the other side of Bruton. The Carmichaels, do you know them?'

She shook her head. 'I don't think so. Should I?'

'Only because Antonia's related in some way to Felicity Carmichael, so as you and Antonia are friends . . . Anyway, I'm acquainted with probably a handful of people through them, but most of them are away for the summer and besides, they're a pretty horsey sort of set which isn't really my thing. Apologies if you're a keen rider.'

She waved a dismissive hand. 'Terrified of them,' she assured him. 'My daughter, on the other hand, says it's the only good thing about us moving here, so she can learn to ride and have her own horse. I'm still trying to pluck up the courage to tell her it's not likely to happen. You'll know when I do, because you'll probably hear the howl from here to Wyke.'

He looked amused. 'How old is she?'

'Twelve. I have a son of seventeen too, who's being very stoic about the move, at least so far.'

'So what exactly are you hoping to do with the shop?' he asked, starting to take another look round.

Wondering if he was genuinely interested, or just being polite, she decided to believe the former and launched into a guided tour of what would go where, once the display cases, plinths and shelves were fully assembled and installed. And how she hoped to exhibit other artists' work too. 'Probably not sculpture,' she said, 'that would be too much of a conflict.'

'Unless your styles are completely different.'

'Of course, but I don't really do much painting any more, so I thought some talented abstracts would be a great way of filling up the walls and helping to get some promising newcomers a little exposure.'

'Have you seen anything that takes your fancy yet?'

She shook her head. 'We only arrived ten days ago, and so far all our energies have gone into sprucing this place up. As you can see, we still have a way to go. When the time's right I'll start hunting down the local talent, then I'll put some notices in local shops and libraries, and the newspapers too, if I can afford it, to let the world know we've arrived.'

Seeming to consider this reasonable, he said, 'Would it be too presumptuous to suggest we combine a talent spot and house search?'

Only just managing not to gush with excitement, she said, 'I'd like that immensely. After all, I can't think of anyone more qualified than you to spot a burgeoning ability, and I can just imagine the impact it'll have on my potential new protégés when the great Cameron Mitchell turns up on their doorsteps.'

He was laughing and starting to protest.

'No, really,' she insisted, 'I know how they'll feel, because it was pretty amazing for me just now. In fact, it still is. Are you actually here, or am I dreaming this?'

'I could pinch you, if you like,' he offered, 'but that probably wouldn't be very gentlemanly.'

She laughed, and realised with an unfamiliar sense of lightness that she was actually enjoying herself. Maybe the glass of wine with lunch had gone to her head, but even if it had, he wasn't coming across as anything like the other art critics she'd met. On the whole they were an extremely pompous, self-aggrandising bunch, far too exclusive even to notice someone outside their rarefied world, never mind go out of their way to be pleasant.

'Well, I guess I've taken up enough of your time,' he said, putting his glass on her cluttered workbench. 'Would it be possible, before I go, to . . .'

'Oh no,' she protested, 'please don't ask me to show you anything now. It's all still in its packaging from the move, and it has to be properly displayed for the best effect. I'm sorry, do you mind? I'm sure you'll hate it anyway, but at least then I'll know . . .' She stopped as his hand went up.

'I understand perfectly,' he told her, 'and actually, I was going to ask if I might use your bathroom before I leave.'

Alicia felt herself blush as she burst out

laughing. 'It's at the far end of the patio,' she told him, pointing outside and wanting to hug Rachel's Uncle Pete with all her might for whipping out the grungy old loo and replacing it with a swanky new buttercup piece that he'd conjured up from . . . she knew better than to ask where. OK, the walls hadn't been painted yet, and Pete hadn't, so far, managed to produce a matching – or not – handbasin to take over from where the old one had dropped off. However, the important thing was it flushed like a vacuum, and the tiny brick cubicle was so much improved from when she'd first forced open the door that she wasn't going to waste time feeling ashamed now.

As he picked his way past the old bird bath and a bench she was in the process of sanding, Alicia pressed her hands to her cheeks, still hardly able to believe he was here. She wanted to snatch up the phone and call Rachel, or better still to thank Antonia, but that would have to wait till he'd gone.

'Alicia? Are you in here?' Mimi called from the door. 'Ah, there you are,' she beamed as Alicia appeared in the arch. 'I noticed the door was open and wanted to be sure it was you, because there was a man hanging around outside a while ago. Never seen him before, and I didn't get a chance to ask what he was doing because I had an order come in. Did you see him? I thought he might be a friend of yours, because he was very smart, and *very* good-looking.' She winked, then her mouth formed an O as Cameron stepped back into the studio. From his expression it was clear he'd overheard.

'Oh, there's me rattling on when you've got company,' Mimi said, starting to edge out.

'Cameron, this is Mimi,' Alicia told him, catching Mimi's hand and pulling her back. 'She has the flower shop next door and I've known her all my life. Mimi, this is Cameron Mitchell.' She doubted the name would mean anything to the old lady, but she liked saying it anyway.

Smiling as he came forward, Cameron said, 'I'm very pleased to meet you, Mimi. I was admiring your arrangements on my way past.'

Mimi flushed with pride. 'That's very kind of you,' she replied, shyly shaking his hand. 'I do me best, and it's nice when folks are appreciative. Anyway, don't let me hold you up. I've got lots to do next door. Pete's coming in later,' she told Alicia, 'to lay them new pipes you discussed.'

'Lovely,' Alicia smiled, but Mimi was already bustling away.

'I guess it's time I was leaving too,' Cameron said, glancing at his watch. 'Jasper's going to be wondering what's happened to me, I've been gone so long.'

Alicia gave him a quizzical look.

'Jasper's a dog,' he explained. 'He usually goes everywhere with me, but he cut his foot on a stone at the weekend, so the vet thought he should rest it . . . Ah, that's who I saw in the pub garden earlier. The vet. I thought I recognised her. And was it you she was with? I'm sorry, I only saw you from the back, but the hair . . .'

'That was me,' Alicia confirmed.

'It's such a small world,' he joked, 'here we are,

we already have two people in common, Antonia and the vet. Who knows where it might end?'

Laughing, she said, 'Who indeed?'

It wasn't until she was standing watching him cross towards the old bank where he'd left his car parked, that she realised she hadn't taken his number. Her first instinct was to go after him, but he knew how to get hold of her, so rather than appear too eager she turned back into the shop, smiling warmly to herself. This unexpected boost to her spirits was so welcome that she wanted to believe it was life's way of showing her that luck could change. It didn't all have to be about loss and struggle, husbands dying too young and sisters-in-law who belonged in hell. Sometimes good things happened, and she couldn't help thinking that Cameron Mitchell showing up out of the blue like this was very good.

'Annabelle, I want you to help me with this please,' Sabrina called from Annabelle's bedroom. Throwing back the sheets, she got to her knees to inspect under the bed. 'My God, how long has this been here?' she demanded, her lip curling in disgust as she dragged out a plate of mouldy food with an encrusted knife and fork and clusters of fluff attached.

'Just leave it,' Annabelle snapped from the bathroom.

'This place is a pigsty and I want it cleaned now, today,' Sabrina told her sharply. 'Rhoda's refusing to come in here, and I can't say I blame her.'

'I like it this way, and it's my room so I'm the

one who gets to say how it is,' Annabelle shot back.

Choosing not to get into such a fatuous argument, Sabrina continued picking up clothes and shoes, magazines, old tissues, dropped make-up, remote controls for the endless electronic gadgetry and a revolting assortment of sweet and crisp bags. 'Do you ever put any of this stuff in the waste basket?' she demanded. 'Or the washing machine?' she added, holding up a badly creased pair of white jeans smeared with lipstick and heaven only knew what else.

'No, I just buy new when I need to,' Annabelle replied, coming into the room in a thin silky wrap. She had a towel wrapped around her head and her toes were padded with cotton-wool puffs while the scarlet varnish dried.

'You're not funny,' Sabrina told her.

'Who's joking?'

Looking at her, so young and pretty and unbearably full of herself, Sabrina was about to launch into another dressing-down over the way she'd defied her and gone to the party on Saturday, when a depressing sense of weariness sank into her bones. They'd only end up screaming at one another, and they'd done so much of that over the last few days that she couldn't face it again. So, turning to strip back the bed, she began bundling up the sheets. 'I'm half afraid of what I'm going to find in here,' she commented seriously.

'Could you just go now?' Annabelle said, sitting down in front of the mirror. 'I need my privacy . . . Oh no, hang on, could you help me with some waxing? I can't do it myself, it hurts too much.'

'You should come with me to the salon at Babington and get it done properly,' Sabrina told her. 'I'm going on Friday. I can book you in if you like.'

'Cool. Are you having a Brazilian?'

Sabrina's eyebrows rose. 'I might.'

Annabelle grinned at her in the mirror. 'Bet Robert gets really horny when you . . .'

'Don't go any further with that,' Sabrina cut in. 'I'm not discussing my love life with you, especially not in that sort of language.'

Annabelle shrugged. 'Whatever,' and peeling off the towel she began brushing out her hair. 'Can I borrow some of your Leonor Greyl stuff?' she asked. 'It makes your hair really shiny and soft.'

'If you were going somewhere special the answer might be yes, but it's too expensive for everyday use, particularly in the heat when you're wearing your hair up anyway.'

Rolling her eyes, Annabelle squirted a large ball of John Frieda mousse into her hand and began smoothing it into her hair. 'Phone's ringing,' she said.

'Thank you, I can hear. Right, I'm taking this lot down to the laundry room,' Sabrina said, scooping up the towel Annabelle had dumped on the floor and plonking it on top of the sheets. 'I shall expect this room to be properly cleaned before you go out, or you won't be going.'

Waiting until the door had closed, Annabelle muttered 'Fuck off,' and began rummaging around for her mobile.

'Hey,' she said, when Georgie answered. 'Are you having a weepy Wednesday?'

'A bit,' Georgie answered dolefully. 'How about you?'

'The same. We need some more E.'

'Or weed, or anything.'

'Are you still up for going to Clark's Village later? Shopping usually cheers us up.'

'OK. Actually, I need to get something for the rave, because I've got absolutely nothing to wear.'

'Me neither. So how are we going to get there?'

'I'll ask my mum if she'll take us, if yours can bring you here. Oh, by the way, my parents are going to be away for the whole weekend of the rave, so you can come and stay here if you like.'

'Brilliant. Count me in, but don't let on to my mum that yours won't be there, or she'll start erupting again. She's been on my case ever since I got back on Sunday about going to the party on Saturday night, stupid bag. It would do her head in if she thought I was going to the rave.' Her eyes closed as they filled with a sudden rush of tears. *Why did everyone always keep picking on her? It wasn't fair, she was only doing the same as all her friends, but her mother, being the narrow-minded uptight control freak she was, who didn't really give a damn about anything anyway, had to keep going on and on like she was talking to some kind of delinquent. God, it made her sick.* 'Actually, I was thinking,' she said shakily, 'I might call Nat to find out what he's doing tonight.'

'Do you have his mobile number now?'

'I can call the house. If Alicia answers I'll just hang up.'

Georgie was sounding dubious. 'I know you're not going to want to hear this,' she said, 'but I really don't reckon he's interested. I mean, he had a perfect opportunity at the party . . .'

'Yeah, and if we'd been on our own . . .'

'He could have taken you somewhere . . .'

'It wasn't his house so . . .'

'Hang on a minute,' Georgie interrupted, and covering the mouthpiece she shouted, 'I'm up here. OK. I'll be down in a minute,' and coming back on the line, 'What were we saying?'

'We were talking about Nat, and I'm telling you he *is* interested, or why would he have come over to talk to me?'

With a sigh, Georgie said, 'Whatever. Let me know how it goes if you do call, otherwise I'll see you here about two.'

After ringing off Annabelle tossed the phone on the bed and went out on to the landing. 'Mum!' she yelled.

No reply.

'Mum.'

'I'm on the phone,' Sabrina said, coming into the hall.

'Sorry. Can you give me a lift to Georgie's in about an hour?'

'Hang on,' Sabrina said to the caller. 'Provided your room's finished,' she told Annabelle.

'Ugh,' Annabelle snorted, and spinning round she slammed the door behind her and began stuffing everything on the floor into wardrobes or under the bed, or behind the drapes. Then, opening a drawer, she scooped all her make-up and perfumes off the dressing table into the tangle of underwear inside, before turning on the hairdryer to blow the remaining dust and debris on to the floor, out of sight. She then dried her hair, taking less care than usual, because, as her mother had pointed out, she was wearing it up a lot lately; ringed her eyes in black kohl, and tugged a short blue halter-neck dress from the back of the wardrobe. Lastly, she laced a pair of Roman sandals around her ankles and stood in front of the long mirror to admire her reflection.

Not bad. She looked at least eighteen, and her tan was really starting to show now. To view the contrast of her white bits she raised the hem of her dress and felt a sharp bite of wickedness as she gazed at her own nudity. She'd *love* to go out with no panties on, it would give her such a kick. Just imagine if the wind blew as a lorry went past, or if she bent over in a café and some bloke was sitting behind her. He'd get a real eyeful and she could pretend she had no idea he was watching.

Deciding to pop a thong in her bag in case she felt like putting one on later, she sank down on the bed and picked up her mobile. As she scrolled through the numbers the urge to cry swept over her again, the way it had all morning, and turning into her pillow she began to sob. She wished Robert would come home and do something to make everything all right again. Her life was horrible, everything was wrong. She wanted to run away with Nat, whose father was dead, and it wasn't fair. He didn't deserve to lose his dad, no one did, and as more waves of wrenching despair came over her she pressed her face harder into the pillow. She hated being rejected. It really sucked, but she wasn't exactly sure that was what had happened on Saturday night, because she couldn't properly remember now. She knew she'd said something about his dad, but she'd only been trying to be nice. Anyway, she knew he wanted her really, he was just playing hard to get, or pretending to be faithful to his stupid girlfriend. Once she got him alone she knew everything was going to happen the way she wanted it to, because men were all the same – all they ever wanted was sex, and since Nat had been dead keen to do it with her before, she couldn't see any reason why he wouldn't want to now.

Finally reaching for her phone again, she used a hand to wipe away the tears, and once she was sure she'd shaken off some of the gloom inside her she pressed in his number.

Chapter Eleven

'Can you get that?' Alicia said, as the main phone started to ring in the kitchen. Her hands were sticky with orange and strawberry juice as she chopped fruit to make a salad.

Tilting his chair back from the table where he was using Alicia's laptop to send emails, Nat reached for the cordless on the counter top behind him. 'Hello, Alicia Carlyle's personal assistant,' he announced.

As Alicia turned round he winked, then his humour faded as the voice at the other end said, 'Hey. It's Annabelle.'

He said nothing.

She took a breath. 'I was wondering if you're free tonight, I thought maybe we could . . .'

'I'm not,' he broke in.

'. . . play some draughts.'

He let a silence run.

'So, do you want to change your plans?' she said huskily.

'No,' he replied, 'but thanks for calling,' and he rang off.

'Who was that?' Alicia asked, going to rinse her hands.

He shrugged. 'Some telemarketer. Did you call Jolyon back to get a time for dinner on Friday?'

'Yes, we're meeting at eight, so we'll have to leave here about six thirty. It's quite a way up to Huntstrete.'

'I'll drive if you want to have a drink,' Nat offered.

She smiled and kissed the top of his head. He couldn't know how much she'd need one to get her over the fact that they might be sitting at the very same table his father had once shared with Sabrina, or looking out at gardens where he might have strolled with her. More likely though, Craig and Sabrina had spent their entire time in one of the luxury suites, rolling around the bed, slick with sweat, breathless with lust, unable to get enough of one another, never sparing a thought for anyone but themselves.

'Mum?'

'Yes?' She kept her back turned as she wiped down the surfaces.

'Are you all right?'

'Yes, I'm fine.'

A few seconds passed. 'Do you want to add something to this email to Grandpa?'

'OK,' she said, 'let me know when you've finished.' Since Craig's father was an invalid now, and unable to travel far, it had fallen to her, after Craig's death, to take the children to see him. For the first couple of months they'd gone every week, but then, for some reason, the old man had seemed to start blaming Alicia for his son's early demise, making their visits difficult and painful all round. So now the contact had dwindled to email, and the occasional phone conversation, mainly with the children, rarely with Alicia, which she found more upsetting than she'd admit, since it was like losing another part of Craig.

As the phone rang again Nat said, 'Can you get it this time? I hate the way those people pester you.'

Drying her hands, Alicia picked up the cordless. 'Hello?' she said, going to rehang the towel.

'Alicia, sweetie. It's Antonia. I got your message. I'm so glad Cameron looked you up. He's divine, isn't he?'

'Yes, uh . . .' Alicia glanced anxiously at Nat, and started into the sitting room. 'It was lovely of you to put him in touch.'

'Oh, no problem. We have to help out our friends in times of need. How's it going down there, darling? Is it very grim?'

'I wouldn't say that. It's just different.'

Antonia gave an audible shudder. 'I'm afraid I don't do the countryside,' she said, 'but Cameron's mad about it apparently. I do so hope the two of you get along. I'm absolutely sure you will.'

'I was wondering,' Alicia said, keeping her voice down in the hope Nat wouldn't hear, 'is he, you know, gay?'

Antonia burst into peals of laughter. 'Oh Alicia, you're so funny,' she cried. 'It's good to know you haven't lost your sense of humour.'

'Actually, I was . . .'

'Oh, darling, I'm sorry, I have to go, someone's just come in, but call any time. It's always lovely to hear you. Mwah, mwah,' and she rang off, leaving Alicia feeling faintly ludicrous and extremely hopeful that her question didn't find its way back to Cameron Mitchell, who hadn't actually come across as gay, but given his profession . . .

'Who was that?' Nat said, as she returned to the kitchen.

'Oh, just a friend from London. Antonia. You might remember her.'

He shrugged. 'Did she come to any of your shows?'

'To all of them actually.' There had only been three, each one held in a small Fulham gallery that used to be a garage until the dealer had converted it into a *salle d'exposition,* as he'd liked to call it, to start up his business. For Alicia, the best part of the shows had invariably been how involved Craig and the children became in setting them up, photographing her sculptures, designing posters, throwing in ideas for publicity, drawing up mailing lists and helping to transport everything from her studio to the gallery. She'd actually sold a few pieces during her first and second exhibitions, though she suspected Craig might have been behind at least one of the purchases since it had gone to his partner in chambers, Oliver Mendenhall. However, after her last exhibition she'd received a commission from an American friend of Antonia's who was a genuine buyer, and the letter the woman had sent when the ballerina arrived in the States had gushed with so much praise and thanks that it had boosted Alicia's confidence for weeks.

'So,' Nat said, still tapping out his emails, 'is he gay?'

Alicia turned round.

'I wasn't eavesdropping,' he assured her, 'but I'm not deaf.'

'You don't even know who I was talking about.'

'No, but I'm guessing it was the bloke who turned up at the shop yesterday. Mimi told me.'

Thanks, Mimi. She'd probably told Nat how good-looking Cameron was too, and topped it all off with a knowing wink. Deciding the only way to play this now was absolutely straight, she said, 'He's an art dealer who might prove very helpful in getting our little enterprise off the ground. In return, I'm going to try to help him find a house.'

Nat slid the mouse around the pad. 'Yeah, right,' he muttered.

'What's that supposed to mean?'

'Nothing.'

'Nathan, if there's something you want to say . . .'

'It's none of my business what you do,' he retorted tersely, 'but Dad's only been dead for six months, so don't you think it's a bit soon to be getting involved with someone else?'

Closing her eyes as she herself recoiled from the idea, she said, 'That's not what the visit was about. No, listen,' she interrupted as Nat started to argue, 'you're right, it's far too early for me to be thinking that way, and I promise you, I'm not, so you've got nothing to worry about.'

As Nat continued typing she could sense his bottled-up frustration and knew he wanted to shout at her for even speaking to another man when his father was the most important person in the world and no one, *no one* could ever take his place. 'So do you think you will ever get married again?' he said shortly.

'No,' she answered. 'I mean, I can't imagine it happening. Actually, I can't imagine loving anyone but Dad.' Since it was true, and undoubtedly what he wanted to hear, she had no trouble saying it, but God knew there were times when she wished betrayal destroyed love as well as trust, because then the loss, and the haunting fear of why Craig had been so stressed during those final months, would be so much easier to deal with.

Nat's expression was still tense as he closed down the laptop.

'Nat, please don't let's fall out over something that's not even an issue,' she implored, as he started to get up.

'I'm not,' he replied. 'It's up to you what you do.'

'Where are you going?'

'To get a drink from the fridge. Is that OK?'

Smiling as she nodded, she decided it was probably best to leave the subject alone for now, and took out a pan to start boiling some eggs. '*Salade Niçoise* for lunch?' she said.

'Cool.' Then, after a beat, 'Darcie's favourite.'

Since those two little words had the feel of an olive branch, she was going to take them as one. 'I'm really starting to miss her now, aren't you?' she said.

'It's pretty quiet without her bossing us around,' he agreed. 'Did you speak to her this morning? She rang while you were in the shower?'

'Yes, I called back on my way up to the shop. She had a few rich comments to make about the permits I need to get the business up and running. I suppose you told her.'

He nodded. 'I don't think she really understands it too much. She got mad because I did.'

Alicia's eyebrows rose. 'We'll get them,' she assured him, 'so I don't want you to go worrying yourself about it. It's just going to take a bit longer than we thought.'

'And what are we going to do for money until then?'

Startled, she turned to look at him. 'We're not broke,' she told him. 'OK, it won't be like it was before, but we'll manage.'

'I don't see how,' he argued. 'You don't sell enough pieces for us to live on anyway, and if you can't put them in the shop . . .'

'There's always eBay, and the website when it's ready . . .'

'It's still not enough. Anyway, I've been thinking, and I've decided I should forget about school and get myself a job. Maybe one of the local factories will have something, or a farm. They might not pay much, but it'll be better than us all starving.'

Alicia was staring at him aghast. 'We're not going to starve,' she told him forcefully, 'and you are going to finish your education the way we've always planned. No Nat, listen to me,' she said as he started to protest. 'Your only responsibility is to yourself and to fulfilling the dream you have of following in Dad's footsteps. It's what he would want, and it's very definitely what I want. So let's hear no more of this nonsense about giving up school and finding a job. Everything's going to work out just fine. I have enough to tide us over at least until the end of the year, and by then the shop's bound to be open.'

'But what if you don't sell anything? I'm sorry, I'm not being rude about your sculptures, because I think they're great, but you don't have that many, and the rate they sell at . . . Well, you know what I'm saying.'

'The shop is not going to be dependent on my sculptures alone. You know that already, so let's drop this now.'

Though he clearly wanted to argue more, he took himself outside instead, and knowing him as she did, she guessed the reason he'd backed down so quickly was because he was afraid of saying something that might hurt her even more than he already had. Though she adored him for how sensitive he was towards her feelings, she hated the fact that he was so worried about their finances, because telling himself he should be shouldering his father's responsibilities wasn't going to help him at all in his A-level year. He needed to be like other boys his age, focusing only on what lay ahead as they prepared themselves to go out into the world.

'Where's Simon today?' she asked, trying to bring things back to a normal level by sounding chatty as he returned with some glasses that had been left outside.

'At home, I guess. I dunno.'

'You're not getting together today?'

'I'm going to make a start on painting the studio this afternoon. I'll need to get more emulsion though.'

'There's no rush now we can't open, so why

don't you take the car and go and do something with Simon?'

'No, it's cool. I like painting, and it'll be good to know it's all done before . . .'

'Nat, this is your summer holiday. It's not that I don't appreciate or need your help, but I want you to enjoy yourself.'

'I am.'

'What, painting, and hanging around here with me? You should be with people your own age.'

'I was at a party last week, I've been to the cricket with Simon, I'm going to this rave at the weekend. I'm doing normal stuff, OK?'

'OK, sorry. I just want to be sure that you're not staying at home so I won't be on my own.'

'That's not why I'm here,' he told her. 'I'm answering emails and doing revision and designing your website. My turn,' he said as the phone rang again. 'Hello? Oh, hey Si. How're things? Yeah, I left my mobile upstairs.'

As he chatted on, Alicia began stoning olives for the salad and chopping tomatoes, but was unable not to listen as he started discussing the rave on Saturday night with mentions of hardcore – which she knew to be a kind of techno music – half a dozen or more performing DJs, the expectation of about a thousand people turning up, and whether the police might come crashing in around midnight to try and put a stop to it.

By the time he rang off lunch was ready, and she was waiting for him to join her at the table outside.

'So,' she said, as he pulled up a chair, 'this rave isn't exactly legal?'

'I've got no idea,' he answered. 'Some are, some aren't.'

'Don't you think you should find out?'

'Mum, it's only over the way in Holly Copse, so it's hardly going to be anything major, is it?'

'I don't know. If there are drugs involved . . .'

'Who says there will be?'

'I thought that was the whole point of these raves.'

'For some it is. For me it's the music and atmosphere. You can get high on that without actually taking anything.'

'What about booze?'

'Well, I'm going to have a drink, obviously.'

'What kind of drink?'

'We're taking vodka so I'll probably have a bit of a hangover on Sunday.'

She rolled her eyes. 'Is it an all-nighter?'

'Bound to be. They always are. At least until five, anyway.'

Wishing she could talk him out of it, but fearing a row if she tried, she said, 'Just as long as you stay away from the drugs. The last thing you need is something like that on your record, if the police do turn up.'

'Will you please stop worrying. It'll be fine. Everything will, you just wait and see.'

Though she was still far from happy about him going, she gave up nagging then, and her eyes went down as his words *it'll be fine, everything will, you just wait and see* echoed out of the past, spoken by Craig, after yet another hysterical phone call from Sabrina.

* * *

Alicia and Darcie were in the den, watching TV, while Craig and Nat shut themselves in the sitting room for one of their usual Thursday-night-debate rehearsals. Since Nat had joined the school team, his father had been coaching him in the art of putting his argument across, and the pleasure they both got from their battles of wits was always written over their faces when they finally emerged.

However, this evening, as the closing credits rolled on *EastEnders*, Alicia heard Nat storm out into the hall, and Craig shouting something after him.

'What's going on?' she asked, coming out of the den.

'It's him!' Nat cried from halfway up the stairs. 'He's not listening. He keeps telling me I've missed points when . . .'

'I'm sorry,' Craig interrupted. 'I know I'm not on form tonight. We probably shouldn't have started. Can we try again tomorrow?'

'I've got rugby tomorrow.'

'OK, then at the weekend. You've clearly researched the subject and you're making a great case, so it deserves to have my full attention. Can we do that? Sunday afternoon?'

'Maybe,' Nat said, and clearly still feeling furious and let down he ran on up the stairs.

Alicia looked at Craig.

He sighed and pushed his hands through his hair. 'I need to do some work,' he said.

Closing the door to the den so Darcie couldn't hear, Alicia said, 'What is it? I knew something was up when you came home this . . .'

'Just leave it,' he barked. 'It's nothing.'

Her face paled as she regarded him. 'She's been

in touch again, hasn't she?' she said, feeling her head starting to spin.

'No! All right, yes she has.'

She tried to swallow but her throat had turned dry. 'Have you seen her?' she asked.

'No, of course not.'

Her face was so tight now that her mouth hardly seemed to move as she said, 'Do you want to?'

His eyes came to hers. 'What kind of question is that?' he demanded.

Pushing him into the sitting room and slamming the door, she said, 'It's a perfectly reasonable question that you seem unable to answer. So I'll ask it again. Do you want to see her?'

'No, I do not want to see her.'

'Then why are you so uptight?'

'Because she won't leave me alone, and she keeps threatening to damn well kill herself . . . What the hell am I going to do if she does?'

Resisting the urge to say *dance on her grave*, Alicia turned away and sank down on a sofa, cradling her head in her hands.

'I'm sorry,' he said, coming to sit with her. 'It's not that I care about her, I swear it, but the way she seems to be suffering . . .'

'Do you think I care about that?' she raged, looking up.

'No, of course not, but for Christ's sake, I don't want to be responsible for someone taking their own life.'

'No! If she commits suicide then that's her decision. It has nothing to do with you.'

'I wish to God I could see it like that, but I can't.'

'Then learn to. You keep telling me it's over, but

the way you are now . . . You're thinking about her all the time.'

'That's not true. Today's the first time she's rung in a week. I was hoping . . . I thought, when I didn't hear, that she'd finally got the message, but it seems I was wrong.'

'Then let me speak to her. I'll make sure she gets the damned message.'

He shook his head. 'You remember what happened the last time you two . . .'

'I'm not going to see her,' she spat. She put out her hand. 'Give me your phone,' she said.

He frowned uncertainly.

'I said, give me your phone. She'll answer if she thinks it's you.'

'Alicia, this isn't a good idea.'

'I want your phone,' she seethed. 'If she thinks she's going to blackmail you into seeing her with ludicrous threats of suicide, which, I might say, she has no intention of carrying out, then she can think again.'

'I'm not giving you the phone.'

Her face turned white. 'If you won't, then I'll know you've got something to hide,' she said in a dangerously low tone.

Sighing, he took it from his pocket and handed it over.

'What's the number hidden under?' she asked, starting to scroll through.

'Keats.'

She looked at him, wanting to hit him. 'The fact that you still have it is bad enough, that it's under the name of a poet . . . How the hell am I supposed to believe it's over?'

'Alicia, stop doing this, please,' he implored.

Finding the entry, she pressed to connect and walked to the window, shaking, as she waited for a reply.

'Darling, at last. I knew you'd call . . .'

'It's not Craig, you whore,' Alicia seethed. 'I know you've rung him again, threatening to kill yourself, well perhaps you could do us all a favour and just get on with it.'

Sabrina gasped. 'You bitch!' she cried. 'I'm not speaking to you . . .'

'You're not speaking to him either. Just leave us alone, Sabrina. You've done enough damage . . .'

'It's not me who's calling him,' Sabrina broke in furiously. 'He's calling me because he can't let go any more than I can. We love one another . . .'

'You're a liar and fantasist,' Alicia broke in, looking desperately at Craig. 'He can't stand you.'

Craig flinched and Sabrina yelled, 'That's what you like to think, but let me tell you this. Every time he makes love to you, he's thinking of me. Whenever he looks at you, he's wishing you were me, and we both know you've been wondering where he really is when he says he's working late at night, well he's with me. It's not over between us, Alicia, and it never will be.'

Alicia was trembling uncontrollably as Craig came to take the phone.

'Sabrina, you have to get help,' he said quietly, and without waiting for a response he ended the call and turned off the phone.

'Did you hear what she said?' Alicia asked hoarsely.

'More or less. It's not true, I hope you know that.'

She turned away.

Catching her, he forced her to look at him. 'It's not true,' he insisted. 'I have not seen her since the day I told her it was over.'

'So where have you been when you're supposed to be working late?'

'There's no supposed about it. That's where I've been.'

'So how does she know . . . ?'

'Alicia, you're falling into her trap. Working late goes with the territory of being a lawyer. Everyone knows that, including her, so she's using it to try and drive a wedge between us again.'

She was shaking her head. 'I want to believe you,' she said, 'but I'm afraid to.'

'If it'll help, go through my phone,' he said, trying to pass it back. 'You'll find one call from her, the one I received today, and that's it. I haven't rung her, I haven't seen her, and I don't want to see her.'

Her eyes were swimming in tears of uncertainty as she looked at him. 'Are you sure?' she asked.

'Of course I'm sure.'

Her head went down, and allowing him to draw her to him she rested a cheek on his shoulder as her mind spun with the chaos of lies and betrayal.

'It'll be fine,' he told her, holding her tight. 'Everything will, you just wait and see.'

'Have you been crying?' Sabrina asked, throwing a quick glance at Annabelle as she drove her to Georgie's.

'No,' Annabelle answered shortly, keeping her face averted.

'Yes you have, I can hear it in your voice. What's wrong?'

'Nothing.'

Sabrina glanced at her again. 'Is it something . . .'

'Just leave it, will you? I'm fine.'

To her relief her mother only sighed and continued to drive. If she'd kept on Annabelle knew she wouldn't have been able to stand it, because she was still so close to the edge that she couldn't allow herself to think about anything, especially Nat, or she'd go over again. He shouldn't have hung up on her like that. It was mean and rude and had made her feel like a stupid minger, and as though she didn't mean anything to anyone. She'd only wanted to be friends, but he'd hardly even spoken to her.

'I expect his mother was there,' Georgie said comfortingly when they were in the privacy of her room and Annabelle related what had happened through a storm of tears.

'Yeah, I thought of that,' Annabelle wailed, dabbing at her eyes. 'It's not that he doesn't like me, is it?'

'No, of course not. I only said he wasn't interested because I was feeling really crap myself. It's weepy Wednesday, remember? We're both on a downer.'

'We need to get some weed.'

'I know. Oh sod Clark's Village, I'll go and tell Mum we've changed our minds, then I'll ring Melody. She usually knows where to get some.'

As Georgie left the room, Annabelle huddled herself up in the window seat and stared absently down into the valley. She was thinking of Nat, and her mother, and how fantastic everything used to be, and wishing with all her heart that it could be like it again.

'This is the best holiday ever, isn't it?' Annabelle sighed happily, as her mother wandered into Annabelle's tower room in the Italian villa.

Sabrina smiled and drew a hand softly round her cheek. 'Absolutely,' she whispered. There was a glow about her that made her appear more beautiful than ever, and Annabelle's heart filled with love and pride that she was her mother. 'It's the perfect place to fall in love,' Sabrina murmured.

Annabelle coloured to the roots of her hair.

Noticing, Sabrina's smile deepened. 'It's OK,' she said kindly, 'I'm not surprised you've fallen for Nat. You two have always been close, and he's very good-looking.'

A delirious glow of infatuation broke through the hesitancy in Annabelle's eyes. 'Do you think he's fallen for me too?' she asked shyly.

Sabrina laughed in a way that always seemed to light up Annabelle's world. 'How could he not?' she answered, hugging her. 'And I won't ask what the two of you have been getting up to when you go walking in the olive groves, or disappear to play some board game or other, Italy's such a romantic place . . .'

'We don't do anything,' Annabelle protested, blushing so hotly it was painful.

Appearing surprised, Sabrina said, 'You mean he hasn't kissed you yet?'

Annabelle's head went down as she started to smile. 'Well, yes, he has,' she confessed. Then, 'Actually, lots of times.'

Sabrina gave another tinkle of laughter, and laughing too Annabelle threw her arms around her and they tumbled in a heap on to the bed. Though she longed to ask her mother's advice on how much further she should let him go, she knew, because she was only thirteen, that her mother would take a very different view of the relationship if she had any idea of the way Annabelle was thinking. But as soon as she was sixteen it would be all right, because then they could tell everyone that they wanted to get married, once they'd finished their studies.

'We have to go to university first,' Nat had insisted, when they'd discussed it earlier in the day, while lying in their secret little niche in the olive groves behind the villa. 'And maybe we should wait until I've passed my bar exams before we make any proper plans.'

'Of course,' she agreed, and felt a burn hotter than the sun slide between her legs as he pulled her to him. 'Do you think they'll be shocked that we want to get married?' she whispered shakily.

'Probably, but who cares?'

Gazing at him adoringly, she said, 'I really love you.'

'I love you too,' he murmured, and covered her mouth with his.

'Is he a good kisser?' Sabrina asked mischievously, as they lay side by side on the bed.

Annabelle blushed again. 'Yes,' she answered. 'I mean, I've never kissed anyone else, but I know he's the best.'

Sabrina's head came round to look at her. 'That's because he comes from the best,' she said softly, 'and nothing else will do for my girl. But promise me it won't go any further than kissing. He's older than you, and you're very beautiful, so he could feel tempted to try and persuade you to do more, especially when you're walking around in a bikini most of the time.'

'Don't worry,' Annabelle said, looking away, and feeling glad that her mother had no way of knowing that Nat was the one holding back more than she was. Then in a rush of euphoria she smiled and snuggled into her, as she said, 'I wish we didn't have to go home tomorrow, don't you?'

'Mm,' Sabrina answered, gazing up at the frescoed ceiling as she idly stroked Annabelle's hair. 'I think we'll both have very special memories of this holiday, my darling, and maybe, one day, we might even come back here. Would you like to live in Italy?'

'To live?' Annabelle echoed in surprise. 'Only if Nat was here.'

Sabrina smiled. 'Of course,' she said, 'and who knows, maybe he will be.'

Chapter Twelve

Sabrina's welcoming smile was fading fast as she looked at Robert. He'd just returned, a day earlier than scheduled, but apparently, instead of coming straight home, where she'd been waiting, he'd dropped in to see his sister first.

'I see,' she said, feeling dizzied and angry and unsure of what to say. 'Well maybe you'd like to go back over there and spend some more time with her,' she blurted sharply. 'After all, I don't suppose it matters that I cancelled my arrangements this morning in order to be here for you?'

Immediately looking contrite, he said, 'You didn't need to do that. I told you when I rang that I wouldn't be staying long. I'm due at the labs in a couple of hours. I only came back to change and pick up my mail. I thought maybe we could go out for dinner this evening.'

Sabrina was still stinging from the slight of having come second to his sister. 'Are you sure you wouldn't rather take Alicia?' she said coldly.

'Darling, don't be childish,' he said. 'Of course I'd rather take you. Anyway, she's meeting one of Craig's old colleagues at Hunstrete House.'

Sabrina stiffened.

Noticing, he felt a fist close tightly in his chest, and wished he could take the words back. 'One of your old haunts?' he said, managing to keep his tone mild, but it was underscored by an acuity that gave a knowing edge to his smile.

She turned away, intending to pick up her car keys.

He didn't want a row, more than anything he wanted to take her in his arms and start his homecoming all over again, perhaps even begin their marriage all over again, but he heard himself saying, 'I hear you've managed to throw a spanner in the works for Alicia's shop.'

Sabrina spun round, outrage not quite managing to mask the guilt in her eyes. 'I'm not the one who makes the rules,' she snapped.

'My guess is you didn't even know what they were until you went looking,' he commented. He looked her straight in the eye. 'It's not going to stop her,' he said evenly. 'She'll get the authorisations or permits . . .'

'Why? Because you're going to help her?'

'I don't have any sway with the local authority. She'll get them through the proper channels, so your only success will be in delaying the inevitable.'

Though her face was pinched, and her eyes were darting about wildly as she tried to think what to say, she knew very well he'd get the better of her if this developed into a full-scale row. So, attempting to turn the tables, she said, 'Is this what you want, Robert? Always to be in the middle, her one side, me the other? Because I hope you realise that's how it's going to be if she stays here.'

Fearing she was right, he said, 'It doesn't have to be.'

'There isn't any other way.'

Sighing, he picked up his mail and started to leaf through. They'd have to find some way of dealing with the situation, but for the moment he was at a total loss as to how they might. 'Where's Annabelle?' he asked. 'I brought her the perfume she asked for.'

Not yet ready to change the subject, she said, 'Tell me, do you defend me when you're talking to *her*? Or do you just stand there letting her play the victim, slagging me off and . . .'

'Sabrina, please don't do this. I'm tired, I've got a lot on my mind and I'm not going to let myself be drawn into this ridiculous campaign you seem to have started. *You* are the one who was in the wrong, when you slept with her husband, and now you're compounding matters by trying to stop her making a living. So why don't you simply get on with your life and let her get on with hers?'

'Before you walk away,' she shouted, as he started to leave, 'maybe you'd like to consider the favour I did her, by bringing the permits to her attention. If I hadn't she'd have been operating illegally and they'd probably have closed her down.'

'Nice try,' he said, turning back, 'but as we both know there was no altruism in your motive.'

'OK, but please try to understand how difficult life is going to be, having her here. Look at us now. You've just come back after ten days away, and we've already fallen out, which wouldn't have happened if you hadn't called in to see her.'

'Actually, it was Nat I dropped in to see. I wanted to invite him to Lord's with me next week, but he wasn't there, so I had a chat with Alicia instead.'

'You're taking *Nathan* to Lord's?' she gasped, looking so shaken he might have hit her.

'He's my nephew,' he reminded her. 'His father has recently died, which means I have a role to play in his life, and I'd like to do so.'

'I see.' Her mind was spinning with dread as the ramifications of what he was saying began crowding in on her. She was going to lose him, she could feel it deep inside her, and she couldn't bear it. 'So what about Annabelle?' she said huskily. 'Or doesn't she count any more?'

His eyes turned hard. 'Don't ever accuse me of not caring about Annabelle,' he growled. 'I'd take her anywhere she wanted to go, if she was willing to go with me, but she's at the age now where she'd rather be with her friends, as you well know. Now, where is she? I was hoping to see her before I set off for the labs.'

'Actually, she's taking my appointment at Babington. I drove her there about an hour ago, then came home, thinking we could spend some time together before I had to go back for her.'

She looked so lost and unsure of herself that he put his mail down and went to gather her up in his arms. 'I'm sorry,' he murmured into her hair. 'It wasn't the best homecoming, was it?'

She clung to him hard, as though afraid he would let her go, then looking up at him she began searching his eyes, but for what he couldn't be sure. 'I love you, Robert,' she said. 'You know that, don't you?'

'Yes,' he answered, certain it was true, but knowing with an old familiar ache that it wasn't the same as she'd felt for Craig.

'I know I've messed things up,' she said brokenly, 'but I'm . . . It's been so hard since . . .' She gasped on a sob, and pressed her fingers to her mouth. 'I'll get it together,' she told him, trying to sound firm. 'It'll be all right.'

'Of course it will,' he said, wishing he could believe it.

Her luminous, but tragic, eyes returned to his. 'Will you help me?' she whispered plaintively.

He swallowed hard as he nodded, wishing he could ignore the doubts that were gathering in his mind. 'I know this isn't easy for you,' he said softly, 'but trying to hurt Alicia is only going to make it worse.'

'I know,' she agreed, 'but I might not find it so difficult if I felt you were fully on my side.'

'I would be, if you were in the right. Which doesn't mean I stand there allowing her to say what she likes about you without speaking up on your behalf, but I have to tell you, Sabrina, the way you're behaving . . . Looking at you now . . . Well, it's starting to worry me in more ways than one.'

Feeling a burst of panic in her chest, she clutched at his shirt and tried to feign confusion as she looked up at him, but they both knew what he meant.

'I understand that his death came as a shock,' he told her, 'but to feel so bitter towards Alicia this long after the affair is suggesting to me that you never really got over him. And if that is the case, I have to ask myself if I want to go on living with someone who's probably only with me because the man she really loves either didn't love her enough to leave his wife – or is no longer around to fulfil the promises he might have made for the future.' As she started to protest he put a finger over her lips. 'Think on it,' he said, torn inside by the truth of his words, and kissing her briefly on the mouth, he picked up his mail again and went off to his study.

'Sabrina, it's me. I'm sorry about last night. Alicia insisted on using my phone to call. Are you OK?'

'I am now,' she answered, sounding clogged and shaky from all the crying she'd done. 'She hates me so much.'

'Don't think about it. Just tell me, please, that you're not going to do anything stupid.'

'I don't want to go on without you . . .'

'You'll get over it, Sabrina, I promise. And think of your family.'

'I can't. All I can think about is you and how wonderful it was when we were together. All the things you said . . . You still love me, I know you do, so don't deny it.'

'I'm not going to, I just want you to accept that we can't see one another again.'

'Darling, I understand about the children, but they'll survive, children always do.'

'Sabrina, listen to me. I'm not leaving Alicia.'

'So why did you say you would?'

'At the time . . . I . . . I shouldn't have said it. I'm sorry that I let you believe we could be together.'

'We still can. I know it's what you want, in your heart. Tell me you don't think about me.'

'Of course I think about you.'

She sat quietly in her car, feeling his words wrapping themselves around her as tenderly and passionately as his embrace.

'Sabrina, please don't tell Alicia I'm with you when I'm not,' he implored. 'It won't make me change my mind about us.'

'Would you like to make love to me again?' she croaked desperately.

There was only silence at the other end.

'It can happen,' she told him, 'it's only you who's stopping it.'

'You know why.'

'But you want to.'

Again he didn't answer.

'You see, I'm still in your heart, and however much you try to deny me, I'll always be there.'

'Let me go,' he said softly.

'Tell me you love me.'

'No.'

'Say it, and I'll never call you again.'

'Is that a promise?'

'Yes.'

'OK. I love you.'

'Alicia. It's Cameron Mitchell. I hope this is a convenient time to call.'

Quickly glancing out to the front of the shop where Nat was mixing paint, Alicia stepped out on to the back patio saying, 'Of course. How are you?'

'Surviving the heat,' he replied. 'I hear it's supposed to go into the thirties over the weekend.'

'Really? Then I must blow up my paddling pool.'

Laughing, he said, 'There's a pool here that you're welcome to use if you'd like to come over. I'm afraid Jasper might keep you company, though – he's rather partial to a swim. And he gives anyone in the vicinity a good soaking when he gets out and shakes himself down.'

Entertained by the image of it, she said, 'What kind of dog is he?'

'A golden retriever – with attitude. But he's not the reason I'm calling. I was just going through my emails and would you believe, the wine club I belong to is holding a champagne tasting at Wells town hall next Thursday evening. If it's not too presumptuous, I was wondering if you might like to come with me?'

Immediately flustered by what sounded alarmingly like a date, she moved further across the patio as she heard Nat carrying the ladder into the studio. She was flattered, of course, who wouldn't be, but it was far, far too soon even to think about . . .

'If you're free, and willing,' Cameron went on, 'I was thinking we might have a bite to eat after and I can show you some of the property blurbs I've received. I'm told the Montague Inn at Shepton Montague is very good.'

'Yes, it is,' she agreed, having been there often in the past, usually with Craig, and seizing on the easiest part of the issue to deal with first. Her mind was spinning, throwing up all sorts of objections: she truly wasn't ready to start seeing anyone else; Nat wouldn't like it; nor would Darcie; she didn't want to lie to her family; but at the same time another voice was telling her to stop overreacting, he was only being friendly, and considering who he was and how helpful he could prove to her little business, never mind her budding career, should he happen to like her work . . . In the end, almost to her own amazement, she heard herself saying, 'Yes, that would be lovely.'

'Excellent,' he declared. 'The tasting starts at six thirty, so I'll pick you up at six and book a table for eight thirty. Does that work for you?'

'Yes,' she said, wondering who'd taken charge of her replies. 'I'll look forward to it.'

It wasn't until she'd rung off that she realised he probably didn't know where she lived, but that was fine. She had his number on her mobile now, so she could always ring back and suggest they meet at the shop, which would be wiser than having him come to the house anyway. Or she could cancel, which was probably more likely.

Going back into the studio, she put her phone on the draining board and was about to continue where she'd left off with some grouting, when she stopped and thought. She didn't want to start keeping secrets from Nat. The invitation was harmless, but it wasn't going to appear that way if he found out about it later and realised she'd deliberately concealed it from him. So, assuming a part-excited, part-surprised sort of tone, she said, 'You'll never guess who that was.'

Nat glanced down from his ladder. 'I take it it wasn't Darcie.'

She smiled. 'No. It was the art critic, Cameron Mitchell, who came into the shop the other day.'

His expression immediately darkened. 'What did he want?' he asked.

'Actually, he was calling to invite me to a champagne tasting in Wells next Thursday.'

His face turned stony.

'Darling, don't look like that,' she implored. 'You're reading too much into it.'

Looking up at the ceiling, he carried on with his painting.

'He's staying in the area for the summer,' she went on, 'and he doesn't know many people, so Antonia gave him my number. That's all there is to it.'

'It's your life,' he retorted, 'if you want to go out with someone it's up to you.'

Taking a breath, she said, 'Look, I promise, it really isn't what you're thinking. He's incredibly influential in the art world. A few words of praise from him and my prices would probably double, even triple, in value. Imagine what a difference that could make to us.'

He returned the roller to the tray, coated it in more paint, and continued with his task.

Alicia watched him, torn between frustration and understanding. 'He has a pool, and a golden retriever,' she ventured a few minutes later, trying to tease him out of his hostility.

'I'm not six any more,' he reminded her. 'And I'm not your father either, so you can do what you want.'

'Actually, maybe you could come too,' she suggested, not sure whether that was a good idea or not.

He gave a mirthless laugh. 'No way am I playing gooseberry, thank you very much. I've got better things to do, like going to Lord's with Uncle Robert, in case you'd forgotten.'

'Oh yes, of course,' she said, wanting to hug

her brother for having made Nat's day, week, whole summer, probably, by inviting him to the one-day international.

Deciding to give up trying to get his approval for now, she returned to the grouting, feeling slightly dispirited and anxious, and started to wonder if Craig would mind about her going. He probably wouldn't be thrilled, because he'd always been very possessive of her; or maybe he'd be fine about it, since the invitation was definitely only platonic – and considering what Craig had done in the past, she couldn't imagine why she was putting herself through this.

For several minutes she and Nat worked on in silence, until, in the end, Nat said, 'You could have gone and I'd never have known.'

Surprised that he hadn't let the subject drop, she stayed focused on what she was doing as she said, 'Wouldn't you prefer I was honest with you, rather than sneaking about trying to hide things?'

It took a moment, but eventually he said, in a slightly grudging tone, 'I suppose so.' Then, a beat or two later, 'Actually, I don't have a problem with you going, but I don't want you taking advantage of me not being here and coming home late, OK? Or staying out all night and getting yourself a bad reputation. Home and in bed by eleven thirty, or there'll be trouble.'

Laughing with relief, she went to the fridge to pour them both a drink. She didn't imagine he was over his resistance to the idea of her having a male friend yet, but he was clearly no happier about having an atmosphere between them than she was. The best thing to do, she decided, as she passed him an ice-cold blackcurrant juice, was introduce him to Cameron as soon as possible – and Jasper, since both her children adored dogs. That way everything would be out in the open, and Nat would see for himself that there was absolutely no need to worry that someone was trying to force their way into his father's shoes.

'OK, time to wrap it up here,' she said an hour later as Nat's phone bleeped with a text. 'We both need to get the paint out of our hair and shower before we set off for Hunstrete.'

When Nat didn't answer she looked up, to find him staring down at the message.

'Is everything OK?' she asked.

'Yeah, it's cool,' he answered, putting the phone away.

'Are you sure? You look a bit . . . annoyed?'

'I said it's cool. It was just Simon about tomorrow night. No big deal. '

Letting it go, Alicia started to clear up as best she could, ready to start again in the morning, while Nat folded the ladder and stowed it on the patio outside. She knew better than to try pressing him as to what the text had really been about. Keeping things to himself was another trait he'd inherited from his father – however, unlike Craig, he usually got round to telling her in the end. He just needed to get there in his own good time.

'Hey, Nat, it's me,' Darcie cried down the line. 'Where are you?'

'Talking to you on the phone,' he replied.

'Funny. I was trying to call Mum but her line's busy all the time. Are you with her?'

'Yep. She's driving and chatting to Rachel using her Bluetooth. How are you?'

'I'm OK. Actually, that's not true. I'm a bit fed up.'

'Don't tell me you're missing us,' he teased. Then, 'Mum! You just got flashed by that camera.'

'I know, I saw,' Alicia muttered, easing off the accelerator too late. 'Just what I need, a speeding fine.'

'Where are you going?' Darcie asked.

'We're on our way to meet Jolyon,' Nat reminded her. 'So why are you fed up?'

'Oh, I just had a bit of a row with Verity. She really gets on my nerves sometimes. I wish I could come home tomorrow instead of next Saturday.'

'You'll make it up with her before then,' he told her.

'Yeah, I expect so. I feel like I've been away ages though. Tell me, what's it like living there instead of London?'

'It's OK.'

'Don't say this to Mum, but I'm absolutely dreading coming back without Dad being there.'

As her words crept over him like an icy stain, Nat turned to look out of the window.

'Is it really bad without him?'

'Sometimes,' he said shortly.

'I've still got his mobile number in my phone. I keep wanting to ring it.'

Nat still had the number too, and had even called it a couple of times.

'I so don't want to change schools,' Darcie complained. 'I hate having to leave all my friends.

I mean, who wants to be stuck in the middle of nowhere? Not me, that's for sure.'

'You've got friends here,' he reminded her.

'Yeah, like one.'

'Una's really looking forward to you coming. I think she and Rachel are planning a party of some sort to introduce you to other girls your age.'

'I know, she told me. That's so sweet of them, isn't it? And I have to admit, it'll be nice seeing more of Una. Actually, that's what Verity got all stroppy about, because I was on the phone to Una earlier. It's like I'm not supposed to have any other friends.'

'She'll get over it.'

'Yeah, I suppose so. Oh, by the way, Una says everyone's talking about Annabelle and how she's got the hots for you. Is that true?'

Nat's jaw tightened. 'Let's not go there, Darce. She's just being stupid, playing games.'

'So what, you don't like her? I always thought you did.'

'That was years ago when we were kids. I'm amazed you even remember.'

'Is she really gorgeous now? I bet she is.'

He swallowed hard. 'She's OK,' he answered, thinking of how smitten he'd once been with her, and sensing that he probably could be again, if it weren't for Summer.

'Una says that some of Annabelle's friends are betting she won't be able to get off with you.'

Since the text he'd received from Simon earlier had told him much the same thing, Darcie's news came as no surprise. 'It's all pretty puerile,' he said. 'I'm trying to ignore it.'

'You know what, you're too cool for your own good,' she told him. 'Speaking for myself, I can't wait to see her. I really wanted to be like her when I was little. Have you managed to find out yet why Mum and Sabrina don't speak?'

'No.'

She sighed knowingly. 'And you wouldn't tell me even if you had?'

'Depends what it was.'

'And Mum's right there, so you can't say anything anyway. I get the picture. How's Summer, by the way? Is she still in Italy?'

'Of course. She only went a few days ago.'

'Are you missing her?'

'Yep.'

Darcie waited. 'Is that all?' she prompted.

'What more do you want?'

'I don't know, something a bit more lonely, or passionate, or *I can't stand being parted from her*, I suppose. Anyway, is Mum still talking to Rachel?'

'She is. I'll get her to call when she's finished, shall I?'

'OK, but not tonight. We're going out in a minute, and I don't want to talk to her while everyone else can hear. Have a nice time with Jolyon. Oh yeah, and I'll want to hear all about the rave when I call on Sunday, you jammy thing. Wish I was going.'

'You're too young.'

'Don't take any drugs.'

'Did you just turn into my mother?'

'I'm just saying . . . Get pissed if you like, but not stoned. That's what Dad always used to say.'

'One of these days you'll grow out of eavesdropping.'

'You wish.'

'Take care now. And go and make up with Verity.'

'She's the one who started it.'

'But you're grown-up enough to let it go. I'll call you on Sunday, but it probably won't be until late.'

As he rang off Alicia cast him a look. 'Is she OK?' she asked.

'I think she's missing us.'

'The feeling's mutual. She's been gone too long.'

He nodded agreement and turned to gaze out at the passing scenery as she ended her call to Rachel. 'Where are we?' he asked, as she removed her earpiece and tucked it into the glove compartment.

'We're here,' she answered, and slowing up she steered in through a set of tree-shaded gates, then began accelerating gently alongside a deer park towards a sleepy-looking Bath stone manor house at the end of the drive. Though she was trying hard not to imagine Craig and Sabrina here together, it was as though their ghosts were all around her, drifting in front of the car, moving invisibly across the lawns, passing windows, strolling through doorways, blending with the very fabric of the place. What had she been doing, she wondered, while they were here satiating themselves on their forbidden love? Had they ever spared a thought for her, or Robert, or what the consequences might have been of their treacherous affair?

'This is a bit awesome, isn't it?' Nat commented,

as they came to a stop in the parking area and he gazed up at the creeper-covered walls of the grand Georgian facade. Grains of quartz were glistening like hidden jewels in the evening sun, and the parkland around was reflected like pieces of a mirage in the half-open windows.

'Dad always had a soft spot for it,' she said, trying not to guess which room they might have stayed in.

'So you've been here before,' he said, turning to look at her.

'Dad used to book in sometimes when he was working on a case in Bristol,' she answered, avoiding the question, and handing him the keys ready to drive home, she opened the car door.

Looking extremely elegant in pale-coloured chinos and a crisp white shirt, Nat offered her his arm as he walked round to join her. Smiling, and feeling very proud of her handsome son, who was already a good two inches taller than her, and apparently not embarrassed to be escorting his mother, she took the arm and told herself firmly that she had to let go of what had happened here before or she'd end up ruining the evening.

Following signs for reception, they passed under an arch into a flagstoned courtyard where a dozen or so tables were sheltered by parasols and several guests were enjoying early evening cocktails. Spotting them, Jolyon Crane immediately got up from his table and came to greet them. He was a large man in every sense of the word, towering over them both and engulfing them, one at a time, in an affectionate bear hug. His smile was wide, his green eyes shone with delight and his wonderfully deep velvet voice seemed to resonate from the very depths of him.

'It's good to see you,' he told them, putting a hand on Nat's shoulder and giving it an avuncular squeeze. 'I must say, looking at you takes me back to my Oxford days. Your father and I would only have been a couple of years older than you are now when we first met. How the years fly. And how kind they're being to you, dear Alicia.'

'And to you,' she told him, taking the hand he was offering to lead her to his table. Though he'd been at the funeral, she couldn't remember now whether she'd spoken to him, or how long he'd stayed at the reception afterwards. However, she was aware that as one of Craig's oldest and dearest friends he'd given a personally penned reading during the service, and together with Robert and Oliver Mendenhall, he'd very subtly played host by mingling with the guests and accepting condolences at the reception.

'Is Marianne not joining us?' Alicia asked, as they sat down.

'I'm afraid not. She wanted to, but she had some medical conference she couldn't get out of. She sends her love though, and says to make sure you know you can come and stay any time while Nat's with us for his work experience, which we're looking forward to very much. It'll be good to have some young blood around the house. Now, what are you going to have to drink? I'm on gin and tonic myself.'

'Then I'll have the same, thank you,' Alicia replied, looking up as the waiter arrived.

'A shandy for me,' Nat said, 'and the men's room.'

'It's through that door there,' Jolyon said, pointing to a far corner of the courtyard, 'and round to your right.'

After both Nat and the waiter had gone, Jolyon bunched his hands on the table and fixed Alicia with his warm green eyes. 'I'm glad to have these few moments alone with you,' he said. 'Oliver and I have been talking and there's something we need to tell you.'

As the fear of more debt, or some unimagined catastrophe rose to the front of her mind, Alicia could feel herself wanting to pull away and run.

'I could be speaking out of turn now,' Jolyon went on, 'and if I am just tell me to stop, but Oliver and I would like to act as mentors as Nat goes through his studies. He's a bright boy, an absolute credit to you, and his father, of course, and if he works hard, which I know he will, he has a great future ahead of him. We don't want that to be hampered in any way by his untimely loss. Training to become a barrister is an expensive business, as you know, all the archaic ritual like the dinners he'll have to . . .'

'Before you go on,' Alicia interrupted, 'Craig's father has offered to pay for that. He doesn't have much, but he's as determined as the rest of us that Nat should go far, and he wants to do his bit.'

Jolyon smiled. 'Good for William,' he said. 'Knowing him, he'll feel proud to be contributing to his grandson's education.'

'He wanted to keep him at Westminster,' Alicia confided, 'but the fees were too steep for him, and then there was the question of where Nat would live once we'd sold the house.'

Jolyon was shaking his head regretfully. 'It was a bad business, having to do that,' he murmured. Then, seeing the way her eyes went down, he cut himself off. 'You don't need me going over all that now,' he said gently. 'Just tell me, how's Nat dealing with it?'

She sighed. 'I'm not sure he is,' she answered. 'He only ever mentions his father in passing, and as far as I'm aware he hasn't cried yet. I think he's afraid that if he does he'll have to admit to himself that Craig really has gone.'

Jolyon's expression was full of sympathy and kindness. 'It was a terrible time to lose him, though I guess there isn't a good one,' he said. 'How are you settling in in Holly Wood?'

'It's still early days, but so far it's not been too bad.'

'Your brother still lives there, doesn't he?'

She nodded.

He gave a deep sigh as he considered the ramifications of that. 'I take it Nat doesn't know anything about that unfortunate business.'

Hating that Craig's friends knew about Sabrina, and still not sure if they'd been aware of the affair while it was going on, Alicia said, 'Absolutely not. It's been hard enough for him as it is, so the last thing he needs is Craig crashing down off his pedestal thanks to her.'

'Of course, and I'm sorry to bring it up, I just wanted to be clear on how the land lies, and to let you know that Oliver and I will offer sponsorship where we can to get him through university.

And of course, we'll always be available if he needs to talk about anything, whether it concerns his studies, or anything else.'

'Thank you,' she said softly. 'It's good to know that.' This kindness, she realised, wasn't only a measure of the high esteem Craig's friends had always held him in, but also of the deeply bonded and exclusive fraternity they belonged to. Simply being Craig's son with an ambition to go into the law meant that Nat had already qualified for their rarefied support.

'Ah, here he is,' Jolyon said, glancing up as Nat returned to the table. 'So, are you looking forward to joining us at the end of the month?'

'Definitely,' Nat assured him. 'Dad was really keen for me to see what happens at the sharp end, as he called it. Barristers usually only get cases once they're preparing for trial, whereas criminal solicitors like you are there right from the start. You know everything a person has been through by the time they go into the dock.'

'I've always felt that it was the time your father spent as a solicitor in the early days that turned him into a first-class barrister,' Jolyon told him. 'He really cared about people and the way the law treated them. And many and splendid were the occasions when an arrogant or sadistic police officer would leave the witness box with his case, and sometimes even his reputation, in shreds thanks to Craig's cross-examination. Ah, menus, excellent.' Then, in a lower voice, 'If they're offering venison, I wouldn't go for it if I were you, one of its relatives might be watching from the park next door.'

Alicia smiled. 'Do you come here a lot?' she asked.

'Not so often now, but Marianne and I had our wedding reception here . . . Well, you know that because you came. Sadly, it's gone downhill a bit since then. The food's generally still good, but the place is looking tired, don't you think? It could do with a major overhaul. I don't know what the rooms are like, but I believe they're still a few hundred quid a night, so I guess we have to hope the beds are comfortable and the facilities are good.'

'I'm sure they're excellent,' she murmured, keeping her eyes on the menu. He'd surely never have made that remark if he'd known Craig and Sabrina used to come here.

'Mum, they've got Parma ham with figs,' Nat piped up. 'That's what she'll have,' he told Jolyon. 'It's one of her favourites.'

'And brill,' Alicia added, feeling certain it was what Craig would have chosen if it had been on the menu when he was here. She tried to imagine what Sabrina's tastes were, until realising she was only hurting herself she put the menu down and picked up her drink.

The rest of the evening passed pleasantly enough, mainly because she loved listening to Nat talking about his ambitions, and felt proud of how closely he listened to Jolyon. This was the most animated she'd seen her son since Craig's passing, and knowing it was his love of the law that was bringing him out of himself, she could only feel grateful to Jolyon for understanding Nat's need and for being there in a way only a man – and a lawyer – could.

He was going to be all right, she told herself, when they finally drove away from the hotel with Jolyon's affectionate farewells still ringing in their ears. She didn't need to worry about him; he was a determined and intelligent young man with his path already carved out and enough people caring for him to make sure he stayed on it. It wasn't that he didn't need his father any more, because that would never be the case, but thanks to Robert's invitation to the cricket, and Jolyon's reassurances tonight, she was no longer feeling quite so weighted by the burden of trying to fill the gap alone.

The following night Georgie and Annabelle were jumping and gyrating with the crowd in the middle of the Copse. There were so many people there already that they were practically dancing as one, their bodies supple and sinewy, lit by darting lasers and shrouded in a viscous haze of fake fog. The beat was electric, thudding and pounding, buzzing through limbs, exploding in heads, jerking its victims in seizures of bliss, while the ground pulsated, the trees vibrated and the whole night came alive with sound. DJs and their high-tech wizardry formed a hexagon around the open glade, tossing, rotating and scratching the rhythm from jungle, to techno, to acid and gabba. A forest of arms reached towards the stars, fingers outstretched as though to catch the electronic blades that fenced the black air. Substances were passing like candy, from Ecstasy, to mushrooms, to cannabis, LSD and cocaine. Empty vodka and sambuca bottles littered the undergrowth, along with Red Bull cans, alcopop cartons and cigarette packs. Couples writhed and laughed, screamed and howled, and disappeared like wraiths into the darker depths to discuss life, politics, the universe, or to make out till the moon faded to nothing and the sun came up like a tangerine cheese.

Annabelle had been rolling around Lovers' Dip with Theo, and she was ready to go again. It was a night for sex, drugs, sounds and more sex. The boy dancing with her now was a god. He was rubbing himself against her and she raised her arms to let him right in. She loved his hands on her hips, shaking and grooving her, she wanted more, more, more.

Georgie slunk off with Carl.

Annabelle continued to dance. Katie and Catrina closed in on her. Melody appeared with Kennedy. Petra disappeared with a new friend. Archie was spreadeagled on the grass reciting poetry to the planets.

Georgie came back and put her arms round Annabelle.

'I love you,' she shouted in Annabelle's ear.

'I love you too,' Annabelle shouted back. She took a joint that was passing, inhaled deeply and handed it on.

'Yeah, yeah,' Georgie sang out at the top of her voice.

'Where's Carl?' Annabelle yelled.

'Who?'

'Carl.'

'Over there.' Georgie waved an arm dreamily, then her head fell back as she laughed.

Annabelle yelped as the boy she'd been dancing with grabbed her from behind and turned her round.

'I'm Neil. What's your name?' he shouted.

'Princess Annabelle,' she answered, shimmying into him.

He grinned and dropped to his knees, holding her hips as she gyrated into his face.

'Are you into vodka?' he yelled.

'Bring it on,' she yelled back.

He plunged into the crowd and she turned back to Georgie. 'This is amazing. I want to have sex with everyone, even you.'

Georgie howled like a banshee and pulling Annabelle into her arms she planted her mouth over hers. As they kissed their hands roamed one another's bodies, and when someone pulled them apart another mouth found Annabelle's. Then she was kissing someone else, and someone else again. The whole party was turning into a great big gorgeous orgy of kissing.

Neil found her again, and hooking her about the waist virtually carried her off into the trees. He had vodka and cannabis and a small supply of C. She drank and smoked and blinked back tears as she snorted the white stuff into her brain. He was kissing her and undressing her and she was loving it all. There were other people nearby, writhing in the grass. The music boomed and thwanged. It was all the way inside her, beating her heart, rushing her blood, pumping air in and out of her lungs. She was the music . . .

On the far side of the Copse Nat was holding a beer and watching the heaving, throbbing throng of dancers. Though the beat was drumming into his brain, and he was moving in rhythm, he felt detached, coldly sober and verging on anger at how hard he was finding it to get into. He'd been to raves before and had easily got off his face with the rest of them, but tonight it wasn't happening. He wanted to let go, to end up so hammered and junked that he'd blend into the anonymous, sweating, pulsating mass of humanity. He wouldn't know where he ended and the next person began. He could stop being him and float off somewhere into blissful ecstasy. The huge hole inside him would be filled up, the blackness would be lightened. No more questions, or doubts, or fears, everything would go back to the way it should be, the way it had been before.

He took another swig of beer, but it tasted foul. He tried the joint Simon handed him, and inhaled right down into his lungs, waiting for the steadying flow of calm. He dragged on it again and again. It wasn't working. His tension was building. He wanted to yell and rage. Words he dared not speak were erupting inside him, screaming through his brain, searing across his chest . . . Everything was wrong, nothing was right any more . . .

'Talk to me, baby,' someone murmured in his ear, but he didn't hear.

He thought he knew her, but wasn't sure and didn't care. He was one of the trees in the wood, she was the ivy, creeping all over him, but easy to tear away. He stopped registering her. He couldn't see any more. He couldn't hear or speak.

He could only feel the lights cutting him open like blades, and the emptiness inside that was growing and growing and filling with frustration and hate. What was the point of anything? The world was a meaningless place. He was useless, his mother was hurting, and his father wasn't coming back . . .

As Annabelle danced back into the party she was jerking around with the beat, eyes half closed, arms outstretched, writhing around everyone she passed. She found Georgie with Theo and Cat, sprawled on the grass, punching hands and nodding heads to the hardcore sound. She sank down with them and grabbed a bottle of Bacardi.

'Have you seen Nat yet?' she slurred as Georgie fell against her.

Georgie's arm carved a semicircle through the flashing air. 'He's over there, somewhere,' she said, pointing nowhere in particular. 'With Melody.'

Annabelle staggered to her feet.

'Cool,' Theo murmured, noticing her lack of panties.

Grinning, she lifted her hem to give him a better look. She'd left them in the grass. She didn't need them any more.

She found Nat on the far side of the Copse with Melody draped around him. Simon was with a girl Annabelle had never seen before.

'Hey,' she drawled, almost lurching into Nat as she tried to drag Melody off him.

'Hey yourself,' Melody slurred, and put her head back on Nat's shoulder.

Annabelle's eyes bored into Nat's. Flashes of red, green, yellow and blue sliced across their faces. Her lips curved in a smile as she lowered her gaze to his mouth.

He turned his head away to drink more beer.

Annabelle reached for Melody again and twirled her into the swaying mass of bodies. When she turned back Nat was walking away, picking a route through the dozens of glowsticks that had sprung up in the undergrowth like electronic mushrooms.

She went after him, keeping her distance, expecting him to look back, but he didn't. *He knows I'm following. It's what he wants. I love him, I love him, I love him.*

She caught up with him on the bank over Lovers' Dip. He was standing still, staring at nothing. The music remained a throbbing presence, sprinkled with talking and laughter. Bodies were all over the place, against trees, under bushes, sprawled out randomly in the grass.

Catching his hand she dragged him down into the dip. Gravity pulled him, but he didn't stop at the bottom, he snatched his hand away and walked on.

'Come on, you know you want to,' she laughed, skipping after him.

He walked on, increasing his pace. He shouldn't be too far from the bridge by now.

'It's only sex,' she cried, trying to take his arm. 'Let's do it.'

He turned round to look at her, his face harsh with frustration. 'What part of no don't you understand?' he demanded.

She laughed happily. 'The part that's a lie,' she told him, and letting herself topple into him she encircled him with her arms and tried to kiss him.

Turning his head away, he grabbed her wrists and thrust her aside.

'What's wrong?' she cried gaily. 'Oh my God, don't tell me you're still a virgin.'

Ignoring her, he kept on going.

'Why don't you let me show you how to do it?' she offered, dancing round in front of him. 'Come on, we both know you want to . . .'

'Get out of the way,' he cut in roughly.

'What's the problem?' she laughed. 'If it was good enough for your dad and my mum, why shouldn't it be for us? It'll be like a generational carrying of the . . .' She stopped as his hand closed like steel on her arm.

'What are you talking about?' he growled, but even as he asked the question memories were rushing and changing and falling like the flashing contents of a kaleidoscope into the base of his skull.

'You're lying,' he raged in a tone that made her face drop.

'Take it back,' he roared. 'Admit you're lying.' Tears were starting from his eyes.

'Don't,' she cried as he tightened his grip on her arm. 'Let me go,' and shoving him away she turned to run, but her foot caught on a root and she crashed to the ground. Her buttocks were exposed, her legs were apart. She tried to get up, but he was on top of her, pinning her down. His hands circled her throat, squeezing and choking her.

She struggled to throw him off, but he was too heavy, she couldn't move.

His rage and grief were out of control. He barely knew what he was doing. He couldn't think. He couldn't do anything except hold her there.

'Nat,' she gasped. 'Nat . . . Let me go. I . . .'

'Take it back,' he shouted, 'take it back.'

The music boomed and throbbed; furious splinters of light sparked through trees, and still there was her, writhing beneath him, shouting, screaming, but all he could hear were the terrible words she'd spoken.

Chapter Thirteen

It was just after nine on Monday morning when Annabelle let herself into the kitchen.

Sabrina was sitting at the table, hanging on the line to BT, ready to tackle them over a decision to scrap rural phone booths. 'You're back early,' she said to Annabelle, barely glancing up as she scanned her list of objections. 'Did Georgie's mum drop you off?'

It took a moment for her to realise that Annabelle was still standing in front of the table, saying nothing. She looked up and her insides slowly to turned to ice. 'My God,' she murmured, putting the phone down.

'Don't make a fuss,' Annabelle said.

'What's happened to you?' Sabrina rasped, so stunned by the injuries to her daughter's face that her mind couldn't function.

Annabelle tried to answer, but the words became mangled in her throat as she struggled not to cry.

'You have to tell me,' Sabrina urged, going to her and pushing back her hair to get a better look.

'It doesn't matter.'

'What happened?' Sabrina said forcefully. 'You have to tell me.'

'I – I was raped,' Annabelle choked.

Sabrina froze with shock. 'What do you mean?' she said stupidly.

'I was *raped*,' Annabelle shouted. 'Don't you know what that means?'

'Oh my God,' Sabrina mumbled, starting to shake. This couldn't be happening. They needed to start this again. 'Are – are you sure?' she stammered.

'How can I not be sure, you idiot!'

'Annabelle, stop,' Sabrina cried, grabbing her as she turned to storm off. 'I'm sorry. I – it's . . . Are you OK?'

'What do you think? Look at me.'

Sabrina was looking. Someone had attacked her baby and all she could think was that it couldn't be true. 'When did it happen?' she asked.

'On Saturday night.'

Sabrina's eyes dilated. 'But why are you only telling me now?' she cried. 'Where have you been?'

'At Georgie's. I couldn't come home, because I was afraid you'd make a fuss.'

'What, and now I'm not supposed to?'

'No, I just . . . Don't shout at me. It wasn't my fault.'

Not realising she'd raised her voice, Sabrina wrapped Annabelle in her arms. 'No, no of course it wasn't,' she said, feeling waves of horror coming over her. 'Oh my baby, my poor baby.' Tears were starting from her eyes. What was she going to do? How could she make this all right? 'We have to call the police,' she said decisively. 'If someone's hurt you . . .'

'What do you mean, *if*? Do you think I'm lying?'

'Of course not. Now I want you to sit down here while I make the call. Everything's going to be all right, OK? They'll catch whoever did it . . .'

'I *know* who did it. I was there, remember?'

Sabrina blinked. Why hadn't she already asked that? What was the matter with her that she couldn't think of the right questions? 'So who was it?' she said hoarsely.

'It was *Nathan Carlyle,*' Annabelle spat.

Sabrina reeled.

Annabelle put her head in her hands.

Hearing her voice as though it was coming from a long way away, Sabrina said, 'Nathan Carlyle did this to you?'

'That's what I just said. What, are you deaf or something?'

'No, I . . . What happened exactly? Where were you?'

'It doesn't matter. Just call the police. They have to go round there and arrest him.'

'Of course, but . . . When did it happen?'

'I just told you, on Saturday night.'

'So why are you . . . ? They'll want to know why you're only reporting it now.'

'Because I was drinking and taking drugs, OK? That's why I couldn't come home, because I knew you'd call the police straight away and if they found all that in my system they'd say it was my fault. They might even arrest me . . .'

Sabrina blinked as the truth hit her. 'You were at that rave,' she said.

'Duh.'

'But you're only fifteen!'

'Exactly! Drink, drugs . . .'

Realising they were getting away from the main issue, Sabrina said, 'But don't you understand? It's illegal for anyone to have sex with you, whether you're under the influence of drugs and alcohol or not. So it can't possibly be your fault. Now, I'm calling the police and that boy is going to pay for what he's done.'

'That's right,' Annabelle growled, 'and so he should.'

More than half an hour passed before a patrol car pulled up outside the house. The officer who got out was young and gangly, and still suffering from a rash of late-teen spots. As soon as she saw him Sabrina wanted to send him away. They needed a female, a detective, with experience and rank and the authority to carry out an immediate arrest.

In the event, PC Mervin Mellows proved surprisingly confident in his manner, and wasn't easily intimidated by the overbearing mother who confronted him as he explained that more senior officers from Bath or Bristol would be contacting them soon. As a local constable, stationed at Wells, he had come to see them to assure them how seriously the police were taking the call. Moreover, he was respectful and gentle with Annabelle as he jotted down the essential details of her story.

'So you know the person who attacked you?' he said, glancing up from his notebook.

'Raped,' Sabrina corrected.

Mellows kept his eyes on Annabelle.

'His name's Nathan Carlyle,' she said.

He wrote it down. 'Is he local?'

'Yes. He lives the other side of the village. He's my stepdad's nephew.'

Mellows squinted as he puzzled it out.

'He's my husband's sister's son,' Sabrina explained.

'Thank you.' He noted it down and was about to address Annabelle again when Sabrina said, 'Aren't you going to arrest him? He lives in the Coach House on The Close. He's probably there now.'

'I'm afraid it doesn't work like that,' he told her politely.

She bristled. 'Well it should. For all you know he could be planning to do it to someone else.'

Deciding not to be drawn into that, Mellows said to Annabelle, 'I'm going to contact the station with everything you've told me so far, then perhaps we can go over to the Copse so you can show me where it happened.'

Annabelle's eyes shot to her mother. 'I don't want to go back there,' she protested in a wail.

'No, of course not,' Sabrina answered soothingly. 'Is it absolutely necessary?' she asked Mellows frostily.

'The Crime Scene Investigation team will need as precise a location as we can give them in order to collect evidence,' he explained.

Unable to argue with that, Sabrina turned back to Annabelle. 'It'll be all right,' she assured her. 'I'll be with you and once you've pointed it out we can leave straight away.'

Annabelle's eyes moved nervously back to Mellows.

'That's right,' he confirmed. 'You won't have

to stay long. I only need you to give me as accurate a placing as you can, then I'll bring you back here. By then someone from SAIT – the Sexual Abuse Investigation Team – will probably be trying to get in touch.'

Annabelle blanched. 'That sounds a bit major,' she said doubtfully.

'Rape is a very serious matter,' he reminded her, and getting to his feet he went off to radio the station.

Annabelle and Sabrina waited in silence, neither of them knowing what to say or do now.

'I should call Robert,' Sabrina said, looking nervously at the phone.

Annabelle didn't respond and Sabrina didn't move.

'We should probably wait until we know what's going to happen,' Sabrina decided.

To her relief, Mellows came back and asked if they were ready to go to the Copse.

Trying not to feel daunted by the thought of the huge police machine that was now reacting to the details of Annabelle's case, Sabrina put an arm round her daughter and took her out to the police car.

Mellows opened the back door for them to get in, then slipping behind the wheel he turned the car around to begin driving along Holly Way towards the high street. Sabrina sat close to Annabelle, keeping her eyes fixed straight ahead, but she was aware of Canon Jeffries looking up from his garden as they passed, and wished she'd thought of taking Annabelle in her car instead.

* * *

Two hours later the clock in the tower over Alicia's shop was striking noon. The sun was blazing down on the high street, baking the old cobbles and causing the flowers around the war memorial to wilt. Once the chimes had finished the village returned to an eerie quiet. Everywhere seemed deserted – there was no sign of life at all, not even at the pub where the doors were open, and a board offering a two-course lunch for seven pounds fifty was propped invitingly outside. Every table and chair in the garden was empty.

At the far end of The Close a crowd was gathering on the riverbank, trying to get a look across the footbridge into the Copse. The area was swarming with police. Yards of blue and white tape were looped around the loose ramble of trees, a dozen or more police vehicles were parked all over the place, some with lights still flashing, others with radios squawking.

From where the villagers were standing there was nothing much to see. The actual crime scene was out of view, as was most of the search. No one knew what had happened yet, but rumours were flying. Someone had overdosed on drugs. A girl had been attacked. A boy had hanged himself. A body had been found.

Not wanting to listen to any more, Alicia pushed her way back through the crowd and started to walk home. It was a strange feeling, having so much attention focused on the periphery of their little village. It was as though an invasion was taking place, and in a way it was, because whatever had brought the police here today, it was almost certain they'd be visiting every home in

Holly Wood to find out what the residents had seen or heard.

The Coach House was quiet when she let herself in. Guessing Nat was still in bed, she decided to let him sleep on and went through to the kitchen to start preparing lunch. Though he'd been at the rave on Saturday night, she'd heard him come home around one, and since he hadn't mentioned anything yesterday about something unusual happening she could only presume that whatever had brought the police today must have occurred after he'd left.

'We can always come to you,' the officer from SAIT was informing Sabrina down the phone, 'but, if Annabelle's willing, she'll need a medical examination and we have all the facilities here. I'll happily drive down to pick her up.'

'It's OK,' Sabrina said, 'tell me where you are and I'll bring her myself.'

After giving her the address the officer said, 'Could you bring the clothes Annabelle was wearing when it happened, please. Have any of them been washed yet?'

'Not as far as I'm aware. I'll make sure I have them.'

Half an hour later Sabrina and Annabelle were driving out of the village. Sabrina's hands were clutching the steering wheel so tightly that she could hardly move to indicate or change gear. She hadn't called Robert yet, but she'd have to, sooner or later.

Beside her Annabelle stared blindly out of the window. The bruises on her face and neck stood out vividly against the pallor of her skin. Her hands were bunched into anxious fists, her knees pressed tightly together.

As she followed the satnav directions through the county towards to a suburb of Bristol called Pilning, Sabrina was still trying to absorb the enormity of what was happening. That Nathan was Craig's son was distorting everything. It was making it impossible for her to think straight, unless she forced herself to remember he was Alicia's, too. Then her fury escalated to a point where no amount of revenge would be enough. How dare that jumped-up, arrogant little bastard lay hands on her daughter?

'Mum, you're driving too fast,' Annabelle complained.

'Sorry,' Sabrina apologised, and easing off the accelerator she cast a quick glance in Annabelle's direction. 'Shouldn't be too long now,' she said, attempting a smile. 'How are you feeling?'

Annabelle's voice was small and thready as she said, 'I don't know. Kind of weird and scared.'

Reaching out for her hand, Sabrina squeezed it comfortingly as she said, 'There's nothing to be afraid of. You just have to tell them what happened and then we can go home again.'

Swallowing hard, Annabelle turned back to the passing countryside. 'Do you think they've arrested him yet?' she asked after a while.

'I hope so,' Sabrina replied, and picturing the way the boy used to look at her, so knowingly and coldly, she could only feel glad that, if it had to be anyone, it was him.

The next instant she was in floods of tears, and having to pull over to try to get herself under control. 'I'm sorry,' she gasped, as Annabelle attempted to comfort her. 'It's just that I can't bear to think of anyone hurting you.' She clutched Annabelle's face between her hands. 'You're going to be all right,' she told her fiercely. 'I don't care that he's Cr— Robert's nephew. He's going to pay for what he's done.'

Annabelle swallowed as tears trickled from her own eyes. 'Yes,' she whispered. 'Yes he should.'

Nat was sitting on the edge of his bed, elbows on his knees, head propped in his hands as though it was too heavy to hold up. His mother had called him several times now to come and have lunch, but he was so bound up with fear that he couldn't make himself leave the room. It was as though if he stayed here, not moving, barely even breathing, the nightmare that was trying to close in and devour him wouldn't be able to reach him.

'I'm going to tell everyone you raped me,' she'd screamed at him as he'd walked away.

Was that what she'd done? Was that why the police were crawling all over the Copse? If she had, why hadn't the search started till this morning? If she'd really meant to carry out her threat surely she'd have gone to the police straight away, so maybe the search wasn't anything to do with him. Maybe something else had happened after he'd left. Everyone knew there were laws against raves, so perhaps the police were out there picking up evidence of drugs before questioning those they could find who'd been there.

It was possible, he kept telling himself, it really was.

Suddenly jerking to his feet, he started to pace the room. Back and forth, back and forth. She shouldn't have mentioned his father. He could have stood anything but that. Those lies should never have escaped her mouth. He'd wanted to push them back down her throat, to make her retch and choke on them, the way he'd been retching and choking on them ever since. His father would never have cheated on his mother. He'd loved her. They'd been happy together, the family had meant everything to him, so there was no way he'd have had an affair with Sabrina. He wouldn't, *couldn't*, think about the fact that his mother and Sabrina detested one another. If he did, he'd have to accept that Annabelle might have been telling the truth, and if she had, everything he'd believed in, his parent's love, the bond that had held his family together, but above all his father's honesty and integrity and everything he'd drummed into Nat about respect, love and loyalty, would all be a lie.

Choking back a sob, he tightened the grip on his head. There was so much anger and confusion inside him that he felt it might explode from his skin. Why wasn't his father here to answer his questions? Why hadn't his mother told him the truth? Did she think he was a child, that he couldn't handle it?

Inhaling deeply, he dragged his hands over his face and felt his head starting to reel again with the horror of what Annabelle might be telling the police. Somehow he had to block it from his mind, or listen to the small voice that was trying to say that the search might have nothing to do with him. However, the raging fear in his head kept beating out the same terrible tattoo. *What was she telling them? How much of it was truth, and how much was lies?*

Detective Sergeant Clive Bevan was at the Avon and Somerset CID headquarters on Feeder Road in Bristol, assessing the information he had so far on the rape case that had just come in. He was a well-groomed man in his early forties, with slick dark hair, a square, firm-set jaw and ruthlessly piercing eyes that generally didn't take long to see through a pile of bullshit when it was being spun.

Since it was far too early for him to form an opinion on what he had in front of him now, he was focusing mainly on the victim's age, because if a sexual act had taken place, consensual or not, a crime had very definitely been committed. However, 'if' was still a key factor, since both parties had yet to be interviewed, and long experience had taught him that cases of this nature, involving two teens at a party, very often went away before anyone was charged.

'Any news yet from CSI?' he asked Morley Croft, his DC, who was reading the same screen.

'They're still combing the scene,' Croft answered. 'Dickon's asking when you're intending to go down there.'

'He knows I can't go near the place till he's finished,' Bevan answered irritably.

'Cross-contamination,' Croft stated.

'Precisely,' Bevan confirmed. 'I'm about to go and see the victim, so I don't want to be walking forensic evidence from the crime scene into the rape suite. That's for her to do. So, my friend, *you* are going to pick up the boy and bring him in for questioning. Where does he live again?'

'Same village as her, near where it happened. A place called Holly Wood, would you believe?'

Bevan screwed up his nose. 'Where the hell's that? And please don't say California.'

'Might just as well be,' Croft answered, 'because it's effing miles away. Past Shepton Mallet, nearly as far as Yeovil according to the map.'

Bevan grinned. 'You'll enjoy a day out in the country,' he told him, reaching for his car keys. 'Take the kid to Bath, if they've got room, and I'll meet you there. Ian,' he said to another DC who was using a black marker to list case details on a whiteboard, 'go with him, and haul a local uniform along to assist with the search.'

'On it, Sarge,' Ian Grange responded, capping his pen.

'If the boy tries to resist, cuff him,' Bevan told Croft, 'otherwise, try to be discreet. And don't forget to bag everything he was wearing on Saturday night.'

'And anything else we think might be relevant,' Croft added, 'but keep the search to the boy's room and communal areas.'

'You got it.' Bevan heaved a sigh of annoyance as the most complicating element of the case returned to him. 'Why did it have to be a sodding rave?' he grumbled. 'If we have to start tracking down all those kids . . . But hey, let's not get depressed yet. There's still a very good chance the girl's having a change of heart even as we speak, so we could all be putting our feet up with a bevvy in front of the football tonight.'

'Are you sure this is where we're supposed to be?' Annabelle said dubiously, as Sabrina turned off a leafy side street into a short tarmacked driveway. In front of them was a large detached house whose cream-painted walls and high, blue-painted window frames made it look much more like a private residence than any kind of police station they'd ever seen.

'This is the address I was given,' Sabrina answered, pulling her gold Lexus up alongside a black Citroën C4. There were other cars on the forecourt, but none with any kind of police insignia. 'Wait here,' she said, 'I'll go and check.'

She was barely out of the car before the front door opened and an attractive young woman with a mop of blonde curly hair and a welcoming smile came to greet her.

'Hi,' she said, holding out a hand to shake. 'I'm PC Lisa Murray. Are you Mrs Paige?'

Sabrina nodded and took the girl's hand.

'We spoke on the phone,' Lisa Murray clarified.

'Annabelle's in the car,' Sabrina said.

Stooping so she could see, the officer smiled warmly as she said, 'Hi, Annabelle. I'm Lisa. Would you like to come in?'

Getting warily out of the car, Annabelle glanced at her mother, then walked round to link her arm as Lisa Murray led the way inside. 'I thought this was someone's house,' she said croakily.

'It's a special place for SAIT,' Lisa explained, 'the Sexual Abuse Investigation Team. We find it easier to talk to people in an environment that's a little friendlier than a police station, a bit more like home.'

Annabelle gave a slight nod and moved even closer to her mother.

'I'm going to take you to the waiting area now,' Lisa informed them, directing them past two closed doors and along a blue carpeted hallway to a room at the end.

Annabelle glanced at Sabrina. It wasn't exactly a scary place, but it was deadly quiet and smelled like a hospital gone fusty.

'Here we are,' Lisa said, showing them into a sort of sitting room with a big comfy sofa, two armchairs, and a coffee table with magazines and a box of Kleenex. Lockers were lined up along one wall and an old-fashioned TV stood between the frosted windows, where vertical blinds were swinging gently in the draught of the door opening. 'Detective Sergeant Bevan is on his way. He's the officer in charge of the investigation.'

Annabelle drew back against her mother. 'I don't want to talk to a man,' she protested.

Lisa smiled sympathetically. 'It's OK, I'll be interviewing you,' she assured her. 'He'll be listening in, though. Now, would you like to sit down? There's a kitchen through there, I can make some coffee if you . . .'

Annabelle was shaking her head. 'I don't want any, thank you.'

'Me neither,' Sabrina said, drawing Annabelle down next to her on the sofa.

Perching on the edge of an armchair, Lisa clasped her hands together and looked at them kindly. 'I'm going to go through the procedure with you now,' she said, 'just so's you have some idea of what's about to happen. The doctor's already here. He's in the medical room which we passed on our way in. Are you OK about being examined?' she said to Annabelle.

Annabelle swallowed and nodded. 'I think so,' she answered.

'Can you tell me, have you washed since it happened?'

Annabelle's eyes widened. 'Of course I have,' she replied indignantly.

Lisa's expression remained friendly. 'That's fine,' she said, 'it just makes the search for DNA a little more difficult, but not impossible.'

Annabelle stopped bristling.

'The doctor will be checking you over for injuries,' Lisa continued. 'Obviously we can see those on your face and neck, but perhaps there are others on your arms or back that you haven't noticed yet. He'll work down your body taking wet and dry swabs – this means that he'll be using distilled water for some, and not for others. He won't be taking photographs. Everything will be marked on a body map. For the internal exam he'll use a speculum – do you know what that is?'

Annabelle shook her head.

'It's a device that will open you up a little to allow him to take both low and high vaginal swabs which may, or may not, produce DNA that can be matched to the assailant's.'

Annabelle seemed to shrink into herself, while next to her Sabrina's whole body seemed cramped by the strain.

'Because the rape took place in the early hours of Sunday morning,' Lisa went on, 'it's possible that no traces exist any more, but that doesn't mean we wouldn't go ahead with a prosecution. Your age alone means that any act of intercourse is illegal.' After watching mother and daughter exchange glances she wasn't quite able to interpret, she continued. 'Besides semen the doctor will also be looking for signs of internal trauma, tearing or bruising, that sort of thing. He'll also take nail clippings and scrapings, and pubic-hair combings – do you have any?' she asked gently. 'I know the trend today is to remove it all.'

'She had a bikini wax last Friday,' Sabrina answered for her.

'Actually, it was a Brazilian,' Annabelle said in a small voice.

Sabrina turned to her, aghast. 'But you're too young to . . .' She broke off, realising this was neither the time nor the place to make it an issue.

Being too well-trained to show exasperation at the lack of pubic hair, Lisa said, 'It's OK. I'm sure there won't be a problem. Now, I have to ask if you've bled since the incident and used a tampon or towel?'

Annabelle shook her head. 'I mean, there was a bit of blood, but I didn't use anything.'

'Did you bring everything you were wearing that night?' Lisa asked, looking at Sabrina.

'It's in a bag in the car,' Sabrina answered.

'OK. Perhaps you can get it while Annabelle's being interviewed.'

'Won't I be with her?' Sabrina objected. 'I think I should.'

'I'm sorry, we have to talk to her alone.'

'But she's under sixteen . . .'

'All the same, we still have to talk to her alone.' Turning back to Annabelle, 'Are you OK with that?' she asked.

Annabelle seemed uncertain. 'I'd like my mum to be there for the medical exam,' she said.

'Of course. Now, the last thing I have to tell you before we go through to the doctor is that he'll be taking two lots of blood. I know the incident happened over twenty-four hours ago, but you still need to be tested for alcohol and drugs . . . I can see by your face that there's a chance something might be found, but don't worry, even if you used illegal substances it isn't of any interest to us. This is simply a formality that has to be gone through that might help us to establish your frame of mind at the time of the incident.'

Annabelle's nails were digging into her palms. She didn't know if she wanted to go through with this now, it wasn't turning out to be anything like she'd expected, with all these tests and procedures and stuff.

Seeming to read her mind, Lisa said, 'I know it can seem a bit daunting at first, but once the exam is out of the way and we've had our chat, you'll be able to go home and leave everything else to DS Bevan.'

Annabelle only looked at her. Then, in a tone that surprised Lisa with its harshness, considering how meek and unsure of herself the girl had seemed up till now, she asked, 'Has he been arrested yet?'

'I'm not sure,' Lisa replied carefully. 'DS Bevan will be able to tell us when he gets here.'

Seeing Rachel's name come up on her mobile, Alicia clicked on straight away. 'Hi,' she said. 'To what do I owe this pleasure in the middle of your surgery hours?'

With an ironic lilt Rachel said, 'Just thought I'd keep you up to speed with what's happening in Holly Wood.'

Alicia laughed. 'And you would know because . . . ?'

'Canon Jeffries has just been in with his cat, and you know how he likes a bit of a gossip. So it turns out that a police car was outside your brother's house this morning.'

Alicia's smile died.

'What's more,' Rachel went on, 'according to the good canon, when the police left the house Sabrina and Annabelle went with them, then came back again about half an hour later.'

Alicia's mind was firing off in too many directions, and none felt good. 'So what do we deduce from that?' she asked, hoping Rachel might have a more optimistic take on it.

'No idea, except whatever the search is about it seems Annabelle could be in some way involved.'

'I'll give Robert a call,' Alicia said, and after a quick goodbye she rang off and scrolled through to Robert's mobile number.

'Now there's a coincidence,' he said when he answered. 'I was just about to ring you. Did you know there's an art fair in Somerton at the end of

August? It's being advertised in the local paper. There might still be time for you to get your sculptures in.'

'Thanks, but I've already tried and the closing date was a month ago,' she told him. 'What's this I hear about the police being at your house this morning?'

There was a beat of stunned silence before he said, 'The police were at my house? Are you sure? Do you know why?'

'That's what I'm asking you. Where are you?'

'At the labs.'

'Well, all I can tell you is that there's some kind of search going on over in the Copse, and apparently Sabrina and Annabelle went off with the police sometime this morning.'

There was another baffled silence before he said, 'I'll give Sabrina a call and get back to you.'

As the line went dead, Alicia clicked off her end, and deciding to abandon the new design she was working on, she closed up her laptop and put it back in its case to carry home. Since it was gone two o'clock Nat would surely be up by now, and if he wasn't she was going to insist he let her into his room, because it wasn't like him to lie around in bed for so long. If he was ill he might need a doctor, and if he was depressed she needed to know.

She was just turning into The Close when a dark blue Ford Focus swept past her, followed by a marked police car. To her alarm both drew up in front of the Coach House, and as two suited men got out of the Focus a terrible foreboding came over her.

'Hello?' she cried, running towards them and trying to keep a rising panic from her voice.

DC Morley Croft turned around. His striking appearance, seemingly with African origins, was marred by the gash of a rose-coloured scar across one cheek. 'Mrs Carlyle?' he said.

'Yes. Can I help you?'

'Would you be Nathan Carlyle's mother?'

'Yes.' Her voice sounded high-pitched and razor-thin.

'I'm Detective Constable Morley Croft,' he told her, 'and this is DC Grange. We'd like to talk to your son, if he's at home.'

Her mind was spinning so fast she could hardly speak. It was all right, she tried telling herself. They were just doing their job. Everyone was being questioned and Nat had no more to hide than she did. These were routine enquiries, because he'd been at the rave. She tried smiling, as though her friendliness might make them rethink any dark intent. 'If you'd like to come in,' she said. 'He was still in bed when I left, but I'm sure he's up by now. Can I ask what it's about?'

'We need to speak to Nathan,' Croft answered evenly.

'But it's connected to what's happening in the woods, I expect?'

The detective didn't answer, only followed her in through the front door with his colleague close behind, while the two uniformed officers waited outside.

Alicia's chest was so tight she'd practically stopped breathing. 'I'll go and get him,' she managed to utter.

'Mum?' Nat said from the top of the stairs.

She looked up, and felt an overpowering urge to push him back into his room, as though hiding might protect him from something she couldn't even put a name to. 'You're up. Good,' she heard herself say. 'These gentlemen would like to speak to you.' She turned to Croft. 'You can go through there,' she told him, pointing to the sitting room. 'Shall I make some tea?'

Croft was watching Nat as he came to a halt halfway down the stairs. His young face turned so white that Alicia almost sobbed with fear.

'Are you Nathan Douglas Carlyle?' Croft asked.

'Yes,' Nat mumbled.

'Can you tell me your date of birth?'

'Tenth of November 1992.'

Croft nodded. 'Nathan Douglas Carlyle, I am arresting you for the rape of Annabelle Preston and must caution you . . .'

'Oh my God!' Alicia cried over him.

'I didn't rape her,' Nat shouted. 'She . . .'

Finishing the caution, Croft said, 'Hang on, son, don't say any more. I have to write down your responses and you might want to wait until you have legal representation.'

Nat's eyes were so wide they might burst from his head. His mouth was trembling in a way that was shredding Alicia's heart.

'He didn't do it,' she insisted shakily. 'If you knew him . . .'

'I'm sorry, Mrs Carlyle. We need to search the house.'

'But she's a liar,' Alicia shouted. 'She's . . .'

'Mum, don't say any more.'

'But you can't let her get away with this. Do you have a warrant?' she demanded, turning back to Croft.

'Under Section 17 of the Police and Criminal Evidence Act, we don't need a warrant at this stage,' he informed her. 'We simply want to take the clothes Nathan was wearing on Saturday night . . .'

'You don't need to search for that. We can just give them to you.'

'If you can show DC Grange your room, Nathan,' Croft said. 'All communal areas will be searched,' he explained to Alicia, 'which will include the bathroom.'

'What exactly are you looking for?' she cried. 'If you just want his clothes . . .'

'We'll need to take his computer and mobile phone, and anything else we feel might be relevant.'

'But I'm telling you she's a liar,' Annabelle almost screamed, as Nat turned backup the stairs.

'Mrs Carlyle, could you come with me, please?' Croft said, taking her gently by the arm. 'I know this has been a shock for you. Is there anyone you can call?'

'My husband's a lawyer,' she blurted.

'Then perhaps you'd like to contact him.'

'I can't,' she said, her voice cracking with despair. 'He's . . .' She put a hand over her mouth to stop herself sobbing. 'He died six months ago,' she managed to say.

'I'm sorry,' Croft responded respectfully. 'Is there someone else?'

'What are you going to do to him? I'm telling you, he's . . .'

'We're taking him in for questioning,' Croft explained. 'Miss Preston has accused him of a very serious offence, so we have to follow it up.'

'Her mother's put her up to this,' Alicia told him urgently. 'She's been trying to get rid of me . . .'

'I think it would be best if you took your son's advice and didn't say any more,' Croft suggested kindly.

'He's a good boy,' she said, starting to break down. 'He wouldn't do anything wrong, I swear it. He wants to be a barrister, like his father.'

'I'm going to assist with the search now,' Croft told her. 'If I were you I'd take a few deep breaths and get on the phone to a solicitor.'

Realising the sense of the advice, she took herself off to the kitchen, but there were so many fears spinning through her mind that when she got there it took her a moment to remember what she was supposed to be doing.

Her bag was still on her shoulder, so taking out her mobile she began searching for Jolyon's office number. Her hands were trembling with shock, but on the third attempt she managed to press to connect. 'Can I speak to Mr Crane please?' she asked when a telephonist answered.

'I'll put you through to his secretary.' A moment later another voice came down the line, asking if she could help.

'I need to speak to Jolyon,' Alicia gasped. 'My name is Alicia Carlyle. Please tell him it's an emergency.'

'I'm sorry, Mrs Carlyle, Jolyon's in court at the moment, but I can get a message to him.'

Alicia was having to fight back the panic again. 'Could you ask him to call me as soon as he can?' she said. 'Tell him it's about Nat.'

'Of course. I'll go over there now and hand him a note myself.'

'Thank you,' Alicia whispered.

After ringing off she stood staring at her phone, thinking about Robert and Rachel, but not quite able to call either of them yet. She was waiting for it all to turn out to be a terrible mistake. They were going to find something that would prove Nat could never have committed such a horrible crime.

However, there was no apology for having got it wrong, nor a miraculous discovery. There was only the sound of heavy treading on the stairs, followed by a thorough search of the kitchen, sitting room and old playroom, with evidence bags being filled and sealed, and finally Nat coming to hug her before they escorted him out to the car.

'It'll be all right,' he whispered thickly. 'Don't worry.'

Gazing up into his eyes, she felt her heart breaking into a thousand pieces. He looked so lost and afraid, so vulnerable, like the child he used to be. 'I'm coming with you,' she told him.

'I don't think they'll let you. I'm not a minor.'

Having overheard the exchange Croft said, 'We're taking him to the station in Bath.' He turned round as one of the uniformed officers came back from the unit car. 'No room at Bath,' he said. 'We'll have to take him to Bristol.'

'That's OK,' Alicia said to Nat. 'I've already called Jolyon, so there's a chance he might be there by the time you arrive. Which station in Bristol?' she asked the officer.

'Southmead,' he answered.

Jolyon would know where that was. She'd call to pass the information on, then she'd get in the car and drive there herself.

'It'll be all right,' she told Nat, hugging him hard. 'We both know she's lying, so we'll get this straightened out and you'll be home again before you know it.'

Chapter Fourteen

'Annabelle, this is Detective Sergeant Bevan who I told you about,' Lisa Murray said, as Bevan joined them in a room that wasn't very different from the waiting area. Except the furniture in this one was brown corduroy and there were two small cameras facing down from the corners, with a couple of microphones strategically placed on the walls.

'Hello Annabelle,' Bevan said, shaking her hand.

Annabelle kept her eyes lowered. 'Hello,' she said.

'The medical's been done, sir,' Lisa told him. 'It wasn't so bad, was it?' she said to Annabelle.

Annabelle shook her head.

'Do you have any questions?' Bevan asked her.

'Where's my mum?'

'She's in the waiting area,' Lisa answered. 'Sergeant Bevan's just taken a statement from her.'

'Are you sure she won't be able to hear anything I say? You said she wouldn't.'

'Absolutely sure.'

Bevan's interest perked up. What didn't she want her mother to know? 'I expect Lisa has explained that her role is to act as liaison between you and CID,' he said. 'She's been specially trained in this field, so don't worry, nothing you say can shock her.'

Annabelle's eyes travelled to Lisa.

Lisa smiled. 'Feel free to use whatever words you're most comfortable with to describe what happened,' she told her. 'As DS Bevan said, I won't get embarrassed, but before we begin I must stress how important it is for you to tell the truth. Rape is a very serious allegation, but lying is also a serious offence for which you can be prosecuted. Did you know that?'

Annabelle half nodded and half shook her head. 'I – I think so,' she answered. She looked at Bevan and seemed to wither.

'Do you understand that based on what you say here today,' Bevan continued, 'you could have to appear in court to undergo a vigorous cross-examination by the defence?'

Annabelle's eyes widened with alarm, but she did know, so she gave a small nod.

'Unless Nathan pleads guilty, of course,' Lisa added.

'He'll say he didn't do it,' Annabelle told her, 'but he did.'

Lisa squeezed her arm. 'Make yourself comfortable on the sofa there,' she said, directing her to the one where the cameras were focused. 'I'm going to have a quick word with DS Bevan next door in the tech room before we get started.'

Once the door was closed behind them, and Bevan was certain they couldn't be overheard, he looked at Annabelle's face on one of the screens and said, 'Well, what do you make of her so far? Is she on the level?'

Though Bevan might be a senior rank, out of hours he was Lisa's live-in partner, so she didn't feel she had to stand on ceremony. 'Actually, Clive, I'm not getting much of a sense of her yet,' she admitted. 'She's clearly nervous, and slightly defensive, which conforms to normal victim behaviour, and you've seen the bruises . . .'

'But,' he prompted.

'I don't know. Something obviously happened to her on Saturday night, or some time over the weekend, but I've had too many convincing liars pass through here to make any snap judgements at this stage.'

Bevan nodded. 'Then I guess it's time to hear what she has to say for herself,' he said, and removing his jacket he settled down in front of the monitor while Lisa returned to the room where Annabelle was waiting.

Several minutes later, with the official reciting of rights and explanations of procedure recorded on DVD, Lisa started by asking who Annabelle had gone to the rave with, and what sort of things she'd been doing before she'd run into Nathan.

'Mainly dancing and . . . getting stoned,' Annabelle answered, letting her eyes drift guiltily to one side.

'Who were you dancing with?'

'Everyone. Georgie. Melody. Theo. Some bloke called Neil.'

'Is Theo a boyfriend?'

'Sort of. We kind of all hang out together.'

'So you were there with him . . .'

'With everyone, but I did go off and have a you know, snog with him quite early on. Well, I suppose it wasn't that early, because I was already a bit smashed by then. Then this Neil started kind of coming on to me, so I went into the woods with him for a while as well.'

'What did you do with him?'

Annabelle blushed furiously. 'This and that,' she mumbled. 'Nothing major.'

'Can you be a bit more specific?' Lisa prompted.

Annabelle shrugged self-consciously. 'A bit of snogging,' she said, 'and he . . . he put his fingers in me.'

Lisa's eyes sharpened. 'Did you have sex with him?' she asked.

Annabelle swallowed and shook her head.

Lisa gave it a moment, then said, 'OK, so how did you and Nat get together at the party? Did he come to find you, or was it the other way round?'

'The other way round. Once I knew he was there I went to find him. He was with my friend Melody, but I knew he wasn't interested in her, so I managed to get rid of her for him.'

'Was he grateful?'

Annabelle nodded. 'I mean, he didn't say thanks I'm grateful, or anything, but I could tell.'

'So what happened then?'

Annabelle's eyes drifted again, as more colour crept up over her neck. 'He walked off into the trees, and I followed him.'

'Why did you follow? Did he ask you to?'

Annabelle shook her head. 'Not really, but I knew he wanted to . . . you know.'

'Wanted to what?' Lisa prompted.

Annabelle's eyes flicked anxiously to the door. 'Are you sure my mum can't hear this?' she asked.

'Absolutely,' Lisa promised.

'OK. Well, I knew he wanted to have sex.'

'Did he say that?'

'He didn't have to. I could tell, and I was OK about it. I mean, it's not as if we'd never done anything before.'

Lisa's eyebrows rose. 'So you've engaged in sexual intercourse with Nathan on previous occasions?' she said.

'No, but we did other stuff.'

'Such as?'

'You know, stuff. We showed one another our rude bits, and did some touching.' She gave an embarrassed smile.

'Could you be more explicit?'

With a sigh and a roll of her eyes Annabelle said, 'I let him see my boobs, and he got out his thing.'

'You mean his penis?'

'Yes.'

'Did he touch you?'

'Ye-ah. And I touched him, but we never went all the way.'

'Did you engage in any kind of oral sex?'

Annabelle's defences were rising. 'Yes, if you must know, but only once.'

'I see. When did this happen?'

Annabelle shrugged. 'About two or three years ago, I suppose. We used to go upstairs at his house, or mine, pretending we were going to play a game, like draughts or something, and then we'd, you know, do other stuff.'

'So you were what, twelve at the time?'

'And thirteen, and he was fourteen, fifteen.'

'Did he ever try to force you to have sex with him then?'

'Not force, exactly, but he definitely wanted to. I did too, but we were both too scared someone might come in.'

'So you were a willing party to these . . . games?'

'Yes.'

'Can you tell me how old you were when you actually lost your virginity?'

'Nearly fourteen.'

'Was it to Nat?'

'No. It was a boy at school called Dean Foster. He lives in Canada now, but he used to be one of our crowd.'

'The same crowd you were at the rave with on Saturday night?'

'That's right. Some of them used to be at our school, before they left to go to uni, but we've all stayed in touch, and we see each other in the holidays.'

'OK. So, going back to Nathan and your early experiences together. Did they continue over a long period of time?'

Annabelle pursed her lips as she thought. 'I suppose it was about a year,' she said. 'I expect it would have gone on longer, he might even have been my first, if our mothers hadn't fallen out. We never saw one another after that, until Nat moved to Holly Wood a couple of weeks ago.'

'So you had no contact with him at all for, how long?'

'About two years, I suppose. Our mothers really hate each other, and I know why. My mum had an affair with his dad.' She smirked. 'Isn't that wicked?'

There were other words Lisa might have used to describe it, but she was much less interested in the adult carryings-on than she was in finding out what had happened this past weekend. 'Let's go back to the party again,' she said. 'You followed Nathan into the trees, certain he wanted to have sex with you. What made you so certain?'

Annabelle shrugged. 'I just was. You know, the way he looked at me. It was like he didn't want to, but he did. And I was high, and so I thought why not? I mean, it wasn't like we'd never done anything before, and I really, you know, fancy him . . . Or I did before he turned on me like that.' She swallowed hard as tears swamped her eyes. 'He shouldn't be allowed to get away with what he did to me,' she said hotly.

Lisa only looked at her.

'He shouldn't,' Annabelle insisted.

'Of course not, and he won't if we can prove he's guilty.'

Annabelle seemed to consider that for a moment, then appearing satisfied she sniffed as she tossed back her hair. 'Anyway, like I said,' she went on, 'I was following him, and he was pretending not to know, but then he stopped by Lovers' Dip and waited for me to catch up. I pulled him down the bank, but then he walked off again. I started to tease him about still being a virgin, and I offered to teach him. Then I told him about my mum and his dad and he suddenly went mental. He got hold of me and said I was lying and tried to make me take it back. He started crying and called me a bitch and other things . . . He was really mad. I tried to get away, but

I tripped up and then he threw himself down on top of me and put his hands round my neck.'

'Were you on your front or your back when he threw himself on top of you?'

'My front. I was choking and trying to scream, but he wouldn't let go. I kept trying to push him off, but he was too heavy. Then he pulled up my skirt and started to push his thing inside me.'

'His penis?'

'Yes. He was doing it really hard. I was shouting for him to stop, but he wouldn't.'

'Did anyone try to come to your rescue?'

'No. The music was really loud, so I don't think anyone could hear.'

'Is there a chance Nathan might have thought he was doing what you wanted?'

'No way! He knew he was hurting me, but then he suddenly stopped and got up. He called me a slut and said he didn't do sluts, and started to walk away. I ran after him and tried to punch him, but he caught my hand and punched me here, by my eye.'

'How many times did he hit you?'

'Two or three, I think. He knocked me over and I screamed at him that I was going to tell everyone he'd raped me.'

'What did he say?'

'Nothing, he just turned around and ran away.'

'What did you do then?'

'I went back to find my friends. I was really shaky and crying, and because of the drink and stuff my head felt all weirded out, but I knew what had happened. I wasn't out of it that much.'

'What happened when you found your friends?'

'They were really shocked and thought it was terrible. Then Georgie took me home to her house.'

'Why not yours?'

'I was supposed to be at Georgie's for the weekend anyway, and I didn't want my mum to know I'd been at the rave, or that I was high.'

'But you'd been raped. Surely she'd consider that far more serious?'

Annabelle swallowed hard. 'I suppose so, but you never know with my mum, so I decided to stay at Georgie's until I'd sobered up.'

'Which was until this morning?'

'That's right. Georgie's parents were coming back from their weekend in Ireland, so I knew her mum would get straight on the phone to mine as soon as she saw me. And anyway, I thought that was enough time for everything to be gone from my system, in case you took any blood.'

'Do you understand now that whatever illegal substances – and in your case alcohol falls into that category – whatever you took is only relevant in so far as how it might have impaired your memory, or sense of what was happening?'

'Yes, but I remember everything. It happened exactly like I just told you.'

Lisa nodded and sat forward. 'I'm going to have a word with DS Bevan now,' she said, 'to find out if there are any specific questions he'd like me to ask. While I'm gone, have a think about everything you've told me and see if there's anything you'd like to change, or add.'

Annabelle's eyes were wide with uncertainty as she watched Lisa stand up. 'You do believe me, don't you?' she said shakily.

Lisa smiled and patted her arm. 'Of course,' she said, and after announcing the time into a mic she left the room.

Bevan waited until the door to the tech room had closed behind her before saying, 'You believe her because the law requires it for someone underage, or because you think she's telling the truth?'

'Actually, more the latter than the former,' Lisa replied. 'She's not trying to paint an innocent picture of herself. She's admitted she put herself on offer, and we can see her injuries.'

'Is the genital area bruised?'

'Yes.'

'Much internal tearing?'

'Some. So, what's your take on what you've heard so far?'

'I don't get the impression she's making it up, but I'd like to know more about what happened when she went off into the woods with the other two. If she had sex with them, it could account for the vaginal trauma.'

'But not the facial injuries.'

'Maybe not, but she could have got them another way. The time she spent with her friend, before she went home to her mother, bothers me,' he said. 'Girls that age can be a bloody nuisance with the mischief they cook up when the mood takes them.'

'No doubt you'll be questioning the friend?'

'Of course. I just wonder if they really understand how serious this allegation is. Does she realise the boy could be facing up to ten years in prison if he's found guilty?'

'I haven't asked her, but if he did it, let the

punishment fit the crime. Anyway, we still don't know yet what he's got to say for himself. He might admit it.'

'If he does, then whether it was forced or not, he could be up on a charge, thanks to her age.'

'If he knows she's only fifteen.'

'They're cousins, more or less, so he has to have some idea, and ignorance isn't a viable defence, as you well know. Anyway, we'll get to it. For the moment, I want to know more about what happened with the other two boys, and if she remembers seeing anyone nearby during the time the Carlyle lad was apparently raping her.'

When she returned to the video room Lisa put the second question to Annabelle first.

Annabelle shook her head slowly as she tried to think. 'I can't remember seeing anyone,' she answered. 'I mean, there were loads of people around, but I think we were the only ones in the dip. It was dark, and he was on top of me, so it was hard to tell.'

'What about when you went after him and told him you were going to report him for rape? Do you recall seeing anyone then?'

'Not really. I was pretty worked up, so I wasn't really taking much notice.'

Lisa smiled. 'Of course not,' she said. 'Now, going back to the other two boys you went into the woods with, Theo and Neil? You say you didn't have sex with them?'

Annabelle's cheeks started to burn again. 'No,' she answered earnestly. 'We just made out, you know, like you do.'

'Explain it to me.'

'Well, with Theo, we snogged and he felt me up, and I felt him too.'

'Did you have oral sex?'

'No.'

'What about Neil? What happened with him?'

'Same sort of thing really, but we did have some oral sex. Oh yes, and like I said before, he put his fingers in me.'

'If we talk to these boys, they'll confirm what you've just told me?'

Annabelle's redness deepened. 'I don't know. I mean, they should, but they were really high, so they might not remember as clearly as I do.'

'Do you have their addresses?'

'I know Theo's, but I only met Neil that night.' Her face started to crumple. 'Now you think I'm a slut, don't you?' she wailed.

'Of course not,' Lisa lied, but being promiscuous did not make the girl immune to rape, which was all that concerned her.

Back in the tech room a few minutes later Lisa waited for Bevan to finish his call to Morley Croft before saying, 'I take it from that the boy's now in custody?'

'At Southmead,' he confirmed. 'So, do you believe that she didn't have sex with the other two?'

'Does it matter if she's not accusing them of rape?'

'It matters,' he said, getting to his feet. 'I've heard enough for now. Time to go and find out what young Nathan Carlyle has to say for himself.'

More than an hour had passed since Nat had been brought into the custody area of Southmead police station, where he'd been read his rights, before his fingerprints were taken along with a mugshot and samples of DNA. He was then made to remove every item of clothing, which was bagged and taken away, leaving him with a pale blue paper overall to cover himself up with, and a pair of cardboard slippers.

Now he was locked in a cell with a single window at the top of the back wall that was too high to see out of, even if it hadn't been made of opaque glass bricks. There was a concrete bunk barely inches off the floor covered by a thin plastic mattress, and a stainless steel toilet with no seat, some squares of hard toilet paper next to it, and a spyhole in the wall to allow the custody officers to see in while the occupant was engaged in his private business.

The hatch in the cell door was firmly closed, and he was deliberately not looking at it, because every time he did feelings of claustrophobia and panic started to engulf him. He was perched on the edge of the bunk which was so low that his knees were almost at the same height as his shoulders.

'It's the only one available,' the custody sergeant had told him. 'It's normally used for drunks, so they don't have so far to fall.'

Nat didn't really want to think about the previous occupants of this cell, but it was better than tormenting himself with the nightmare he was facing. Except that was all he could think about. He was so afraid now that it was virtually impossible to stop himself crying. He wouldn't, though, because tears wouldn't make this go away, any more than they'd bring back his dad. They were useless, childish, and weak.

He wondered, angrily, if his father was up there somewhere watching this horror unfold. He'd wanted Nat to see what happened at the sharp end, what an accused person had to go through before a barrister took charge. Well, he was certainly getting his wish now. Had he seen what had happened on Saturday night? What might he have to say about that? Did he want to deny he'd had an affair with that bitch Sabrina? Nat's fists clenched with fury. How could his father have done that to his mother? He was a liar and a hypocrite, and he was glad he was dead.

Swallowing another onrush of emotion, he pressed his knuckles to his forehead and dug in hard. He couldn't bear to think of his mother being hurt, least of all by his father. It destroyed everything Nat believed about him, turning his integrity into a sham, and making a mockery of the honour he'd set so much store by. There was no point to grieving for him now, he wasn't worth it, and yet his mother, for all she must have suffered, still missed him and longed for him with all her heart. It made Nat hate him all the more, because he didn't deserve to be loved by someone who was as good and decent as the wife he'd betrayed. How could he have done it? And why wasn't he here to answer for his crimes? He'd taken the coward's way out, abandoning them all to the heartache and sorrow he'd caused, his a legacy to them nothing but lies and deceit.

Hearing the sound of footsteps outside, Nat

lifted his head, and as the hatch suddenly clanged open his insides turned to liquid.

A shiny face with bulging eyes peered in. 'Your brief's here,' the custody sergeant told him.

Nat's heart rose to his mouth as he forced himself up. He watched the door swing open, and his knees almost buckled when he saw Jolyon's strong, familiar face. For one bewildering instant he thought it was his father.

'Nat, my boy,' Jolyon said, coming to embrace him. 'Don't worry, son, everything's going to be all right. We'll have you out of here in no time.'

'You can use the interview room at the end,' the sergeant informed them.

A few minutes later Nat and Jolyon were sitting either side of a scratched Formica table in a soundproof room that was no bigger than the cell Nat had just left, and had no windows at all.

'Sorry it's taken me a while to get here,' Jolyon said. 'I came as soon as I could. Are you OK? Do you need anything?'

Nat shook his head. 'Only for this to be over.' His eyes burned with emotion. 'I didn't rape her,' he said fiercely.

'Of course you didn't,' Jolyon assured him, seeming to think it went without saying. 'Now, I've had a chat with the custody sergeant and DC Croft, so they've brought me up to speed with everything so far. I'm told Detective Sergeant Bevan's handling the case. He's on his way, and should be here in the next ten minutes or so, but you don't need to worry about that. We can take as long as we like to go over this, and then we're going to prepare a statement to hand him. This means you won't have to answer any questions if you don't want to. Do you understand that?'

Nat nodded. 'Do you know him?' he asked. 'What's he like?'

'I'd say he's tough, but he listens and I've generally found him to be fair.' Reaching into his briefcase, he took out a legal pad and a pen. 'Right,' he said in a businesslike fashion, 'let's get straight to it, tell me what happened, starting from the beginning.'

Nat sat forward, clenching his hands on the table, and rocking back and forth as he psyched himself up to begin. After a few false starts he managed to tell Jolyon what time he'd arrived at the rave, who he'd gone with and how much he'd had to drink by the time he saw Annabelle. He then went on to describe how she'd come up to him and dragged another girl away.

'She was totally out of it,' he said, watching Jolyon's hand moving across the page.

'Do you know what she'd taken?'

'There was loads of E around, and cannabis.'

'Did you actually see her taking anything?'

Nat shook his head.

'OK, go on.'

'I could tell by the way she was looking at me that she was going to start coming on to me, so I turned around and walked away. I didn't really want to be there anyway, so I thought I'd just go home.'

'Has she ever come on to you before?'

'Kind of, yes.'

Jolyon nodded and made a note in the margin. 'We'll come back to that,' he said. 'What happened after you walked away?'

'She followed me, but I didn't know that until I stopped at the top of this bank. She came up behind me, grabbed my hand and dragged me down into the dip. At the bottom I snatched my hand away and tried to walk on, but she kept coming after me. She was saying, "Come on, you know you want to do it." I told her to leave me alone, but she wouldn't. She started going on about me being a virgin and did I want her to show me how to do it. I was getting pretty mad by then, because she wouldn't take no for an answer. She just kept on and on, saying stupid things . . . All this rubbish was coming out of her and in the end . . .'

'What kind of rubbish?'

Nat's head went down. 'I don't really remember,' he mumbled. 'It was crazy stuff, and I couldn't make her shut up. I got hold of her . . . She pushed me off and started to run away, but then she tripped and fell. I was so mad I hardly knew what I was doing. I wanted her to take back everything she'd said, but she wouldn't, so I threw myself down on top of her to try and make her. She was . . .'

'What had she said that you wanted her to take back?'

'I can't remember now, it was just getting to me at the time, like she was really trying to wind me up.'

Jolyon's eyes came up from the page.

Nat swallowed and clenched his hands more tightly.

Jolyon continued to regard him. 'OK,' he said finally, 'was she on her front or her back when you threw yourself on her?'

'Her front.'

'And what did you do then?'

'I put my hands round her neck. She was choking and shouting at me to get off. Then I realised what I was doing and took my hands away. She started to laugh then and said, "Come on, do me. You know you want to." His mouth trembled as he stared down at his hands. 'She wasn't wearing any underwear and her skirt was up around her waist,' he said raggedly.

'So she was inviting you to have sex with her?'

He nodded. 'I didn't want to, but at the same time I did.'

'So you were sexually aroused?'

'Yes, no, I can't really remember. I only know that I wanted to get away from her. I stood up and she rolled over on to her back. Her face looked as though it was bleeding, but she was still laughing and telling me to do her. I called her a slut and said, "I don't do sluts." Then I started to walk away, but she came after me again. She tried to punch me, but I stopped her and pushed her away. I think I hit her face as I pushed, I'm not sure. It happened really quickly. She fell over again and started screaming at me, saying she was going to tell everyone I'd raped her. I couldn't listen to her any more. It was all too crazy. She was stoned and drunk and saying things . . . I just wanted to get away from her, so I ran home and turned off my phone in case she tried to call.'

'Did she?'

'There weren't any messages when I switched it on again in the morning.'

'And that was the last time you saw her? When you left her, half naked in the woods?'

'Yes.'

Jolyon scanned his notes quickly and sat back in his chair. 'I don't think we have too much of a problem here,' he declared. 'As long as you didn't have sex with the girl, there's no case to answer.'

'Robert, it's me,' Alicia said, using her Bluetooth to talk to him as she drove. She knew she was breaking the speed limit and presenting a danger to other drivers, but she had to get to Nat.

'Hi,' he responded. 'I still haven't got hold of Sabrina . . .'

'So you don't know Annabelle has accused Nat of rape?'

'What?'

'They arrested him a couple of hours ago.'

'Jesus Christ . . .'

'Your bloody wife is using her daughter to try and ruin my son,' she cried.

'Where are you?' he demanded.

'I'm going to Southmead, in Bristol. It's where they're holding him.'

'There has to be some kind of mistake,' Robert said.

'I know that,' she shouted. 'Annabelle's lying, and if she gets away with this she's going to ruin his whole life. Just tell your damned wife to back off or she'll be sorry,' and unable to speak to him any more she tore out her earpiece and threw it on to the passenger seat.

* * *

DS Bevan was pacing up and down the custody area, glancing impatiently at his watch.

'How much longer are they going to be in there?' he demanded irritably.

'They'll be preparing a statement,' Croft told him.

'Yeah, thanks, I'd worked that much out,' Bevan retorted, flipping open his mobile as it started to ring. 'Bevan,' he barked into it.

'Clive,' a female voice came down the line. 'I hear you're investigating a suspected rape.'

Bevan's insides sank. Just what he needed, input from Detective Inspector Ash. 'Hello ma'am,' he said, 'yes, you heard right.'

'And the boy you have in custody goes by the name of Nathan Carlyle.'

'He does indeed.'

'Doesn't ring any bells?'

'Should it?'

'If you're me, it does. His father is – or was – Craig Carlyle, QC.'

Bevan almost groaned aloud. Not only did he hate cases where the families of prominent lawyers were involved, but when the full might of the legal establishment came at him like a tank, there wasn't a detective in the department who didn't know how Caroline Ash felt about Craig Carlyle, and it wasn't good. 'I see,' was all he muttered.

'You'll need to watch yourself on this one,' she warned. 'Keep me posted every step of the way, because if that boy's guilty I don't want his father's cronies opening up loopholes for him to walk through. Do you hear me?'

'Loud and clear, ma'am.'

'How's it looking so far?'

'I haven't spoken to the boy yet, but the girl's got injuries and she sounded plausible.'

'Who's the young Carlyle's lawyer?'

'Jolyon Crane.'

'Of course. Only the best for Daddy's boy.'

'Actually, ma'am, the best has just come out of the interview room, so I'll have to go,' and with a curt goodbye he rang off.

'Jolyon,' he said, holding out a hand to shake as the lawyer came towards him.

'Clive. Good to see you,' Jolyon responded. 'We've prepared a statement. It shouldn't take long to read.'

Bevan nodded and signalling to Croft to come too, he followed Jolyon back into the interview room. This time Jolyon sat the same side of the table as Nat, and spoke to him quietly about what was going to happen next, as Bevan broke the seals of two audio tapes before slotting them into the machine.

After everyone present had identified themselves, and Bevan had cautioned Nat and made sure he understood his rights, Jolyon read out the prepared statement, giving Nat's account of what had happened on Saturday night, while Bevan made notes.

When Jolyon had finished Bevan said, 'Thank you. Can we have a copy of that?'

'Of course,' Jolyon agreed.

Bevan turned his attention to Nat, regarding him intently.

Nat could feel his insides churning. Sweat was making the paper overall cling to his body.

His chest was too tight, he needed some air, but he only went on staring at the detective in a way that made his eyes look glassy and wild.

'OK, so you're denying you had sex with Annabelle Preston on the night of the twenty-ninth of July,' Bevan began.

Since it wasn't a question, Nat said nothing.

'Is that true?' Bevan asked.

Nat's face turned crimson. 'Yes,' he said faintly.

'You say she was egging you on, inviting you to have sex with her, but you turned her down. Is that right?'

'Sergeant, you have the statement,' Jolyon reminded him.

Bevan's eyes remained on Nat. 'You and Annabelle Preston are cousins by marriage, aren't you?' he said.

Nat nodded.

'Can you answer in words, please,' Bevan said, glancing towards the mic on the wall.

'Yes,' Nat said.

'So you've known her for what . . . ? Most of her life?'

'Yes.'

'Have you ever had any kind of sexual relations with her? I mean, prior to Saturday night.'

Nat flushed again. 'No,' he answered. 'Well, I guess we messed around a bit when we were younger.'

'What do you mean by messed around?'

'It was like kids experimenting, you know.'

'No, I don't know. Tell me.'

'Sergeant, this isn't relevant,' Jolyon interrupted.

Though Bevan begged to differ, he decided not

to pursue it for the moment. After a beat he said, 'You say she made you really angry when she followed you from the party, but you don't explain what she said to make you . . .'

'Irrelevant,' Jolyon cut in.

Bevan looked at him.

'My client has denied raping Miss Preston, so whatever she might have done or said to make him angry is beside the point,' Jolyon expounded.

Bevan sucked in his upper lip as his eyes slid back to Nat. 'You admit hitting her?' he said.

'Accidentally,' Nat replied. 'I think, when I pushed her . . .'

'You also admit trying to throttle her.'

'Yes, but not for long. I just . . .'

'That's enough,' Jolyon cautioned, putting a hand on Nat's arm. 'You don't need to say any more.'

Bevan shot the lawyer a virulent look. 'You say when she rolled over and looked up at you her face was bleeding,' he said to Nat. 'How do you suppose that happened?'

'I don't know. Maybe she hit it on a stone when she went down.'

'Are you sure you didn't knock her down, with your fist?'

'I'm *sure*. I didn't hit her at all, not deliberately.'

'And you didn't rape her either?'

'No. Definitely not.'

Bevan sat back. 'OK,' he said shortly, 'I think we're finished here,' and after stating the time for the record he turned off the tapes.

Nat looked at him warily, unable to believe it was over so soon, but it seemed to be because everyone was getting to their feet.

'What happens now?' he asked Jolyon as they followed the detectives into the corridor.

'The nice custody sergeant here is going to bail you,' Jolyon replied. 'Isn't that right, Bob?'

The custody sergeant, who was at his desk behind a high counter top, looked at Bevan who was coming in through a side door of the office. Bevan gave a brief nod of his head. 'We need to set conditions,' he said.

'Of course,' Jolyon replied affably. 'Is my client's mother here yet?'

'She's waiting in the front office.'

'Mum's here?' Nat said. He didn't want her to see him like this, but at the same time he could hardly wait to feel the familiar comfort of her arms around him.

'I asked her to bring you some clothes,' Jolyon told him, 'so I'll go and get them. When do you want him to report back here?' he asked the custody sergeant.

'Let me see,' the sergeant said, consulting the bail diary. 'About a week?' he said to Bevan.

Bevan nodded.

'OK, next Monday at four o'clock,' the sergeant announced, 'if that works for everyone. In the meantime you're not to go anywhere near Annabelle Preston, or have contact with her of any kind. Do you understand that?'

'Yes,' Nat answered.

Leaving the sergeant to explain the consequences of breaking bail terms, Bevan went back to shake Jolyon's hand, said a polite goodbye and used his swipe card to exit through the back door.

'You seemed to let him off pretty light there,

Sarge,' Croft said, as they walked to their cars. 'What happened with the girl?'

'She says he did it, of course, and frankly, as things stand, I'm inclined to believe her, because my gut instinct is telling me that boy's lying. However, let's keep our minds open, shall we? At least until Wednesday evening.'

'Why then?'

'That, my friend, is when the all-important DNA is due back.'

Chapter Fifteen

Robert was waiting as Sabrina and Annabelle came into the kitchen. 'What on earth's going on?' he demanded. 'I've been trying to call you . . .'

'I'm sorry, I had to turn my phone off,' Sabrina apologised. 'Are you OK?' she asked Annabelle.

'I think so,' Annabelle answered in a thready voice.

Robert's eyes dilated with shock as he registered her bruises. 'I didn't realise . . .' he stammered, a chill of horror going through him. Surely to God Nat hadn't done that? 'Are you badly hurt?' he asked, not sure whether to go to her, or what to do.

Sabrina put an arm round Annabelle, saying, 'It's been a long day. You must be exhausted. Do you want anything to eat or drink?'

'No, I think I'll just go up and lie down,' Annabelle answered.

Alarmed by the uncharacteristic meekness, and still thrown by the injuries, Robert watched her walk to the door. Suddenly, to his surprise, she came back and hugged him. 'I don't want to be a nuisance,' she said, squeezing him tight.

'You're nothing of the sort,' he assured her, smoothing her hair. 'If someone's hurt you . . .'

'I don't want to talk about it,' she said, pulling back. 'I'm going to my room.'

For several seconds after she'd gone Robert stood staring at the door, afraid to assimilate his thoughts because of where they were heading. Then, turning to Sabrina, who was unpacking all the literature she'd been given by Lisa Murray, he said, 'Is she all right?'

'You saw her, so what do you think?' she replied crisply.

Feeling horribly out of his depth, he said, 'You should have called me. When Alicia rang to tell me . . .'

'Don't mention her name to me,' Sabrina cut in.

At a total loss how to handle this, he let a few moments pass before he said, 'So what happened exactly?'

Sabrina's head came up, her eyes dark with loathing. 'He raped her, is what happened,' she seethed. 'Your nephew, her son, sexually assaulted my daughter.'

'But if that's true . . .'

'What do you mean, *if* it's true?' she snarled. 'Are you saying Annabelle's lying?'

'No, of course not, I . . .'

'Well that's what it sounded like, and since we know you've always put your sister first, I guess it stands to reason that her son's innocent and my daughter's a liar. I wouldn't expect anything else from you.'

'That's not what I'm saying,' he protested. 'I'm just trying to . . .'

'No! I don't want to hear any more,' she snapped furiously, and cutting him a scathing look she returned to what she was doing.

He watched her helplessly, trying desperately to think of something to say that wouldn't trigger another explosion. 'I thought she was at Georgie's for the weekend,' he ventured finally. 'So how did . . . I mean . . .'

'She was at Georgie's, but they went to that damned rave.'

His eyes widened.

'Don't look at me like that,' she cried defensively. 'I didn't know she was going. For God's sake, you surely don't think I'd have allowed it if I had?'

'No, of course not,' he answered, 'but I've been trying to tell you for a long time that she should be mixing with girls her own age.'

'You think I don't know that? But try telling her, when she's known Georgie since they started school, and you know how headstrong she is.'

'All the same, we have to be stricter.'

'Thank you for your advice, but it's a bit late now, and I hope you're not trying to blame me for this . . .'

'Stop, stop,' he broke in, putting up a hand, 'of course I'm not, but you have to admit we're not as in control as we ought to be, so that has to change. Now tell me, what happens next?'

Taking a moment to back down from her temper, she said, 'They're waiting for the DNA results to come in and then they'll charge him.'

Wanting to resist the mere thought of that, he rubbed a hand over his unshaven chin as he said, 'Do you know where he is?'

She gave a growl of disbelief. 'How would I?' she demanded. 'I've been with Annabelle all day, trying to get her through this terrible ordeal. I would do that, because I'm her mother, whereas you, as her stepfather, are clearly more concerned about the fiend who attacked her.'

'That's not true,' he protested, glancing at the phone as it started to ring. 'They're children . . .'

'*He* is not a child. Hello,' she snapped into the phone. 'Oh yes, hi. How are you?' A moment later her voice softened as she said, 'It's so kind of you to be concerned. Yes, I'm afraid you did hear right. Well, she's very badly shaken up, obviously. Oh yes, he definitely raped her . . . I know, it's terrible. I can hardly believe it myself. OK, thank you for your call, and of course I'll let you know if there's anything you can do. It's lovely of you to offer.'

Robert's face was taut as he watched her put the phone down. 'Was that absolutely necessary?' he asked.

'People are concerned, and they have a right to know what's happening.'

'You're trying to inflame the situation,' he accused, 'and whatever you might think, that won't help Annabelle. If she's experienced a trauma, and merely looking at her tells us she has, then the last thing she needs is to be used as a weapon in her mother's vendetta.'

Sabrina's jaw dropped. 'How *dare* you say that?' she cried. 'In all the . . . all the time I've known you . . . I never . . . Oh blast,' she choked, breaking down. 'I can't believe this is happening,' she sobbed, covering her face with her hands. 'It's all so horrible, and now you're making it worse.'

Understanding at last what a terrible ordeal this was for her too, and distressed by the dreadful mess he was making of things, he went to gather her into his arms. 'I'm sorry,' he murmured, holding her close. 'We're all overwrought and in a state of shock.'

'Of course we are, because it's horrible, *horrible*, and for you to suggest that I might be glad Annabelle had to go through that . . .'

'That wasn't what I was trying to suggest at all,' he assured her. 'Everything's coming out the wrong way at the moment, so maybe we should pour ourselves a drink and try to calm down before we go any further.'

Using her fingers to wipe away her tears, she looked up into his eyes.

As he gazed back he was searching for hidden truths, or the merest trace of malice, but there was only a kind of helplessness and a need for his support that stole deeply into his heart. He hugged her again, wanting more than anything to try and get this right for them all, but for the moment he could think of nothing to say that might help in any way.

'Thank you,' she said, when he passed her a glass of wine. 'I'm sorry, I shouldn't have been hostile when I came in. I was so afraid you'd take Nathan's side . . .' She sipped her drink. 'I understand what a difficult position this puts you in, and I know you don't want to believe the worst of him, but I promise you, Robert, she's not lying. I can always tell when she is, and this time I know she isn't.'

Swallowing a mouthful of his own drink, he stood looking at her, not doubting her sincerity, but at the same time desperately not wanting to believe this of Nat. In the end he said, 'Have the police put you in touch with Victim Support?'

She nodded. 'They'll be contacting us, apparently. I brought home some leaflets and things as well. Perhaps we can look at them together.'

'Of course. Maybe we should ask Annabelle if she'd like to look at them with us.'

Sabrina was about to reply when the phone rang again.

'If that's another neighbour,' Robert said, 'please don't do the same as you did before.'

Sabrina stiffened. 'If they ask me what's happened I have to tell the truth,' she said, reaching for the receiver. 'Hello?' Her eyes went to Robert's. 'Ah, Canon Jeffries, how lovely to hear you. Yes, everything's fine thank you. More or less, anyway. Yes, I'm afraid Annabelle has been the victim of a crime. No, it wasn't very pleasant. Yes, I believe Nathan has been arrested. I can't really say . . .' Her face suddenly dropped. 'Oh really,' she said coldly. 'I see. Well, thank you for letting me know.'

'What's happened?' Robert said as she rang off.

'Apparently your nephew is back at home,' she said tartly.

Finding himself trapped in the minefield again, he took another sip of his drink rather than risk saying the wrong thing.

'I'd like you to tell me that you won't be going over there,' she demanded.

Having sensed this coming, he inhaled deeply before saying, 'Maybe if I spoke to Nat . . .'

Sabrina stared at him fiercely.

'This is no easier for Alicia than it is for you,' Robert reminded her gently.

'And you think I care about that?'

'I know you don't, but I do. No, please don't let's argue about it when the situation hasn't even arisen yet. Let's focus on Annabelle now, and take a look at the information you brought home so we'll be better informed about what we need to do.'

Alicia was studying Nat across the kitchen table. His head was down, his hands linked loosely together in front of him. Though he'd all but fallen into her arms when they'd finally released him, he'd barely spoken a word the whole way home, and he still didn't seem to want to talk now.

'Are you sure I can't get you anything?' she asked again. 'You haven't eaten all day.'

He shook his head. He looked so tense, and so very close to breaking, that she was afraid the slightest word or even gesture might push him over the edge.

'What if I throw something together?' she suggested. 'Then you can make up your mind.'

'I don't want anything,' he said.

Biting her lip, she turned to glance out at the garden. She was trying to imagine what Craig would do, to seek some sort of guidance from what she remembered of him, but every time she thought of him she wanted to curse the unfairness of life that he wasn't here now, when his son needed him most. 'Do you want to tell me how it went with the police?' she probed gently.

His head stayed down. 'They didn't say much.'

Since Jolyon had told her, while Nat was dressing, that they'd handed over a prepared statement, she guessed the police probably hadn't put him through too much questioning, but she still didn't know what he'd told Jolyon – except that he'd denied it, and Jolyon believed him.

'Jolyon can't go into any detail,' she said to Rachel, when she came round later to lend some moral support and they strolled up to the pub garden in order to talk without Nat overhearing. 'And Nat doesn't seem to want to tell me anything.'

'Did Jolyon give you any idea what happens next?'

'Apparently the police are taking statements to find out if anyone saw anything, but he said not to worry, it'll probably all go away as soon as the DNA results come back.'

'When's that likely to be?' Rachel asked, glad that Alicia had her back to a couple from the new estate who were looking their way and whispering.

'On Wednesday, apparently.'

Rachel was surprised. 'So soon? I thought those tests took ages.'

'So did I, but apparently for something like this they turn them around pretty quickly.' She gave a protracted sigh, then looked up as Maggie came out of the pub.

'Hello my love,' Maggie said, giving her a hug. 'I heard you were out here. How are you?'

'I've had better days,' Alicia answered, guessing the entire village must know what was going on by now.

'It's all a load of nonsense,' Maggie informed her hotly. 'I don't care what everyone's saying, I know your Nat would never do anything like that.'

Alicia's face drained. 'Are people saying he did?' she asked shakily.

Realising she'd blundered, Maggie reddened. 'Well, only some,' she said, trying to backtrack. 'But mark my words, no one's allowed to say it around me. We all know what young Annabelle's like, ten to one she did get herself assaulted, and now she's trying to blame it on Nat. And we all know who'd have put her up to that.'

Alicia swallowed and lowered her eyes.

Suspecting she'd hit another wrong note, Maggie glanced at Rachel. 'I best be getting back in now,' she said awkwardly. 'I'll send out a couple more drinks, OK?'

Rachel nodded her thanks and turned back to Alicia. 'She could be right,' she said. 'Sabrina might be blowing this up into more than it is.'

Alicia didn't disagree, but all she could really think about right now was Nat and what he was going through. 'I just don't understand why he's clammed up on me the way he has,' she said.

'He's probably embarrassed. After all, it's a sexual thing, and you're his mother. Boys can be very self-conscious over things like that, especially at his age.'

'But he's always been quite open with me before. True, he'd probably go to his dad first. I keep thinking of how much he must be missing him now. I know I am.'

Rachel smiled and squeezed her hand. 'Have you spoken to Robert?' she asked.

'Not since I called to tell him what was happening. He was as shocked as I was, obviously. Odd that Sabrina hadn't told him, don't you think?' Her eyes fluttered closed, as the enormity of it all swamped her again. 'Just to think of what they're doing to my son,' she said, putting a hand to her head as a sharp pain shot through it. 'I'd like to go over there and wring that bloody woman's neck. This could ruin Nat's entire life.'

'It can't if Annabelle's lying,' Rachel reminded her, 'and as we know she is, you can put that fear out of your mind now.'

'It was seriously full on,' Annabelle was saying to Georgie, who'd come round to find out how she'd got on with the police. 'We had to go all the way up to Bristol to this special unit for victims of sexual abuse. It was a bit weird, actually, like it was someone's house – not that you'd want to live there. Anyway, I had to have a medical so they could take all these swabs and blood and stuff, then they took me into a room where there were cameras so they could video everything I said. It was really out there, you know, all these detectives and special officers.'

Looking faintly horrified, Georgie said, 'So what did you tell them?'

Annabelle shrugged. 'Everything,' she answered. 'I had to, didn't I, or there was no point in going.'

Conceding that, Georgie lit a cigarette and went to open the window. 'Do you know what they're going to do to him?' she asked, blowing the smoke outside.

'They arrested him, apparently, but Mum said just now that they've let him go again.'

'So what, they're going to let him get away with it?'

'She doesn't think so. He's probably on bail, or something.'

Georgie nodded and took another drag. 'Everyone's talking about it,' she said. 'The police are going round taking statements . . .'

'Oh my God! That reminds me. Give me your mobile. I have to ring Theo. Do you know if he's spoken to them yet?'

'They're seeing him tomorrow, he said. Where's yours?' Georgie asked, handing over her phone.

'They kept it. Have you got his number programmed?' Finding it, she pressed to connect and put the phone to her ear. 'Damn! Voicemail!' she muttered. 'I'll have to leave a message. Theo, it's me, Annabelle. Georgie says you're seeing the police tomorrow, so just tell them we snogged and made out, OK? You don't have to say anything about us going the whole way. I didn't, so our stories have to match, and this way you won't have any problems because of my stupid age. Oh, and can you text me if you know someone called Neil? Use Georgie's phone, OK?' Snapping the mobile shut, she grabbed a cigarette from Georgie's packet and lit up. 'I should have given them a false name instead of saying it was someone called Neil,' she said, blowing out a cloud of smoke, and annoyed with herself for only thinking of it now.

'He might have made it up himself,' Georgie pointed out, taking the positive view.

'True. Let's hope you're right. So when are you supposed to be seeing them?'

'They're coming round in the morning about ten so Mum can be there too. I have to tell you, she's not at all happy about this. She didn't want me to come over here tonight, so I said I was going to Cat's and got my neighbour to drop me off on her way to Bruton.'

'What's her problem?' Annabelle demanded frostily. 'Does she think I'm contaminated or something?'

'No, she just thinks you're leading me astray, going to raves and stuff, like I don't have a mind of my own.'

Annabelle's face was turning pale, her eyes showed her confusion.

'Forget her,' Georgie said, waving a dismissive hand. 'She'll get over it.'

Deciding to take the advice, Annabelle picked up a hand mirror to inspect her bruises. 'The swelling's not going down much,' she said, touching a finger to the puffiness over one eye. 'So what are you going to say to the police when you see them?'

Georgie shrugged, and flicked her ash into a cup. 'Whatever you want me to.'

Annabelle considered how Georgie's evidence might help her, but after running several possible scenarios through her mind, she thought of her own statement and said, 'I think you just have to keep it simple, like we said yesterday.'

'Whatever, just as long as we don't let him get away with it.'

A pale circle formed around Annabelle's lips as they tightened angrily. 'No way,' she snorted. 'He raped me and he knows he did, so as far as I'm concerned he's going to prison – and with any luck it'll be for the rest of his stupid life.'

* * *

Nat was lying on his bed, wearing only boxers. His limbs were spread out across the rumpled sheets and his face was turned to the wall. He needed to shave and shower, and his dark hair was greasy, but he didn't care. What was the point of being clean when he only wanted to be dead?

Part of him wanted to ask his mother about his father's affair, but another part would rather die than go there. She should have told him. OK, he kind of understood why she hadn't, but if she had . . .

Hearing a knock on the door he said, 'I don't want any breakfast, thanks.'

'It's me,' Simon said, putting his head round. 'OK to come in?'

Forcing himself to sit up, Nat rubbed his face with his hands. 'Sure,' he said.

Closing the door, Simon went to sink into one of the beanbags next to Nat's desk. 'So, how are you doing?' he asked.

A bitter smile twisted Nat's mouth. 'I'm just great,' he answered. 'This is the best, being accused of something I didn't do.'

Simon regarded him sympathetically. 'The police came round to see me yesterday,' he said.

'They didn't waste much time.'

Simon shrugged. 'I told them what she's like, and how high she was when she followed you into the woods. Oh yeah, and how she dragged that Melody girl off you so she could get in.'

Nat nodded and swallowed a rising knot inside him. 'So what's everyone saying?' he asked. 'That I did it?'

Simon grimaced. 'Some,' he answered honestly,

'but most reckon she's lying, and even if she's not she had it coming.'

Nat's face turned stony. 'That really helps,' he said bitingly.

Looking chastened, Simon said, 'So what *did* happen when she followed you? She's got bruises on her face, apparently . . .'

'I don't want to keep going over it,' Nat interrupted. 'She's lying, all right?'

'Yeah, well, I know that, but what grounds is she basing this on? They're not going to . . .'

'We had a scene, OK? She really wound me up, and somehow she ended up on the ground and I grabbed her round the neck. It was a seriously dumb thing to do, and when I realised what I was doing I backed off. Then she started going on about screwing her again, so I told her I don't do sluts and walked off. That's when she said she was going to tell everyone I raped her. Obviously she doesn't like being called a slut. Did you see her again after I'd gone?'

'I think so, from a distance. She was with that friend of hers, Georgie.'

'What were they doing?'

'Drinking, dancing a bit . . .'

Nat's eyes narrowed. 'She was dancing after I'm supposed to have raped her?' he said scathingly. 'That doesn't sound like someone who's suffering, does it? Did you tell the police that?'

'Sure. I figured it was something they'd want to know, and that it would help you.' Simon's eyes started to shift a little. 'Between us, mate, with all the booze and stuff it's kind of hard to remember exactly what happened when. I mean, I know I saw her, but to be honest, it might have been before she followed you. The police don't need to know that though, do they? All that matters is getting you out of this mess.'

'How are you feeling this morning?' Sabrina asked, going to open Annabelle's curtains.

'OK, I think,' Annabelle answered, turning on to her back. 'What time is it?'

'Almost midday. Are you hungry?'

'I don't know.'

Sabrina went to sit next to her and smoothed the hair back from her face. 'Are you hurting at all?' she asked.

'Not really. I mean, a bit.' She frowned and closed her eyes as though her head ached.

As Sabrina watched her she was thinking of Craig and what he'd be doing if he were here. Knowing he would almost certainly defend his son made her heart churn with awful emotions. It was too painful to imagine them being torn apart by something like this.

Eventually Annabelle opened her eyes, and Sabrina smiled at her tenderly. 'Would you like to stay in bed for today?' she asked. 'It'll probably do you good to get some rest.'

Annabelle nodded. 'Yeah, maybe,' she said faintly.

Leaning forward to kiss her forehead, Sabrina rose to her feet.

'Mum?' Annabelle said, as Sabrina reached the door.

'Mm?' she answered, turning round.

Annabelle's face started to crumple. 'It wasn't

my fault,' she wept. 'I mean, maybe a bit of it was at first, but I didn't expect him to . . .'

'Sssh,' Sabrina soothed, coming back to the bed to comfort her, 'whatever you did, even if you sent out the wrong signals because you'd had too much to drink, what he did can never be your fault.'

Annabelle sniffed, and looked at her with big, haunted eyes.

'Would you like me to sit with you until you fall asleep?' Sabrina offered.

'No, it's OK. I'll be fine.'

After kissing her again Sabrina picked up a cup containing the dregs of a drink and three cigarette ends, but deciding now wasn't the time for discipline, she simply took it away.

As soon as the door closed behind her Annabelle fished out the mobile Georgie had left with her and called Theo. 'Have the police been yet?' she asked when he answered.

'They've just left, and don't worry, I said exactly what you told me to.'

'Great. Thanks. What about this Neil guy, do you know him?'

'Never heard of him, why?'

'It doesn't matter. I'll work it out. Is everyone still going to Wells on Friday night?'

'Yeah, but I don't think it's a good idea for you to come too.'

'Why not? I'm not an invalid.'

'No, but you're underage and no one wants to risk it again. Come back when you're a grown-up, Annabelle,' and the line went dead.

* * *

Jolyon looked up as his wife put her head round his office door. Beckoning her in he said into the phone, 'I'm sorry, Alicia, there's nothing more I can tell you at this stage. The police have to gather evidence and take statements . . .'

'But they wouldn't have to if they waited for the results of the DNA,' Alicia protested. 'The whole village is being questioned . . .'

'I know it must be difficult, but they have to follow procedure.'

With an anguished sigh, Alicia said, 'I know, and I'm sorry to bother you. It's just that I'm going out of my mind here. Rumours are flying, people are already taking sides, and Nat won't leave the house.'

Saddened, but not surprised to hear that, Jolyon said, 'How is he today?'

'A very good question. I've no idea. He won't speak to me. At least not about how he is, or what's going on.'

Feeling for her frustration, he said, 'It'll be over soon enough. The results are due back tomorrow, so we should have more information by Thursday, Friday at the latest.'

'Should I expect a call? How will I find out?'

'You might not know anything until Nat answers his bail on Monday, but I'll do my best to get something out of them before that.'

'Thank you,' she said warmly. 'Actually, there's one other thing, before you go. I'm afraid it might take me a while to pay you . . .'

'Put that out of your mind now,' Jolyon interrupted.

'But . . .'

'No arguments.'

'Thank you,' she said again, and after apologising once more for being a nuisance she rang off.

'I take it that was Alicia,' Marianne Crane said, as Jolyon put the phone down. She was a slight, pale-skinned woman in her early forties, with a neat auburn bob, intense dark eyes and a lively smile.

'It was,' he confirmed, 'working herself up into a bit of a state, I'm afraid.'

'With something like this hanging over her, I'm not surprised. Have there been any developments since yesterday?'

'Who do you think would tell me if there had?' he said sardonically.

'Oh, I know you, Jolyon Crane,' she teased, 'a spy in every camp.'

'And don't you forget it,' he warned playfully. 'So what brings you to Small Street in the middle of the afternoon? No babies coming into the world today?'

'None that are scheduled,' she replied, going to the window to find out what all the fuss was about outside. 'Is there a big case going on over at the court?' she asked. 'The press seem to be gathering.'

'One of the Bristol City players is up for assault,' he answered. 'So, what are you going to do with your time off, Mrs Crane?'

'Go shopping, I think, until my husband is ready to take me for dinner. I fancy the Hotel du Vin, if that's OK with you?'

Since it was less than a five-minute walk from his office, on the edge of the city centre, he had no problem agreeing.

After she'd gone, he continued mulling over the unfortunate situation Nathan Carlyle had managed to get himself into. He'd been in this job long enough to know how grief could unhinge people, and drive them to behave in ways they never would otherwise – in fact, his files, and the nation's prisons, were full of them. Not that he thought Nat had raped the girl, but he had it on good authority (DS Bevan during an off-the-record chat outside the courts that morning) that Annabelle had told Nat about Craig's affair with her mother during the build-up to the disputed encounter. There was no doubt in Jolyon's mind that this had played a big part in tipping Nat over the edge into trying to throttle the girl, and it was almost certainly why the lad was finding it so hard to talk to his mother. He hadn't even been able to mention it to Jolyon yesterday, which told Jolyon how hard the boy must be struggling with this suddenly tarnished view of his sainted father's character.

With a sigh, Jolyon turned back to his computer and called up the notes he'd taken the day before to go over them again. He'd got no further than the first page when his secretary announced a call from Oliver Mendenhall.

Picking up the phone, Jolyon swivelled in his chair to face the window. 'Oliver,' he said, to Craig's former colleague in chambers.

'I got your message about Nathan,' Oliver told him. 'How's it looking?'

'To be frank, I'm worried,' Jolyon answered. 'The DNA results are due back tomorrow, but whatever they are, given the girl's age, and the history between the two mothers, I have a nasty feeling this isn't going to go away easily.'

'Then we'll have to make it,' Mendenhall stated.

Lisa Murray was in the back garden of the red-brick semi she shared with Detective Sergeant Clive Bevan, whose divorce was still pending in the acrimony tray. The house, which she'd managed to buy with a small inheritance from her gran and a hefty mortgage, was in the Bradley Stoke area of Bristol, whose dubious claim to fame was being one of the largest private housing estates in the country, or certainly in the South West.

Since it was a lovely balmy evening Lisa was setting the table on the patio in preparation for a barbecue she and Clive were hosting for a few friends from outside the force. It did them both good to get away from the job whenever they could, even though the conversation invariably found its way round to the cases they were working on – no names mentioned – since Joe Public's fascination with crime seemed to have no saturation point.

Hearing the front door slam shut, she finished clipping the tablecloth in place and went back inside for the plates.

'Hey,' she said, as Bevan came into the kitchen looking hot, tired and unusually dishevelled for him. 'Bad day?'

'You could say that,' he answered, coming to kiss her briefly on the mouth. 'The psycho foot-baller got off with a fine, some idiot cameraman nearly knocked me out with his sodding camera, my soon-to-be-ex-wife has raided the joint account and taken the lot, and the statements coming out of the teenage contingent of the Holly Wood case are a bigger load of bunkum than those soaps you watch.'

'Let me pour you a drink,' she said soothingly.

'Make it a stiff one,' he responded, tugging off his tie. 'What time's everyone arriving?'

'Not until eight, so plenty of time to relax and shower. Go and sit in the garden. I'll bring the drinks out.'

A few minutes later they were lounging side by side on a swinging hammock chair, absorbing the earthy smell of gardens recently watered and the mouth-watering drift of someone else's barbecue.

'So,' she said, 'what's new in the Holly Wood case?'

With a protracted sigh he said, 'They're having the devil of a time tracking everyone down, as you might imagine, but going by the statements so far we don't have any witnesses to the actual event. What is becoming clear though, is that our Annabelle and her chums are a pretty racy bunch, who go in for all kinds of stuff, from partner swapping, to topless parties, to spit-roasting . . .'

'Spit-roasting?'

He cocked an eyebrow. 'Think about it.'

She did, and as the image of two boys either end of one girl came into her mind her eyes closed. 'Delightful,' she murmured.

He grinned. 'So you're not up for it?'

She glanced at him sideways. 'I could be, if you managed to clone yourself,' she challenged.

'Is the right answer,' he laughed, and kissed her.

'Anyway, it's all hearsay and to a large degree irrelevant,' he continued. 'CSI on the other hand have turned up a couple of interesting items in the woods, not the least of which was a girl's thong.'

Lisa's eyebrows rose, already guessing where this might be going.

'It's been sent to the labs for analysis,' he continued, 'but I'm thinking of Nathan Carlyle's claim that our Annabelle wasn't wearing any underwear, so, presuming he's telling the truth and didn't take it off her himself – and she's not saying he did, so I guess we can count that out – did she turn up to the party like that, or did it come off when she was making out with one of the other two and she didn't bother to put it back on again?'

'And I'm thinking,' Lisa said, 'that there was a thong among the clothing Annabelle brought with her when she came to the suite.'

Bevan nodded. 'So either the one being tested isn't hers, or it is, and she popped another in from the laundry basket at home. I guess we'll know soon enough. Now, I'm going upstairs to shower, then I'll come back down and get the barbecue going.'

After he'd gone Lisa continued swinging in the chair for a while, mulling over their conversation and her initial instincts regarding Annabelle Preston. While the girl was beautiful, and, like most teenagers, probably a great deal more full of herself with her peers than she'd exhibited yesterday at the suite, Lisa had sensed a genuine vulnerability about her that was far more in keeping with her age than her rumoured behaviour. The mother had interested Lisa, too. Another beauty with cracks beneath the surface, was Lisa's opinion, and she couldn't help wondering if the mother's inner problems were connected to the affair Annabelle had told Nathan Carlyle about on Saturday night.

Whether they were or not wasn't particularly relevant in itself – everyone who walked the planet bore the scars of previous experience – what the issue was doing for Lisa, however, was firming up her belief that Annabelle Preston had triggered something in Nathan Carlyle that had turned her into the victim of a spontaneous, and fairly violent rape.

The following evening just after five o'clock Bevan was in DI Caroline Ash's office, updating her on the Holly Wood case, when a call came in from the labs with the DNA results.

As he listened Bevan's expression went into shutdown. DI Ash watched him intently, her flinty lichen-coloured eyes raking his face as though trying to find a way in. She was a formidable woman of ample proportions and a fierce ambition that might have hoisted her several rungs higher by now, had Craig Carlyle QC not brought her promotion trajectory to a sudden and tragic end. The fact that she'd screwed up over an accused's civil rights, allowing Carlyle to get him off on a technicality, was not the issue, as far as she was concerned. It was the fact that Carlyle had known full well that his client was a compulsive arsonist with three previous convictions and should, for society's sake, be behind bars. However, instead of doing the right thing and overlooking the procedural gaffe, he'd used the miserable specimen of pondlife to slap her down for having got one over on him during an earlier trial. The pondlife had then walked, and less than a month later Caroline Ash had been one of the officers called to the scene of a fire on Fishponds Road, where a mother was screaming hysterically because her two children were trapped in a blaze set by Carlyle's despicable client. Both had subsequently perished.

'Well?' she prompted when Bevan tucked his mobile back into an inside pocket.

When he gave her the answer a frown line deepened between her eyes.

Bevan got to his feet and returned to his desk. After filling in the rest of the team he picked up a phone to call Lisa. 'The results are back,' he told her.

'And?'

'Turns out they're both lying.'

Chapter Sixteen

'I'm not sure about this,' Alicia was saying to Nat. 'We'll have to cover the carpet and find somewhere to put all the furniture.'

'We can get plastic sheeting for the floor,' he suggested, 'and why don't we just let the furniture go? No one ever comes in here, and it's not valuable, is it?'

As Alicia shook her head she was gazing round the disused wing of the Coach House that used to be her father's waiting area and surgery, until her mother had turned it into a playroom for the children with a small study for herself at the garden end. 'I think we should keep Grandma's things,' she said, opening up a wooden chest to check what was inside. Old board games and books. 'But the toys and play furniture can go.'

Since it would have been too awkward for both Nat and Robert to go to the cricket, as planned for today, Nat had insisted that he and Alicia make a start on turning the wing into a temporary studio until she could legitimately use the one at the shop. It would mean transporting her workbench and a few materials back to the Coach

House, but Nat was certain Simon and a couple of other friends would help out.

'You have to focus your mind on something else, Mum,' he'd told her last night, 'or you're going to drive us both nuts, the way you keep worrying.'

'You're right,' she'd agreed, 'and I'm sorry. I know everything's going to be fine, it's just hard to think about other things while it's all still up in the air. I hope they don't make us wait till Monday to hear the results.'

Now, as she watched him moving about the room, so like a man in his build, and attitude, and yet still her precious boy, she felt a sob of pure love forming in her throat. He was so much a part of her that sometimes it was as though they were still joined. Her blood ran in his veins, he saw the world through eyes identical to hers, and he shared a sensitivity with her that his father had adored in them both. Only the mother of a son would ever really understand the complexity of the relationship she shared with him, and know how utterly indestructible the bond was that secured them.

'What?' he said, realising she was watching him.

Smiling, she resisted the urge to go and hug him, and gave a brief shake of her head. *Please God,* she murmured inside as she carried on sorting through dolls' clothes and Action Men, *don't hurt him any more. He's a good person who's never caused harm to anyone. He doesn't deserve what's happening now, especially while he's still trying to get over losing his dad.*

Hearing a car pulling up outside, she glanced round to check if it was someone coming into the

Coach House. They weren't expecting anyone, but with any luck Rachel had found a few spare minutes to drop in. However, when she saw who it was she felt the bottom drop out of her world. Why was DC Croft here again, with another man she didn't recognise? Surely they wouldn't come in person to deliver the results. Something else must have happened.

Sensing Nat coming to stand behind her she glanced up at him, and for one disorienting moment she felt as though she'd been struck. He was so white it was as though the blood had been sucked from his veins. His eyes were burning and wide, and his mouth was disappearing in a thin, tight line.

'It's all right,' she said, squeezing his arm, 'they're probably just in the area and have a couple more questions they need to ask.'

By the time she reached the front door DC Croft was already there, but it was the other man who spoke.

'Mrs Carlyle,' he said, his tone as grim as the Reaper's. 'I'm Detective Sergeant Bevan. Is Nathan at home?'

'Uh, yes, he . . .' She turned as Bevan's eyes moved past her.

'Nathan Carlyle,' Bevan said, stepping in through the door, 'I am arresting you for the rape of Annabelle Preston on the twenty-ninth of July . . .'

'No!' Alicia cried. 'It's not true. *Please* . . .'

Bevan continued. 'You do not have to say anything, but it may harm your defence if you do not mention when questioned something which you later rely on in court. Anything you do say may be given in evidence.'

Stricken with horror, Alicia watched as Croft went to take Nat by the arm. Nat's face was a mask. It was as though he'd withdrawn deep inside himself, leaving only a shell.

'Don't worry, darling,' she said, hearing the roar of a distant storm as they led him past her. 'We'll sort it out. I'll call Jolyon now.'

Nat mumbled something to Bevan, who nodded, then he turned round and drew his mother into an enveloping embrace. 'I love you,' he whispered into her hair, 'I really love you.'

Alicia stayed at the door, watching the Focus drive away. She could see Nat in the back seat with Croft, but he didn't look round. As soon as it disappeared from view she dashed into the kitchen and snatched up the phone. Her hands were shaking so hard she couldn't dial the number. She took a breath, pressed her hands together and tried again.

'Is Jolyon there?' she said when the telephonist answered. 'I have to speak to him. It's Alicia Carlyle.'

'I'll put you straight through.'

'Alicia,' Jolyon said moments later.

'Jolyon, they've taken him,' she cried, her voice ragged and shrill. 'They've charged him . . .'

'Hang on, hang on. Tell me the wording they used.'

'They said they were arresting him for the rape of . . .'

'OK, that's enough, it's not a charge. I'll find

out what's going on. Do you know where they're taking him?'

'I didn't ask. I . . . It happened so fast. Jolyon, they're making a terrible mistake . . .'

'Try to stay calm,' he advised firmly. 'Obviously some new evidence has come to light.'

'Do they have the DNA?'

'I don't know. Leave it with me.'

'It can't be that. He didn't do it.'

'I'll get back to you as soon as I know what's going on.'

As she rang off Alicia tried to make herself breathe deeply, but her chest was too tight. She was seeing Nat in the back of the car, lonely and afraid, the victim of an injustice too terrible to contemplate. She shouldn't allow anyone to do this to him. Wasn't he already going through enough? What was to be gained from destroying his life? Nothing, unless you were an adulterous bitch avenging herself on his mother.

She was out of the door and across the village without allowing herself any time to think. The gates to Robert's house were open. The three strikes she gave the knocker were so forceful they might have splintered the wood.

When the door opened Sabrina's eyes dilated with shock. 'What the hell . . .'

'Where is she?' Alicia seethed. 'I want to speak to her.'

'How dare you . . . ?'

'She's lying and you know it. You put her up to it. You're . . .'

'He *raped* her,' Sabrina cut in furiously.

'You're ruining an innocent boy's life because

you can't stand the fact that Craig didn't leave me,' Alicia yelled. 'He's Craig's *son*, for God's sake. Why do you want to hurt him?'

'You should be asking him why he wanted to hurt my daughter. He attacked and assaulted her, then he forced himself on her like a wild animal.'

'I want to speak to Annabelle.'

'She's not here.'

'You're a liar. You're . . .'

'I don't need this,' Sabrina cut in and started to close the door.

Alicia jammed a foot against it. 'Where is she?' she screamed. 'I have to . . .'

'You stay away from her,' Sabrina hissed. 'She's suffered enough from your family.'

'Why don't you think about what this is doing to her? Using her like this . . .'

'No one's using her. She's got the injuries to show what he did to her.'

'She didn't get them from Nat. You're sick, Sabrina, do you realise that? You're obsessed and *sick*. This should be between you and me. To drag the children into it . . .'

'Your son did the dragging. Now get away from here before I call the police.'

'I'm not leaving until I've seen Annabelle.' She was walking backwards, looking up at the house. 'Annabelle!' she shouted. 'Please. I need to see you.'

'How many times do I have to tell you, she isn't here. Now go home and don't come near us again.'

Before she could slam the door Alicia threw her weight against it. 'If my son is found guilty of a crime he didn't commit, I'll come back here and *kill* you,' she raged.

'That's it. I'm reporting you for threatening me. My God, it's no wonder Craig couldn't wait to be free of you. You're crazy. Crazy or dull, that's what he used to say about you.'

'And do you know what he used to say about you? That you were only good for one thing, and you weren't even very good at that. Now it seems you're teaching your daughter to be the same, because everyone knows she's a slut . . .'

She drew back as Sabrina raised a hand. 'I should never have let him stay with you,' Sabrina snarled. 'It was only because of the children. He couldn't wait for them to grow up so he could be free of you. Do you know the last words he said to me? They were, I love you. That's how he felt about me. What were the last words he said to you?'

Alicia started to shout back, but Sabrina couldn't stop.

'You're the reason he was so stressed that his heart gave out. You killed him, you bitch, and now you've got the audacity to come round here, accusing me of lying and my daughter of . . .' She broke off as a car swept into the drive.

'What the hell's going on?' Robert cried, leaping out.

'Why don't you ask her?' Sabrina shouted. 'She came over here trying to force her way in . . .'

'Alicia?' he said, turning to his sister.

'They've arrested him,' Alicia said brokenly. 'They've taken him away. Oh God, Robert, I can't bear it. You've got to make her stop. She ruined my life once, please don't let her do it again.'

* * *

'We've brought him to Bath,' Bevan was telling DI Ash on his mobile. 'We couldn't get him into Trinity Road.'

'OK. I take it Jolyon Crane's on his way.'

'So I believe.'

'That boy's not getting out of this,' she stated. 'That's not a threat, it's a fact.'

Knowing she was right, Bevan said, 'The father's dead, ma'am, it'll be a pyrrhic victory.'

'All I care about, Sergeant, is that justice is done. Learn from my mistakes, no cock-ups in procedure, everything by the book. Where is he now?'

'Being processed. Kevin Wheeler's on today, so we know he'll be thorough.'

'Good. Get back to me when the interview's over.'

After ringing off Bevan turned towards the custody desk where Nat, ashen-faced and mute, was listening to the custody sergeant asking him if he understood the rights that had just been explained. As Nat nodded Bevan's mobile rang again.

'Bevan,' he barked into it.

'Sarge, I've got a very irate Mrs Paige on the line, the mother of . . .'

'I know who she is. What's her problem?'

'I'm not sure. She's insisting on speaking to you . . .'

'Patch her through,' he interrupted, and walked away so Nat couldn't hear.

A moment later Sabrina's hysterical voice came down the line. 'Sergeant, I have just been threatened in my own home by Nathan Carlyle's mother,' she seethed. 'I want to press charges and I need to know . . .'

'Hang on, hang on,' he said. 'What do you mean, threatened?'

'Exactly what I said. She came round here like a mad woman, accusing my daughter of lying, and then saying she was going to kill me. I hope you're going to arrest her, Sergeant, because she's . . .'

'Where is she now?'

'My husband has taken her home. She was completely out of control. She's insane. Dangerous.'

'OK, I'll send someone round there.'

'Thank you. And I hope you're going to impose some kind of restraint on her . . .'

'Mrs Paige,' he interrupted, 'I take it you haven't received a call from Lisa Murray yet?'

There was a beat before Sabrina said, 'No. Should I have?'

'She'll probably be in touch sometime in the next hour,' he told her. 'We need to speak to Annabelle again.'

'Why?'

'Lisa will explain when she rings. Now, I'm afraid I have to go. Someone will be round to deal with your complaint,' and before she could go off on one again he cut the connection.

Finding Croft alone at the custody desk while the sergeant escorted Nat to a cell, Bevan told him about Sabrina's call, adding, 'We've got a right bloody hornet's nest where that family's concerned, but you'd better get one of the local uniforms to go and have a chat with Mrs Carlyle. A gypsy's warning will do, but make sure she knows she's lucky not to be under arrest.'

'On it, Sarge.'

'Before you go, no sign of Jolyon Crane yet?'

'Apparently he's stuck in traffic, should be here in about half an hour.'

'Are you sure you're all right?' Robert was saying to Alicia. 'Can I get you anything?'

'No, I'm fine,' she said dully, keeping her head in her hands as she sat at the kitchen table.

Watching her anxiously, Robert reached out to smooth her hair.

She sat back. 'Please don't,' she said shakily. 'You should go home. Sabrina won't like it if you stay too long.'

'I can deal with Sabrina. It's you I'm worried about. What are you going to do?'

'You mean now? Or about Nat?'

'Both.'

'I don't think there's anything I can do except wait to hear from Jolyon. Apparently they're holding Nat in Bath.'

'Do you want me to drive you up there?'

Slowly, she shook her head. 'Jolyon said I won't be able to see him, and they might keep him in over . . . night.' As a sob mangled her last word, she pushed a fist to her mouth. 'I don't know what they've found,' she said raggedly, 'but whatever it is it won't make a difference, he didn't do it.'

Because neither Annabelle nor Sabrina was there to hear, he was able to say, 'Of course not. There's obviously some kind of misunderstanding . . .'

'You have to talk to Annabelle,' she implored,

grabbing his hand. 'Sabrina's pushing her into this, but if you can get her alone . . . You have to make her understand how serious this is, what it could do to Nat's future.'

'I'll try,' he promised, feeling such a tearing of his loyalties that he hardly knew which way to turn. 'I should probably get back,' he said, after a while. 'Shall I call Rachel and ask her to come over?'

'It's OK, I'll do it. Thanks for bringing me home. I hope she doesn't make it too difficult for you. I'm sure she feels your place was at her side, not mine.'

He smiled weakly. 'Call me as soon as you have any news,' he said, and kissing her briefly on the cheek, he left.

'It never fails to amaze me,' Bevan was saying to Jolyon as they walked towards the interview room, 'how stupid supposedly bright kids can be.'

Since Jolyon had come across the anomaly often enough himself, he could only shake his head in shared dismay. That Nat was falling into the category wasn't something he'd expected, and it wasn't pleasing him at all.

As they reached the door, Bevan held Jolyon back. 'I shouldn't be telling you this,' he said, keeping his voice down, 'but my DI's after a conviction, and right now I can't see any way she's going to be disappointed.'

Jolyon's expression remained impassive as he said, 'I take it we're talking about Caroline Ash?'

Bevan nodded.

Jolyon made no further comment on that. 'This

could take a while,' he warned, as he went to open the door.

'I was figuring it would,' Bevan replied.

Jolyon found Nat inside the interview room slumped in a chair with his arms clutched around his chest, and his knees spread wide. His head was hanging forward, but he looked up when Jolyon came in.

'Are you OK?' Jolyon asked, lifting his briefcase on to the table.

Nat replied with a half-shrug.

Knowing it was shame and embarrassment, as much as fear, that was making him withdrawn, Jolyon took out his yellow pad and a pen, clipped shut his briefcase, and sat down. 'I know Sergeant Bevan's explained to you that your semen was found on a high vaginal swab,' he said, coming straight to the point, 'so maybe you can tell me why on earth you lied when you must have known what the DNA results would show.'

Nat's head stayed down. His knees began swinging back and forth. 'I thought . . .' he said haltingly. 'I didn't come, so I thought . . .' He jerked a shoulder.

Learning, yet again, never to assume a person knew something just because he did, Jolyon said, 'You don't have to orgasm to leave traces of semen behind.'

Nat continued to hang his head.

Jolyon sighed. 'Well, I guess you've learned that the hard way,' he said. 'So now we move on to the good news, which is that yours wasn't the only semen that turned up.'

Nat looked at him warily.

Feeling wretched that the good news ended there, Jolyon said, 'The bad news, I'm afraid, is that you're the only one she's accusing. So, Nat, I have to ask you, did you *force* yourself on her?'

Nat was shaking his head. 'No,' he answered earnestly. 'It happened exactly the way I told you.'

'Except you *did* have intercourse with her.' It was no longer a question.

'Yes, but . . . She was asking for it. She was there with her legs open telling me to do it, so I . . . I was doing it before I realised . . . I mean, it's like I was out of my mind, but as soon as I came to my senses I got up. I hated myself for even . . .' He stopped as Jolyon put up a hand.

'I have one very important question to ask you now,' Jolyon said. 'Did you know, at the time you were doing this, how old she was?'

Nat swallowed dryly, and put a hand to his face. 'I think, I'm . . . She's about sixteen, isn't she? Or . . .'

'That's far enough,' Jolyon cut in sharply. 'Proving a vagueness about her age is probably the only thing that'll save you now, and God knows that's going to be hard when you're practically cousins. You see, Nat, whether or not she was willing, it's illegal to have sex with a girl of fifteen, and I'm afraid that's how old she is.'

Nat looked as though he'd been struck.

'I'll have to give this to you straight now,' Jolyon continued, 'then we'll start trying to sort it. First, anyone who has committed this crime is automatically put on the Sex Offenders Register.'

Nat's face drained. 'But . . .'

'No, hear me out. Consent is no longer an issue,

because even if she admitted it wasn't rape, and there's no saying she will, there's still the problem of her age. There's also the bruising to her face and genitals to consider, which could jeopardise a lesser charge of unlawful sex. Basically, Nat, they can throw the book at you now, and I'm afraid you haven't helped yourself at all by lying.'

Nat was looking so stunned that Jolyon eased the severity from his tone as he went on. 'We're going to do everything we can to get you out of this mess, but you haven't made it easy.'

Nat's eyes seemed hollow, his mind was dulled by shock. 'How – what if she keeps claiming I raped her?' he said. 'How long would I have to go to prison for?'

Seeing no point in scaring him half to death with the maximum possible sentence, Jolyon said, 'Let's not dwell on that now. We'll be working towards getting everything thrown out if we can, because the last thing you need, son, is to go into the future with your name on that register.'

Nat's hands suddenly pressed in each side of his head. 'I can't stand this,' he choked, his voice cracking with terror. 'If she'd left me alone, but she wouldn't. She kept on and on and then she said Dad and her . . . Oh God,' he gulped, burying his face in his hands. 'I shouldn't have listened. I should have just kept walking . . .'

Very gently Jolyon said, 'She told you about the affair her mother had with your father.'

Nat kept his face down.

'You had no idea until then?'

He shook his head.

Though provocation was no defence in the circumstances, right now Jolyon was more concerned about the personal trauma the boy was suffering.

'He said . . . He used to bang on about respect and loyalty,' Nat croaked. 'How could he . . .' His voice fractured and he clutched his head still tighter.

'He was a good man, Nat, in spite of what he did.'

'Does Mum know? She does, doesn't she?'

'Yes, she does.'

Nat growled in fury and despair.

After a while Jolyon said, 'I'm going to get you some water now, then we'll make a start on a new statement for Sergeant Bevan. Is there anything else you need?'

Nat finally looked up at him. 'Is Mum outside?' he asked.

'No. I'm not sure how long you're going to be here, so I told her to wait at home.'

'Good,' he said distractedly. 'That's good.'

'No, no news yet,' Alicia was saying to Rachel down the phone, 'but Jolyon said there probably wouldn't be any until much later tonight.'

'OK. I'm going to be with you just as soon as I can, but someone's bringing a dog in who's been hit by a car, and I won't know till it gets here whether I'll have to operate or euthanise – hopefully neither, but the latter will be quicker. What are you doing now?'

'Nothing. Just waiting. Darcie rang a few minutes ago, she knew something was wrong, but how could I tell her what's happening?' Tears were stinging her eyes. 'She's due back on Saturday and I thought . . . I really believed all this would have blown over before she got here.'

'Anything could happen between now and then,' Rachel said reassuringly, 'so don't start stressing yourself over her too. You've got enough to be going on with . . . Is that someone ringing your bell?'

Alicia was staring down the hall. 'I'd better go and find out who it is,' she said. 'I'll see you when you get here,' and putting the phone down, she dashed the tears from her cheeks and took several deep breaths as she went to the door.

For a moment, as she looked at the man standing there, she couldn't think who he was.

'Alicia? Are you all right?' he asked.

As recognition dawned, a jolt of despair hit her heart. 'Cameron,' she said, trying to assemble her thoughts. 'I'm sorry . . . I . . . I lost track of the days.'

'Has something happened?' he asked. 'You look upset.'

She almost laughed, but sobbed. 'It's . . . I'm afraid I can't come with you this evening. I should have called . . .'

'It doesn't matter. Is there anything I can do?'

Her eyes closed. Should she invite him in? Try to excuse herself? She didn't know what to do. Then to her horror a police car turned into the street.

'What is it?' Cameron asked, following the direction of her eyes.

She didn't answer, only went on staring at the

car, her hands bunched at her throat. They were bringing Nat home. They'd realised a terrible mistake had been made and now they were letting him go. But when the car drew up, only a uniformed officer got out.

'Alicia, let me help,' Cameron said, as she started to shake. 'Tell me what's going on.'

'I can't,' she said, her eyes fixed on the policeman. Why was he here? They already had Nat, surely they didn't want to search the place again.

'Mrs Carlyle?' the officer asked.

'Yes,' she almost whispered.

'I'm PC Darren Whitby. Could I come in for a moment please?'

'Oh my God, there's been an accident,' she cried, pressing a hand to her mouth.

'No, no,' he assured her. 'It's nothing like that.'

Seeming unsure what to do, but reluctant to abandon her, Cameron said, 'I'll wait in the pub in case . . .'

'No, come in,' she said suddenly. What did it matter that she barely knew him, or that he would probably drop her like a hot brick once he found out what was going on? Right now she couldn't face dealing with the police alone.

After showing them through to the sitting room, she perched on the edge of the sofa, while the young officer took an armchair, and Cameron stood slightly apart close to the window.

'I'm afraid,' PC Whitby began, 'that we've received a complaint about you from Mrs Paige.'

Alicia's head started to spin.

'She says you went round there and threatened her . . .'

'She's making her daughter accuse my son of rape,' Alicia cut in furiously. 'I needed to speak to Annabelle . . .'

'We all understand how difficult this is for you,' Whitby sympathised, 'but I have to caution you to stay away from your sister-in-law and her daughter during this time. If you don't, I'm afraid we'll have to arrest you and I'm sure that's the last thing you want.'

'What about her daughter staying away from my son?' Alicia cried desperately.

The officer rose to his feet. 'Your brother has persuaded his wife not to press charges,' he said, 'so please, do as I say, and don't go round there again.'

As he let himself out Alicia stared at the fireplace, unable to look at Cameron, or to think of what to say next.

'If you can tell me where to find it, I'll go and fix us both a drink,' he suggested calmly.

Glancing at him quickly, she forced herself up. 'I only have wine,' she said. 'Is that OK?'

'Perfect. Red or white? And please stay there, I'm quite capable of opening a bottle, just as long as I know where it is.'

Managing a weak smile at his irony, she gave him instructions and sank back against the cushions as he went to do the honours. This was all a nightmare, she was telling herself, it had to be, or she was losing her mind.

DS Bevan didn't like being lied to, and though he'd been prepared to hear the boy out, perhaps even give him the benefit of the doubt, the way the kid was prevaricating and mumbling like a moron, with Jolyon Crane constantly reminding him he didn't have to answer, was getting right under his skin.

'Are you really asking me to believe that you didn't know Annabelle Preston's age until today?' he said scathingly. 'You're practically related to her. You've known her for most of her life, and yet . . .'

'Sergeant, he's already answered the question,' Jolyon interrupted.

'With another lie,' Bevan retorted, his eyes boring into the top of Nat's head. 'How many more have you told, son?' he demanded. 'You said you didn't have sex with her, but we know now that you did. Now you're trying to tell me you thought she was sixteen. Do I look stupid? Do I have gullible stamped across my forehead? You knew damned well how old she was . . .'

'What's your question, Sergeant?' Jolyon asked.

Bevan shot him a look. 'My question is,' he said to Nat, 'did you rape Annabelle Preston? We know you had unlawful sex with her, but she says you raped her. Is that true?'

'No,' Nat said vehemently, before Jolyon could remind Bevan again that the question had already been answered.

'I don't believe you,' Bevan told him, 'and do you know why? Because I think you've been wanting to have sex with her ever since she was twelve years old, when you used to mess around together in her bedroom. She'd tease you, let you go so far, and then she'd pull back. I think that's what she did on Saturday and you'd had enough.

You weren't going to let her get away with it again. You wanted her, so you took her, even though she was trying to prevent you. Isn't that how it happened?'

'No! I mean . . .'

'Yes? What do you mean?'

'She was asking me to do it, and when I did she was . . .'

'What was she? Struggling to get away? Shouting for you to stop?'

'No. She was telling me to keep going.'

'So she's urging you on, telling you you're great, and you suddenly decide, hey, I think I'll smack her around a bit now?'

'No! When I realised what I was doing I stopped.'

Bevan couldn't have appeared more incredulous. 'When you realised what you were doing?' he repeated scathingly.

Nat's head went down. 'It wasn't like you're trying to make out,' he said.

'Then tell me how it was.'

'It's in his statement, Sergeant,' Jolyon told him.

'Yes, but I'd like to hear him say it.'

'You don't have to,' Jolyon advised Nat.

Nat's eyes moved back to Bevan. 'She told me my dad had an affair with her mother,' he said. 'I didn't want to believe her. I hated her for even saying it . . .'

'You hated her,' Bevan cut in, aware of Jolyon's eyes closing in despair. 'So feeling that way about her, you had sex with her and now you're asking me to believe that there was nothing violent in the act. It was what she wanted, someone who hated her pinning her to the ground, grabbing her round the throat and pushing himself into her so hard that her genitals turned black and blue . . .'

'I don't know how that happened,' Nat said. 'I wasn't being rough, or not like that.'

'Really? Well, I think you were so angry that you had no idea how rough you were being, and nor did you care. As far as you were concerned she had it coming. She's been leading you on for years, and you were going to give it to her whether she wanted it or not. And the fact that she didn't was as irrelevant to you as her age. You couldn't have cared less whether she was sixteen, fifteen or twelve, you were going to have her.'

'We're waiting for a question,' Jolyon told him sharply.

Bevan sat back in his chair. 'Do you know what,' he said, 'I don't think there are any more questions, because it's all perfectly clear to me. Nathan here raped his cousin on Saturday night, and his sudden memory loss over her age won't wash at all, because he's been having unlawful sex with her since she was a twelve-year-old child. And do you know what that makes you, Nathan?'

'If I were you, Sergeant, I wouldn't go any further with that,' Jolyon warned.

'I know you're trying to say I'm a pervert,' Nat cried, 'but it's not true. We only messed about like kids do when she was that age . . .'

'How do you know other girls that age do those things?' Bevan cut in. 'Because you were there, making them? Is that who you're growing into, Nathan? A pervert? A paedophile?'

As Nat's face turned white Jolyon banged an angry fist on the table. 'This interview is over,' he told Bevan.

'You don't get to make that decision,' Bevan snapped.

'My client is not answering any more questions, so it's over,' and hoisting his briefcase on to the table he began packing everything away.

Bevan got sharply to his feet and walked out of the room.

He found the duty sergeant making tea in the custody area's kitchenette.

'I want the Carlyle boy kept in,' Bevan said shortly.

The duty sergeant's eyebrows rose. 'On what grounds?' he asked.

'That he's likely to harass the victim. His mother threatened the victim's mother today. They live in the same village, and I don't think he can be trusted to stay away.'

Binning a tea bag, the duty sergeant started back to his desk. 'Better get Mr Crane out here,' he said.

Back in the interview room Jolyon was explaining to Nat what was likely to happen next. 'They'll probably want to keep you in,' he said, 'but given the fact you have no previous convictions, I might be able to swing it so you can be released into my custody.' He wouldn't tell him that his mother had caused the biggest obstacle to his release by threatening Sabrina, because Nat didn't need to know that. 'I think it'll be easier for you to be as far away from Holly Wood as possible for the time being,' he advised.

Nat didn't argue. He only felt relief that he wasn't having to face his mother yet. Anything beyond that was too terrifying to allow into his head.

Chapter Seventeen

'Well, I expect you're sorry you ever came to see me now,' Alicia said, trying to smile at Cameron across the table. 'And I can't believe I actually told you all that.'

His dark eyes were still conveying the depth of understanding that had encouraged her to say more than she might otherwise have done. 'You're going through a very rough time,' he said, refilling their glasses, 'and you obviously needed to talk to someone, so I'm glad I came.'

She looked at him, then away again, wondering what he was really thinking, and if she should drink any more.

They were in the garden now, sitting in the limpid glow of outside lights with an almost finished bottle of wine between them, and the whole sorry tale of Craig's affair with Sabrina and Nat's arrest fully aired. She'd held nothing back, and now she could only think that on a subconscious level she'd been trying to push him away, to destroy any chance of him helping with her work, because she'd become so used to everything falling apart that she wanted to get this next blow over with as quickly as possible.

'So you won't know what happens next for Nat until Jolyon calls,' he said, picking up his glass.

She shook her head. 'The fact that he lied to the police . . .' She swallowed hard. *He hadn't raped her, he just couldn't have.* 'Jolyon didn't mention this when he rang, but Annabelle's age . . . Even if she can be persuaded to drop the rape charge . . .' Her voice faltered, unable to utter the words that formed her dread.

Cameron was looking at her with the utmost compassion. 'He'll have the best lawyers defending him,' he reminded her, 'and if the rape comes down to her word against his, there's every chance the police will drop the case.'

'Her mother won't let that happen,' she said. 'Even if we can make the rape charge go away, she'll insist they prosecute for unlawful sex. So either way he's . . .' She put a hand to her mouth. 'If they put his name on the Sex Offenders Register . . .'

'I think you should stop scaring yourself with thoughts like that for now,' he advised gently. 'You don't know if it's going to happen, and I can't imagine your husband's colleagues allowing it to. They'll find a way of sorting this out, you'll see.'

Attempting a smile as she glanced at him, she said, 'You're being very patient and kind, and you must be extremely hungry by now.'

He cocked an ironic eyebrow. 'Ravenous,' he admitted.

The lightness of his tone put a little warmth into her smile. 'I'm sorry I kept you here all this time,' she said, 'going on and on . . .'

'We still have a reservation at the Montague

Inn,' he told her, 'if you're feeling up to it. If not, maybe we can rustle something up here. I'm a bit of a wow in the kitchen, even if I do say so myself.'

Still smiling, she said, 'I couldn't possibly let you wait on me, but I would rather stay here, if you don't mind, in case Jolyon calls.'

'No problem, and we can cook together. How does that sound?'

Apart from being told she was in a nightmare and would wake up any minute to find Nat upstairs in his room, she couldn't imagine anything sounding better. 'Is pasta OK? I have some smoked salmon and crème fraiche, and there's a blackberry crumble in the fridge that your fan, Mimi, brought round earlier.'

His eyes creased at the corners. 'Good old Mimi,' he said, picking up both their glasses and the bottle as he got to his feet. 'One of my favourites.'

'Actually,' she said, as they walked back inside, 'my friend, Rachel, the vet?'

He nodded.

'She should be over at some point, so we ought to make enough for her too.'

'No problem. It'll give me the opportunity to thank her for squeezing Jasper in at short notice the way she did. That's as long as you don't mind me being here. Maybe the two of you would like to talk . . .'

'No, please stay. She'll enjoy meeting you properly, and giving you dinner is the least I can do to thank you for listening.' She smiled wryly. 'Actually, I dread to think what you've made of it all, but I can promise you, until a few months ago we were a very normal family.'

His eyes lit mischievously. 'I have to challenge you on that,' he said, 'on the grounds that all the evidence suggests that no such thing exists.'

'OK,' she conceded, pouring olive oil into a pan, 'you win, but we were definitely all alive and on the right side of the law. It's hardly credible how quickly life can change, is it?' she added, shaken by the way she'd just more or less joked about Craig's death. Then Sabrina's terrible diatribe came back to claw through her heart. *It was only because of the children . . . He couldn't wait to be free of you. The last words he said to me were, I love you. What were the last words he said to you?* She put a hand to her head as though to stop the screaming echo. Had Craig really been waiting for the children to grow up to go to Sabrina? Were they truly the only reason he'd ended the affair? The last thing he'd said to her was that she was wrong to think the affair wasn't over . . .

'Does Rachel have an especially big appetite?' Cameron asked, interrupting the torment.

She looked at him blankly. 'Not really,' she answered, confused. 'Why?'

He nodded towards the pan where almost a pint of olive oil was starting to heat.

Quickly she removed it from the flame and took the jug he was passing to empty most of it out again. 'Sorry, I suddenly went . . .'

'Don't apologise,' he told her, going to the fridge, 'just tell me where to find some onions. Ah, smoked salmon, crème fraiche,' he said, taking it out, 'and unless I'm greatly mistaken that's a doorbell.'

She blinked, half expecting him to take it out

of the fridge, then registering that it had rung, she went to let Rachel in.

'We have company,' she told her, as they embraced. 'Cameron Mitchell's here. I forgot about the champagne tasting this evening . . .'

'Actually, I remembered it on my way here,' Rachel said, 'and wondered if you'd thought to cancel. I'm glad you didn't, because it means you've had some company. And I hope,' she continued, walking into the kitchen and smiling at Cameron, 'she's been showing you what a brilliant artist she is. Hi, good to see you again. How's Jasper?'

'I'm amazed you remember his name,' Cameron replied, clearly pleased that she had. 'He'll be most impressed when I tell him, when he gets over sulking because I didn't bring him this evening, that is.'

'You should have, Alicia adores dogs, don't you darling? Has all the wine gone? I hope you have some more.'

'There's plenty,' Alicia assured her. 'I hung on to half of Craig's cellar, which is now in the cellar here.'

'I'll go, if you tell me how to get there,' Cameron offered.

'There's some here in the cupboard,' Alicia told him, 'but only red. Is that OK for everyone?'

'It will be when it's open,' Rachel retorted, rummaging for a corkscrew. 'I'm whacked and in sore need after almost losing the dearest little spaniel to a ruptured spleen. I think she'll be all right, though. We'll see in the morning.'

As she passed over a wine bottle, Alicia said,

'I'm afraid I've been boring Cameron with my woes all evening, and I didn't spare much detail.'

Rachel turned to look at him in surprise. 'She's normally very secretive and shy of people she doesn't know, so I'm not sure how you got her to open up . . .'

'He was here when the police came to tick me off for threatening Sabrina,' Alicia told her.

Rachel's jaw dropped. 'She reported you to the police?' she said. 'The cow. I think I'll go over there and whack her one, that'll give her something to complain about.'

'She already has that,' Alicia reminded her darkly. 'Now, could we change the subject please, the image of two grown women screaming at one another isn't one I'd like Cameron to dwell on. Let's talk about him instead, since you know everything about me, Cameron, and all we know about you is that you have a dog called Jasper and you're hoping to buy a house in Somerset.'

'What do you mean, that's all we know about him?' Rachel protested. 'I thought you said he was God as far as the art world's concerned, so . . .'

'Yes, I did say that,' Alicia cut in before she could go any further, 'but he'll have people trying to push their work on him all the time, so I was trying to be different by peddling my problems and pretending not to know who he really is.'

Apparently enjoying the moment, he said, 'I can be anyone you like as long as you feed me. Do we have some snacks to be going on with?'

'There must be crisps here somewhere,' Rachel answered, tugging open a cupboard. 'This family has a passion for them. Ah, here we are, good old salt and vinegar. Gosh, it takes me back, foraging about in this kitchen, gossiping and cooking and getting pissed as we go. That's one thing I have to say about your husband, Alicia, he always had a great nose for wine. Are you married, Cameron?'

'You don't have to answer that,' Alicia told him, shooting Rachel a meaningful look.

'I'm happy to,' he insisted. 'My wife and I separated about a year ago. You could say she traded me in for a younger model, because her new partner would probably still be in short pants if he weren't so precocious. Not that I'm bitter, you understand, but I wouldn't have minded giving him a bit of a duffing-up when it first happened.'

Rachel and Alicia were laughing, but acknowledging the seriousness of it, Alicia said, 'Are you still in contact with one another?'

'Only if it concerns the children, or the divorce.'

'How many children do you have?'

'Five or six,' he said airily.

Alicia's jaw dropped, until catching the twinkle in his eye she started to laugh.

'OK, three,' he admitted, 'but it often feels like five or six, they have so many friends. They're all girls, and they've all flown the nest now, except when they need money or a shoulder to cry on, then Dad's place is the best pad in town.'

'Do you have any photographs?' Rachel asked.

'Not with me, but I have a whole album full where I'm staying, if you're ever passing.'

Choking on a laugh, she put her glass down and started to pull out place mats and plates to set the table outside.

By the time they sat down to eat it was almost

nine thirty, and not having realised how late it was until she happened to glance at the clock, Alicia felt a bolt of fear for Nat. Why hadn't Jolyon called yet? What was delaying him?

'It'll be all right,' Rachel whispered, sensing her distress.

'But look at the time.'

'Jolyon will call as soon as there's some news.'

Alicia looked at Cameron, and alongside her concern she felt a swell of gratitude for the welcome distraction of these past few hours. Had she been alone she'd probably have chewed her nails to the knuckles by now, or paced a rut into the carpet, or torn out half her hair. As it was, she'd managed to go a few minutes at a stretch without even thinking about Nat, or Craig, and during the moments when she had, she'd been able to disguise her anguish with a smile.

However, the heaviness of her concern for Nat began weighing on her heavily now. How could she have spent this time enjoying herself while her son was going through such a terrible ordeal? Even if she couldn't be with him, she should at least have been calling Jolyon to find out what was happening, or sitting by the phone waiting for a call. Instead, she'd invited a man who was practically a stranger into her home, let him ply her with wine and sympathy and cook her a meal, while she indulged in a horrible rant of complaint and self-pity. She was obviously losing her grip, unable to get anything into a proper perspective, or even to know how to behave. She could hardly believe now that she'd started a brawl with Sabrina. What the hell had she been thinking? All this time she'd managed to avoid her, then like the crazy woman Sabrina had accused her of being, she'd had to go and create the kind of scene that was so degrading she wanted to bury herself away never to come up again.

'Alicia,' Rachel said gently, 'you're not eating.'

Alicia looked at her. 'I'm . . .' Her heart wrenched as the phone inside started to ring.

'Shall I get it?' Rachel offered.

'No, I will,' Alicia said, and putting down her napkin she ran into the kitchen and closed the door.

'Were you sleeping?' Jolyon asked when she answered.

'No. How is he? What's happening?'

'He's tired, and a bit shell-shocked by everything, but on the whole he's bearing up.'

'Did he lie?' she asked, in spite of knowing it was a pointless question now the DNA was back. Maybe there had been a mix-up, or a cross-contamination . . .

'He seemed to think that because he didn't ejaculate, there would be no trace of semen, so that's why he lied,' Jolyon told her.

Alicia was struggling. 'So he did have sex with her?'

'I'm afraid so.'

'Oh my God,' she murmured, clapping a hand over her mouth. 'And was it . . . ? Was it . . . ?' She couldn't bring herself to say the word.

'That's still in dispute,' Jolyon answered, 'but he's admitted to hating her when he did it, because she'd just told him about Craig and her mother.'

Alicia's eyes closed in despair. Her throat was

so tight she couldn't speak. She'd always known it would devastate Nat if he found out, but for it to have come to this . . . 'Have they formally charged him yet?' she finally managed to ask.

'No. They're interviewing Annabelle again in the morning, so a lot will depend on what she says now. Off the record I've been told that Nat wasn't the only one she had sex with last Saturday night.'

Alicia's heart gave a small leap of hope. 'Do you mean someone else could have caused the bruising?'

'It's possible, but I don't want to put too much store by it at this stage, because there's still a way to go, and there's still the problem of her age.'

Remembering that was a horror that wouldn't go away, she said, 'No matter what Annabelle says, Sabrina won't let him get away with . . .'

'Don't think about her now,' Jolyon advised. 'Just concentrate on yourself and try to get a good night's sleep. I'm taking Nat home with me.'

Immediately understanding why, she said, 'You mean he can't come here because I went over to Annabelle's earlier?'

'It didn't help the situation, but don't be too hard on yourself, most of us would have done the same in your shoes.'

Taking very small comfort from that, she said, 'Can I speak to him?'

'Of course. I'll get him to call you from the car when we're on our way home, but I wouldn't expect too much if I were you. He's not only exhausted, he's deeply ashamed for having lied, and feels that he's letting you down badly.'

'But you have to tell him he's not,' she cried. 'If anything it's the other way round.'

'Actually, I think Craig's the one who did the letting down,' Jolyon said soberly, and with a quiet goodbye he ended the call.

As she replaced the receiver Alicia was registering only those final words. He was right, of course, Craig had let them down. If he hadn't cheated on her with Sabrina, or remortgaged their house, or taken the easy way out by dying, none of this would be happening. They wouldn't even be in Holly Wood, never mind facing the kind of threat to Nat's future that was going to utterly destroy it if Jolyon couldn't make it go away.

Yet she wanted Craig more now than she ever had in her life, because she was absolutely terrified that Jolyon wouldn't be able to achieve what she could only feel would be a miracle.

Lisa Murray was always interested to see where, and how, the victims who made up her caseload lived. Sometimes it could add a whole new dimension to her character assessment, or at least a new insight into what made them tick. When in their own environment they generally became more confident, she found, and opened up in a way that the sterile atmosphere of Pilning, for all the efforts to make it feel like home, sometimes prevented. In some instances she'd found another personality altogether emerging from the protective shell adopted in the rape suite, and in Annabelle Preston's case that was starting to happen.

There was no doubt the girl led a privileged existence out here in this leafy backwater, with all the trappings most girls her age could only dream about. Whether she appreciated how fortunate she was seemed doubtful, since her attitude towards it all seemed to be one of indifference, or perhaps entitlement. However, when children grew up with all the advantages money could buy, to them it was the norm. So Lisa wasn't about to judge the girl harshly for not seeming to realise that not everyone lived in an exquisitely restored Queen Anne house with at least six bedrooms, a Mercedes and a Lexus in the drive and fastidiously achieved detail in every room.

What she wasn't prepared to give Annabelle a break over, however, was the way she'd lied during her initial interview, because one lie in a statement was like one drop of poison in a water glass. The drink might still look safe, and ultimately, it might do no harm, but only a fool would trust it without finding out first why it had been put there and how damaging it could be.

Annabelle's expression was edged with surliness and defiance as she regarded Lisa across a gilt-edged coffee table carefully positioned between the twin japanned sofas they were sitting on. The room was pure Classical Revival, from the arabesque wall decorations, to the maplewood secretaire, to the very grand marble and limestone fireplace. Its colours were muted and tasteful, with an ivory-wash carpet, sofa accessories in the same shade, and peppermint-striped wallpaper that blended perfectly with the copious silks swagging and draping the windows.

Repeating her question, Lisa said, 'Why didn't you tell us you had sex with the other two boys?'

Annabelle was still scowling, but behind it Lisa was detecting an uncertainty and defensiveness that interested her far more than the typical teenage attitude. 'You're not going to tell my mother any of this, are you?' she demanded.

'No, now please answer the question.'

'OK, if you must know, I didn't tell you because I knew you'd end up thinking I was a . . . Well, that I, you know . . . Went with anyone, and even if I did, which I don't, it wasn't them who raped me. It was Nathan Carlyle.'

Lisa gazed directly into her eyes, half expecting her to look away, but she didn't. 'Could you have acquired the bruising to your genitals while having intercourse with them?' she asked.

'*No-o*, because they weren't *raping* me.'

'Did you ask Theo to lie in his statement?'

Annabelle flushed. 'I had to, didn't I, or we wouldn't be saying the same thing.'

'Have you contacted Neil to ask him to do the same?'

In an effort to cover her embarrassment Annabelle tilted her head cockily and pursed her mouth. 'No,' she answered.

'Why?'

Annabelle didn't reply.

'Is it because you don't know where to find him? In fact, you're probably not a hundred per cent certain his name's Neil, are you?'

'That's what he said it was, and I don't see any reason why he'd lie.'

'Are you in the habit of having sex with boys you don't know?'

Annabelle's nostrils flared. 'It wasn't like that,'

she retorted. 'When you're at a party and the music's going and everyone's having a good time, it's like you're in love with the whole world, so it's not about who you know, or what their names are, because everything's cool and you just do it with whoever you want.'

'And you wanted to do it with him, and Theo McAllister, but not with Nathan Carlyle?'

'That's right.'

Lisa waited for her to realise her mistake.

It didn't take long. 'I mean, I wanted to with Nat,' she corrected, 'right up until he turned feral. Then he scared me and I wanted to get away, but he wouldn't let me. I told you already, I thought he was going to kill me. Look, I've still got the bruises on my neck to prove it.'

Since Nathan had admitted to grabbing her round the throat, Lisa didn't ask if she might have got the markings from the other boys. Instead she said, 'The thong you brought with you to Pilning on Monday wasn't the one you were wearing on Saturday night, was it?'

Annabelle baulked as the colour deepened in her cheeks. 'What do you mean?' she said stiffly.

'I think you understand the question.'

Annabelle's lips were pursing more tightly.

'We have the one you were wearing,' Lisa told her, 'it was found by one of the forensic team in the woods.'

Annabelle swallowed hard as her eyes went down.

'I thought I'd made myself clear on Monday about the seriousness of lying to the police,' Lisa said sharply. 'This isn't a game, Annabelle. A young man's future is at stake and now we know you're lying about how many sexual encounters you had, and that you've planted false evidence, you're making it very difficult for us to believe anything else you've told us.'

Annabelle sat very still, her beautiful young features a mask of resentment and guilt.

'Annabelle?'

She started to answer, but then her face crumpled and tears swamped her eyes. 'I'm not lying about that,' she insisted. 'I swear I'm not. He got hold of me like he was going to kill me and I was really scared. He was off his head, and . . .'

'. . . so were you,' Lisa cut in, 'so are you sure you really remember what happened? Might he have been play-acting, and you, under the influence of drugs, misunderstood . . .'

'If that's what he's saying he's lying,' Annabelle cried. 'He was deadly serious and I'm lucky to be alive.'

Lisa only looked at her.

'I don't know why you're being so mean to me,' Annabelle wailed. 'I'm the one who got raped. It was me he threw down on the ground and tried to strangle.'

'In your original statement you said you tripped, then he threw himself on top of you,' Lisa reminded her.

'Yeah, well that's what happened.'

'That he threw you down, or threw himself on top of you?'

'The second one.'

Lisa nodded.

She allowed several moments to pass, interested

to see if the silence would put Annabelle even more on the defensive and perhaps push her into entangling herself even further in the web of lies she'd spun. Not that she doubted the girl had been raped, or at least she clearly believed she had, it was all about trying to get her story straight for a jury, because the shape it was in right now meant she wouldn't even see the inside of a court.

Eventually, Annabelle's eyes came up, and to Lisa's surprise the antagonism and hostility had gone. In their place was a lost young girl of fifteen who was no longer at all sure of herself. 'I'm really sorry,' she said in a tremulous voice. 'I shouldn't have lied to you. It was wrong, and I wish I hadn't done it, because I can see how stupid it was now. It's just . . . I mean . . . I didn't want you to think I was . . .' She shrugged rather than say the word slut, or slag, or slapper, which was what Lisa imagined was on the tip of her tongue. 'And I didn't want Theo to get into trouble because of my age,' she added.

'Well, it's a little late for that now,' Lisa told her. 'Anyone who has sex with a girl under sixteen is breaking the law . . .'

'But I wanted to do it.'

'It doesn't matter. It's still an offence, so now it'll be up to the Crown Prosecution Service to decide whether or not they want to press charges.'

Annabelle could hardly have looked more desperate. 'Please don't,' she implored. 'I'm losing all my friends as it is.'

'Annabelle, you're an intelligent girl. You know you're too young to be having sex . . .'

'But everyone does. It's not just me . . .'

'It's you we're talking about, and I can't press home strongly enough how much you've weakened your case by lying. If all this goes in front of a jury, it's going to be very difficult for them to bring a conviction for rape when you've lied and tampered with evidence. A charge of unlawful sex probably won't even be contended, because Nathan is no longer denying that intercourse took place. So now, Annabelle, I want you to think about this very carefully before you answer, and then I want you to tell me the absolute truth. Did Nathan Carlyle rape you?'

Annabelle's head came up. There was no hesitation at all, though her words were quiet and slightly shaky, as she said, 'Yes, he did. He definitely raped me.'

Detective Inspector Caroline Ash wasn't particularly fond of the Crown Prosecution Service lawyer who was assessing the Carlyle case, and she was going to like the weasel-featured excuse of a man a whole lot less if he decided there was not enough evidence to go forward with. Damn the Preston girl. If she hadn't lied during her initial statement, this could be sailing straight through to Crown Court. As it was, the weasel was not sending out many vibes of encouragement.

Contrary to what Clive Bevan thought, sitting there with his immaculate hair and soap-star looks, this wasn't a grudge prosecution as far as she was concerned. It was a straightforward determination to seek justice for a girl whose behaviour might be questionable, and whose veracity was as dodgy as a three-legged donkey, but SAIT officer Lisa Murray was convinced she was being truthful about the rape, and given Lisa Murray's track record that was good enough for Caroline Ash.

'But you don't have any actual evidence,' the weasel pointed out, for the umpteenth time. 'This is a classic "he said, she said" and if that's all you've got it'll be thrown out before you . . .'

'How many more times,' Bevan interrupted, launching into his own repeat, 'there's the bruising, the semen, Carlyle's admission he hated her . . . The boy's lying, I'm telling you. There was nothing consensual about that shag, and once we get him up on the stand, believe me, the jury's going to see straight through him.'

In the end, after hours of arguing, bullying, cajoling and even, occasionally, reasoning, the weasel finally signed off on the prosecution, leaving Detective Inspector Ash with a smug hope that Craig Carlyle was looking down from his cloud, and DS Bevan with a phone call to make.

It wasn't often one of the country's leading barristers turned up to make an application for bail, so when Oliver Mendenhall QC strode into the custody area with Jolyon Crane and Nathan Carlyle there was a moment's stunned silence. At six foot three Mendenhall cut an intimidating figure, with owlish brown eyes, a magnificent Roman nose and a thin, uncompromising mouth, much improved by a smile. However, there was no sign of one now as he spoke quietly to his client before presenting him to the custody sergeant for charging.

Murmuring to Croft, Bevan said, 'They must be worried if they're wheeling in the big guns already.'

As Nat stepped forward, his face was so drawn it was almost possible to see the bones through the pallor of his skin. His eyes were luminous with dread, and spiked with panic. This was a formal charging. He really was going to stand trial for rape.

Bevan began by cautioning him. At first the words seemed to glance off the shock that encased him, then, like a radio tuning in and out, they started to penetrate . . .

'. . . may harm your defence if you do not mention now something which you later rely on in court . . .' They disappeared again, and the next thing he heard was, 'Do you understand, son?'

Nat looked at him.

'He understands,' Mendenhall spoke up. Nat felt the lawyer's hand on his shoulder, then he was numb again.

The custody area felt crowded and alien, part of a world that he'd stumbled into by mistake and strangely couldn't escape. It was as though he'd become caught up in a net and every attempt to break free was binding him tighter and tighter. His father was there, but he couldn't get to him. The struggle was turning into a panic as his father turned his back . . .

Oliver's hand pressed his shoulder again and he became aware of the custody sergeant watching him, and Croft. There was a woman he'd never seen before. Somewhere in the background officers were coming and going. A drunk in a cell was shouting for God.

'Nathan Douglas Carlyle,' Bevan said gravely, 'you are charged that on the night of the twenty-ninth of July in the village of Holly Wood, Somerset, being a person under the age of eighteen, namely seventeen, you intentionally penetrated the vagina of Annabelle Preston, aged fifteen, with your penis, when she did not consent, and not reasonably believing she was aged sixteen or over.' He stopped and stared hard at Nat. 'Is there anything you want to say?' he asked.

'No,' Mendenhall answered.

The reply was entered into the computer and the custody sergeant then pressed a button under the desk with his foot. 'If you could sign please,' he said, as a small electronic pad lit up on the counter in front of Nat.

Taking the stylus Mendenhall put into his hand, Nat looked at it blankly. Mendenhall murmured in his ear and he moved forward to inscribe a shaky imitation of his name on the pad.

Feeling as though he was about to throw up, he stood back again and tried to listen as the custody sergeant and Mendenhall spoke to one another, but the words were like arrows failing to pierce the surface. There was something about no previous record followed by a setting of bail with conditions, and then a date: the 6th of August.

As Jolyon and Mendenhall guided him towards the back door of the station he heard DS Bevan saying to someone, 'It's an indictable offence, so it'll be a committal straight to Crown Court.'

Mendenhall turned round, treated Bevan to a withering look, then nodding to the officer who was waiting to release the door, he stepped outside and glanced at his watch.

'I have to get back to London,' he told Nat, 'but I don't want you to worry about anything. We're going to get this sorted out.'

Nat regarded him with traumatised eyes.

Mendenhall gave him a rare smile. 'You understand what's happening now, do you?' he said. 'I came to make the application so you can be released into Jolyon's custody until Wednesday, which is when you're due to appear before the Youth Court. Jolyon will be with you for that, because it's just a formality. He'll let me know the dates for the serving of papers, which we'll do together, unless I can get the CPS to see sense and throw the case out before it gets that far.'

Taking heart from the confidence of his tone, Nathan's voice was less shaky as he said, 'Thank you.'

Mendenhall nodded, and after a quick word with Jolyon he pumped both their hands and got into his car.

As he drove out of the station car park Mendenhall pressed to connect to Alicia. 'He's with Jolyon,' he told her when she answered. 'They've set the Youth Court hearing for next Wednesday in Wells. It won't be a big deal, just a setting of dates, and there's a good chance I'll be able to make it go away soon after.'

'Thank you,' she whispered.

'Don't worry,' he said, 'he's in safe hands,' and

clicking off he connected to his clerk, ready to give him instructions on whom to call and where to go for the backup he might need in the coming weeks.

Chapter Eighteen

Alicia woke with a start. Her heart was thudding like a drum, her skin was drenched in sweat. In her dream Nat had been raping Annabelle, his face contorted with fury, his rage hammering into her as Annabelle choked and screamed and begged him to stop. Then it was no longer Nat, it was a stranger, a monster, and the girl being attacked was Darcie and Sabrina was watching, trying to pull Craig away as he attempted to save his daughter.

Taking several deep breaths, Alicia dashed a hand through her hair, waiting for the lingering images to fade. Then, still trembling and disoriented, she swung her legs off the bed and padded downstairs to make some tea. It was five o'clock in the morning, and the sun was coming up, so she wouldn't go back to bed again now. God forbid she should make a return to that terrible nightmare. She had a lot to do today, so in an effort to clear her mind, and assure herself that she really didn't believe Nat had done it, she kept reminding herself of Oliver Mendenhall's matter-of-fact calmness when he'd rung last night. After speaking to him she'd no longer felt as though she and Nat were trapped in front of a speeding train – though God knew her terror had hit new heights when Jolyon had rung to tell her Nat was to be formally charged.

Now she must prepare herself to face the next hurdle, that of picking up Darcie from the train and deciding what to tell her when she asked where Nat was. Knowing how badly Darcie was likely to take it, she'd need to put as light a spin on it as she could, or maybe she'd simply tell her that Nat had gone to work with Jolyon earlier than expected. She might get away with that, because no matter what evidence the police thought they had, Oliver and Jolyon would be sure to tear so many holes in it that the courts would wonder how the case had ever reached them, if indeed it did. The spectre of unlawful sex would continue to loom, she knew that, but when she'd spoken to Jolyon before going to bed last night he'd been almost dismissive about it, telling her to put it out of her mind, because they'd find a way of making sure that didn't stick either.

Deciding not to torment herself with what Sabrina might have to say about that, she went upstairs to shower and dress. It was as she was reaching into her wardrobe for a clean blouse to put on over her jeans that she thought she caught the faintest whiff of Craig's cologne. Though she knew it was probably lingering on one of her dresses, she found herself thinking of him so intensely then, and feeling his presence so strongly, that she turned around, almost expecting to see him. The room was empty, but when she closed her eyes to push back the tears she was overcome by the memory of how he used to hold her, his thighs pressed to hers, his hips, his chest, his entire body wrapped so lovingly and protectively around hers that she almost lifted her arms to embrace him.

'If you're there, if you can hear me,' she whispered in her mind, 'please tell me what to do. We have to help him.'

There was no answer, nor had she really expected one, but the silence seemed to feel denser, strangely closer and as full as her heart.

After putting on her blouse, she brushed out her hair and went across the landing to Darcie's room. For a long time she simply gazed around at Darcie's things, wanting to think only about her daughter for a while. She'd been away for so long, and so much had happened during this last week, that she felt guilty now for a neglect that, luckily, Darcie knew nothing about.

'Mum, Dad, I have to write a riddle for English, so here it is,' Darcie announced, coming into the den where Alicia and Craig were sprawled together on the sofa watching TV.

Hitting the mute button, Craig said, 'OK, squirrel, shoot.'

Darcie stood in the centre of the room holding her notebook and twisting her spindly little body from side to side as she read aloud. 'What has no concept of time or place, can make you cry and laugh, and are always with you, even though you can't see or touch them? Oh yes, and you can share them, but I might not add that bit.'

Puzzled, Craig glanced at Alicia.

Alicia was thinking hard, but ended up shaking her head.

'Shall I give you a clue?' Darcie offered.

'Yes please,' Craig replied.

'Lane, card and stick.'

'Mm, lane, card and stick,' Craig repeated.

Alicia smiled, suspecting he'd guessed the answer by now, but she knew he wouldn't dream of stealing Darcie's thunder.

Darcie's pretty face was shining with excitement as her eyes stayed glued to her father. As always, he was the one she really wanted to impress.

'OK, give up,' he said in the end.

'Memories,' she cried, jumping up and down in triumph.

Craig looked totally blown away. 'Of course,' he said. 'Memories. Did you make that up yourself?'

Darcie nodded with pride.

'And you're only nine?'

She nodded again.

'Then I think that deserves a very special Dad hug,' he declared, and leaping to his feet he swept her into his arms and swung her round and round as she squealed with delight.

Alicia was smiling now, as she tucked in the corners of Darcie's bed. How appropriate that she should be recalling that clever little riddle, considering how drawn into her memories she'd found herself earlier. Darcie was right, they didn't have much concept of time or place, because they could turn up at the mention of a single word, or the mere drift of a scent.

Hearing the phone ringing in her own room she

left Darcie's bed half made to go and answer, hoping it might be Nat, or Darcie, or maybe Robert.

'Hi, Mrs Carlyle, Alicia, it's Summer. How are you?'

'Oh, Summer,' Alicia said, somehow managing to keep her tone light. 'I'm fine. How are you? How's Italy?' *Italy, where Craig and Sabrina had started their affair.*

'Very hot and very boring most of the time. I've been trying to get hold of Nat for ages, but he's not answering his phone. Is he there?'

Already reasonably prepared for this, since lots of Nat's London friends had called over the last few days, trying to track him down, Alicia said, 'He's managed to lose his mobile, I'm afraid, and he's staying in Bristol with Jolyon Crane for the next few days helping him with a case. Some early work experience. I'll be speaking to him later though, so I'll ask him to call.'

'Is there any chance I could have the number?' Summer asked. 'It's been almost a week since we spoke. I was starting to get worried he might have found someone else.'

Not wanting to think about how she'd react if she knew the truth, nor feeling it her place to tell it, Alicia said, 'Of course you can have the number, but I'm afraid I've left my address book up at the shop, and I have to leave soon to collect Darcie, so I'll text you later, if that's OK.'

'Sure, that's fine. Say hi to Darcie for me, won't you? I expect you'll be really pleased to see her after all this time.'

Alicia smiled as her heart softened. 'You're right,

I will,' she said truthfully, though she knew the reunion probably wasn't going to be easy. Darcie was too attuned to her mother's moods for Alicia to be able to hide much from her, and there was still her reluctance to moving here to get past.

After promising again to send a text, Alicia rang off and returned to Darcie's room. She hated lying, about the text and about what was happening, but what choice did she have? She couldn't tell Summer or any of Nat's friends the truth, it would be the last thing he wanted, nor could she face trying to find the right words to say it. All she could hope for was to get these next few days over with and then try, if they could, to return to normal.

Hearing the phone ring again, she went back to her room and to her relief this time it was Rachel.

'Hi, how are you doing?' Rachel asked.

'Not too bad, thanks. Steeling myself for the whirlwind.'

'What time are you picking her up?'

'In about an hour. The family she's been staying with will be on the same train, but they're going on to Dorset.'

'That's worked out well. So, will you bring her over later? Or would you rather we came there?'

'Either way. Actually, we'll come to you. I need to get out of the house for a while, and away from the phone.'

'No problem. Shall I invite Cameron? Dave would love to meet him.'

'No,' Alicia answered, knowing full well that Rachel was trying to matchmake and not going for it at all. 'I don't want Darcie getting the wrong idea, or him, come to that. Anyway, he's gone to London for the weekend.'

'Really? And you would know this because?'

'He rang yesterday to thank me for dinner on Thursday and to ask if there was any news about Nat.'

'Did you tell him he'd been charged?'

'Yes. I'm not sure what he said now, because I was on the ceiling at the time, having just heard from Jolyon, but by the end of the call I think I was managing to sound marginally less hysterical.' She took a breath as an all-too-familiar dread stole back into her heart. 'It's going to be fine,' she said firmly, more for her own sake than Rachel's.

'Of course it is,' Rachel agreed. 'Now, before I go, what news from Robert?'

'None really. He rang last night, after I sent him a text about the charge, to tell me to call if I needed anything, but I guess there's not much more he can say at this stage. He's in a horrible position, and I can't imagine she'd take very kindly to him coming over here.'

'It beats me why he stays married to the witch,' Rachel grunted.

'I think it's called love, and as they say, there's no accounting for it.'

'Isn't that the truth? Anyway, Oliver's on the case now, so time for you to relax and let your sister-in-law start worrying about what she's going to do when the police press charges against her daughter for lying.'

* * *

'Annabelle? Are you OK? Can I come in?' Sabrina said, putting her head round Annabelle's bedroom door.

'Yes, I'm all right,' Annabelle answered, sweeping the hair from her face as she turned on to her back.

'It's gone midday,' Sabrina told her, starting to pick up the clothes Annabelle had dropped on the floor.

'Really?'

Concerned by how lifeless and disinterested she'd become these last few days, Sabrina went to sit on the bed and put a hand to her forehead. 'Do you feel unwell?' she asked.

'No, I'm just tired and fed up with the way everyone keeps talking about what happened.'

'Of course you are,' Sabrina said, stroking Annabelle's face gently. 'It's best to put it out of your mind now until Lisa comes to start preparing you for court.'

Annabelle's eyes lingered on hers for a moment, then she let her head drift to one side.

'Shall I run you a bath?' Sabrina offered.

'No.'

'How about something to eat?'

'Not hungry.'

'So are you going to stay here all day?'

'I might.'

'What about coming to Babington tomorrow with me and June? Or we could go shopping if you like.'

'I don't want to do anything,' Annabelle said, turning over. 'I just want everyone to leave me alone.'

Understanding that the reality of what had happened to her, combined with what she was facing in the months ahead, was finally coming home to roost, Sabrina stroked her hair as she said, 'Remember, you don't actually have to go into the courtroom when the time comes. If you don't want to see him, and I'm sure you don't, you can give your testimony by video link.'

'Will you just *shut up*,' Annabelle seethed into her pillow. 'You're as bad as everyone else. I told you I don't want to talk about it and you just go on and on and on. It's not you who was raped. And it's not you people are calling a liar.'

Sabrina frowned. 'Who's saying that?' she asked.

'It doesn't matter.'

'Yes it does. I suppose it's Nathan's friends?'

'Yeah, and some of mine as well. They think I'm making it up because he . . . because he didn't fancy me, but if that's true then how did I get the bruises? And how did his, you know, stuff end up inside me? It can't get there on its own, can it?'

'No, of course not, but you don't have to justify yourself to them. They'll eat their words when he's sent to prison, and by then you'll have found out who your real friends are.'

Annabelle rolled over and looked up at her. 'I don't think I've got any,' she said tearfully. 'Everyone's turning against me. They're all on his side and it's not fair.'

'I'm sure you're exaggerating,' Sabrina told her gently, 'because Georgie keeps calling to find out how you are. Catrina too. They're really worried about you . . .'

'Yeah, but they don't come over, do they, because their mothers won't let them.'

Sabrina's expression froze. 'What do you mean, their mothers won't let them?' she demanded.

'What I said. Oh God, don't start going off on one. I couldn't care less, OK? They can all drop dead as far as I'm concerned.'

'Would you like me to speak to their mothers?' Sabrina offered, incensed to think that anyone would spurn her child, as though she were in some way to blame for what had been done to her.

'*No!* Don't you dare speak to anyone. I'd rather be on my own anyway.'

Not ready to give up yet, Sabrina said, 'Isn't there someone else you can invite? You have so many friends, and it would show Georgie and Catrina's mothers that not everyone is as stupidly misguided as they are. Do they think being the victim of rape is catching, or something?'

'Will you just leave it?' Annabelle growled angrily. 'I told you, I couldn't care less about them.'

'Maybe not, but I find it utterly unacceptable . . .'

'This isn't about *you*.'

'No, of course not, but I'm thinking of you, and how nice it would be for you to have some company tonight while Robert and I go to the Willoughbys.'

Annabelle looked up at her, a mix of resentment and pleading filling her eyes. 'Do you have to go out?' she asked, her tone suggesting she already knew the answer.

Sabrina sighed gently. 'Darling, you know I'd stay with you if I could, but Helen Willoughby's gone to a lot of trouble to . . .'

Annabelle turned over. 'It doesn't matter,' she said into her pillow.

Sabrina sat looking at the back of her head, feeling exasperated and guilty and horribly torn. 'It's too short notice to let them down now,' she said. She wouldn't remind her that one of the minor royals whose book club she was hoping to join was going to be at the dinner, because she didn't imagine it would go down too well right now.

'You'd have to if you were sick,' Annabelle pointed out.

'But I'm not.'

'You could always pretend.'

'That would be dishonest, and as we're already having an issue with that particular . . .'

'Oh fuck off,' Annabelle snarled. 'I don't know why you're acting like you care when we both know you don't. No, don't touch me. Just go. I don't want you in here any more.'

'I'm not leaving you like this,' Sabrina argued. 'You're not being reasonable, and it's just plain silly to suggest I don't care when you know very well that no one means more to me than you.'

Annabelle spun over on to her back. 'You're such a liar!' she cried. 'The only person who matters to you is *you*. And what about all those times you pretended to be ill after Craig packed you up? You didn't mind about letting everyone down then, did you? You just lay in bed all day . . .'

'What are you talking about?' Sabrina cut in, aghast. She'd had no idea that Annabelle knew about Craig, and for it to be coming out like this now . . .

'As soon as I knew about your affair,' Annabelle spat, 'all sorts of things started falling into place, like the rows you and Robert used to have, the way you wouldn't eat and kept moping about the place, crying and saying you'd rather be dead. Did you ever stop to think how that made me feel? You told me nothing mattered any more and there was nothing to live for. So that's how much I matter to you. I'm not even worth living for. Everyone kept saying you were in a depression, but really you were all screwed up over him, so don't you dare try saying you're not a liar, because I know you are.'

'Annabelle, listen . . .'

'No!' Annabelle raged. 'Let go of me, I'm not interested in anything you have to say,' and tearing herself free she leapt up from the bed and ran into the bathroom, locking the door behind her.

Dizzied by shock and guilt Sabrina continued to sit where she was, not sure what to do next. She couldn't just walk away, but nor, unprepared as she was, could she explain anything to Annabelle. In any case, Annabelle was in no mood to listen. She turned round as Robert came into the room and her heart contracted.

'Did . . . Did you hear any of that?' she stammered.

'Enough,' he answered.

She pressed her hands to her cheeks.

'Come on,' he said, 'leave her for now. I'll try to have a chat with her later.'

Lifting her head to look at him, she felt her emotions swelling and roiling inside her. He'd always had a way with Annabelle, so yes, it was best to leave it to him. 'I don't deserve you,' she said, going to him.

'No,' he answered, turning from her kiss, 'I don't think you do.'

She looked at him uncertainly, but he only stood aside for her to pass, and once she was out on the landing he closed Annabelle's door and started back down the stairs.

'Robert,' she said.

'Not now,' he replied.

She watched him until he'd disappeared from view, feeling disoriented and afraid and angry with herself for not knowing what to do. Everything was going horribly wrong. Her life seemed to have so many cracks running through it that it might disintegrate at any moment. Somehow she had to hold it together. She needed Robert to understand that none of this was her fault. She hadn't made that boy attack Annabelle, nor had she meant any of the things she'd said to Annabelle after her break-up with Craig. She hadn't been in her right mind then. Robert knew that, so surely he couldn't blame her for what was happening now.

Once alone in her own room she began pacing up and down, trying to think what to do about Annabelle, but it was as though Annabelle's accusations had opened a floodgate, because her mind, her heart, her whole body was filling up with Craig and how much they'd meant to one another. To those on the outside the way she'd gone to pieces at the end of their affair might have seemed too dramatic, an overreaction, even a monstrous self-indulgence, but if they'd understood how intense it was, how desperate they'd always been to see one another, how they'd never been able to get enough of one another and then to be torn apart the way they were . . .

'Sabrina, it's me,' he said quietly. 'I have to see you.'

'Of course,' she murmured. Two weeks had gone by since Alicia had found them together, and a week since he'd told her it was over, but the only good it had done was to make their mutual need burn hotter than ever. 'When?'

'Tonight. I won't be able to stay long. Can you meet me at the motorway service station?'

'The same one we met at before?'

'Yes. It's driving me crazy not seeing you.'

'It's the same for me. I think about you every minute of the day and night. When Robert touches me I have to pretend it's you. It's the only way I can bear it.'

'Don't tell me about him. I want you all to myself.'

'That's how I want you. We should be together, always.'

'Yes.'

'We can make it happen.'

There was a pause. 'Be there tonight,' he said softly. 'Don't wear anything under your coat.'

Their reunion that night had been fiercer and more tender than ever before. Passing cars had filled theirs with light, illuminating the insatiable demands they made on each other. She hadn't cared who saw them, she wanted the world to bear witness to how wildly and passionately she loved him.

They'd gone on meeting after that night,

knowing it was pointless trying to stay apart. But then Alicia had started snooping around Craig's mobile phone and credit-card statements, and it hadn't taken her long to come up with the truth.

When he'd called to tell her for the second time that it was over she'd begged him to see her, but he wouldn't. He'd known what would happen if he did, they'd never be able to let each other go, and because he couldn't risk it, he made himself say goodbye on the phone. She'd felt certain he wouldn't be able to go through with it, that like the last time he'd soon be on the phone to her again, but as the days passed and he hadn't rung or texted, or taken any of her calls, the awful truth of how impossible it was going to be to continue without him had started to dawn.

Somehow Annabelle must be made to understand that what had happened during those terrible dark months after Alicia had stolen Craig back had been a desperate, agonised fight for survival. Without Craig her life had lost all direction and meaning, nothing seemed worthwhile, all that mattered was getting back what was rightfully hers. Which wasn't to say Annabelle hadn't mattered too, it was simply that, at the time, Sabrina had been incapable of showing it.

'Mum!' Darcie yelled, waving from an open window as the train pulled into Castle Cary station. 'I'm here.'

Laughing as the door was flung open and Darcie leapt on to the platform, Alicia ran to scoop her into her arms. 'Hello darling,' she cried, squeezing her tight, then holding her back to get a good look at her. 'Wow, what a tan,' she declared, cupping Darcie's lively young face between her hands, 'and your hair's so blonde,' she added, bouncing the wayward clusters of silky white curls. 'You look gorgeous.'

'I do my best,' Darcie chirped. 'Where's Nat?'

'He's in Bristol for a few days.'

'What? You mean he's not here to greet me? That really sucks. Wait till I see him, I'll really . . . Oh my God, quick, we have to get my luggage.'

Verity's father was already hefting a large suitcase and a flower-power holdall down to them, while Verity struggled to burst past for a final hug.

Minutes later the doors were slammed shut, and as the train started to chug out of the station Alicia and Darcie stood, arm in arm, waving Verity and her family goodbye.

'No tears?' Alicia asked, glancing down at Darcie.

'No, I'm cool. We did all that last night.'

Alicia smiled, and feeling profoundly thankful that the monstrosity of a suitcase had four wheels of its own so that they didn't have to try to carry it up the stairs and over the footbridge, she began steering it along the platform towards the exit. 'So you had a good time?' she said, as Darcie gamely shouldered the holdall.

'Fantastic. I mean, there were the odd blips, you know, when I felt homesick, or Verity got on my nerves, but on the whole it was the best.' She turned her pretty face up to her mother. 'I really missed you, if that's what you want to know, so I hope you missed me too.'

'Oh, I think I managed to once in a while,' Alicia teased.

Darcie laughed and nudged her. Then her face fell as Alicia stopped next to the old Renault. 'I'd forgotten we had that now,' she said dismally. 'Don't you feel embarrassed being seen in it?'

'No, and if you do, you can always walk,' Alicia told her, not liking her snobbery.

Darcie slanted her a look, and as her smile made a mischievous return she grabbed her mother in a bruising embrace. 'I am so glad you're my mum,' she said, as Alicia opened the boot, 'you should hear the way Verity's goes on and on. If you were like that I'd leave home.'

'If I was like that I probably would too,' Alicia quipped.

Laughing delightedly, Darcie dumped her holdall, helped crane the suitcase in after it, then skipped round to the driver's side. 'Oops, got to get used to being back,' she chuckled, realising her mistake. 'Actually, this car's not so bad really, is it? It'll probably be great for when you take your stuff to the foundry. Have you done any work since you've been here? How's the studio coming on? Is the shop open yet? You have to tell me everything. I'm so out of touch.'

Waiting for her to buckle up on the passenger side, Alicia started the engine and at the end of the parking area turned right towards home. 'Rachel's invited us over this evening,' she said. 'Una's dying to see you.'

'Oh, fab, because I'm dying to see her too, and little Todd, he's so cute, but I'm still really ticked about Nat. Fancy him not being here for my homecoming. He said he would, and I haven't even spoken to him since Monday. Why did he have to go up to Bristol?'

'He's helping Jolyon prepare some cases. It's good experience and I think the change of scenery is doing him good.'

'But he's hardly been here three weeks. Is it really that bad?'

Rolling her eyes, Alicia said, 'It's not bad at all. You'll like it once you get used to it.' How easily the words were tripping off her tongue, while the dread of reality was lurking in the background, ready to swoop like an avenging ghoul.

'I don't suppose I've got any choice, have I. Still, at least I'll have all my own stuff around me. Is my computer set up yet?'

'Nat did it last week. And your TV, and the DVD.'

'He's the best. I'm really glad he didn't go to Italy with Summer. We should all be together now, shouldn't we?'

Smiling at how conveniently she'd glossed over her month in France, Alicia said, 'We should, and there's still plenty to do around the house and in the shop if we're all going to pull together.'

'No problem. I'm definitely up for that. It's never going to be the same without Dad,' she said, suddenly glum, 'but I still want him to be proud of us, you know, just in case he's looking down, and I really think he is, don't you?'

'I'm sure of it,' Alicia said, partly because it was what Darcie wanted to hear, and partly because she wanted to believe it too. 'I need to call into the village shop on the way through to pick up some milk and a card for Todd's birthday tomorrow. Would you like to choose it?'

'Sure, why not? Have you got him a present?'

'Yes, it's all wrapped ready to take with us tonight.'

Twenty minutes later, still listening to Darcie chattering on about her French adventure, Alicia pulled up outside Mrs Neeve's shop and kept her fingers crossed, as she always did in the high street now, that she wouldn't run into Sabrina – or any of the neighbours whose loyalty had been bought, at least to her mind, by one of Sabrina's charitable acts.

'Hello,' she said, walking in to find Mrs Neeve behind the counter, as usual, and another neighbour, Sally Hopkins, leaning against the customer side. As both women looked round Alicia felt her smile starting to fade. Neither one of them was attempting to say hello back.

'Uh, I'll help myself to some milk,' Alicia said, pointing to the fridge. 'Darcie's looking for a birthday card. She's just come back from France, haven't you darling?'

'There's no more milk,' Mrs Neeve said as Alicia started to open the fridge.

'But it's right . . .' Realising what was happening, Alicia let go of the door, and putting an arm round Darcie she steered her back on to the street.

'What was all that about?' Darcie said in a loud whisper. 'There was loads of milk, you could see it.'

'I know.'

'So why didn't you say something?'

Not sure whether she was more offended by the two women inside, or relieved to have had it pointed out so soon that Darcie needed to be told what was happening before hearing it from someone else, Alicia said, 'Come on, get in the car, I'll take you home.'

She waited until Darcie had been upstairs to inspect her room, and check her email, then sitting her down at the kitchen table with a glass of juice and some biscuits she said, 'There's something I have to tell you, darling, which isn't . . .' As Darcie's face drained she broke off quickly, realising her mistake. She'd sounded too gloomy, making Darcie think the worst.

'It's Nat, isn't it?' Darcie said, rising to her feet. 'Oh my God . . .'

'Ssh, no, I promise, Nat's fine,' Alicia insisted. 'We can speak to him on the phone if you like and he'll tell you himself.'

'So what is it?' Darcie said, looking horribly anxious and close to tears.

'Sit down again,' Alicia said, pulling out a chair for herself. 'It does concern Nat, but not in the way you're thinking.'

With wide eyes fixed on her mother, Darcie sank back down again.

'Something happened at the rave last Saturday,' Alicia continued, feeling slightly stunned that it was only a week ago, when it felt like a lifetime. 'I'm not sure what exactly, but I do know that things got out of hand and Annabelle ended up accusing Nat . . . Well, she's accused him of raping her.'

Darcie's jaw dropped.

'Of course it isn't true,' Alicia went on hurriedly, 'but the police have become involved and now they're intending to prosecute Nat for something he didn't do.'

Darcie began shaking her head vehemently. 'No, they can't,' she declared hotly. 'He'd never do anything like that. They've got it wrong. You have to stop them, Mum. If Dad was here, he would . . .'

'Oliver and Jolyon are taking care of it,' Alicia told her, grabbing her hands. 'It's partly why Nat's with Jolyon now . . .'

'But she's *lying*,' Darcie cried. 'Why are they listening to her? Can't Uncle Robert make her stop?'

'I'm sure he's trying, but . . .'

'I'm going round there,' Darcie said, shooting to her feet. 'I'm going to . . .'

'No, darling,' Alicia said, pulling her into her arms. 'You can't go over there, none of us can.'

'But you have to do something,' Darcie insisted. 'You can't just let her get away with it.'

'For the moment there's nothing we can do,' Alicia explained, 'apart from put our trust in Oliver and Jolyon. If we go near Annabelle, or her mother, we'll make it worse for Nat, and that's not what we want, is it?'

'No, but . . .' Her eyes suddenly widened. 'Oh my God, that's what was going on in the shop, isn't it? Mrs Neeve wouldn't let you have any milk because she thinks Nat did it. You have to tell her she's wrong, Mum. Nat would never hurt anyone and she's got no right to make judgements like that. The law says he's innocent till proved guilty, so she should mind her own business.'

'Maybe, but people always have opinions, we can't stop that, and . . . Oh darling, don't cry. It'll be all right,' Alicia soothed, holding her close.

'We didn't want to come here in the first place,' Darcie wept, 'and now they're doing this to Nat . . . It's not fair, Mum.' She turned her face up to Alicia's. 'Can't we go back to London? Please. They won't be able to get to him there.'

'Ssh,' Alicia murmured, pressing a kiss to her forehead, and stroking her hair.

'Annabelle is such a cow,' Darcie said fiercely. 'She won't get away with it. She won't. And shall I tell you why? Because *I* won't let her.'

As Annabelle wandered into the kitchen, wearing a sleeveless blouse over a long, pale blue pareo, her eyes were bloodshot and tired and her face was blotched with uneven patches of red. 'Where's Mum going?' she asked Robert, as Sabrina's car left the drive.

'To pick up Bethany Cottle,' he answered, engrossed in the paperwork spread out on the table in front of him.

'What for?' Annabelle protested. 'I don't hang out with *her*, and anyway, I already said I'd rather be on my own tonight.'

Robert gestured towards the phone. 'You can always call and tell her to come back,' he said, turning over a page.

Ignoring the suggestion, Annabelle padded to the fridge and took out a large block of Cheddar cheese. After cutting a thick slice, she glanced at him sideways. 'Fancy a toasted sandwich?' she asked, her tone daring him to say yes.

'No thanks,' he replied, hiding his surprise, since she rarely waited on anyone but herself these days.

After finding a bap, she cut it in half, put the cheese in the middle, and jammed the whole thing into the toaster.

'That's not how to do it,' Robert said mildly.

'I know.'

He made a few notes on a page, then turned to another. 'Like some help?' he offered.

'It's OK, I can do it.' A moment later she popped the sandwich out of the toaster and stuffed it into the panini grill.

'What are you doing?' she asked, glancing up from the study of her nails.

'I'm one of the judges for a young scientist award,' he answered, 'so I'm having a look through some of the entries.'

'Mm,' she grunted. Then, 'Are they any good?'

'Some, yes.'

With a sigh, she wandered over to the window and stood staring out at the garden.

To Robert's mind she seemed tense and angry, or perhaps she was nervous, he couldn't quite tell. Then suddenly she said, 'Why didn't you leave her?'

Knowing exactly what she meant, but continuing to appear partially engrossed in his papers, he said, 'It wasn't as simple as that.'

Her back was still turned. 'Why not? Oh, you mean this is your house, so you'd have had to throw her out. So why didn't you? I know I would if I was in your shoes.'

'It didn't have anything to do with whose house

it was,' he answered, 'it was about your mother and me, and the bond we share in spite of everything.'

After digesting that, Annabelle turned round and leaned against the counter top. 'Didn't it bother you that she was all cut up over another man?' she asked testily.

'Of course it did.'

'So I don't understand why you didn't just tell her to go.'

Deciding to put his pen down now, he sat back in his chair and regarded her steadily. Though she was trying to make this all about her mother, he knew it was really about her, and how she'd dealt with the last two years. 'What your mother felt for Craig,' he said, wanting to be as open and honest with her as he could, in spite of how much it was hurting him, 'was like an obsession. It consumed her, so she could hardly think about anything else. There isn't really a way to explain how, or why, these things happen, they just do. You can call it a grand passion, a great love, a whirlwind romance, whatever you like, but while it's happening those who are involved can't see anything else. It's as though there *isn't* anything else. When your mother's affair with Craig ended it was more than she could bear. For a long time she really wasn't in her right mind, so all the times she ignored you, or pushed you away, or said things to hurt you, none of it was meant. She couldn't help the way she was, she was suffering a kind of illness that needed time to heal.'

'I think she was just being selfish and seriously

up herself and couldn't care less about anyone else,' Annabelle declared tartly.

'Love is very selfish,' he agreed, 'which is partly why I didn't ask her to leave. I was being selfish too, because I wouldn't only have lost her, which I really didn't want to happen, I'd have lost you too and for me that wasn't an option. I know I'm not your real father, but I think of you as my daughter, and before . . . Well, before things started going wrong, I don't know if you remember, but you used to call me Dad from time to time. I liked that. It made me feel very proud indeed to think of you as mine.'

Annabelle's face tightened to hide the confusion she was feeling. 'I still think you should have thrown her out,' she said belligerently. 'She doesn't deserve someone like you.'

He smiled.

'I mean it,' she insisted. 'She doesn't care about anyone else. She's only ever interested in herself.'

'She cares a great deal about you.'

Her lip curled. 'Yeah, it really shows,' she sneered sarcastically. 'It wouldn't bother her if I walked out of that door right now and never came back.'

'Actually, it would bother her a lot. It would bother me too, so I hope you're not thinking about doing it.'

She turned her head impatiently to one side.

When she seemed to have no more to say, he said, very gently, 'Can I give you a small piece of advice?'

She immediately stiffened.

'The panini grill works better when you turn it on,' he told her.

Her eyes darted to it, and determined not to laugh, she said sharply, 'I'm not hungry now, anyway,' and with a toss of her hair she flounced off back to her room.

'Nat, darling, it's Mum. Are you OK?'

'Yeah, I'm cool. What about you? Is Darcie back?'

'She's right here, but I wanted to have a quick word first. Summer's called a couple of times asking for your number and I can't keep stalling her. What do you want me to do?'

Nat was standing in front of the huge picture window of Jolyon and Marianne's apartment, gazing out at a spectacular view of the Clifton suspension bridge and Leigh Woods beyond. Way down at the bottom of the gorge, so far he could hardly see it, was the thin, sludgy meander of the River Avon, where all the suicides ended up when they jumped from Brunel's masterpiece. 'I guess you'd better give it to her,' he said, his eyes barely focused on anything.

'OK, if you're sure. Is everything all right with Jolyon and Marianne?'

'Yeah. They're out doing some shopping. We're going to the Colston Hall tonight to see Billy Bragg.'

'Really? You'll enjoy that.'

'I expect so. Shall I speak to Darcie now? You haven't told her anything, have you?'

'I had to,' Alicia replied. 'I didn't want her finding out from anyone else.'

A pale line showed around his mouth as he said, 'OK. Put her on then.'

A moment later Darcie's bossy voice came down the line. 'Nat, I don't want you to worry about anything,' she told him. 'I'm not going to let her get away with this. I'm going to talk to her . . .'

'Darce, stop,' he interrupted. 'You mustn't get involved. It's too complicated and there's too much at stake, so please, promise me you won't try to interfere.'

'But someone has to. I know Jolyon and Oliver are doing everything they can, but I think someone has to talk to Annabelle.'

'Maybe, but it can't be you. We're not allowed to go near her, and if you try you might end up making things worse. So stay away from her, Darce, OK? Just take care of Mum and make sure she doesn't get too down. Now, tell me what you're planning to do for the next few days.'

'I don't really have any plans yet,' she answered, sounding less sure of herself now. 'I thought you were going to be here and we'd help Mum with the shop and stuff.'

'She still needs help, and it'll be good for her to have something to distract her. I've been trying to talk her into using Grandpa's old surgery as a studio until she can use the one at the shop, so offer to help set it up.'

'I really wish you were going to be here,' Darcie wailed.

'I'll probably come back on Wednesday, after the hearing,' he told her. 'I just can't go within a hundred yards of Uncle Robert's house.'

'Who'd want to with her there?' she snapped. 'Anyway, what hearing?'

'I have to go to court on Wednesday. It's no big

deal, just a referral kind of thing, so I don't want you to come, OK? And try to get Mum to stay away too, it'll only upset her.'

'What does a referral mean?'

'It's where they set dates for the next hearings and for when everyone has to serve papers, all boring stuff, so nothing to get excited about.' He turned around at the sound of the front door opening. 'Jolyon's back now,' he said, 'so I should go. Can I have a quick word with Mum first?'

A moment later Alicia was saying, 'Hi darling. Everything OK?'

'Stop asking me that,' he suddenly snapped. 'No, it's not OK, but right now there's not a whole lot I can do about it.'

'I'm sorry,' she said, 'force of habit.'

He was sorry too, and feeling guilty for biting her head off, and angry for being in this stupid position. 'Just make sure Darcie doesn't try to take matters into her hands,' he said. 'I want to come home on Wednesday, but I won't be able to if she goes over there trying to talk to Annabelle.'

'Don't worry, I'll make sure she understands how important it is that she doesn't.'

After passing the phone to Marianne so she could have a chat with his mother, Nat went to help Jolyon bring in the shopping. It was good being here, not having to deal with his mother worrying and fussing, but at the same time he hated being away from her. It was his duty to try to take care of her, and to be strong for her, especially now he knew what his father had put her through . . . Every time he thought of that a surge of rage caught in his heart. His father was a hypocrite, a liar, an adulterer. He wasn't the man Nat had always believed him to be, so who was he? He was tempted to ask Jolyon, but couldn't bring himself to mention it. He only wanted to protect his mother so that no one could hurt her like that again. Yet every minute of the day was a living hell for her now, as she worried about what was going to happen to him.

He was scared out of his mind too, not only of being found guilty of rape, but of what he'd decided to do if he was.

Chapter Nineteen

It was Tuesday evening and Alicia was in the playroom-cum-study with Darcie, sorting through old toys and games to pass on to charity, when the phone started to ring. Being the closest, Darcie dragged the handset across the floor towards her and clicked on.

'Hello,' she said, lifting a foot for her mother to tug free the bin bag trapped under it.

'Hello,' a man said at the other end. 'I know that's not Alicia, so would it be Darcie, by any chance?'

'Yes, it is,' she replied, frowning as she tried to recognise the voice, until her suspicions kicked in and a troubled light flickered in her eyes. Was this the man Nat had warned her about? 'Do you want to speak to Mum?' she said cagily.

'I'd love to, thank you. Please tell her it's Cameron Mitchell.'

She stiffened. Yes, it was him, and Nat didn't approve, so neither did she. 'I'll see if she's here,' she said frostily, and covering the mouthpiece with one hand, she whispered to her mother, 'You don't want to talk to anyone tonight, do you?'

Alicia blinked. 'Depends who it is,' she responded.

'It's no one. Don't worry, I'll tell him you'll ring back another time.'

'Hang on, hang on,' Alicia said quickly. 'Who is it?'

Darcie slumped her shoulders. 'Someone called something Mitchell,' she said wearily.

Getting to her feet, Alicia took the phone and carried it out to the kitchen. 'Hi,' she said, tucking the receiver under her chin as she filled the kettle. 'Are you back in Somerset?'

'I am,' he confirmed. 'We arrived a couple of hours ago so Jasper's having a bit of a lie-down after the long drive, and I'm having a drink – not from his bowl, I hasten to add. I was calling to wish you and Nat luck for tomorrow, and to see if there's anything I can do, like drive you there, or pick you up, or anything at all. You just have to say the word.'

'That's so kind of you,' she responded warmly, realising that part of her would actually like to take him up on his offer to play chauffeur. However, being in little doubt of how her children would react if she did, she simply said, 'Everything's already arranged, thank you.'

'Well, you know where I am. How's Nat feeling about it all?'

'He won't discuss it much, but I can tell he's as nervous as heck, even though it's only a formality. He doesn't want us to go to the court, but I think he might regret that when the time comes, so we're going anyway, and if he's upset we'll wait outside.'

'So Darcie's going with you?'

'I'm afraid there's no talking her out of it.'

Sounding both empathetic and amused, he said,

'Having had some experience of girls her age, I know sometimes it's easier simply to give in than to carry on the fight. The hearing's at Wells, isn't it? I hadn't realised the court there was still active.'

'Apparently it only sits once a month, so we're quite lucky to get in – if you can call it luck. Otherwise we'd probably have had to go to Bristol or Bath. Anyway, the important thing is, he's coming home with us after. I've really missed him these last few days, though it's wonderful having Darcie back. She really livens the place up, and needless to say, she's dying to see him.'

'I'm sure.' Then, with a sympathetic sigh, 'Let's hope your husband's friends can put an end to this soon, so the three of you can get on with your lives.'

'Hear, hear to that. Anyway, I guess I should be sorting something out for dinner. Thank you for calling. I really appreciate it.'

'No problem. I didn't want you to think I'd forgotten. I also wanted to tell you about an idea I've had concerning your shop, but now's not the time, so I'll wish you bon appétit and perhaps we'll speak sometime tomorrow.'

After ringing off Alicia replaced the phone on its base, and pulled open the fridge door to start seeking some inspiration for dinner. Though she was touched by Cameron's thoughtfulness, and intrigued to know what his idea might be about the shop, her thoughts were soon swamped by the ordeal Nat was facing the following day, and how desperately worried she was about him and how the next few weeks were going to unfold.

* * *

'But you can't,' Sabrina cried aghast. 'You're Annabelle's stepfather. How's it going to look if you turn up in support of her attacker?'

'Her attacker, as you like to put it,' Robert responded evenly, 'is also my nephew, but the support is intended for my sister.'

'And who's going to know that? Or will you wear a badge?'

Ignoring the sarcasm, he said, 'I'm simply going to offer to drive her there and back. I don't intend to go into the court.'

'But she's got a car. She can drive herself. No, Robert, I'm sorry. I won't let you do this. Annabelle's in a very vulnerable state at the moment, she needs to know she can count on us, and if she finds out you're taking her violator's mother to the court she's going to think the same as everyone else, that you don't believe her. I take it that isn't the case.'

Not wanting to be drawn on that, since he barely knew what to think from one day to the next, he said, 'A jury will decide who's telling the truth, if it gets that far.'

Sabrina's eyes widened. 'And what's that supposed to mean?' she demanded angrily.

'It means that the defence lawyers will do everything they can to get the case thrown out, and for all we know they might succeed.'

'Over my dead body.'

Rather than pursue the fatuousness of that, he said, 'Did you see the message from Joanne Willoughby? It seems you're being invited to join the *royal* book club.'

Her pleasure at being accepted was spiked with annoyance at the deliberate barb.

'So it was worth going on Saturday night,' he added.

'Apparently so,' she retorted, 'but you think I should have stayed here with Annabelle.'

'As a matter of fact, I do.'

'She had Bethany to keep her company, so it's not as though she was on her own.'

'She could have done with you being here.' Speaking over her as she started to protest, he said, 'You don't, or shouldn't, need me to point out that she's going through an extremely difficult time at the moment, added to which she needs to understand what's gone wrong between you two. I know you're trying to avoid it, but only you can tell her.'

Sabrina looked astounded. 'Just because you took ten minutes out of your busy schedule to have a chat with her on Saturday night doesn't give you the right to accuse me of avoiding or neglecting her. I've been there for her through every step of this, and I will continue to be until justice is done, which is a damned sight more than I can say for you, signing up for your sister's pathetic little entourage at the first opportunity.'

'In those ten minutes I managed to learn quite a lot about what's going on inside her,' he replied smoothly. 'Not that I hadn't suspected it before, but it was interesting to hear it from her.'

'OK, parent of the year, what did you learn that you think I don't already know?'

'Actually, I think you do, you just don't want to face up to what you put her through after your affair came to an end. I know, better than anyone, how hard it was to cope with you when you were trying to get over it, the way you screamed and ranted, begged me to take you to him, threatening to kill yourself, and hardly letting anyone near you. Annabelle was in the house too, remember, so to try telling yourself that it went over her head, or that she's somehow magically forgotten it by now, would be self-deception of stupefying levels. She was no doubt scared witless when it was happening, had either of us bothered to notice, so I'm blaming myself for this too. I was so caught up in what it was doing to me, how rejected, and worried, and useless I was feeling, that I couldn't see anything clearly. And there she was, as vulnerable and impressionable as any girl her age could be, and faced with your theatrics and rejection it's hardly any wonder she started to seek attention elsewhere. So whether you like it or not, you and I have to take our share of the responsibility for how she's ended up in the mess she's in now.

'Now, I don't wish to discuss this any more tonight. I'm going to sleep in the guest room to give you some time to think about what I've said, and to contemplate your relationship with your daughter. And before you ask again, I won't be offering Alicia a lift. I can see it would send out the wrong message, and though I don't give a damn about anyone else, I most certainly do about Annabelle,' and leaving her staring after him, her face pinched with shock, he walked out of the room and closed the door.

The following morning Alicia and Darcie set off early, wanting to make sure they arrived at the court in plenty of time. They were both dressed in sombre colours with their hair tied up, as though any flash of colour or perky curl might show some disrespect for the proceedings.

As they drove out of the village Darcie began jabbing at the radio, flitting through stations, as unable to make a choice as she was to sit still. Alicia stared straight ahead, not wanting any eye contact with her neighbours this morning, even those whose good wishes were going with them.

Thanks to a brief call from Marianne earlier, she knew that Nat and Jolyon were already on their way, and she'd felt buoyed by Marianne's assurance that she was doing the right thing in ignoring Nat's instructions to stay away.

'Jolyon thinks he's trying to shoulder everything himself, when really, like the rest of us in times of trouble, he's very much in need of his mum,' Marianne had told her.

Wanting nothing more than to support him in any way she could, while feeling that she could shake him senseless for having been so stupid as to have sex with a girl who was so volatile and vulnerable, thanks to her nightmare of a mother, and, worst of all, underage, Alicia put her foot down as they wound erratically through the country lanes. However, on reaching the main road she eased off again, knowing that the highway was littered with cameras all primed to go off the instant she pushed past the limit.

A little over half an hour later they were driving into the cobbled market square at the heart of Wells, where the town hall presided in all its pomp and stateliness over the olde English quaintness around it. It was a large eighteenth-century building with noble Romanesque pillars flanking its portico, tall arched windows and a yellowy limestone facade that was colourfully decorated by hanging baskets of flowers and an array of giant flagpoles soaring majestically over those who came and went.

The court was inside, to the right of the main lobby, with a small waiting area adjacent to the main door, where Alicia and Darcie sat down quietly, able to hear voices echoing through other parts of the building, though no one was actually in sight. Then they heard footsteps crossing the flagstones towards them, and Alicia's heart flooded with love and anxiety as Nat and Jolyon appeared in the waiting-room doorway. Even though Nat held back from hugging her, he didn't utter a word of rebuke about her being there, but there was no time, anyway, because Darcie flew straight into his arms to hug him with all her might.

'Hey, squirrel,' he said, hugging her back.

'Hey, yourself,' she said. She drew back to look at him and her face started to crumple. 'Everything's going to be all right,' she told him through her tears. 'I just know it is. I have this feeling, and you know when I get them I'm always right.'

His eyes were shining as he looked down at her. 'I thought it was me who was always right,' he teased.

'No, never,' she assured him. 'It's definitely me.'

Handing her the victory, he said, 'That's quite a tan you've got there.'

She glanced down at her arms. 'It's fading already,' she complained. Then, dismissing it, she looked up at him again. 'You're coming home after, aren't you?'

He nodded. 'Unless they lock me up straight away.'

'Don't even joke about things like that,' Alicia chided, as she and Jolyon embraced. 'Thanks for letting him stay,' she murmured. 'I'm sure it did him good.'

'It's been a pleasure having him,' Jolyon told her, 'apart from the awkward little moment when we were kicking a football around the Downs yesterday and he lobbed it into the windscreen of a passing police car.'

'Obviously something in me can't stay away from them,' Nat quipped.

Chuckling, Jolyon gave him a brief pat on the shoulder, and glanced at his watch. 'Almost time,' he said. Then, seeing Alicia's face, 'It's all going to be very informal, so don't worry,' he told her. 'No stodgy judges or standing up in the dock. This is purely a process that has to be gone through. Now, I'll find out what's going on, so you wait here, and don't run away.'

Fifteen minutes later they were entering the claustrophobic little courtroom where the air of its chequered history assailed them, seeming to seep up from the shadowy cells below, and clamber like cobwebs over the dark wood panelling. The windows were tall and frosted, allowing views to nowhere, the smell was stale and dusty, and the lawyers' benches were cramped so tightly together that there was barely room for Jolyon to squeeze in alongside prosecuting counsel.

As Alicia, Nat and Darcie made their way into

the row of seats Jolyon directed them to, Alicia felt a strange sense of dissociation trying to pull her from reality. It was as though they'd lost their bearings on a journey that should have had no stops, and were now being swept along the wrong tracks. There was no way to change course, no chance of turning back. It shouldn't be happening. Her son wasn't meant to be in court like this, he should be here as a lawyer, not the accused. Something was going horribly wrong and she needed to find a way to make it right.

Feeling Darcie's hand slip into hers, she struggled past the panic rising inside her and tried to force herself to get a grip.

The lawyers in their dark suits stood as the Youth Panel began filing in, coming to perch like jackdaws on the high bench over the court. To her, they were hanging judges with only one outcome in mind, whereas in reality they were three very ordinary-looking middle-aged people, two men and a woman, who undoubtedly had families and issues of their own tucked away behind their implacable facades.

Nat was asked to stand and feeling him rise beside her, Alicia forced herself not to reach for his hand. After he'd confirmed his name the charge was read out, and Alicia felt sick. Had she known it would be so explicit she'd have put her foot down about Darcie coming here.

'. . . in that you did intentionally penetrate the vagina of Annabelle Preston aged fifteen, with your penis, when she did not consent, and not reasonably believing she was aged sixteen or over.'

Nat's face was taut and pale, his hands bunched

into iron tight fists. He wasn't expected to plead, so he remained silent.

'Thank you, Nathan,' the chairman said mildly, 'you can sit down.'

It didn't take long for the prosecuting lawyer to lay out the case, his words swooping around the old room like bats. Alicia, feeling Nat beside her, stiff and unmoving, found herself thinking about the wretched souls who'd appeared here before, the evil and oppressed, the terrified and the insane. There would be more stories attached to this place than could ever be told, more secrets hidden in its cracked wood panels and underground chambers than would ever be known. She felt as though they were impostors, or actors who'd stumbled on to the wrong stage. They were out of sync with a reality that was trudging on somewhere, regardless of them.

Jolyon rose to outline the current bail conditions and requested that the same terms be granted, with the exception of custody. Nat wanted to return to his home.

After consulting his colleagues, the chairman levelled a grave look Nat's way. 'Nathan, I hope you understand that if you breach your bail you'll be arrested and held in custody until the time of your trial,' he said.

Nat nodded.

After murmuring to his colleagues again, the chairman said, 'Then you can be released into the custody of your mother.'

Next came the setting of a date for the service of papers, which was to be in exactly four weeks, five days before Nat and Darcie were to start their new school. Then proceedings were ended by the chairman saying, 'Nathan, you are to report to the Youth Court in Taunton at eleven a.m. on Thursday the eleventh of September for your case to be committed to Crown Court. Do you understand?'

'Yes,' Nat answered huskily.

'Thank you, you may go.'

Outside on the market square uninterested shoppers were going about their chores, and a newly married couple were posing in front of the town hall for photographs to capture their special day. As Alicia waited for Nat to finish speaking to Jolyon she found herself watching the newlyweds and thinking of her own wedding, almost twenty years ago. She'd been happier that day than she ever had in her life, and only having Nat and Darcie had managed to eclipse that joy. She wondered, if she'd known then what she knew now, would she have married Craig, and the answer was immediately yes, because in spite of the affair she'd loved him with all her heart, and still did, and without him there would be no Nathan or Darcie, and without them, there would be no point to anything at all.

Turning to find out where they were, she felt a trip in her heart as she spotted them wandering, arm in arm, towards the gate of the Bishop's Palace. Nat seemed unaware of the way he was turning passing girls' heads, as did Darcie, who was apparently engrossed in whatever he was saying. Towering behind the medieval buildings they were heading towards was the magnificent cathedral, where, until recent years, they used to attend midnight mass every Christmas Eve. It was a tradition Craig had loved, even though he hadn't been particularly religious. It was a time for family, he used to say, and an opportunity to give thanks for how blessed they were to have one another.

'Are you OK?' Jolyon asked, coming to rest an arm on her shoulders.

'Mm,' she murmured, still watching Nat and Darcie. 'I was just thinking that no matter how well you think you know someone, or how much you trust them, you can never really be sure of what they might do.'

'Are we talking about Nat?' he asked in surprise.

'No, no,' she assured him. 'About Craig, actually.'

'Ah, yes,' he said regretfully.

In a sudden spurt of need, she said, 'What do you think drove him to have an affair? Was it me, because he didn't . . .'

Jolyon's hand closed tightly around hers. 'Put that thought out of your head now,' he urged. 'Whatever else might have gone on, Craig was devoted to you and the children, and don't ever doubt it.'

Feeling steadied by his assurance, and embarrassed by her outburst, she tried to smile as she returned her attention to Nat and Darcie. 'I wonder what those two are gassing about,' she said, trying to lighten the moment.

Following the direction of her eyes, Jolyon's lit with fondness to see the youngsters in such an earnest exchange.

At the other end of the square Darcie was saying, '. . . but I thought you were dead set against this Cameron bloke.'

'I am, I mean, I was,' Nat replied, 'but I've been

thinking about it. I know Dad's not been gone all that long, but there are things . . . Look, she's probably not interested in him anyway, so what I'm saying is, he can really help her as far as her art's concerned. Think about it, it would be great if she could make a go of the shop, wouldn't it? And we have to ask ourselves, is it fair to want her to be on her own just because we don't want anyone to replace Dad?'

Darcie looked appalled. 'But she doesn't want anyone to replace him either,' she protested.

'Not now, obviously, but later she might, and we have to think about when I've gone off to university and you're more interested in your friends than staying at home. She'll want some company then.'

Darcie stopped walking and when he turned to look at her, to his surprise her confusion had gone and she was grinning.

'What?' he asked.

'You said, when you go to university, which is only next year, so it means you think everything's going to be all right too.' She threw her arms around him in joy. 'I told you it would be,' she said, 'all you have to do is believe it.'

Sabrina gave a cluck of appreciation as she gazed out over the perfectly pampered gardens of Babington House. 'Isn't it wonderful having *The Buzz* meetings here instead of at the office?' she commented, watching a family of doves pecking about the lawn.

'Heaven,' June agreed, sipping an iced lemonade. 'Makes me feel quite decadent.'

Sabrina smiled, showing nothing of the angst she was feeling about Robert and his continuing coolness towards her. And about Annabelle and how far apart she and her daughter had drifted. She was constantly trying to think of ways to repair the damage, but it wasn't easy, and to her mind Robert was being far too hard on her anyway, trying to load her with guilt for behaving in a way she hadn't been able to control.

'Wasn't Nathan Carlyle due in court this morning?' June said, letting her head fall back to expose her face to the sun. 'I wonder how he got on.'

Sabrina shrugged. 'I've no idea,' she replied, 'but please don't mention it in front of Annabelle when she comes out, she's being very touchy about it all at the moment.'

June looked sympathetic. 'I expect she's worried, and nervous about the time when she'll have to go in front of the judge herself,' she said.

'She'll probably do it by video,' Sabrina informed her, wanting to get off the subject. 'It's not so traumatic that way.' After finishing her drink, she pulled a handful of files out of her Prada briefcase and set them down on the table. 'OK, let's take a look at what we have for the next issue,' she said, crisping up proceedings with a businesslike manner. 'I still haven't heard back from BT about the rural-phone-box issue, so I'll chase that up. I've been in touch with our useless MP to get his comments on the affordable-housing problem in the area. With any luck he'll be voted out next time, because the answer's definitely *not* to extend that ghastly estate on the outskirts of

Holly Wood, which he's currently proposing. Now, what else do we have here?' she went on, continuing to leaf through her files. 'This is all "what's on" stuff, oh yes, here are some notes I've made on starting a volunteer recruitment drive to spare time for the elderly. Perhaps you could take that over while I'm away.'

June looked up. 'Away? Oh yes, I'd forgotten you're going to France. When do you leave?'

'Next Monday. I can hardly wait. Ten days on the French Riviera. All those gorgeous yachts and fabulous beach restaurants.' She gave a shaky sigh of rapture. 'Have you fixed things up with your sister yet?' she remembered to ask.

June pulled a face. 'Actually, I was thinking I might just stay here,' she said bleakly.

Spotting Annabelle sauntering towards them, Sabrina affected her best motherly smile as she said, 'Ah, there you are, darling. How was your massage?'

Annabelle slumped into a chair and picked up Sabrina's glass. 'It was OK,' she answered. 'What's this?'

'Lemonade, but there's not much left, so let's get some more.'

After summoning a waiter and giving him their orders, Sabrina returned to her files, hoping to find something that might interest Annabelle.

'I expect she's been telling you all about her new book club, has she?' Annabelle said to June.

Sabrina's eyes darkened. 'I haven't been to a meeting yet,' she said, 'so there's nothing to tell.'

'Which book club is this?' June enquired, all interest.

'Robert calls it the *royal* book club,' Annabelle informed her, 'because someone eighty-fifth in line to the throne belongs.'

Sabrina rolled her eyes. 'Actually, she's married to someone who is *fourteenth* or fifteenth in line,' she told Annabelle, 'but that's not why I joined.'

'Pffft!' Annabelle snorted. 'You don't even read, so I can't think why else you signed up.'

'Please ignore her,' Sabrina said to June, 'she's clearly in one of her moods again.'

'So how did you manage to join this club?' June wanted to know.

Sabrina waved a dismissive hand. 'It came up when we were at the Willoughbys' having dinner the other night, so I said I would. You know how these things happen, you're on the spot, so you have to say yes, or it would seem rude.'

Annabelle was regarding her incredulously, but before she could say anything June was lamenting her fate.

'This is the trouble with being divorced,' she grumbled, 'I never get invited to anything any more.'

Sabrina was all compassion. 'It's very difficult when you're on your own,' she agreed. 'I have to admit, we were all couples on Saturday night, with not one unattached person to be seen. It's going to be just the same at the Bingleighs' in France, apart from madam here, of course.'

Annabelle's face told how much she was looking forward to it.

'You know, June,' Sabrina continued, 'Joanna Willoughby was talking about someone on Saturday who might be interesting for you to meet.'

Her eyes were narrowing as she tried to remember exactly what had been said. 'Apparently she'd invited him to join us,' she continued, 'but he couldn't make it. He's staying in the area, though, somewhere over Wyke way, and from what she was saying, he's going to be here right through the summer.'

June didn't bother to hide her interest. 'Do you know who he is? Did she tell you anything about him?' she demanded.

Now it was coming back to her, Sabrina's expression was lightening with eagerness. 'Actually, he's quite a catch,' she replied, 'and I think you'll probably have heard of him. Cameron Mitchell? The art critic.'

June pulled a face as she thought. 'The name does ring a bell,' she admitted, 'but art critic sounds decidedly gay to me, and having already been there with my ex . . .'

'Apparently his marriage broke up about a year ago,' Sabrina told her, 'and there was no mention of anyone else being on the scene, male or female. He's very presentable, from what I've seen of him on TV, but you know how diminished people can seem in the flesh, so perhaps we should make up our minds about that when we meet him.'

'Can you set it up?' June asked excitedly.

'I'll certainly try, but it'll have to wait till we're back, I'm afraid. There won't be time before.'

'That's OK. It'll give me something to look forward to.'

As she listened to their middle-aged drivel Annabelle was tapping her foot impatiently, wanting to be gone from here, in spite of having nowhere to go. Maybe she could talk her mother into paying for another massage. Actually, she wouldn't mind having her nails done, and her hair blow-dried. There was a party at Melody's tonight, everyone was going, and she still hadn't worn the D&G dress she'd bought in Bath a couple of weeks ago. She wondered if it would be OK for her to go, but even if it was, no way was she going to call anyone to find out, especially when no one was bothering to call her. Except Bethany, who was more boring than blah, and Georgie, who she had to admit had rung yesterday to ask how she was. Georgie hadn't mentioned anything about the party though, but that was OK, because Annabelle didn't really want to go anyway.

'When's Robert leaving for Paris?' she suddenly blurted.

Sabrina turned to look at her. 'Tomorrow,' she answered. 'Why?'

'I thought I might go with him.'

Sabrina gave an exasperated sigh. 'He'll be in meetings the whole time . . .'

'I can go shopping and look at the sights.'

'Not on your own, you can't.'

'So why don't you come too?'

'Because I've got far too much to do here before we go away. Now, will you please stop tapping your foot. It's very annoying.'

Annabelle turned to June. 'Everything about me is annoying to my mother.'

'I'm sure that's not true,' June protested.

'Of course it isn't,' Sabrina said, sounding

crosser than she intended. 'Why don't you go for a swim, or see if they can fit you in for a manicure, while June and I plan what's going in the next issue.'

'Actually,' June said, before Annabelle got up, 'I was going to mention this before, but I wondered if Annabelle might be interested in writing something for *The Buzz*. It might help our circulation a bit to have some young input.'

Sabrina looked decidedly impressed. 'That's a great idea,' she responded enthusiastically. 'What do you think, Annabelle? Would you like to do it?'

'I don't know,' Annabelle answered, slightly thrown. 'What sort of stuff would I have to write?'

Sabrina looked at June.

'You could do something on what people your age are up to,' June supplied. 'You know, the kind of events you go to, like festivals and concerts, and where's good to shop. Anything you think's suitable really.'

Annabelle turned to her mother.

Sabrina smiled encouragingly.

'Tell you what,' Annabelle said, 'I'll think about it,' and picking up her lemonade she wandered back inside.

With a sigh, Sabrina said, 'Thank you for that, June. I've been trying so hard to think of ways to include her since Robert gave me a dressing-down for neglecting her. He's wrong, of course, because I'm always there for her, and the reason she's being rude and stroppy at the moment is because she's going through a very tricky time with all this unpleasant business.'

Not even starting to get into the understatements

and denial going on there, June said, 'Does she know Nathan was in court today?'

Sabrina nodded. 'I tried to have a chat with her about it this morning, but all she said was, "Everyone'll know the truth soon enough, and then you'll all be sorry for not believing me."'

'But I thought you did believe her.'

'Of course I do, but for some reason she's telling herself I don't.'

It was late on Sunday morning. After the boom and crash of a thunderstorm during the night, everything was peaceful now. The clouds, having emptied themselves lavishly over the countryside, had contracted into small white ruffles floating through a swathe of perfect blue sky, while the ground steamed as it dried, filling the air with a fresh, earthy scent.

Nat was alone in the house, lying on his bed trying to read and listen to music. He'd been out a few times since he'd returned on Wednesday, mostly with Simon, when they were always careful to leave the village by the bottom road, and to keep well back as they waited for a bus to take them into Bruton, or Bath. Last night his mother had driven him and Darcie over to a pub in Somerton for a change of scene, and to meet up with Rachel and her family. They weren't sure if the Traveller's was the requisite hundred yards from Annabelle's house, but even if it was, the way some people in the village were staring and whispering whenever they saw them, or blatantly blanking them, made it too uncomfortable for them to go out anywhere nearby.

Picking up his mobile as it bleeped with an incoming text, he clicked it open and seeing it was from Summer, his expression darkened with anguish and guilt. *What have I done? Why won't you speak to me? Sx*

He was still looking at it, trying to think how to answer, when someone knocked on the front door. Dropping the phone, he swung his feet to the floor and went out on to the landing. He didn't want to answer in case it was someone come to shame him, and tell him to eff off back to London, the way a gang of young kids on the new estate had the other day, when he and Simon were waiting for the bus. 'Dirty rapist,' one girl had screamed. 'Sex maniac,' another had yelled. 'Go back where you belong.'

Whoever it was knocked again.

Half afraid of something unpleasant or dangerous coming through the letter box, he went partway down the stairs and shouted, 'Who is it?'

'Nat? It's Uncle Robert,' came the reply.

Allowing relief to overcome his misgivings for the moment, he ran down to the hall and pulled open the door. 'Sorry I took so long,' he said, standing back for Robert to come in. It was better than being abused by the locals, he thought, but maybe his uncle was here to lay into him over Annabelle. Did he believe what she was telling him? Was he going to read the riot act and say how ashamed and disgusted he was by what his nephew had done? If he did Nat was ready to defend himself – he might even dare to ask his uncle how he could have stayed with that bitch Sabrina after what *she'd* done.

'No worries,' Robert told him mildly. 'Are you on your own?'

Nat swallowed. 'Yes. Mum and Darcie have gone to a flea market in Frome. Not really my thing. I thought Mum said you were in Paris.'

'I got back last night,' Robert answered, following him into the kitchen. 'We're off again tomorrow so I thought I'd come and see how you are before I left. I don't suppose there's a cold drink going?'

'Oh, yeah, sure. What would you like? We have squash, I think, lemonade and there's probably some fruit juice.'

'If it's blackcurrant I'll have squash,' Robert replied.

As Nat dug some ice cubes from a tray and topped the squash with water from the tap, Robert pulled out a chair and sat down.

He didn't seem angry, Nat was thinking, but since that wasn't really his uncle's style there was still no knowing how this might go.

'So, how are you?' Robert asked, as Nat brought two drinks to the table.

Nat shrugged. 'I'm cool,' he answered, not really knowing what else to say.

Robert regarded him closely, then took a sip of his drink. 'We're off to France for ten days tomorrow,' he said, 'so hopefully that'll make things a bit easier for you around here.'

Nat's cheeks flamed with colour.

With a sigh, Robert put a comforting hand on his shoulder. 'I'm sorry all this is happening,' he said, 'for both of you . . .'

'If you don't mind,' Nat interrupted, 'I'd rather not discuss it.'

'I can understand that, but I'm here in the hope that we can do something to resolve this unfortunate business before either of you has to face the ordeal of going to trial. It won't be a pleasant experience . . .'

'I'm not the one who's making it happen,' Nat broke in angrily. 'It's her you should be speaking to.'

'And believe me, I'm going to try. Perhaps, while we're away and in a different environment, she might be more willing to talk. Meanwhile, I can't help wondering if perhaps you might have misunderstood what she . . .'

'I didn't misunderstand anything,' Nat cried bitterly. 'I couldn't make her leave me alone. She kept coming after me, and then she was there with no underwear on, behaving like the slut she is. Everyone knows what she's like, because they've all been there, and she couldn't stand it because I didn't want . . .' He broke off as frustration and embarrassment swallowed his words.

Robert looked away, hating hearing his stepdaughter being spoken about that way, in spite of having suspected for a while that her virtue was a thing of the past. It was like being punched in the face with his own shortcomings, shown exactly how ineffective he had become as her parent and moral guide. However, he had to remember who he was hearing this from, so hopefully the picture wasn't quite as profligate as Nat was painting it. 'You two used to be very fond of one another once,' he said.

'That was a long time ago. She's a different person now. We both are.'

'But underneath, I think in many ways you're still the same.'

Nat shook his head.

Robert sighed, and tried a different tack. 'I'm ready to admit that Annabelle has her problems,' he said awkwardly. 'The past couple of years haven't been easy . . .' He stopped as Nat rose to his feet. Then, realising his mistake, he said, 'I know they've been difficult for you too, but you're older and . . .'

'I'm not bringing this suit,' Nat reminded him sharply. 'She is, so like I said just now, it's her you should be talking to.'

The spectre of Craig and Sabrina's affair was looming large now, but unless Nat mentioned it, Robert wasn't going to complicate matters even further by doing so himself.

Giving himself something to do, Nat walked over to the door and pushed it open. It was on the tip of his tongue to ask his uncle why he'd stayed with Sabrina, how he could even bring himself to look at her after what she'd done, but knowing his father was as much to blame, he didn't want to risk hearing his uncle saying so, any more than he wanted to hear how hurt Robert might have been too. He was a kind and decent man, and Nat just knew he would never behave in an underhand or disloyal fashion with anyone. To think of his father making a fool of Robert was almost as bad as thinking of what it had done to his mother. It made his father the very kind of person Craig himself had always claimed to despise.

Feeling a choking misery burning in his chest,

he was about to walk outside when Robert said, 'How's your girlfriend? Summer, isn't it?'

Nat's eyes closed as he took a breath. As difficult a topic as Summer might be, he could handle it a whole lot better than a discussion about his dad. 'Yeah, that's right,' he said, turning round. 'She's OK. She's with her family in Italy.' He thought of how he'd been invited to join them and wished with all his heart now that he had.

'Does she know what's going on here?' Robert asked carefully.

Nat shook his head. 'I don't know what to do,' he admitted. 'Every time she rings . . . She thinks she's done something wrong. I keep telling her it's not her, but she won't believe me. She thinks I've met someone else, and if I have I should just be honest and tell her. It's getting so I don't take her calls any more or answer her texts, and that's not right. You shouldn't treat someone like that, but I don't know what else to do.'

Feeling for his dilemma, Robert said, 'You have to tell her the truth, Nat. I know it'll be hard . . .'

'She'll end it if I do, I know she will, and who can blame her? She hated Annabelle. I'm sorry, but Annabelle was so rude to her, and the way Annabelle kept coming on to me when Summer was there . . . If you'd seen it, you'd know what I mean.'

Taking a breath and blowing it out slowly, Robert said, 'I'm afraid you still have to tell her the truth. How she deals with it will be up to her, but if you continue avoiding her, calls it'll only make it worse.'

Nat's eyes went down. He knew his uncle was

right, but the problem was finding the right words that would enable him, in spite of everything, to hold on to the threads of a relationship that were already starting to fray.

Glancing at his watch, Robert said, 'I should be going.'

Nat walked with him to the front door, wishing he didn't have to leave, but not saying so. He liked his uncle being around, in spite of his connection to Annabelle, and though there were subjects he really didn't want to discuss, he'd have liked to talk some more. 'I'll tell Mum you dropped in,' he said.

'I'll give her a call later,' Robert replied. 'And you have my number, so if you want to chat, any time . . .'

'Thank you. I hope you have a good holiday.'

Robert's smile was wry as he hugged his nephew, then turned to start down the path. He wasn't sure if he'd done any good in coming here, but it had felt important for him to try and keep a channel open between his stepdaughter and nephew, and he was reasonably confident he'd succeeded, even though he himself had ended up feeling more torn than ever. In his heart he knew that if it went to the wire he'd support Annabelle, but he was praying to God it wouldn't come to that, because the mere thought of turning his back on Nat was almost as bad as how he'd feel if he turned it on her.

After closing the door Nat went back upstairs to his room, his head crowding with thoughts of Annabelle and the times they used to spend together before their parents had stopped visiting one another. They'd been really close then, and he supposed he'd meant it when he'd said he wanted to marry her when they were older, because as young as they both were, he wasn't going to deny that she'd been his first love. Or his first crush, anyway. In spite of her age she'd have had sex with him then, any time he wanted, or so she'd said, and that was just what had happened that Saturday night. She'd wanted to have sex, and he'd tried to get away, but she wouldn't let him go, and then everything had got out of hand, and now she was accusing him of rape and that *wasn't* what had happened at all.

Slamming the bedroom door behind him, he threw himself down on the bed and tried to push her out of his mind, but images of how she'd looked that night, laughing and teasing, shouting, sobbing and then laughing again with tears and blood on her cheeks, kept flashing before him like a grisly film. She knew what had happened, they both did, and it wasn't rape, so why was she doing this?

Putting on some music in an effort to blot out everything else, he lay down on his bed and picked up his mobile phone. Though he scrolled to her number he wouldn't risk trying it, because if she reported him he'd be arrested and taken into custody until the trial. The mere idea of that dredged an icy wave of dread all the way through him, and as though to escape it he jerked himself up from the bed to kill the music. Then, scrolling on through his numbers, he stopped at Summer's, and without giving himself any time to think he pressed to connect. Though he still had no clear idea of how he was going to tell her what had happened, he knew he had to take his uncle's advice and stop stalling, and the sooner he got it over with the better.

'Nat, hi,' she said happily when she heard his voice. 'At last. Where have you been? Why haven't you . . .'

'Summer, listen, there's something I have to tell you.'

'Oh my God. You *have* met someone else,' she cried.

'No. No, not at all, well, not the way you're thinking.' He took a breath. 'It's just that well, Annabelle . . .'

'No! Don't tell me it's her, I won't be able to stand it.'

Desperate to get it out now, he said, 'She's accused me of raping her, and the police arrested me, but it's not true, Summer. I didn't force her, she was coming on to me the way she does. You've seen how she is, and well, it wasn't rape. I swear it.'

For an excruciatingly long moment there was nothing more than a stunned silence at the other end, then she said, 'So what you're saying is that you had sex with your cousin Annabelle?'

'Yes, but not the way you're thinking. I mean, it wasn't rape, but it didn't mean anything either.'

'Do you know what,' she said, 'it's not the rape that bothers me – I mean, it does, of course, but at least it wouldn't have been an act of love. The fact that you're saying it wasn't rape, though, means you had sex with her because you wanted to.'

'No! It was spur of the moment . . . I just said, it didn't mean anything . . .'

'But you had sex with her! Do you realise what that tells me? It tells me you got excited by her, and if someone like that turns you on, Nathan, then all I can say is good luck to you, because if you're that shallow, then tramps like her are all you deserve.'

As the line went dead Nat threw down his phone and dropped his head in his hands. It was as though his entire world was falling apart, and he didn't know how to make it stop. He thought about his mother and how badly he was letting her down, when all he wanted was to be a strength and support to her. Instead, he'd brought her this, and as each day, each hour, passed he was becoming more terrified than ever of how far it might go, and what needed to be done to stop it.

Chapter Twenty

As August drifted on the world seemed to adopt a surreal sort of quality for Alicia, with the sun continuing to blaze as though time had become snagged on the hottest day of the year, while life moved forward in its usual impervious way. Since Robert had taken his family to France it had been possible to venture up to the high street, but unless they were going to the shop, they rarely did. It was better to continue keeping a low profile, they'd decided, that way Nat wouldn't have to encounter people's spitefulness and prejudice, nor would Alicia and Darcie have to suffer the intolerable experience of watching him endure it. Though some of her neighbour's behaviour was shocking and offensive in the extreme, Alicia refused to challenge them, because it would do nothing to help Nat if she got into some kind of showdown, nor was it likely to change their minds. She simply had to be thankful that they wouldn't be on the jury when the time came, a thought that in itself caused her heart to churn with dread.

Though they were in regular contact with Jolyon, so knew that he and Oliver were working hard preparing the defence papers, Nat almost never discussed what was happening, and Alicia didn't try to make him. He'd never mentioned Craig's affair either, but it was there between them, like a barrier they could see through, but didn't know how to cross. She tried once or twice, but as soon as he realised where she was going he put up a hand and walked away.

It was hard to find the right way to handle this, when she knew he must have so many questions and confusions, but even if he were prepared to discuss them, she wasn't sure what she could tell him that might give him a better understanding of his father's behaviour. After the horrible showdown with Sabrina Alicia's own doubts and insecurities had resurfaced with a vengeance, and she didn't want Nat to sense them. Knowing she was still suffering over his father's betrayal would be sure to make his own bewilderment and disillusion even harder to bear.

So she could only watch him withdrawing more deeply into himself, particularly after Jolyon's calls, when she knew that he was wondering why they hadn't managed to get the case thrown out yet. There was little, or nothing, she could say to alleviate their fears. They simply had to live through this now, pretending to themselves, and the rest of the world, that everything was going to work out just fine, when in truth they were becoming increasingly terrified that it might not.

It wasn't until ten days after Nat's first court appearance that Alicia saw Cameron Mitchell again, though he'd rung a few times to find out how she was and to let her know he was there if she needed to escape for a while. Though she'd have dearly loved to spend a few hours talking about art, or house-hunting, or anything at all that didn't concern the upcoming trial, she was too afraid of how Nat and Darcie would react if she took him up on his offer. Besides, it wouldn't be fair to leave them, when the world had become a pressure cooker for them too, and no one was offering them an escape.

'I was wondering,' Cameron said when he called one evening, 'if you were at all intrigued to know what my idea is concerning your shop – or perhaps you've forgotten I mentioned I'd had one.'

'Actually, I do remember,' she admitted, 'but I didn't like to ask in case it might seem . . . I don't know, pushy I suppose.'

He gave a laugh. 'I think that's the last thing anyone could accuse you of being,' he told her. 'Anyway, I'm keen to run this idea past you, but before I do, it's important that I see your work. I've checked online, but couldn't find anything.'

'That's because Nat's still in the process of designing a new website for me, but I'd love to show you what I have. I'm not sure it'll be quite to your taste though, and considering how famously outspoken you are when it comes to talent, or lack of it, I'm afraid my sensibilities might not be able to take it.'

'OK, if I promise not to give you a hard time, no matter what I think, will you set a day for me to come over?'

After searching in vain for an objection that wouldn't entail telling him how set against him her children were, she said, 'OK, but if you don't like what I'm doing, how will that fit with your idea?'

'Very easily, but I'll be able to explain better once I've seen it – and, for the record, I'm sure it'll be right up my street.'

Not anywhere near as convinced herself, since she'd checked out his gallery online so knew his tastes ran more to abstract and postmodernism than to the offbeat kind of figurative style that was hers, she said, 'Nat and Darcie are going to a horse show with Rachel on Tuesday, so if you're free then . . .'

'Give me a time and I'll be there,' he told her. 'Oh, and I have some property brochures I'm hoping you'll glance over while I'm sizing up your sculptures, if you wouldn't mind.'

'I'd be happy to,' she told him, and after confirming the date and time again she rang off and stood thinking about the arrangement, and how she was going to break it to Nat and Darcie.

In the end, she wandered out to the garden where they were playing badminton using the worn racquets and shuttlecocks they'd unearthed while clearing the playroom-cum-study. Since Nat and Simon had transported some of her equipment from the shop by now, the space had begun to resemble a temporary studio, but before she attempted to start work again she wanted to sort through her mother's little cubbyhole of a study in order to turn it into a store.

As she watched them play, she was trying not to focus too much on Nat, knowing he would sense it and immediately withdraw, the way he always did lately when he felt her eyes on him.

Fortunately he wasn't the same with Darcie, because they seemed as close as ever, if not closer.

'I didn't see you there,' Darcie called out. 'Fancy a game? You can be on my side and help me thrash him, because he keeps beating me.'

'You're the one who told me to stop letting you win,' Nat reminded her, belting the shuttlecock over the net.

'That was too fast,' Darcie complained as she missed it. 'Come on, Mum, save me from complete annihilation. There's another racquet on the table.'

Going to fetch it, Alicia took up position on Darcie's side of the makeshift court, and twenty minutes later, after much grunting, running, voluble protesting and cheering, Nat was rolling his eyes at the pathetic performance of the female opposition.

Laughing, as he went off to hose himself down in the shower, Alicia flopped into a deckchair, attempting to fan herself with her racquet, while Darcie lay spreadeagled on the grass getting her breath back. A few clouds were starting to gather, casting a bulbous shadow over the house, but it was still warm and the feeling of cool grass prickling softly between her toes was as refreshing as the thought of an ice-cold drink, which she was trying to summon the energy to go and get.

'Mum?' Darcie said, turning her head to squint up at her mother.

'Mm?' Alicia responded, idly batting away a fly.

'I keep trying to work out why Annabelle's doing this. I mean, she always used to be dead keen on Nat, so why's she saying he hurt her when everyone knows he'd never hurt anyone?'

Loving her unfailing loyalty, and wishing there was a way to take the confusion from her heart with a few simple words, Alicia sighed as she said, 'I don't know, sweetheart.' She didn't want to explain to Darcie all the possible complications of Annabelle's motives, or to try to imagine what might be going on in the girl's mind when she could only guess what it must have been like for her after Sabrina's break-up with Craig. 'I wish I did.'

'He had sex with her though, didn't he?' Darcie said. 'Or this wouldn't be happening?'

'I'm afraid so,' Alicia replied, keeping her eyes closed so Darcie wouldn't see the frustration and anger she felt on top of all the concern.

'Una says Annabelle's got a bit of a reputation for going with boys,' Darcie went on, 'even though she's only fifteen.'

Alicia sighed again. 'Yes, I've heard that too,' she said, 'and if it's true, which it seems to be, it's a great pity Nat didn't control himself a little better – and that Annabelle doesn't value herself more highly than to sleep around with anyone.'

'Except Nat's not just anyone.'

'No, but that's not the point. It was wrong of him to have sex with a girl who's underage, and who's not even his girlfriend.'

'Because it's important to be in a special relationship before you do anything like that?'

'Exactly. And over sixteen. I'm not sure Nat actually realised she was still only fifteen, but it doesn't make a difference. She is, and now he's in terrible trouble because of it.'

Hearing Nat rattling about in the kitchen

Darcie let the matter rest there, and when he came out with three glasses of blackcurrant squash, Alicia avoided his eyes as he passed her one, so he wouldn't see how disappointed and angry she was with him for having got himself into this mess.

'Oh yeah,' Darcie said, shifting round to prop her head on Nat's chest as he lay down on the grass beside her, 'who was that on the phone just now? No one for me, I suppose?'

Alicia swallowed some squash. She didn't want to lie, but she was afraid that any mention of Cameron would start making them feel protective towards their father and end up causing another kind of friction that they just didn't need right now. However, in the end, because she didn't want to start hiding things from them, she said, 'Actually, it was Cameron Mitchell. He wants to take a look at my work.' She tried not to sound defensive as she went on, 'I'm sure he'll hate it, but if he doesn't, who knows, he might be willing to help me try to sell it.' She wouldn't add how much they needed the money, because they really didn't need to know how little there was left in the pot now.

The answering silence stretched on long enough to make her want to shout at them to give her a break, but then to her surprise Nat said, 'That's great. So when's he coming?'

Stunned into confusion, it took a moment for her to say, 'Next Tuesday. I thought while you two were at the show with Rachel, I could brace myself for the worst and take him to the shop.'

'Isn't everything still packed up?' Darcie said.

'Yes, but . . .'

'I know,' Darcie broke in, 'we should help you jimmy open the crates and set it up like a little show. We've got loads of white sheets upstairs that we can put over tables and boxes, and Nat can do some blurbs about each piece on the computer.'

'I could design a brochure,' he said, picking up the theme. 'Do you know where the digital camera is so we can take some shots? We need some for your website anyway, so this could be the perfect opportunity.'

Amazed, and still not quite able to believe this was happening, Alicia said, 'I've only got six pieces . . .'

'That's enough,' Nat told her. 'If we price them at four grand each and you sold only one . . .'

'What?' Alicia laughed. 'I don't sell them for that much. Nothing like.'

'Then it's time you did. Art is worth what someone will pay for it, and if you start low, so will they.' Craig's words to the letter.

'But he's not buying,' she said, aware of the emotions swirling about inside her. This was starting to feel like the few other occasions she'd exhibited her work, when Craig and the children had thrown themselves into staging it all.

'Doesn't matter,' Nat told her. 'It's important to show that you value yourself. Darce, go and find the camera while I dig out something we can use as a crowbar.'

'He's not coming until Tuesday,' Alicia reminded them.

'That gives us three days to set up a private show to blow his mind,' Nat decided, 'come on, it'll be like old times,' and after planting a kiss on her forehead he took off to the shed to rummage through the tools, while Darcie went in search of the camera and Alicia fought back tears of guilt for getting angry with them, and relief that she hadn't let it show.

'We're getting damned good at this now,' Craig declared, standing back to admire their handiwork after they'd finished setting up her third show. 'I'm starting to think we could go into business.'

'That would be so cool,' Darcie agreed, clapping her hands, 'but Mum's the only artist we want to promote.'

'Of course,' he said seriously. 'We're very exclusive and only ever work with the best.'

'Keep saying that,' Alicia encouraged them. 'I don't care if you're family, I'm ready to believe it.'

'I've had a great idea,' Nat piped up, 'why don't I write your reviews? I could sell them to a paper under another name and make some money.'

Laughing excitedly, Darcie said, 'And I can be your publicist, keeping the paparazzi at bay.'

'Excellent idea,' Craig remarked approvingly, 'and I shall be her umbrella carrier, because it's belting down outside and we're due in the restaurant in ten minutes for our pre-show dinner. Everyone ready?'

'Yes,' Nat and Darcie chorused.

'Then go and find us a cab while I have a little smooch with our number one client.'

'Oh yuk, gross,' Darcie retorted, screwing up her nose.

'You two are so embarrassing,' Nat informed them, as Craig swept Alicia into a romantic embrace.

'And you two are extra to requirements,' Craig murmured against Alicia's lips, 'so hop it and get a cab.'

After they'd gone he kissed Alicia deeply, pressing his whole body to hers and seeming to wrap her in so much love that he made her feel like the most treasured woman alive.

'How do you do that?' she whispered as he pulled back to look at her, his dark eyes gazing lovingly into hers.

'What?'

'Make me feel so special after everything that's happened.' She swallowed. 'Tomorrow I'll be terrified again that you're thinking of going back to her, but right now, I can actually believe you might still love me.'

His tone was dark with sincerity as he said, 'I've always loved you, Alicia, from the day we first met. Nothing's ever changed that, and nothing ever will. One day you'll know that's the truth and won't doubt it any more.'

Alicia's heart fluttered as she recalled that evening, and wished it was possible to replay memories like a film, so that Nat could remember it too, and hear what his father had said to her after he and Darcie had left the gallery that night.

She wouldn't tell him how she'd then asked Craig if he'd switch off his mobile for the evening in case Sabrina called to ruin it all. He'd agreed, and had even given her the phone so she could be sure he wasn't sneaking outside to check if there were any messages or texts. She'd dropped it into the bottom of her bag and they'd both forgotten about it until after he'd left for work the next morning, when he'd called from chambers to ask if she could take it to Knightsbridge Crown Court, where he was going to be all day. Inevitably, she'd turned the phone on, and had immediately felt sick with anger and dread to find two messages from Sabrina. The first was telling Craig that she'd be in London the following Wednesday, so could he please call to let her know if he was able to see her? The second gave details of the hotel she'd booked them into.

'She does this all the time,' he cried, when Alicia confronted him outside the court. He was wearing his wig and gown, and looked both impressive and frustrated. 'Just delete them. She's crazy. She thinks if she just turns up that I will too, but it's not going to happen. I swear it.'

She'd believed him then, until he spent the night away from home the following Wednesday. In spite of calling the hotel near Winchester Crown Court and being put through to his room where he'd answered her call straight away, she'd had no way of knowing whether or not Sabrina was with him.

'This is a *stupid* house, full of *stupid* people, in a *stupid* place,' Annabelle seethed furiously.

'Will you please keep your voice down,' Sabrina hissed through her teeth.

'Why? No one's here.'

'The staff speak English,' Sabrina reminded her, 'and I don't appreciate being shouted at anyway. Now will you please do as you're told?'

'No! I don't want to go to the Eden Roc for lunch, and that's that. I hate it here. I want to go home.'

'Don't be ridiculous. You can't possibly hate this place. Look at it.' The sheer luxury of Annabelle's room was indeed breathtaking, with all its pale grey marble, copious mauve silk drapes and Louis Quinze-style bed, but it was only one small part of this palatial villa, secreted away in its own parkland garden on the western side of the Cap d'Antibes.

'I don't care what it looks like, I don't want to have lunch with all those stuck-up people.'

'Then come to the yacht later.'

'No! Same people. And anyway, I get seasick.'

'We didn't even leave the port yesterday,' Sabrina pointed out impatiently, 'so how could it have made you feel sick?'

'I don't know. It just did, and I'm not going on it again.'

Sabrina was close to stamping a foot in frustration. 'Honestly, most girls your age would give anything to be having a holiday like this,' she fumed, allowing her temper to rise over all the fear and guilt bottled up inside her. She couldn't deal with Annabelle and everything that had gone wrong between them while they were here, in someone else's home. They needed to be good guests, appreciative of the honour being bestowed on them, and do everything they could to keep their skeletons hidden from view. There would be plenty of time, when they got back to Holly Wood, to give them an airing. 'Why do you have to be so difficult?' she asked plaintively. 'I've really been looking forward to this holiday, and now you're spoiling it . . .'

'I didn't ask to come,' Annabelle shouted. 'They're your friends, not mine, and I hate them. They're really up themselves . . .'

'And you're not, with this attitude?'

Annabelle's eyes flashed, and sensing another explosion, Sabrina quickly said, 'Look darling, I know you're worried about the case, we all are, but every time I bring it up . . .'

'I don't want to talk about it,' Annabelle seethed.

'You see, you won't discuss it. So why don't we try to forget about it for a while and enjoy ourselves?'

'I can't just forget about it, you idiot. I was raped, OK? And if you don't want your stupid friends to know, you shouldn't have made me come here.'

Sabrina regarded her in overwhelming despair. She knew she was handling this badly, and had been ever since they'd arrived, but short of taking Annabelle home again, she was at a complete loss as to what to do with her. Struggling to keep the emotion from her voice, she said, 'I haven't brought you up to be rude about people and hostile like this. I've always taught you the proper thing to do, the right way to be . . .'

'Oh yeah, you always get it right and proper, don't you? Nothing you do is ever wrong. I don't expect you even think having an affair was out of order. And it wasn't just any affair, because you had to really go for it and pick on your sister-in-law's husband. That makes you a great role model, doesn't it?'

Sabrina's face had turned white, her whole body was starting to shake. 'What I did,' she began, 'the relationship between Craig and me . . .' Suddenly she couldn't go any further. The effort to hold everything back, the grief, the loss, the bewilderment and terrible sense of failure over Annabelle, came flooding so fast to the surface that she started to sob. 'You have no idea what I've been through,' she choked raggedly. 'You seem to forget that I have feelings too, and the way you treat me . . .' She grabbed a tissue from a box and blew her nose. 'I'm trying to help you, don't you realise that? I want us to be close again, but you keep attacking me – and to bring up the relationship I had with Craig, to throw it in my face like that . . . I loved him, Annabelle. It wasn't just some sordid affair, the way you're trying to make out. We meant everything to one another, and now we'll never be together, so how do you think that makes me feel?'

Annabelle's face was strained and confused. 'Why don't you just go and join your friends?' she said bitterly. 'I'm staying here, and if you start arguing again, I swear I'm going to run out on to that balcony and jump off.'

Sitting where he was, further along the same balcony, outside his and Sabrina's room, Robert couldn't hear everything that was being said, but enough was reaching him for him to get the gist. She and Annabelle had been struggling dreadfully with one another almost as soon as they'd arrived, so he'd more or less been expecting the showdown – however, he hadn't considered how revelatory it might prove. Though he'd known Sabrina was grieving for Craig, he'd evidently been blinding himself to the extent of her grief, or he simply hadn't wanted to see it. However, this time, instead of the old wounds opening up with the same bitter and dull pain of rejection and fear of losing her, the way they usually did at any mention of his brother-in-law, he was finding himself far more concerned about Annabelle and how the continuing strain of it all was starting to affect her now.

Hearing Sabrina coming into the room, he gave it a few moments, then put his book down and went back inside. He wasn't surprised to find her in the bathroom repairing her make-up. She'd need to hurry now to join the others for lunch.

'Are you ready?' she asked his reflection as he came to stand in the door.

'You go,' he said, 'I'll stay here with Annabelle.'

Though her eyes showed a moment's unease as she realised he must have overheard the row, she covered it quickly as she said, 'She's a teenager, everyone will understand if she doesn't come, but if you don't it'll just look rude.'

'You can tell them I have to make a phone call for work, or that I have a headache.'

She turned round to face him, looking nervous and very unsure of herself. 'Would that be the same headache as the one you've had several nights in a row?' she asked hoarsely.

Knowing she didn't really want to get into his reluctance to make love to her now, he simply said, 'Go and join the others.'

'Robert, I . . .' She was so close to breaking down again that her words were swallowed by a gulf of emotion, and she quickly pressed her fingers to her lips to try to stifle a sob.

Reaching for her, he hugged her to him, and kissed the top of her head, trying to give her some reassurance, while knowing that he needed to sort out what was going on in his own mind before he could talk to her about what was, and wasn't, starting to happen between them.

'I'll stay here, if you want me to,' she whispered, looking up at him with misty eyes.

He shook his head. 'No, you go and enjoy yourself,' he said, and kissing her briefly on the cheek he left her to return to reassembling her mask of total happiness and fulfilment, while he went in search of Annabelle.

It was two thirty on Tuesday. Rachel's husband, David, had come to collect Nat and Darcie half an hour ago, only minutes before Cameron had turned up with Jasper. Alicia was now playing with the dog at the front of the shop, unable to bear witness to Cameron's scrutiny of her work in the back.

Between them Nat and Darcie had made a great job of turning the studio into a trendy-looking mini gallery, covering everything with crisp white bed sheets, and borrowing a black filigree three-fold screen from Mimi to mask the boiler and sink. Mimi had also provided some trailing greenery to help with the decor, and to Alicia's amazement, Nat and Darcie had managed to dig out some old photos of her in the process of creating her pieces to scatter around the place (though in truth, in her welding helmet, flame-resistant coat and heatproof gloves, the artist at work could have been anyone). Shots of her moulding plasticine to form the bronze element of the pieces, however, were much more obviously her, but not particularly flattering, if the truth be told.

The sculptures themselves had each been allocated a stand of some sort, anything from a packing case to an upturned flower pot to a pile of bricks that might topple at any moment, all carefully disguised by the minimalist robing of white cotton sheets. The order of viewing Nat had provided in the brochure he'd printed off that morning was 1) *Alligator Shoes*; 2) *Darcie Dreaming*; 3) *Bird in the Hand*; 4) *Ballerina Blues*; 5) *Snail Mail*; 6) *Wedding Night*.

Keeping her back turned and hands busy with Jasper's insatiable appetite for tummy rubs, Alicia waited in silence till she could bear it no more.

'OK, I'm a big girl,' she said, going to stand in the arch between the two spaces, 'you can give it to me straight. They're really amateur, aren't they? Or maybe even that's flattering myself.'

Cameron's attention was focused on the ballerina as he regarded it from all angles, a deep furrow between his eyebrows, a loose fist in front of his mouth.

'I know they're not really your thing,' she gabbled on, 'but some people have liked them. Actually, I've sold quite a few . . . Well, four, but I only started . . .'

'This skirt is made entirely of steel,' he said, as though not quite believing it. 'It's so fine . . . I thought it was fabric when I first saw it. You have all the folds, the shadows, the movement . . . And her stance is almost fluid. This position is called arabesque?'

Alicia nodded.

He went on absorbing every detail, from the carefully shaped fronds of the dancer's hair, to the willowy grace of her neck, to the leaf-like form of her bodice, right down to the sharply pointed tips of her toes. 'This is so exquisitely executed,' he said finally, 'that whether or not it's a piece you'd want to own, you could never tire of looking at it.'

'Which means you don't like it, but . . .'

His hand went up. 'Will you please stop trying to put words in my mouth,' he barked.

Alicia looked down at Jasper and pulled a naughty face.

'You've chosen an unusual medium,' Cameron went on, moving along to *Snail Mail*. 'I'm enjoying the wit as well as the *tendresse*. This works,' he said with feeling, as he smoothed his fingers over the snail's steel shell. 'A Fibonacci sequence.'

Impressed that he knew that, until she remembered who he was, she found herself daring to hope that her little show wasn't an all-out flop.

Pointing back to the alligator, he said, 'Putting him in shoes made of the same skin is an effective statement. The scales are very lifelike, so's his expression.' Taking a moment to assess his judgement, he said, 'I get the feeling you're more comfortable with steel than with bronze, which isn't to say that Darcie's head doesn't work, because it's actually probably one of the more saleable pieces.'

Holding her breath now, Alicia continued to watch him, and felt so much elation struggling to rise up inside her that it was hard to keep it down. It wasn't only, she realised, that he was seeming to like her work, it was also the wonderful feeling she was experiencing of being an artist for a few minutes, a woman even, a person other than a grieving widow, or an anxious mother.

'Do you know what I think?' he said, standing back to get an overall view. 'I think if you were to reproduce the steel sculptures at ten times the size they are now, turning them into installation art, you could find a lot of interest coming your way from the billionaire set. They're perfect garden or entry-hall pieces for large homes, which doesn't mean they won't sell as they are now, because I think they will, but I'm getting the sense that they need to be bigger.' He glanced at her and grimaced when he saw her look of shock. 'Not what you wanted to hear?' he said.

'No, yes, I mean, I've always wanted to do something huge,' she admitted, 'but I've never had the courage, or the space.'

Turning back to *Wedding Night*, he said, 'The embrace here draws you around the figures, and around again, kind of like a waltz, so it would have to be displayed on a three-sixty or you'd lose the flow. At ten times the size, it might even make you dance.'

Alicia was smiling as her heart tripped with so much pleasure that she was close to dancing anyway. It was Craig's favourite, and she'd modelled it on the way he used to embrace her. 'I don't think I'll hang up my welding torch just yet,' she murmured to Jasper.

Clearly delighted to be spoken to, Jasper leaned against her and nudged her with his head.

'Stop flirting,' Cameron scolded.

'I can't help it, he's irresistible,' she apologised.

Laughing, he returned to his perusal of her works, starting at the beginning again and taking another ten excruciating minutes to reach the end. 'OK,' he said finally, ruffling Jasper's ears as the dog came to stand next to him. 'I confess you've surprised me, Alicia. I really wasn't expecting to be this impressed, which probably isn't very flattering, but I'm afraid I'm far more frequently disappointed by what I see than I am the reverse. I'm not going to try telling you that what you've created is perfect, but I think that's because you're not giving them full expression. You could do that by letting rip with the size. Just go for it. A ten-foot alligator in matching shoes in the garden at a cost of a hundred thousand pounds or more could be just what Mr and Mrs Moscow are looking for. A ballerina of that subtlety and beauty will be a must for anyone with a discerning eye and unlimited budget. However, as I said, the sculptures also work very well as they are, and you could probably sell them for upwards of three thousand pounds a piece, but I'd love to see the drama and power you could get into them if you magnified their size.'

Too overwhelmed to say very much, Alicia threw out her hands in an apologetic sort of delight. 'This is where I work,' she told him, 'or in the space at home, which isn't much bigger.'

'That's fine. There'll be plenty of barns, or established workshops, around that you could rent at a reasonable price, and once you start selling the smaller pieces you'll have the funds to do it.'

Feeling like a child who'd been visited by three Santas in one go, only to find they'd forgotten to leave gifts, she said, 'And therein lies the rub, selling anything, when I can't open the shop yet, and getting noticed on the Internet is like asking a grain of sand to make itself stand out on a mile-long beach.'

'Ah, but if the grain of sand is displayed in the right window, to the right sort of clientele,' he countered, 'it'll stand a much greater chance of achieving its allotted fifteen minutes. And so we come to my idea for your shop. Now I've seen your work I have no problem at all about putting this to you: why don't you let me exhibit these pieces in my gallery in London until you can open for business? I have staff running it six days a week with access to collectors and dealers all over the world, so if nothing else, you'll certainly get noticed. Meanwhile, you and I will go on a double hunt around Somerset, you for local talent assisted by me, me for the right house assisted by you, and with any luck we'll both end up with what we're looking for at the end of the day. Or summer. Or year, however long it takes.'

Alicia was sure there must have been stars in her eyes as she looked at him, or bats in her belfry, because this was simply too good to be true. As far as she could make out she had everything to gain and nothing to lose, so why wouldn't she take him up on the offer? 'I don't understand why you're doing this,' she said in the end. 'You hardly know me, and it's not as though I have an exceptional talent . . .'

'As a matter of fact, I think you do,' he interrupted. 'And as for knowing you, let's just say if you've got the thumbs up from Jasper, which you seem to have, then you've got it from me.'

Laughing, and refraining from pointing out that this was the first time the dog had ever clapped eyes on her, she said, 'So I guess I should take a look at your property details to get that part of the show on the road. But first I need to know your budget, so we don't waste any time.'

'Not a penny over a million,' he told her.

Trying not to reel, she said, 'Are we looking for a stately home?'

He chuckled. 'I'd need considerably more than a million for that,' he replied, going to fish in his bag for the brochures. 'What I'd like is something with character, but not too old; elegant in an understated way, with a huge sitting room and fireplace – a must for the girls – a kitchen/dining room, we're not too big on formal, and at least four bedrooms so we can all have one each when they come to stay. Oh yes, and a minimum of three bathrooms.'

'Tennis courts? Swimming pool?'

'If we can squeeze them into the price,' he answered seriously. 'And it must have a view.'

'I see,' she said dubiously. 'I'm starting to think you might have the easier task, but I'm definitely up for the challenge,' and suddenly realising she was on the brink of crying with pure relief that something seemed to be going right for once, she stooped quickly to Jasper to bury her face in his fur.

* * *

To Robert's surprise, and delight, Annabelle had sought him out this morning, asking if she could take him up on the offer he'd made yesterday, which she'd turned down, to drive her into the old town of Antibes for lunch. He had no idea what had happened to change her mind, nor did he much care, he was simply glad that she had, and after informing Sabrina that she'd need to make his excuses to the rest of the party again today, he went to make sure that his car was brought round to the front of the house by midday.

Now, as he and Annabelle journeyed along the Cap, with the stunning blue Mediterranean sparkling like polished diamonds alongside them, their progress was made tediously slow thanks to all the tourist traffic. However, since he was amongst their number he couldn't really complain, unlike Annabelle, who grumbled ceaselessly the entire way round to the port, and she was still going strong when they finally sat down outside a red-painted café in the heart of the old town.

After deciding on one of her favourites, moules marinière with *frites*, Annabelle smiled charmingly at the extremely attractive young waiter and asked for a beer.

'Make that two *panachés*,' Robert said to the waiter who, to his relief, seemed not to notice Annabelle's interest.

'But I don't want shandy,' Annabelle protested.

Robert nodded to the young man, confirming the order, and said, 'When the food comes I'll order a pichet of rosé wine, and you can have some of that.'

Appearing satisfied with the compromise, she

looked around the square, taking in the centuries-old buildings with their various-coloured shutters and ground-floor shops which included fashion boutiques, jewellery stores and typical Provençal marts. Her survey complete, she promptly launched into another negative diatribe about sailing, France, stuck-up people, her life in general and her mother in particular.

Robert said very little, merely listened, or nodded, or asked a question in the appropriate places. The food and wine arrived. She ate everything, and tried to talk him into ordering another pichet when theirs was empty. He refused and suggested they take a walk along the ramparts, and maybe drop into the Picasso museum to have a look round. Though she screwed up her nose as though unable to think of anything more boring, she ended up agreeing to go, making it sound as though it was only as a favour to him, certainly not something she'd ever consider were something more exciting on offer.

By the time they returned to the villa in the late afternoon Annabelle had long since run out of complaints, and was now chattering on and even laughing about a holiday they'd had five years ago in Spain when she was ten. Though he was impressed by her memory, he was sure she had a few facts wrong, and they fell into a good-natured tussle about who was right, and who was making things up to suit themselves.

Since the others were still on the yacht, Robert and Annabelle were the only ones for tea, which they took in the summer house, down by the beach. Still Annabelle ran on with whatever came to mind, but as repetitive and, it had to be said, boring, as she was, Robert couldn't help being amused by how adept she was at keeping up the flow. He guessed this was probably the first time in far too long that she'd had the undivided attention of an adult, and though he'd have liked to try and draw her on more serious matters, he didn't even attempt it. It was doing her the world of good to let go the way she had today, and hopefully it was helping her to rebuild her confidence in him in a way that might, eventually, enable him to broach the subject of Nathan and the upcoming trial.

Then suddenly, to his surprise, she said, 'I know you're making friends with me because you want me to drop the charges against Nat, but I can't. It wouldn't be right. When someone commits a crime they should pay, and so I'm going to make sure he does or he might think he can get away with doing it to someone else.'

'I'm sorry, Alicia,' Rachel declared hotly, 'I'm not arguing about this. You are going to let me pay for those sculptures to be transported to London, and that's final.'

'But you . . .' Alicia began.

'Mum!' Darcie protested. 'You can't pass on this just because we don't have the ready cash. And if they're going to sell the way he seems to think, you can always pay Rachel back.'

'Yes, but what I . . .'

'Will you please stop with the buts,' Rachel interrupted. 'I've made my decision, so now all we have to do, Darcie, is find a company to transport them. It'll have to be someone bonded, now we know they're valuable.'

'Nat can pack them up,' Darcie decided. 'He knows how, because he did it when we moved them here. What does bonded mean?'

'Insurance. Actually, I'm rather tempted to buy one myself. Not that I didn't want to before, but why pay a few hundred quid when you can pay a few thousand, is what I say. There you are,' she said to Alicia, 'you have your first sale, so you can already pay me back and you haven't even borrowed it yet, so stop complaining.'

Laughing helplessly, Alicia said, 'I wasn't objecting, you just wouldn't let me get a word in. I'm happy to take a loan to get them to London, but I'm drawing the line at charging you for a . . .'

'Here she goes again,' Rachel said to Darcie. 'Shall we go outside and continue this or she'll just end up getting on my nerves, trying to give me a piece of art for nothing when I want to pay a small fortune.'

As Darcie linked Rachel's arm and walked her out to the garden, Alicia turned to Nat, who'd said nothing since she'd told them about Cameron's reaction to her work. 'You're very quiet,' she ventured, hoping the last few frivolous moments hadn't made his problems seem any less important to them all.

'I'm cool,' he said.

'So do you think this is good news, or am I getting carried away?'

'Sounds good,' he responded.

Still not able to gauge what he was thinking, but feeling sure it must be about his father, she said, 'If you don't want to pack them . . .'

'It's no problem, I'll do it. When do you need it done by?'

'I'm not sure yet.' Sitting down at the table she put her hands over his, then started as he moved quickly away.

'I'm going upstairs,' he said. 'I need to make a call.'

Watching him go down the hall, she said, 'Have you spoken to Summer?'

To her surprise he turned round. 'Why? Did she ring?'

'No, I just wondered if you got back to her last week, and how she's getting on in Italy?'

His eyes went down. 'It's over,' he mumbled, and before she could say any more he took the stairs two at a time up to his room.

Alicia stood staring along the hall. That had to be an end to his bad luck, she was pleading silently. It had to be, because he couldn't take any more – and if he couldn't, then nor could she.

Chapter Twenty-One

Alicia had spent the last two weeks driving around the countryside with Cameron in search of million-pound houses and untapped artistic talent. More often than not Darcie and Jasper came along too, and even Nat had joined them on a couple of occasions. Having struck up quite a bond with the dog, Nat generally took it for walks and tirelessly threw the ball while the others inspected dilapidated old farmhouses and some jaw-droppingly awful pieces of art. However, the talent quest wasn't entirely without fruit, as they'd happened upon a wonderfully flamboyant sixty-year-old hippy with a large collection of watercolours Alicia felt sure would sell, and a rather gifted old bumpkin of a potter who, for reasons they didn't go into, called himself Flash Gordon.

Though her own work had now been transported to London, Cameron was keeping it in store until she could spare the time to go and take part in organising its display. It wasn't that she was so busy in Somerset, it was more the children being reluctant to visit the capital for fear of not wanting to leave again that was holding her back. Though they never really discussed with her how much they wished they were returning to their old schools and friends after the summer, she'd heard them talking to one another, and her heart ached with the longing to make their wishes come true. There was nothing she wouldn't give to be able to change the course of the months ahead, particularly if it would make the forth-coming trial go away, but Robert had called from France to warn her that he was making no headway with Annabelle, so Nat must prepare himself for this to go all the way.

'If I thought Sabrina was pushing her into it,' Robert had said, 'I'd tell you and put a stop to it, but as far as I can make out this is Annabelle's decision and she's sticking with it.'

Dismayed and angered by the news, Alicia tried throwing herself back into the double search, but as the day of Annabelle's return drew closer, everyone's mood started to change. It was as though the summer was coming to a premature end, and dark clouds were masking the sky, when in reality it was still pristine and blue. However, the day before she was due back the heavens opened, and after that the sun didn't seem to have the energy to stage much of an encore.

The only good part of Annabelle's return was that it coincided with Nat's official work-experience period at Jolyon's office. For the next two weeks he would be in Bristol, no longer having to endure the divided loyalties of the village, or the incon-venience and humiliation of being unable to go up to the high street. By the time he came home he'd know his AS results, which were expected to be good, and there would be only three days left before he was due to join the Upper Sixth at Stanbrooks and Darcie was to start year eight. Alicia wasn't sure who was dreading it the most, though guessed it had to be Nat, since half the sixth form probably already knew what he was facing.

'If only I could get him enrolled somewhere else, miles from Somerset,' she lamented to Jolyon when she drove Nat up to stay with him. 'He shouldn't be having to go through this. It could damage him for life.'

'It's certainly going to be an experience he won't forget,' Jolyon agreed, 'but Oliver's in regular touch with the CPS and we're still hopeful we can get the rape charge dismissed. Of course, there'll still be the matter of unlawful sex, but we need to deal with the big issue first.'

'Oliver has to succeed,' she said urgently. 'There can't be a trial. There just can't.'

Though Nat was unable to hear what his mother and Jolyon were saying as he unpacked in his room, he knew what they'd be discussing, because after what had felt like a two-week respite, with Annabelle away, his own sense of doom was returning, big-time. Starting school was the first hurdle he'd have to overcome, where no doubt everyone would take sides, just as they had in the village, but worse, far, far worse, was if he ended up having to stand trial. The fact that seventy per cent of rape cases were thrown out before they got that far was small comfort when he'd expected, hoped, Oliver would have got it dismissed within days of the first hearing. Instead, time was running on, and still the prosecutors seemed to believe there was a case to answer. The horrific, unthinkable prospect of standing in the dock as an accused rapist, being judged by a jury, then possibly sent to prison for the next five years at least, when he should be at university and law school, was starting to crowd in on him with a terrible, suffocating might.

'Mum, look what I found in the bottom drawer,' Darcie said, coming out of her grandmother's study to where Alicia was in the playroom, sorting through the books and files she'd taken from her mother's desk.

Glancing at the small square box Darcie plonked on the workbench, she asked, 'What's in it?'

'Mostly letters from Grandpa,' Darcie said, pulling one out.

Seeing her father's familiar hand spread across the page Darcie was unfolding, Alicia felt her heart swell with nostalgia. 'How many are there?' she asked, taking it.

'Loads. The box is full. Isn't it sweet that she kept them?'

Alicia smiled. 'I wonder when she last read them,' she said, looking at the date on the one she was holding. To her surprise it went back to a time before her parents were married.

'People don't really write letters any more, do they?' Darcie said.

Alicia shook her head. 'It's a pity, but you're right.'

'So you don't have any from Dad?'

Wishing she did, Alicia said, 'I've kept all the cards he sent me over the years, and even some of the notes he left saying he'd be late, or could I pick up his dry-cleaning, or asking me to record a programme.'

Darcie screwed up her nose. 'You kept dumb notes like that?' she said.

Smiling, Alicia said, 'That's not all they said. The rest is for me to know and you to find out a long time from now. I wonder if we should read these.'

'Oh, I think we have to,' Darcie said, clearly sharing none of her mother's scruples. 'I mean, we can't just throw them away, it would be like we didn't care, and that wouldn't be right at all. Honestly, I bet if Grandma was here she'd tell us to go ahead. After all, if she didn't want us to see them, why keep them when she had plenty of chances to get rid of them?'

'Put like that, I suppose we could have a look through,' Alicia said. 'I'm just intrigued to know why you're so keen.'

Darcie's face was all innocence. 'I never knew Grandpa,' she reminded her, 'so this is a way of hearing him speak, well, sort of, if you know what I mean.'

Stooping to kiss her, Alicia said, 'I know exactly what you mean, and it was very well put. Now, go and answer the phone and we'll tuck these back in the drawer until we have time to get round to them properly.'

Returning to the room a few minutes later, Darcie said, 'It was Cameron. He said to tell you he's on his way and if we want to go out to eat it'll have to be a pub, because Jasper's with him.'

Smiling, Alicia said, 'Are you going to come

with us, or do you want us to drop you at Rachel's?'

Darcie looked at her with uncertain eyes. 'Is it OK if I come?' she asked.

Surprised by the tentativeness, Alicia said, 'Of course. Why would you think it wasn't?'

Darcie shrugged. 'I don't know. I suppose you might think I was a gooseberry and you'd rather be on your own.'

Alicia's mouth fell open as she laughed. 'Cameron and I aren't dating,' she told her firmly. 'We're just friends, and besides, if he can bring Jasper I'm very sure I can take you. In fact, I know he'll insist.'

Darcie immediately brightened. 'I really, really love him,' she said warmly. 'He's so funny, isn't he, always running after that ball, and trying to make friends with everyone we meet. I wish we could have a dog, don't you?'

Since she'd started out thinking Darcie was talking about Cameron, Alicia was over her double take by the time she said, 'As a matter of fact, I've been giving that very subject some thought, and maybe, once we're up and running, with our finances a little more settled, it might not be out of the question.'

Darcie started to jump up and down. 'Let's get one like Jasper, please, please. They're the best, and Nat's really keen to get one too.'

Hugging her, Alicia said, 'As soon as we're able we'll go online to find out if anyone in the area's expecting a litter. Or maybe there'll be one we can rescue.'

'Oh yeah, that would be really cool,' Darcie

agreed. 'Provided it's not nutso, or anything. We could give it a really good home, couldn't we?'

'I think so,' Alicia said, suddenly feeling the poignancy of expanding their family without Craig. Her first instinct was to retract what she'd promised, rather than take another single step into the future without him, but making herself smile past the ache inside she said, 'I guess we'd better go and make ourselves presentable, don't you?'

As Darcie charged up the stairs ahead of her she followed at a more leisurely pace, aware of how her reluctance to plan a life without Craig was still pulling her back, as though her dreams were all now trapped inside her memories.

'OK, you've got one each,' Darcie announced, handing out single sheets of paper to her father, her mother and Nat. Then suddenly she snatched them back again. 'No, I'm going to read them out myself,' she decided, making them into a neat little pile.

'What is it?' Nat asked, stretching luxuriously, then losing it in a laugh as Alicia poked his hairy tummy.

It was Sunday morning and she and Craig were still in bed, with Nathan, in boxers and a T-shirt, sprawled out next to his mother, and Darcie, who'd dug her brother out of a lie-in for this big event, sitting cross-legged up against the foot rail. '*Duh*, they're the poems I was writing for you all,' she reminded him.

Nat turned his head towards Alicia. 'Can't wait for this,' he muttered, and earned himself a warning nudge in the ribs.

'I heard what he said,' Darcie complained, looking at her father.

'Ignore him, squirrel,' Craig told her. 'He has an underdeveloped sense of the arts, unlike you, my darling. So, come on, hit us with your rhythm stick.'

Darcie bubbled with laughter. 'OK, here goes,' she said, looking down at the first sheet of paper. 'This one's for you, Dad.

'"My dad is a lawyer, tall and strong,

He gets people sent to prison when they do things wrong,

I love him very much with all my might,

Having him as my dad means I'm getting things right."'

She looked up, beaming with delight.

'Fantastic,' Craig enthused. 'Well done, squirrel. Can I keep it?'

'I'll get you a copy,' she told him. 'Now, here's yours, Mum,' she said to Alicia. 'Are you ready?'

Still smothering a smile at the 'copy' line, Alicia said, 'Ready.'

'"My mum is a sculptor, pretty and slim,

She makes things out of steel and bronze, all from a whim,

I love her very much with all my heart,

Having her as my mum means I've had a great start."'

Her eyes were shining with pride as she looked at Alicia.

'Brilliant!' Alicia declared. 'I love it. Can I have a copy too?'

Darcie nodded importantly. 'I was going to end it with the line, "Even though she's turned me into a work of art,"' she said, looking down at it again. 'I still might, I'll think about it. OK, Nat, it's your turn. Are you ready?'

'Bring it on,' he encouraged.

'"My brother is a pain, but I love him all the same,

His name is Nat and he's definitely not fat . . ."'

'Definitely not *fat*,' he scoffed. 'What kind of . . .'

Darcie looked up, stricken, as her mother clapped a hand over Nat's mouth.

'Go on, sweetheart,' Alicia said softly.

Darcie glowered at him, then went back to her poem,

'"His name is Nat, and he's very, very fat,"' she amended.

'"He's tall and he's dark and he's great at sport,

If ever I get into trouble, I want him on my side in court."'

Her eyes came up uncertainly.

'Bloody fantastic,' Nat declared, clapping his hands. 'You're a laureate in the making, squirrel. Can I have a copy too?'

'No, because you'll say you're going to use it in the loo.' Her eyes lit up. 'That rhymed too,' she said to her father.

Laughing, Craig swung her into his arms and kissed her roundly on the cheek. 'I'm going to get them all framed,' he told her, 'and we'll hang them in our bedrooms.'

She seemed to like the idea, until her nose wrinkled a protest. 'I won't have one,' she pointed out.

'Oh yes, you will,' he told her, 'because Nat's going to write one for you, aren't you, son?'

'Get lost,' Nat cried. 'I'm . . .'

'*And*,' Craig cut in, 'he's going to make it up right now. So off you go, Nat. Wow us all with your poetic genius, see how much better you can do than your sister.' In a whisper to Darcie he said, 'He'll be rubbish, so don't worry, you'll still be the best.'

'Oh yeah?' Nat retorted. 'OK, so, off the top of my head, here goes . . . My sister is a cutie, all cuddly and sweet, her name is Darcie and . . . she lives on our street . . .'

Craig winced and Darcie giggled. 'Told you,' Craig whispered.

'She's good at acting, dancing and song,' Nat pressed on, 'and typical of a girl, she's never in the wrong.'

Darcie burst out laughing. 'That was quite good,' she told him generously. 'Except the bit about our street, that was really dumb.'

'Yeah, like the line about me being fat.'

'I said you weren't until you were mean,' she reminded him.

'OK, before this develops into an argument,' Craig interrupted, 'who's going to walk down to the bakery with me to get some croissants for breakfast?'

'Not me,' Nat said. 'It's freezing out there. I'm going back to bed.'

'I'm doing my homework,' Darcie told him.

Craig looked at Alicia.

'Seems you're on your own,' she told him, snuggling back under the sheets.

He turned on to his side so his face was close to hers. 'Bet I can clear this room of children in three seconds flat,' he murmured.

'I'm gone,' Nat cried, even before his parents started to kiss.

'Me too,' Darcie said, taking off after him.

Laughing as the door closed behind them, Alicia

said, 'Isn't it amazing, the way she remembered what you said about me creating on a whim?'

'Mm, amazing,' he murmured, running a hand up over her thighs.

Her eyes fluttered closed. 'So no croissants?' she said faintly.

'No croissants,' he confirmed, and turning her mouth to his he kissed her deeply as he pulled her on top of him.

The poetry morning had been a mere two days before he'd died, and it was the first time in over a year that Alicia hadn't wondered, while he was making love to her, if he was thinking about Sabrina, and maybe wishing he was with her instead.

Taking a deep breath now, as though to draw the memories back into the past, she refused to allow herself to think of how cruel fate had been to have taken him when they were finally starting to put it all behind them, and returned her mind to the present.

It gave her a jolt when she remembered that they were about to meet up with Cameron, and for a moment she felt herself pushing that away too. It seemed wrong to be waiting for someone who wasn't Craig, to be seeing another man at all, even if he was just a friend. But then, reminding herself of how kind and supportive Cameron had been through this dreadful summer, and how he never uttered a single word or made even the slightest gesture to suggest that he might be trying to insert himself more permanently into their lives, she felt herself relaxing again. She liked him enormously, there was no doubt about that, but for the time being at least she was still very much Craig's wife – and perhaps as wedded to her grief now as she'd once been to him.

Besides, until she knew what was going to happen to Nat she couldn't allow herself to think very seriously about anything else at all.

Sabrina was in an excellent mood. For once everything seemed to be going right. All the friends she wanted to invite for cocktails, the second weekend of September, were able to make it, the caterers and bartender were booked, and Robert was due back from yet another trip to Washington two days before, so would be home in plenty of time. Added to the success of her own party plans was the pleasure of knowing her first book-club meeting had now been scheduled for the end of next week (so she'd better get reading fast); *The Buzz* had achieved a higher than usual advertising take-up thanks to June's hard work these past three weeks; and she'd received a very welcome invitation to an end-of-summer party at the Roswells, who were always extremely particular about who made their list. Not that she and Robert were ever left off, but being at the centre of all this unpleasant business of police inquiries and court appearances, they might have found themselves *personae non gratae* as far as the county elite were concerned.

Fortunately that hadn't happened, and since she'd heard last week, just after arriving back from France, that Nathan Carlyle had been shipped off to Bristol, and that Annabelle's supporters in the village had remained true throughout, she'd felt as though her cup was truly running over. All she had to do now was get Annabelle through the ordeal that lay ahead, and if justice was done it might, with any luck, help to bring her and Annabelle closer together without having to go into all that painful business about what she'd been like after Craig. At the same time, it might even make it impossible for Alicia to remain in the village.

Two birds with one stone, marvellous.

'Mum!' Annabelle shouted from somewhere in the house.

'I'm in here,' Sabrina shouted back from the small parlour she used as a study. Following their dreadful showdown in France there had been an uneasy sort of truce between them, mainly, Sabrina suspected, because they were both still afraid of it happening again. In a way, her relationship with Robert was travelling along the same lines, much sweetness and light on the surface, while behind the scenes something else altogether was going on. She'd tried talking to him about it, but he kept brushing it aside, saying he was too hot, or too tired to make love, or she was making too much of it.

'Of course I still find you attractive,' he'd assured her only last night, 'I'm just not really in the mood at the moment.'

'Mum!' Annabelle shouted again.

With an exasperated sigh, Sabrina got up from her computer and went to the door. 'Where are you?' she said.

'I'm upstairs. I need you to come here.'

'I'm busy. What do you want?'

'I just told you. I want you to come here.'

'I will when I've finished. What time is your dental appointment, so I know when to be ready?'

Annabelle came out on to the landing and looked over the banister. 'I'm pregnant,' she announced.

Sabrina turned very still as all the signs she'd tried to ignore started clashing about in her head like a bizarre sort of circus, and turning into an unimaginable reality. 'If that's meant to be a joke,' she croaked.

'Look for yourself if you don't believe me,' Annabelle cried, and she tossed the white wand with its telling blue line down to the hall.

Going to pick it up, Sabrina registered it and felt her head spinning. She looked up at Annabelle, whose eyes were like deep, haunted pools in her ghostly white face, then back to the blue line. She wasn't sure how long she went on standing there, she only knew that when she looked up again Annabelle had returned to her room, and that she couldn't get her mind to function beyond the fact that what she was holding in her hand was the first evidence of a child that had her and Craig's blood running in its veins.

Oliver's Mendenhall's forbiddingly hawkish eyes were regarding Nat across Jolyon's desk. 'We're still putting pressure on the CPS to drop the rape charge,' he told him, 'but unfortunately he's digging in his heels. It's likely he's getting pressure from other quarters,' he added. He wouldn't tell Nat about his father's history with Detective Inspector

Caroline Ash, because he hadn't yet been able to discover how much sway that was having with the prosecutor, and besides the boy didn't need to know. It was enough that Mendenhall knew, and though he wasn't completely without sympathy for Ash's position on what had transpired after Craig had got the arsonist's case thrown out, the law was the law. She hadn't done her job properly, so in Mendenhall's book that made her every bit as responsible for the tragic deaths that had occurred, possibly even more so. And just in case she *was* leaning on the prosecutor, he was ready to play her prejudice as a trump card should the CPS make the grand mistake of going to trial.

'So I still have to attend the committal,' Nat said, his dark eyes partly concealed by an overly long fringe.

'Yes,' Oliver replied, 'but it'll be brief and quite informal again. They'll set the date for the Plea and Case Management hearing, which should probably be around four to five weeks later.'

'And that'll be in the Crown Court?'

Oliver nodded.

'So that's when I have to stand in the dock and plead not guilty?'

Again Oliver nodded, picking up on the boy's dread as Nat looked away.

'There's a judge in Taunton now who can hear these cases,' Oliver told him, 'but I think it's more likely you'll be referred here to Bristol. This is presuming it gets that far, and I'm still very hopeful it won't.'

Nat looked at him, then at Jolyon who was standing against the windowsill listening.

'I'll be with you for the committal,' Jolyon told him. 'Oliver will take over at the PCMH.'

Oliver glanced at his watch. 'I'm afraid I have to go now,' he said, 'I'm due back in court at two. I'm glad I've had this opportunity to see you,' he told Nat, getting to his feet. 'The case I'm here for is likely to go on for a few days, so if you want to get together at any time, just let me know.'

'Thanks,' Nat said, standing up too and shaking Mendenhall's hand. 'I'm going back to Somerset tomorrow. School starts next Tuesday.'

'Ah,' Mendenhall responded. 'Well, good luck with that.'

Nat's expression remained taut.

'I'll be at the end of the phone if you have any questions,' Mendenhall assured him, 'or if you simply want to talk. Otherwise Jolyon will keep you abreast of developments, especially if we receive some good news from the CPS. Oh, and by the way, Jolyon tells me you've been extremely helpful around here these last two weeks. Well done.'

Nat glanced at Jolyon and tried to smile a thank you.

Much later in the day, having taken the bus back to Jolyon's flat while Jolyon went to a meeting at the Law Society, Nat sat in his room for a long time trying to decide what to do. In the end, knowing Marianne was about to come home, he let himself out of the flat and walked across the road to the bridge approach. With rush hour still under way traffic was streaming by, slowing to a stop at the red brick towers that housed the toll-booths before speeding on to the other side.

It was cloudy and dull, but not cold. The air smelled of fumes and seaweed from the river, way below, and the roar of engines was drowning the sound of gulls and footsteps. He wasn't really registering much – his mind was strangely empty, his thoughts, his decisions had ground to a halt.

It was free for pedestrians to cross the bridge, so he walked on past the Clifton-side tower, feeling a warm blast of air on his face as a lorry went by. The walkway was separated from the road by solid casings, and the rails between him and thin air were thick iron struts that soared like bastions to the sweep of the suspension. He'd studied the construction of this bridge once, in year eight or nine. He knew Isambard Kingdom Brunel had designed it, and that it had first been opened in 1864, after Brunel's death. A local wine merchant had financed it, but he couldn't remember the merchant's name.

He was standing three hundred feet over the gorge now, halfway across the bridge and wondering if he could really feel a sway, or if it was just his imagination. He was so high that the river below was no more than a ribbon of sludge in the mud banks, and the cars clogging up the Portway were like toys. He looked out over the city, his eyes travelling from the tangled roads that made up the Cumberland Basin, across a myriad Victorian rooftops to the Mendips in the distance. Somewhere beyond those hills his mother and sister were going about their day.

His eyes dropped down through the gorge again, passing over the cragged rock face much faster than anyone could fall. At the bottom a blade of light struck the grimy water and was gone.

Suddenly his mind was filling again, a clamouring chaos of thoughts that seemed to have no beginning or end. *Not guilty . . . Forced himself on me . . . She was begging me . . . Why did you lie? Penetrated with your penis . . . Nathan Douglas Carlyle, you are accused of the rape . . .* His eyes closed. He felt sick and giddy. The world was swooping and pitching. He could sense everyone watching him. Accusatory and contemptuous eyes. His mother would be in court, torn apart with grief and shame. She'd hear how he'd touched Annabelle when she was twelve. It would all come out. Everyone would know and call him a pervert, a child molester, a rapist.

His hands gripped the rail. He squeezed it so tight his knuckles cracked. His mind was emptying again, like a chorus pausing for breath. Then he could hear his father's voice, but not what he was saying. He wanted his father so much it seemed to hurt in every part of his soul. He'd have the answers, he'd know what to do. Yet how could he? His father wasn't who he'd pretended to be. He was a fake, a liar, a cheat. He hadn't loved his wife, and thinking of his mother unloved, when he knew how deeply she'd loved his father, wasn't something he could bear. The mere thought of anyone causing her pain made him want to hurt them in every possible way, but his father was no longer here to face his shame. In dying he'd cheated his family again.

He looked up at the security caging, the uncompromising bars that attempted to keep people in and death out. If he went to prison he'd be treated like scum. They'd beat and rape him and turn him into a miserable, toadying fag. The dream of a career in the law would end the day he was convicted, and for the rest of his life he'd bear the label of a sex offender. No one would want to live near him, wherever he went frightened parents and vigilantes would drive him out. He'd never find a job or a wife, he'd have no friends or children of his own.

And all because of that one crazy moment with Annabelle.

Why was she doing this?

Would he, if he could break through the bars, make the jump?

The answer, he realised to his shame, was no, because he didn't have the courage. Or maybe it was because he knew what it would do to his mother. And there was still, please God, a very slender chance that he might not be punished for a crime he hadn't committed.

Though she was scared and horrified by her pregnancy, Annabelle knew exactly what needed to happen. Her mother would make an appointment at a clinic in London, then she'd drive her there and a couple of hours later they'd come home again. 'It's easy,' she declared. 'I know three people who've done it, and they only had a day off school.'

Sabrina was appalled. 'Who are they?' she demanded, casting a nervous glance at Robert. Since he was paying for Annabelle's education he'd surely take a very dim view of the kind of trouble the girls were getting into.

'I can't tell you that,' Annabelle answered, starting to colour, 'but don't worry, they're not at Bruton, if that's what you're thinking. Sadie Virran's the only one who's ever got pregnant there, and if she hadn't been stupid enough to tell everyone she probably wouldn't have been expelled.'

Sabrina's eyes rounded. 'Is that why she . . . ? I thought it was to do with drugs.'

'It was, but . . .'

'We're getting off the subject,' Robert told them. 'As much as I dislike the idea of Annabelle having to go through a termination, I think she's right, it's what needs to be done.'

'Absolutely,' Annabelle agreed. 'I mean, I can hardly have a child at my age, can I? It would ruin my whole life. Plus, who's going to look after it while I go to school and uni?'

'Hang on, before we start making rush decisions,' Sabrina said. 'An abortion is a very serious issue, and not one to be taken as lightly as you seem to be . . .'

'Oh my God, you're not saying I should keep it, are you?' Annabelle cried. 'There's no way . . .'

'I know you don't want it now,' Sabrina interrupted, 'but later on, when your studies are over and you're a little more mature, you might feel differently. In fact, I know you will when you see it, because every mother does.'

'Yeah, I'm sure it'll be really sweet and gorgeous and everything, but I can hardly walk around school with a great big pregnant belly, can I? And what about breast-feeding and stuff?'

'All I'm saying is let's consider this rationally.

I understand that it'll be inconvenient to be pregnant while you're at school, you probably won't be able to do games and a few other things, but it happens, other girls have . . .'

'I'm not other girls! I don't even want anyone to know, so . . .'

'And after,' Sabrina pressed on, 'when the baby comes, you can fit back in with everything and I'll be here to take care of it.'

Annabelle's jaw dropped. Was this really her mother speaking?

'I think you're missing the point, Sabrina,' Robert said. 'It's not about games and other things, it's about how she came to be pregnant in the first place.'

'I was raped, in case you've forgotten,' Annabelle threw at her mother.

'Yes, but this is a totally separate issue,' Sabrina insisted.

Robert was stunned. 'How can you say that?' he protested. 'They're one and the same, and I can't quite believe we're having this conversation. Are you really saying you want her to carry a child that was conceived through rape?'

'Well, it's not as if Nathan Carlyle's some kind of monster, or from the wrong sort of background, is it?' Sabrina pointed out.

Robert's shock hit new heights, until a horrible understanding dawned. He couldn't continue this in front of Annabelle, but continue it he would, and Sabrina had better be prepared to start thinking straight or he'd be taking some drastic measures to make her.

'What are you on, Mother?' Annabelle cried.

'One minute he's the Devil incarnate and you can't wait to drive him and Alicia out of town, now, suddenly, you're going on like he's . . .' She stopped suddenly as the penny dropped for her too. 'Oh my God,' she said incredulously. 'You want me to have this baby because Nathan is Craig's son.'

'Don't be ridiculous,' Sabrina snapped. 'It's got nothing to do with that.'

'Yes it has. In your head you're starting to think of this as the baby you and Craig never had.' She looked at Robert and saw, to her horror, that he wasn't going to contradict her.

'Will you please stop talking nonsense,' Sabrina growled angrily. 'I'm only thinking of you . . .'

'That is such crap. It's yourself you're thinking about, as usual, and . . .'

'I've had enough of this,' Sabrina raged, springing to her feet. 'I'm just trying to get you to see alternatives and you start accusing me . . .'

'Alternatives that suit you and no one else,' Annabelle broke in.

'They might suit you too, one of these days. You have no idea what's going to happen in the future. What if, for some reason, you're not able to have any more children? You'd really regret letting this one go then.'

'And what if I told you Nathan Carlyle might not be the father?' Annabelle shouted.

Sabrina's mouth fell open as her face drained of colour.

Annabelle's face was turning white too. It was too late to take that back, and she couldn't think how she was going to get out of it.

'So if – if it isn't his, who else's could it be?' Sabrina stammered.

'I don't know. I . . .'

Sabrina reeled. *'You don't know?'* she cried. 'How can you not know?'

Annabelle tightened her mouth and tilted her head away.

'I want an answer,' Sabrina demanded.

Annabelle looked at Robert, whose head was in his hands. 'I don't know, because I don't want to tell you,' she retorted. 'Anyway, it could be Nat's, but I bet you don't want me to go through with it now you know I'm not sure.'

Feeling a desperate need to lie down, or at least to get away from her daughter, Sabrina said, 'I think we should all try to forget everything that's been said in the last few minutes and carry on as we were before.'

She'd got as far as the door when Annabelle said, 'Does that mean you're going to make an appointment for me or not?'

'If that's what you want,' Sabrina answered, keeping her back turned, 'I'll do it tomorrow,' and before either of them could say anything else to stop her she left the room.

'Wouldn't you love us to have a baby together?' she murmured, running a hand over Craig's face as she gazed sleepily into his eyes.

He smiled. 'You have the craziest ideas,' he told her.

'It would be so good-looking,' she said. 'And intelligent, and witty and sporty . . .'

'. . . and unbelievably sexy, if it's like its mother,' he interrupted, touching his lips to hers.

'If we were free to have children together,' she said, after they'd kissed for a long and deliciously sensuous time, 'would you want them with me?'

'Of course,' he murmured, and pulling her closer still, he kissed her again – and then he made love to her with all the tenderness of a man whose only thought was to create a perfect child with the woman he loved.

From the moment she'd collected Nat from Jolyon's that morning, Alicia had sensed a change in him. Though he was obviously anxious about starting a new school next week, and still bound up in the horrible prospect of a committal looming only a week later, with her mother's instinct she'd known right away that there was more. He wasn't only quiet and withdrawn now, there was an air about him that made him seem even more strained and fragile than before, as though his whole body was cracking with the effort to hold on to his emotions. She was almost afraid to touch him in case he broke down, and yet in her heart she knew it was what he needed to do. The pressure on him was enormous now, and whether he was trying to prove himself a man by holding it all in, or if he was too afraid to let go for fear of his entire world falling apart, she had no idea, but suspected it was both.

Throughout the day on Saturday he kept mainly to his room, while Alicia and Darcie went to Bath to buy all kinds of stationery and the requisite plain black shoes that couldn't be ordered from the school shop. Being in the sixth form Nat wouldn't have to wear a uniform, but there was still a long list of items he needed, sports gear, new shirts and trousers, a new holdall and coat. However, he showed no interest in coming to choose them himself, which wasn't like the normally image-conscious Nat at all. He was cool about leaving it to his mother and Darcie, he said, as though they were going to a supermarket to choose something for supper.

To Alicia's relief, when she and Darcie returned from their shopping trip just after six, Nat was in the kitchen making himself cheese on toast, and when Darcie began showing him what they'd picked out for him he was kind enough to tell her she had great taste. Darcie glowed, and after hugging him with all her sisterly might, she cut herself two slices of bread and stuck them under the grill.

'I thought you two were having fish and chips tonight,' Alicia commented, as she stuffed all the credit-card receipts in a drawer and prayed they'd have managed to pay themselves by the next time she looked.

'We are,' Darcie confirmed, 'but I'm starving now, so I can't wait that long.'

Alicia glanced at Nat who pulled one of his comical faces, but there wasn't the usual light in his eyes. 'Are you sure you don't mind me going out?' she said, aiming the question at Darcie, but meaning it more for Nat.

'Of course not,' Darcie answered, breaking a corner off Nat's cheese on toast and scoffing it.

'What are you going to do with yourselves?' Alicia asked.

Darcie shrugged and looked at Nat. 'Watch a movie, hang out, I don't know,' she replied.

'Is Simon coming over?' Alicia said to Nat.

'No, he's going to some party in Shepton.'

Still trying to keep it casual, she said, 'If you want to go, I don't mind cancelling this evening and staying with Darcie.'

'You can't do that!' Darcie protested.

'It's fine, I'm cool hanging out with Squirrel,' Nat told her.

'You've been looking forward to tonight,' Darcie reminded her, 'and you can't let Cameron down now. That would be mean – and rude.'

'Is he leaving Jasper with us?' Nat asked.

'I think so.'

'Great, we can take him for a walk before it gets dark.'

Knowing she didn't have to remind him about his limits, or his curfew, she dropped a kiss on his head, and went off upstairs to put the new clothes away. Then she'd really have to get her skates on if she was going to be ready by the time Cameron came to pick her up.

An hour later, hearing Cameron arriving with Jasper, she slipped on her silver slingback shoes, applied a few quick dabs of Hermès Faubourg Vingt-Quatre, and stood back to survey herself in the mirror. The instant she saw her reflection, a feeling of resistance tugged at her. This was the first time in months that she'd dressed up to go out, and seeing herself looking so elegant in the figure-hugging grey metallic dress with its sparkly chain straps and low-cut back that she'd last worn to a charity banquet with Craig, was unsettling her badly. For a fleeting moment she almost gave in to the urge to strip it off again, but she was rescued by a spark of common sense reminding her that there was nothing to be afraid of. It was only a party, and it wasn't as if she'd never been to one without Craig before, so this wasn't the first time . . .

Hearing a knock on the door, she spun round and called for whoever it was to come in.

'It's me,' Nat said, putting his head round. 'Cameron's downstairs.'

'Yes, I heard him arrive. I'm ready now. So,' she said, giving him a twirl, 'will I do?'

'You look great,' he assured her. 'Your hair suits you up. Are those the earrings you had for Christmas last year?'

Touching the small diamond drops, she felt a flush of colour in her cheeks as she nodded. He knew they were a gift from Craig, and she couldn't help wondering how he was feeling about her wearing them tonight.

'Come on, or you're going to be late,' he said, and turning away he went back out to the landing.

Grabbing her purse, she checked she had everything she needed inside, and after coating her lips in a soft pink shimmer she picked up her wrap and followed him downstairs.

'Has anyone seen my phone?' she said, to cover her embarrassment as she walked into the kitchen.

'It's here,' Nat said, unplugging it from the charger.

'Mum, you look ay-mazing,' Darcie cooed.

'Jasper, no!' Cameron cried, grabbing the dog as he came bowling in from outside.

Jasper's eyes were gleaming as he regarded

Alicia, his tail wagging so eagerly that Darcie gave him a shove as it thumped her legs.

Feeling Cameron's eyes on her too, Alicia quickly dropped the mobile in her bag. 'OK, I'll leave my phone on in case you need to get hold of me,' she said. 'The Friary should be open by now, so if . . .'

'Mum, will you just go,' Darcie told her.

'Of course. So you'll be all right?' she asked, needing to be sure.

Darcie looked at Cameron and rolled her eyes.

Apparently amused, Cameron said, 'I can't promise to have her home by midnight, but I'll try.'

'Do it,' Darcie told him seriously, 'because honestly, you won't want to see what she turns into at the strike of twelve.'

With a cry of laughter, Cameron handed Jasper's lead to Nat, and taking a scowling Alicia by the elbow he steered her towards the front door.

'Your carriage awaits,' he told her as they stepped outside, 'and by the way, you look stunning.'

The Roswells' end-of-summer party was one of the county's major events. Everyone who was anyone was invited, from the landed and titled, to political high-flyers and A-list celebrities, to the very rich and stupendously well connected. Robert always made the list thanks to his frequent hobnobbing with presidents and prime ministers, and as his wife Sabrina was naturally expected to come along too. In fact, no amount of wild horses – or wayward daughters – could have kept Sabrina away tonight, because being present at this event was absolutely vital to a couple's standing in the county. And for her and Robert to have the right standing was of paramount importance to Sabrina.

Though it had rained on and off throughout the day, now, as the two hundred or more glittering guests mingled about the stately mansion's superb long gallery, the south wall of French doors was thrown open to allow access on to the terrace for an excellent view of the gardens and sunset.

As Sabrina wandered through she was chattering away gaily with Archie Roswell's sister, Camilla, whose husband was being tipped as the next British Ambassador to China, a position of immense significance in today's new world. At the mermaid fountain, which had recently been restored at great expense, they paused to admire the sinuous stone sirens with feathery jets spurting from their upturned mouths, before moving on to join Felicity and Bodwin Singer-Smythe. The Singer-Smythes were closely related to one of the country's most prominent dukes, and were known to be worth somewhere in the region of half a billion.

With the conversation flowing as pleasingly as the champagne, Sabrina looked around for Robert and smiled approvingly as she spotted him strolling through the parterre with Archie Roswell, apparently engrossed in whatever Archie was saying. It was a pity he had to make a call to the States at nine thirty, just as everyone was sitting down in the great hall for dinner, but she knew he'd handle this so discreetly that he'd be back before anyone noticed he'd gone. He really was the most perfect husband, she decided with a shaky little sigh, loyal, supportive, attentive and above all tolerant of her silly aberrations.

Since the awful scene with Annabelle on Thursday he hadn't embarrassed her once by mentioning it again, other than to agree that it should, indeed, be a closed book. He'd then promptly offered to drive Annabelle to London himself for her little procedure, and to Sabrina's surprise and confusion Annabelle had accepted. As Annabelle's mother it should be her place to take her, and she was more than willing, but Annabelle's mind was made up, she wanted Robert to hold her hand. So they were going as soon as he returned from Washington the week after next. By then Annabelle would have had a little time to settle back into school before taking a day off 'to consult a specialist about a tiny internal problem', Sabrina would tell the house mistress.

On second thoughts, she decided now as she laughed and chatted on with the county elite, she might say it was something to do with the brain or back, because she didn't want anyone even suspecting it might be what it actually was, or equally as bad, an STD.

'Sabrina, darling, you're looking absolutely scrumptious,' Emily Roswell barked in her manly voice as she swept towards Sabrina's little group. 'That colour is a delight on you. Personally I look like a corpse in cream, but with that wonderfully exotic dark colouring of yours, you can carry it off like no one else.'

Treating Emily to one of her most charming smiles, Sabrina said, 'Thank you. It was a gift from

Robert while we were in France. Actually, if I'm going to be strictly accurate, we were in Monaco at the time.'

'Oh poor you, dreadful place in the summer,' Emily grimaced. 'Wouldn't catch me within ten miles of it, unless we were on the yacht, of course. Our daughter, Jacoba, has a little place there actually. She adores it. Commutes every day to the university in Nice. Speaking of daughters, how's dear Annabelle? I heard what happened. Nasty business, poor thing. How's she coping? I imagine she's horribly traumatised. In fact, I was half expecting you and Robert to back out this evening.'

'Oh, we'd never do that,' Sabrina assured her. 'We so look forward to your parties, and Annabelle's coping very well, I'm happy to say. She's being very brave about it all, and she absolutely insisted we come tonight.' By the time she'd finished Emily's attention had already drifted to the next group of guests, and as she wafted away, all handkerchief chiffon and L'Air du Temps, Camilla said, 'Sabrina, there's someone over there I absolutely must say hello to. Why don't you come along and let me introduce you. Between us,' she said under her breath as they floated through the party, 'I have a bit of a crush, but please don't give me away. *Cameron,*' she crowed delightedly, throwing out her arms. 'How utterly splendid to see you. Emily mentioned you might come.'

Turning to her, Cameron's eyes crinkled in a smile. 'Camilla, what are you doing here?' he said warmly. 'I thought you were in Beijing.'

'Not quite yet,' she replied as they embraced. 'Is it true you're looking for a house in the area?'

'I am, but not having much luck so far, I'm afraid. Is Ronald here?'

'Oh, he's around somewhere, I'm sure you'll run into him sooner or later. Now, do let me introduce a good friend of mine. Sabrina Paige, this is Cameron Mitchell. Cameron's one of our foremost authorities on modern art. Actually, you might already have met,' she added, the thought apparently just occurring to her.

'No, unfortunately we haven't,' Sabrina murmured, affecting her best sultry tones as she moved forward to shake his hand, 'but I've heard of you, of course. It's a pleasure to meet you.'

'Likewise,' he responded politely. 'It would seem our reputations go before us, because I've heard of you too.'

Sabrina smiled and almost batted her eyelids. 'I hope you're not going to believe all you hear,' she said playfully.

'Oh, but I probably should,' he assured her.

Warming to the flirtation, she said, 'Actually, I'm very glad to run into you, because I'd love to invite you to a soirée on the twelfth if you're still going to be around these parts.' It would be crass to mention anything about June just yet, but June was going to be over the moon when she saw him, he was so attractive.

'I'm due to go back to London on the fifteenth,' he told her, 'so that should work out, but I'll need to check with my partner to make sure we don't have anything else on that evening. I believe you've already met her . . .' and reaching behind him for Alicia's hand, he kept hold of it as she excused herself to the couple she was talking to and turned around.

Sabrina's face went ashen.

As Alicia's paled too, Cameron tightened the grip on her hand.

'What are *you* doing here?' Sabrina hissed.

'We were invited,' Cameron cut in, before Alicia could respond.

'Does Emily Roswell have any idea who you are?' Sabrina threw at Alicia. 'She can't, because she'd never let the mother of a rapist . . .'

'My son is nothing of the sort,' Alicia cut in furiously. 'It's your daughter who's a liar and a whore, like her mother.'

Sabrina almost exploded with outrage. 'How dare you . . . ?'

'Come on, Alicia,' Cameron said, trying to ease her away.

'Aren't you ashamed of the way you're using your own daughter to punish me because Craig wouldn't leave me?' Alicia challenged. 'You could have kept it between us . . .'

'It was your son who attacked my daughter,' Sabrina said scathingly. 'He's a sick, perverted boy . . .'

'He's a boy whose father has just died, and you are trying to ruin his life. Why can't you leave him alone?'

'He deserves everything that's happening to him. He's been interfering with my daughter since she was twelve, so if I were you I'd keep an eye on Darcie, or the next thing you know he'll be molesting his sister.'

Alicia's hand swung so hard that Sabrina reeled back into the people behind her.

Then suddenly Robert was there, and before Sabrina knew what was happening he'd emptied a glass of red wine down the front of her dress.

'Oh my God,' she gulped, 'what have you . . . Look at me.'

Seizing her arm in an iron grip, he began steering her through the crowd.

'Are you OK?' Cameron murmured, pulling Alicia into a protective embrace.

'What she said,' Alicia gasped. 'How could she . . . ? It was so . . .'

'Ssh, I know. Come on, let's go inside.'

'I think I'd rather go home.'

'Whatever you prefer.'

As they turned away the guests who'd been close enough to hear watched them leave, some murmuring to others in voices muted with shock. One woman, whom Alicia had never seen before, stepped forward and put a friendly hand on her arm, but another pointedly turned her back as Alicia caught her eye.

On reaching the front of the house they saw Robert and Sabrina on the forecourt below, getting into their car. After tipping the attendant Robert closed his door and drove away.

'I'm sorry you had to go through that,' Cameron said, as they waited for his car to be brought round. 'I blame myself . . .'

'No, I'm the one who should be sorry,' she interrupted. 'I guessed she'd be here, but I foolishly hoped we'd manage to stay out of one another's way.' As another wave of horror came over her she covered her face with her hands. 'How could she have said that?'

'She disgraced herself far more than you,' he told her, 'so try to put it out of your mind.'

Inhaling deeply as she looked up, she said, 'Listen, you don't have to leave. Let me get a taxi . . .'

'I'm coming with you,' he said firmly, and as the parking attendant brought the car to a halt he walked her round to the passenger side.

Robert's silence was terrible as he drove them home, far worse than when he shouted, because at least then Sabrina could have a say. This way there was no reaching him. He was angrier than she'd ever known him, and it was unnerving her badly.

Though she'd like to believe that he hadn't heard what she'd said, she knew he must have, or he wouldn't have tipped his drink down her dress. It was his way of making sure she left the party, she understood that, but why wasn't he saying anything?

'I think you should at least . . .'

His hand went up, cutting her off.

Annoyed, but too nervous to argue, she turned towards the dusk, watching, but not seeing, the countryside speeding by. Her mouth was swollen and throbbing from where Alicia had punched her, and her dress was ruined. The wine had soaked in now, plastering the silk to her skin. It was like blood, thick and red and completely indelible. If they were stopped, the police would think she'd been shot, or stabbed. She wondered if she wished she had.

Maybe she had gone too far with the remark about Nathan and his sister, but actually, who was to say she wasn't right? The boy might be a budding pervert, and if he was, it would be as well to get him off the streets now. She imagined saying that to Robert and felt the words wither inside her.

The dread of what everyone might be saying now began digging like spikes into her head. She could be dropped for this, and if she was, Alicia would be to blame. The wretched woman shouldn't have been there, she wasn't a part of the county set, and none of it would have happened if she hadn't somehow smarmed her way in with Cameron Mitchell. The woman was a menace, an intruder, a damned nemesis, who should get the hell out of a place she no longer belonged.

As Robert swung the car into the drive his expression was completely closed, betraying nothing of what he was thinking or feeling inside. Without waiting for Sabrina to get out, he pushed open his own door, slammed it shut, and walked into the house. There was no sign of Annabelle, but the mess in the kitchen showed that she'd made herself some dinner sometime during the evening.

After filling a glass with water, Robert was on his way to the hall when Sabrina said, 'Aren't you going to say *anything*?'

He didn't turn round, only kept on walking, up the stairs, past his and Sabrina's door and along the landing to the largest of the guest rooms. Once inside he put the glass down next to the bed and tore off his bow tie. No, he wasn't going to say anything, not because he didn't want to, but because he was so angry he didn't trust himself to know when to stop. He needed to calm down first, then focus his mind on what had to be achieved in Washington over the next two weeks, before returning to sort out Annabelle. After that he was going to have a great deal more to say than Sabrina would ever want to hear.

Chapter Twenty-Two

Keeping her head down and hands over her ears Darcie ran out of the school gates, weaving a path through straggling clutches of students and across the road to where Nat was waiting in the shade of a huge brick wall. Una was right behind her, her pretty freckled face stricken with worry.

'They've been really mean,' Una gasped, as Darcie buried her face in Nat's shoulder. 'You know, calling her names and stuff. It was horrible.'

Having experienced his own share of abuse in the sixth-form block, Nat tightened his arms round Darcie, saying, 'I'm sorry, squirrel, you shouldn't be having to put up with this . . .'

'It's not your fault,' Darcie cried, bringing her head up. 'They're just stupid and don't know any better.'

'Exactly,' Una agreed. 'They'll be sorry one of these days, when someone picks on them.'

'Come on,' Nat said, taking Darcie's bag and swinging it over his shoulder, 'let's go and wait for the bus.'

'Where's Mum?' Darcie objected, almost in a panic. 'Why isn't she here to pick us up, like she said she would?'

'Didn't you get her text?' Nat replied. 'She's seeing someone at the District Council about the shop. She'll be home about five.'

Staying close to his side, with Una linking her other arm, Darcie deliberately avoided looking at anyone else as they started down the hill towards the bus stop. The road was really crowded now, with pupils from two nearby schools spilling out of their respective gates, and dozens upon dozens of parents coming to pick up their offspring.

Annabelle was walking along the high street with Georgie and Catrina, who'd been waiting outside her classroom a few minutes ago, apparently dead keen to find out how she was and what was happening with the rape thing, as Catrina had put it. It seemed they didn't mind hanging around with her after school, but no mention had been made yet of whether they'd be inviting Annabelle to parties, or back to their houses, or any of the other places they used to go before Annabelle's age had become an issue.

This first day back hadn't been easy for Annabelle either, being stared at and talked about, as though she couldn't see or hear anything. Did they think she was stupid, or something? Just because she'd been raped didn't mean she was blind now, or deaf, or didn't have any feelings. Just as well no one had tried coming up to her and saying something, she'd have given them a good slapping if they had. It was none of their business what had happened to her, so they should just keep out of her face.

'Oh my God,' Georgie muttered, coming to a sudden stop. 'Look who it isn't.'

Annabelle followed the direction of her eyes and froze. Nat was barely twenty paces away, on the other side of the street, next to the bus stop.

'Hey, Nathan,' Georgie sang out nastily. 'Raped anyone lately?'

As Nat turned away, Annabelle saw Darcie starting to cry. Nat tried to comfort her, but Darcie suddenly swung round in a rage,

'This is all your fault,' she screamed at Annabelle, 'telling lies about my brother. You should be ashamed of yourself.'

Grabbing her, Nat turned her back towards the school. 'Come on, we can't be near her or I'll get into trouble,' he said.

'But it's not fair!' Darcie protested. 'She's the one who caused it . . .'

'Don't do this now,' Nat pleaded. 'Everyone's looking. Let's just get out of here.'

'That's it, run away,' Georgie shouted after them.

'There's Robert,' Annabelle said, spotting the Mercedes. 'Come on, quick.'

Having witnessed some sort of exchange between Annabelle and Nathan, Robert got out of the car not knowing what on earth he was going to do, but his niece was crying, and his nephew looked stricken – he couldn't just let them go. On the other hand, Annabelle was already running towards him, appearing none too happy herself, and if he turned his back on her now the little trust he'd built up with her would be wiped out in an instant.

In the end, as Annabelle and her friends piled into the car, he accepted that there was no way he could offer Nat and Darcie a ride home too, and as he wasn't even sure they'd seen him, he got back into the driver's seat vowing to do something to make this up to them.

'What happened?' he asked, catching Annabelle's eye in the rear-view mirror.

'Nothing,' she answered. 'Where's Mum?'

'She had to wait for a phone call,' he lied. He wouldn't tell her the truth, since Sabrina hadn't actually admitted she was afraid of running into Alicia at the school, but he knew it was the real reason she'd asked him to come in her place.

When they got home, having dropped off Georgie and Catrina along the way, there was no sign of Sabrina. Her car was gone, and there was no note letting them know where she was or when she'd be back. 'Give her mobile a try,' Robert said to Annabelle as she went to the fridge. 'I still have a paper to finish before I leave tomorrow, so I'm going back to my study.'

'How long are you going to be away?' Annabelle asked.

'Not as long as I'd intended,' he answered. 'I'll be back on the tenth.' He was about to add that they'd go up to London the day after for her 'little procedure' as Sabrina had taken to calling it, but stopped himself. She knew the date of her appointment, so didn't need reminding.

He was halfway across the garden when Darcie's tears and Nat's pale face struck his conscience again, and knowing he couldn't continue without going to find out if they'd got home all right, he redirected his steps out into Holly Way and across the high street to The Close. It was unlikely they'd be back yet, but he could always wait if they weren't.

Since Alicia's car wasn't in its usual place he didn't have much hope of the door being answered when he knocked, but to his surprise he heard footsteps on the stairs, and then Nat was there. From the expression that came over the lad's face, Robert knew right away that he'd seen him at the school.

'You're home already,' Robert said awkwardly.

'Simon's mother saw us and gave us a lift,' Nat replied.

Robert nodded. 'Good.' Then, 'Where's Mum?'

'At a meeting about the shop.'

'I see. Well, as long as you're all right.'

'We're fine, thanks.'

Robert raised a hand in a kind of wave and turned back down the path. The fact that Nat hadn't invited him in told him more clearly than anything how hurt the boy was, and Robert didn't blame him. In Nat's shoes he'd no doubt feel let down and betrayed too, but then he only had to think of Annabelle with her pregnancy, and not knowing who the father was, and Sabrina's refusal even to acknowledge the fact that her daughter had behaved like a tramp, to know where he belonged right now.

'Where have you been?' Annabelle asked, looking up from her second bowl of frosted cornflakes as Sabrina came in the door.

'I popped out to the supermarket,' Sabrina answered, hefting a couple of bags on to the table. 'How was your first day back?'

'Horrible,' Annabelle replied with her mouth full.

Sabrina looked at her.

'I don't want to talk about it,' Annabelle said, and carried on eating. 'The swelling's going down on your lip now,' she commented. 'Are you sure you walked into a door and Robert didn't whack you?'

'Don't be ridiculous.'

'So why isn't he speaking to you?'

'He is speaking to me. Where is he?'

'In his office. He's got some paper to finish, he said.'

Nodding, Sabrina put on the kettle and started packing the groceries away.

'Mum?' Annabelle said after a while.

'Mm?'

'What do you think would happen if I said I didn't want to go to court?'

Sabrina turned round, aghast, but needing to be certain where this was going before she got off on the wrong foot. 'You've already been told you don't have to appear,' she reminded her. 'You can give your evidence by video.'

Annabelle looked down at her bowl, but all she was seeing was Darcie's face as she'd screamed at her across the street.

'What's the matter?' Sabrina asked warily.

'Nothing, I just . . .'

'Just what?' Sabrina prompted.

'Well, I was thinking, maybe we should just forget about it all now.'

Sabrina's head started to spin. 'Rape doesn't just go away,' she said angrily.

'I know that, but everyone's talking about it and it's getting on my nerves.'

Sabrina opened her mouth, but didn't know what to say.

'Anyway, I saw Darcie earlier,' Annabelle went on. 'Someone said people are calling her names, and she looked really upset. So did Nat . . .'

'You saw Nathan,' Sabrina interrupted. 'That boy's supposed to keep . . .'

'I know, I know. He was waiting for the bus, so it wasn't like he was trying to hassle me or anything.'

'Nevertheless, he's in breach of his bail . . .'

'Oh shut up, I wish I'd never said anything now.'

'Annabelle, what is going on in that head of yours?'

'Nothing. I just felt bad for Darcie, OK?'

'Well, I'm very sorry if she was upset, but Nathan should have thought about that before . . .'

'Just leave it,' Annabelle cried. 'I can't talk to you about anything, so forget I ever mentioned it.'

Stiff with tension, Sabrina turned back to carry on unloading the shopping, until, unable to keep her frustration to herself a moment longer, she suddenly shouted, 'Did that boy rape you, or didn't he?'

'Yes, he did,' Annabelle shouted back.

'Then there's no more discussion to be had. You did the right thing in reporting him, and now you need to see it through. I understand it's not easy, so maybe we should give Lisa Murray a ring. She can have a chat with you, and put your mind at rest, because I'm sure a lot of victims go through the stage you're going through now.'

'Whatever,' Annabelle said, glancing at Sabrina's mobile as it started to ring.

Seeing June's name come up, Sabrina clicked on saying, 'Hi, how did you get on with Canon Jeffries?'

'Great as usual, he's such an old gossip. I swear he's gay, you know. Anyway, I can now round off my Glastonbury versus God piece, and then all we need is the scoop on the Roswells' party. How was it, by the way? I suppose the whole world was there, except *moi*, of course. Let me tell you, it's no fun being Cinderella at my age, even fairy godmothers are looking for younger models.'

Casting a sideways glance at Annabelle, Sabrina said, 'I'll put something together and email it over. When are we due to meet?'

'Some time next week, Thursday I think, to put the next edition to bed. So tell me, was Cameron Mitchell at the party? Did you meet him?'

'Kind of,' Sabrina answered. 'It'll have to wait until I see you, I'm afraid, Robert's leaving for Washington tomorrow, and I want to cook something special for tonight.'

As she rang off Annabelle got up from the table and went to put her bowl and spoon in the sink. 'You must have done something really bad if he's not speaking to you and you're sucking up to him with special dinners,' she commented, 'but I don't suppose you're going to tell me what it was, so I'm going upstairs to my room.'

'Before you go,' Sabrina said, 'how are you feeling now? Any more nausea?'

'I'm cool, apart from first thing, but you were

there when I chucked up, so you already know about that.'

'Have you told anyone?'

'No way. Not even Georgie. I don't want to end up being stared at even more than I was today. Or expelled, thank you very much. Anyway, here comes Robert, so I'll leave you to your sucking up. Good luck,' and waving her crossed fingers, she left.

Feeling a horrible fluttering inside as Robert opened the door, Sabrina smiled affectionately as she said, 'Hi, everything OK?'

'Everything's fine,' he answered shortly, going to unplug his phone charger from the wall.

Breezing over his abruptness, she said, 'I thought I'd do a rack of lamb in the rosemary and mint pesto you like for dinner. Would you prefer dauphinois or roast potatoes to go with it?'

'Actually, I'm driving up to Heathrow tonight,' he told her. 'My flight's at nine in the morning, so it makes more sense for me to stay at a hotel nearby.'

'I see,' she said carefully. 'OK, well I can always freeze the lamb and we can have it when you come back.'

Making no response, he picked up the newspaper he'd left on the table and went on upstairs to start packing.

'Mum just rang,' Nat said, going to stand in Darcie's bedroom doorway. 'She'll be home in about ten minutes.'

Darcie looked up from her computer. Her eyes were still pink from crying, but she was putting a braver face on things now. 'Did she say how it went?' she asked.

'Only that progress is being made and she'll fill us in when she gets here.'

Darcie nodded. 'Are you going to tell her Uncle Robert came over?'

'No. I don't think we should tell her anything. She'll only worry and get upset and she's already got enough to be dealing with.'

'What, you mean we should let her think everything's all right at school?'

Realising how hard that was going to be for her, he said, 'Well, that's what I'm going to do, but obviously, if you want to . . .'

'No, I'll do the same,' she cut in. 'I don't want her to worry either, or you. I can deal with it, honestly,' and getting up from her computer she came to give him a hug. 'I wish Dad was here,' she said brokenly. 'I keep trying to think it's not horrible without him, but it is.'

His arms tightened around her. 'I know,' he whispered, resting his head on hers. Then, 'I'm really sorry about the way everyone's being with you. You shouldn't be having to put up with all that crap because of me.'

'It's because of *her*,' she reminded him hotly. 'If she hadn't told all those lies this wouldn't be happening.'

'I know, but . . .'

'I'm really glad I shouted at her,' she ran on. 'I wish I'd gone over there and punched her now. I *hate* her for what she's doing, and I don't like Uncle Robert very much any more either. He should make her tell the truth so all this can be over.'

'It will be soon,' he said, 'just hang in there and let Mum think everything's OK.'

Returning to his room, he closed the door and went to sit at his own computer. There were a lot more suicide websites than he'd expected, so many that he hardly knew which one to choose. The one on the screen now though was probably the one he'd go with, because the way out they were suggesting seemed quick and easy and wouldn't, so they said, be too traumatic for those left behind. Thinking of his mother and Darcie and how they'd react when they found him brought a lump to his throat. He didn't want to do this to them, he wanted to be here to take care of them, to make sure no one ever hurt them, but they were suffering because of him, so what choice did he have?

If he had the courage and tools he'd do it right now, but he didn't, so bookmarking the site, he closed it down and sent an email to Jolyon. *Things getting a bit tough for Mum and Darcie. Any news from Oliver?*

'The weasel isn't going to have much trouble deciding whether to prosecute this one,' DS Clive Bevan was remarking, as he and Lisa went back into the rape suite after seeing out a frightened young boy and his mother, both victims of sexual assault by the live-in boyfriend. 'Bet our shifty little CPS wishes it was as cut and dried in the Carlyle case. He's coming under some serious pressure now to reduce the charge.'

'Funny you should mention that one,' Lisa remarked, leading him through to the tech room where one of her colleagues was spot-checking the most recent video recording. 'I had a call from Sabrina Paige this morning, asking if I'd talk to Annabelle.'

'Oh?' he said, perching on the edge of a desk.

'According to her mother, Annabelle's starting to feel sorry for Nathan and his sister, so she's considering dropping the charge. Mrs Paige thinks this might be typical behaviour for a victim, so she'd like me to persuade Annabelle to see it through.'

Bevan pulled a face. 'So what are you going to do?' he asked.

'Talk to Annabelle, and find out how she's really feeling. She's at school now, and my schedule's chock-a-block here, so it'll probably have to wait till next week.'

He glanced at his watch, checking the date. 'I think the Carlyle boy's up for committal some time soon,' he said, 'unless the CPS cracks and gives his lawyers what they want. Ash has got herself totally involved in it, of course. She thinks the same as me, that the boy's lies at the start are going to hang him, so she's not letting up on the weasel either. Wouldn't want to be in his shoes, that's for sure, but it'll be interesting to find out what young Annabelle has to say when you do manage to talk to her.'

'Alicia, I'm sorry I'm late,' Jolyon apologised, hurrying into the Hotel du Vin's restaurant where she was already sitting with the menus and a glass of wine. 'It's been hectic around here these last few days. How are you?' he said, kissing her on both cheeks. 'Thanks for driving all this way. I'd have come to you, but I'm in court for the next three days, and then it's the committal, and I wanted to talk to you before . . .'

'It's fine,' Alicia assured him. 'I'm happy to get out of Holly Wood once in a while, especially when you're treating me to lunches like this.'

He smiled, and after ordering a glass of wine for himself, he said, 'I know the menu pretty well, so I'm ready to order when you are.'

After choosing an arugula salad with pears, tomatoes and pine nuts, she handed the menu back to the waiter and gazed intently at Jolyon. 'Since I got your call I've been torn between intrigue and nerves waiting to find out what this is about,' she confessed. 'I keep telling myself if it was good news you wouldn't have made me wait, but I don't think you'd have put me through this for bad news either, so . . .' she shrugged, 'over to you.'

With an affectionate smile he said, 'First of all, it's looking as though we'll have to go through with the committal. As you know, Oliver's doing his damnedest to get the case thrown out, or at least to reduce the charge, and he's still confident he can make one or other happen. It's just unlikely to be before Thursday, which is a shame, because, in my opinion, Nat's already been through enough.'

Alicia was in total agreement with that. 'You got my email about how tense he is, did you?' she asked. 'He's so close to breaking, I'm not sure how much more he can take.'

'Yes, I got your email,' he told her, 'and I also

received one from Nat, who's worried about you and Darcie. He's not telling me anything about how he's feeling himself, but it's there, between the lines. He's understandably very frightened, and I agree with you, I think he's close to breaking. That's why I wanted us to talk.'

Swallowing dryly, Alicia kept her eyes on his.

'I'm assuming you've still not discussed the affair with him,' Jolyon said.

She shook her head. 'I've tried a couple of times, but he won't let me go there, and to be honest, I don't know what to say about it that might make him feel any better.'

He nodded soberly, seeming to understand her predicament. 'The point I'm getting to,' he said, 'is that Oliver and I both think he needs to start dealing with his grief before this goes any further. In many ways he's like a ticking bomb, and it won't help him at all if he explodes in front of a judge.'

Alicia's eyes went down. 'No, of course not,' she mumbled.

'He's never discussed this with me,' Jolyon went on, 'but I know he's very angry and confused. His father's come crashing off that pedestal we mentioned before, and Nat doesn't know how to pick up the pieces. I can understand that he doesn't feel able to talk to you, because he won't want to remind you of how hurt you were by the affair, and I'm pretty sure that a part of his problem is trying to deal with your pain. You mean more to him than anything, and all he can see right now is that his father, his idol, has behaved in a way that's gone against everything he's ever preached to his son. I've no doubt he thinks he hates Craig and wishes he could find a way to punish him, but death doesn't allow for that, so along with everything else, grief, love, fear of what's going to happen in the future, it's all staying bottled up inside him. Somehow, we have to find a way to help him let it go, and you're probably the only one who can do it. As his mother, you can, to some degree, speak for his father, and that's what would help him more than anything right now, to hear something from his father that will enable him to deal with everything else.'

Sitting back as their food arrived, Alicia barely even saw it as she tried to think what to do. Though Jolyon's words were making sense, and she was ready to do anything to help her son, she hardly knew where to begin. Once the waiter had gone she said, 'If I can manage to get him to talk about the affair . . . Do I tell him . . . ? What kind of detail should I go into?'

'Probably not too deep,' Jolyon replied, 'but treat him as an adult. Admit that it was really hard for you, which will be tough for him to hear, but if he knows you continued to love his father in spite of what he did, he might find it easier to forgive him. Tell him what it was like between you and Craig *after* the affair. He needs to know that his father died loving you and his family, and not wishing he was with someone else.'

Her heart was thudding painfully. 'I understand what you're saying,' she told him, 'but I don't know if that's the truth. The things Sabrina's said, the stress he was under towards the end. I can't help thinking it was because he wanted to be with her.'

Squeezing her hand, he said, 'I really don't think that was the case, but it's important for Nat to start seeing his father as a man who was every bit as capable of character weaknesses as he was of being the pillar of strength Nat knew.'

Already dreading the encounter, she said, 'How soon do I need to do it?'

Jolyon sipped his wine as he thought. 'It wouldn't be wise just to wade on in there, that way you could do more harm than good. Give yourself some time to think it over, decide what you want to say and how you're going to say it, then make sure you're alone in the house when you sit him down. Meantime, feel free to call me 24/7 if there's anything you want to ask or discuss.'

'Yes, this is Mrs Paige speaking,' Sabrina said into the phone.

'Hello, I'm calling from Dr Feverel's office,' the voice at the other end told her. 'I'm just confirming Annabelle's appointment for the day after tomorrow at ten o'clock.'

'Oh yes, thank you,' Sabrina said. 'She'll be there.'

'She knows she mustn't eat or drink anything during the twelve hours before, does she?'

'Yes, she does. Um, actually, her father will be bringing her.' She wouldn't say stepfather, because things being what they were these days, someone might presume Robert was the rapist.

'That's fine,' the receptionist assured her.

Sabrina wanted to explain why, as Annabelle's mother, she wouldn't be there, but unless she lied, which she'd considered, she'd have to admit that Annabelle didn't want her to be. Those weren't words she could speak aloud to anyone, even herself, so after thanking the receptionist politely she put the phone down and heaved a tremulous sigh.

Then, doing her best to push aside the rejection she was feeling from both her husband and her daughter, she turned to a problem that she might be more easily able to cope with: the printer and his exorbitant new prices.

Alicia was sitting on the floor in her mother's study, surrounded by her father's old letters. The urge to read them had suddenly come over her while she and Cameron were looking around a half-derelict barn that morning, and by the time she got home it still hadn't gone away.

It was strange, she was thinking now, as tears rolled down her cheeks, how feelings could come out of nowhere and with such force that they seemed to have words to make themselves heard. There was no explaining the need she'd suddenly felt to have the only contact she could with her father, it was simply there, a solid yet gentle insistence that had remained with her until she'd sat down half an hour ago with this cluttered little box.

The handwritten lines were too blurred for her to read the letter she was holding for a second time, but she would when she'd managed to pull herself together. There were whispers of gratitude inside her that wanted to be spoken, but when she tried they were broken apart by sobs. Was it really her father who'd brought her to this box today? Had he, from some other dimension, in some mystical way, managed to communicate his advice into her thoughts, so that she'd find this letter at a time when she couldn't have needed it more?

'Thank you,' she finally managed as she pressed the letter to her chest. 'Thank you, thank you.'

For days, since she'd spoken to Jolyon, she'd been trying to find a way to approach Nat, and now, having read this letter, she knew exactly how to do it.

Chapter Twenty-Three

'Sabrina, why do you keep checking the time?' June complained. 'Are you expecting someone? Or do you have to be somewhere?'

'Sorry. I'm waiting for a call from Robert, but it's probably still too early.'

'I'll say. It's still only half past four in the morning on the East Coast.'

'He came back yesterday,' Sabrina told her. 'He's had to go up to London . . . There's an important meeting he had to make and I . . . Well, I just keep wondering how it's going.'

'So why don't you call him to find out?'

'It won't be over yet. I'll try in about an hour. So, do you think we're about ready with the next issue?'

June sat back and folded her arms. They were in their usual office space at the back of the stately home where she rented a flat, and where a huddle of tourists was, at that moment, strolling past the window having a good look in. 'More or less,' she replied, ignoring their audience, 'except the piece on the Roswells' party isn't quite complete, or not from what I've been hearing.'

Sabrina shifted uncomfortably, as the bruise on her upper lip seemed to throb like a beacon.

'Felicity Singer-Smythe's hairdresser, who also happens to be my hairdresser,' June said smoothly, 'informs me that Alicia socked you one, then Robert spilt his drink down your dress and bundled you off home. So what on earth happened?'

'That's about it,' Sabrina answered, making a show of getting on with the work in front of her.

'But what made her hit you?' June wanted to know. 'Surely she didn't just come up and land one . . .'

'I said something,' Sabrina interrupted. 'I mean she did, then I did, and it got out of hand, and being the hysteric that she is she let fly with her fist. I fell into Robert, and his drink went all down my gorgeous cream dress, which is completely ruined, all thanks to her. Over a thousand pounds straight down the drain. Anyway, Robert only heard the tail end of it, so he's holding me responsible for what happened, and *she's* the one who lashed out, for goodness sake. It makes me sick the way he always defends her. I've a good mind to leave him. It might shock him into being more appreciative of a wife who's always supported him, no matter what.'

Except when you were having an affair with his brother-in-law, June wanted to point out, but it would have been cruel, so instead she said, 'I'd do some serious thinking before you embark on anything rash like moving out, in case he doesn't let you back in again.'

Sabrina shuddered at the thought of it. 'I didn't actually mean it,' she assured her. 'I'm just reaching my wits' end with him and I'm running out of ways to get through to him. Something's going on his head, I can tell, but he won't tell me what it is. All I know is that he seems to have struck up some sort of bond with Annabelle, which is a good thing, obviously, but it's starting to make me feel excluded in my own home.'

'He's probably feeling a bit stressed about something,' June said kindly, 'you know, the way men do.'

'Mm,' Sabrina murmured doubtfully. Then, after a shaky sigh, 'It's funny, isn't it, the way you always seem to want someone more when you think you might be losing them?'

'Tell me about it,' June said with a roll of her eyes. 'And you would know, having been there with Craig.'

Sabrina's eyes darted to her, then away again. 'What I had with Craig was . . . Well, it was different,' she said. 'I mean it was special, and passionate . . . It meant everything, obviously, but Craig's no longer here, and what I have with Robert . . . What we share is . . . Well, I guess it means everything.' It was only as she was speaking the words that their truth was beginning to dawn, and suddenly she felt more afraid than she ever had in her life.

Dr Feverel was a kindly looking middle-aged woman with neat silvery hair and a ready smile. 'You don't need to worry about a thing, Annabelle,' she was telling her warmly. 'A couple of hours and you'll be on your way home again.'

Annabelle's worried eyes moved to Robert.

He smiled reassuringly and squeezed her hand. 'I'll call Mum, shall I, and let her know we're here?'

Annabelle nodded. She couldn't speak, she was

too nervous about what was going to happen, and whether or not it might hurt.

After the doctor had taken her through, Robert wandered out to the street and flipped open his phone. There were two messages from Sabrina, and four missed calls, also from her, but Nat was due in court at ten and there were only a couple of minutes to go, so he must call Alicia first.

'Robert,' Alicia whispered into her mobile, 'there's been a bit of a delay. We're still in the lobby, waiting to go in, but I'm not supposed to use the phone out here.'

'OK, I just wanted to let Nat know I'm thinking of him. Is he OK?'

'I think so.' She looked at her son sitting on the hard leather sofa opposite the one she was on, his elbows on his knees, his head hanging down. This court at Taunton felt a whole lot more intimidating than the one at Wells. Lawyers in black gowns and wigs were coming and going, the gold-leaf signs were to public galleries, or the jury assembly room, or judge's chambers, and the marble busts looking over them were as formidable a bunch of dignitaries as any court could produce. The Shire Hall was used for no other purpose than to serve as courts of law, and though Nat was appearing before a youth panel again, this was his first taste of how it was going to be when it came to the actual trial.

'I'll call you later,' she said, catching the scowl of an usher who'd just noticed her transgression, and clicking off the line, she shut the phone down and slipped it into her pocket.

Nat didn't look up when Jolyon signalled Alicia to join him at the foot of the cantilevered staircase, nor did he exhibit any signs of trying to eavesdrop as Jolyon said, 'I take it you haven't had a chance to show him the letter yet?'

'No. Darcie's feeling very insecure at the moment, so it's been difficult to find some time on our own. He's taking the rest of the day off though, so I'm hoping to do it this afternoon. It doesn't matter for this morning, does it?'

'It shouldn't,' he replied, 'but the sooner you do it the better.' His eyes met hers and looked into them deeply. 'Thank you for letting me see it,' he said. 'I imagine it's had a fairly profound effect on you.'

She nodded as she swallowed. He was certainly right about that. 'What matters, though, is what it does for Nat,' she said.

He didn't disagree, and as the usher was calling them into court one, he gestured for her to fetch Nat and waited for them to join him to lead the way in.

This wasn't the easiest task Robert had ever undertaken, but there again he hadn't expected it to be, since he'd had next to no experience in dealing with teenage girls' gynaecological issues. However, as he drove Annabelle back through a rainy London towards the M3, he realised he wasn't expected to be an authority on what she'd just been through, he was simply required to ask the right sort of questions and listen whenever she felt like talking.

'It wasn't really that bad,' she was telling him, while shifting slightly in her seat. 'I mean, it didn't hurt or anything. Not that I'd want to do it again, mind you, but at least it's all over now, so we can get back to normal.'

That's never going to happen, he thought sadly to himself. 'Are you uncomfortable?' he asked as she shifted again.

'A little bit, but no, not really. I've got some painkillers, so I can always take one if it gets too bad.'

She was quiet for a while then, with her head lolling against the seat back, and her eyes half shut against the cluttered high streets of south-west London. 'We should probably call Mum,' she said for the third or fourth time.

'She'll be waiting to hear from you,' he told her.

She turned to look at him. 'I'm supposed to be seeing that Lisa from SAIT tomorrow,' she said. 'She's coming to the house.'

He nodded, and put his foot down as they reached the start of the motorway. 'What are you going to talk about?' he asked evenly.

She shrugged. 'I don't know really. Mum thinks I'm going through some sort of *victim* phase, so she wants Lisa to sort me out, as she puts it.'

'Do you think you're going through a phase?' he said. 'Or is it that you'd simply like all this to be over?'

'Well, of course I'd like it to be over, but I'm not sure if I should let him get away with it. I mean, I'd feel terrible if I found out later that he'd done it to someone else, and I could have stopped it.'

Throwing her a quick glance, he said, 'Is that you or your mother speaking?'

She thought about it. 'A bit of both, I suppose, but she's right, isn't she, you can't let someone get away with something as serious as rape.'

It was on the tip of his tongue to ask her if she really knew what rape was, but sensing she might find the question insulting, he said, 'Did you know Nathan's in court today?'

The way she turned away suggested she did.

'It's going to get very serious from now on,' he told her gravely. 'Not that it hasn't been already, but the next time he appears a real judge will be presiding, and the barristers will come in to start arguing the case. It's not going to be pleasant, having all your secrets talked about openly in court. It'll be the job of Nat's lawyer to paint as black a picture of you as he can.'

She sat quietly with that, before finally saying, 'I'm not actually going to be there. I'm doing it by video so that won't be as bad.'

'No, it's Nat who'll have to face the jury.'

'But all criminals do,' she reminded him.

'Indeed, but innocent people can find themselves there too sometimes, and that's probably a whole lot worse than if you committed the crime, to be charged with something you didn't do.'

'That would be terrible,' she agreed, 'but he did do it, Robert. Honestly.'

It wasn't the answer he'd hoped for. 'Really?' he prompted dejectedly.

As she swallowed, her eyes went down. 'Yes,' she said, 'but . . . Well, anyway, I don't want to talk about it any more,' and turning on her mobile, she pressed to connect to her mother.

* * *

As Jolyon and Oliver had promised, the committal proceedings turned out to be yet another formality to be gone through, this time to set a date for the Plea and Case Management hearing, which was scheduled for 7th October, just over four weeks from now.

After they had joined Jolyon for a pub lunch, Alicia drove Nat back to the Coach House, all the time wishing there was something she could say to lighten his mood, if only for a moment. However, instead, she was about to present him with something that was likely to plunge him even deeper into the darkness of his despair, and though she'd give anything to be able to go there for him, she knew that he had to do this alone. She'd be there for him, of course, and she was praying that by releasing all the pent-up emotion inside him he would find new reserves in himself to help him get through the ordeal ahead.

'Before you go upstairs,' she said, as she let them in the front door, 'there's something I want to show you.'

Not seeming particularly interested, he merely shrugged off his coat and started towards the kitchen.

'Why don't you go into the sitting room,' she suggested. 'I'll bring it in there.'

Doing as he was told, he slouched down at the end of the sofa and rested his head on one hand as he waited. When she came in he watched her put a slightly tatty box on the coffee table in front of him before coming to sit on the sofa too. 'What is it?' he asked, as she lifted the lid.

'They're letters Grandma kept from over the

years,' she told him. 'Most are from Grandpa, but there are others too, even some from you and Darcie when you were little.' She passed him a crumpled sheet of paper covered in a childish scrawl with spiky stars and a big half-moon drawn at the top. *Dear Grandma,* he read, *thank you for my fuzzy felts and the trip to the zoo. It was very nice and I loved all the animals especially the lions. Thank you for taking me. I love you, Nat.*

With a small raise of his eyebrows he handed it back.

Taking it, she braced herself as she said, 'There's one letter in particular that I'd like you to read.'

Shrugging, he held out a hand.

She didn't pass it over, but looked down at it herself as she said, 'It's from Dad, to Grandma, written just over a year ago.'

She saw his hand withdraw and when his eyes came up there was a heartbreaking expression of wariness, and even hostility, glowing in their depths.

'I think it'll explain things far better than I can,' she told him softly.

He started to shake his head.

'Please,' she insisted, gently pulling him back as he made to get up. 'Do this for me. I know it won't be easy, but I'd really like you to try.'

His eyes went back to the letter. His face had lost its colour now and he was looking more strained than ever. 'What does it say?' he asked tersely.

Taking a breath, she braced herself again and said, 'He's talking about what happened with Sabrina, and why . . . No, Nat, sit down, please,' she cried, grabbing him before he could get up. 'I know you know about the affair, so you need to read this. It's the only way you're going to understand and maybe forgive Dad, if you let him speak for himself.'

His eyes were still shining with angst and resistance as he looked at her.

'Here,' she said, taking his hand and putting the letter into it.

For a long time he simply sat with it, staring at his grandmother's name and address on the front of the envelope. The handwriting was so familiar to him that it was hard to look at, but at the same time he couldn't take his eyes away. He was too afraid to do this. He didn't have the courage to read his father's words and hear his voice in his head, and know it would be for the very last time. It would be as though he'd come back to life, only to die again. Nat wanted him back so much that it hurt all the time. He couldn't even look at photographs for more than a moment, so how could he possibly read an entire letter?

Taking the envelope back Alicia slipped the pages out, unfolded them and returned them to his hand. 'It's all right,' she promised. 'You'll see.'

Trying to swallow the growing lump in his throat, Nat looked down at the first two words, *Dear Monica,* and then, after a beat, he found himself reading on.

I've sat down many times to start this letter, but could never find the right way to begin, much less to explain the madness that came over me that ended up causing so much pain to your family and the rift that now exists between you and Alicia. Although the two of you speak regularly on the phone, and you know you are always welcome in our home, it is very difficult for her not to visit you in yours. She understands why you've asked her to stay away, and because she has no wish to run into Sabrina in the village, or to cause you any more worry or upset after the dreadful scene between them in front of you, she isn't insisting on coming. Nor am I seeking to change your mind. My aim is solely to try to apologise for all the anguish and unhappiness my actions have brought to you all. It would be too much to expect your forgiveness when I am unable to forgive myself, but I do hope I can convince you that my love for you all is, if anything, more profound than ever.

What happened with Sabrina was, as I said, a madness. Even now I am at a loss to explain how or why I lost all reason and judgement. All I can say is that there was a compulsion inside me that seemed oblivious to integrity, or loyalty. The entire time it was happening I hated myself for it, and yet I was unable to stop. No longer being in the grip of it makes it hard to describe how I was feeling or what I was thinking as it unfolded, I only know now that I wish with all my heart that it had never begun.

Ever since I first came into Alicia's life you have made me feel a welcome and cherished member of your family, so knowing how I've repaid you makes the burden of my guilt even harder to bear. I ask for no sympathy, I simply want you to know how deeply I respect and love you, and how truly sorry I am that all the wonderful times we have spent together in Holly Wood have come to an end. I know how much Alicia and the children miss coming to see you, but I hope that your health will soon improve enough for you to resume your visits here. If you would prefer me not to be around when you do, then I shall understand completely and make myself scarce.

Monica, there are no words to describe how much I love your daughter, and please believe me when I tell you that throughout the entire affair with Sabrina that never changed. The feelings I had for Sabrina were completely separate, as though they belonged to another existence, perhaps even to another man. They connected with a weakness inside me that I never knew was there until it was taking control. Whether that weakness, or the other man, still exist is difficult to say. I like to think not, but being in the profession I am I know how frail even the strongest character can be at times, and how capable we all are of doing things that in the normal course of events would be unthinkable, even abhorrent. I am relieved to say that my aberration didn't drive me into the realms of serious crime, though I sometimes wish that there was a punishment to fit my actions that might eventually release me from my guilt and return real happiness and trust to Alicia's heart.

I am sure that every day for the rest of my life I will ask myself how a man who had everything could have risked losing it all the way I did, and for so little. It's not my intention to diminish Sabrina with that comment, I am only trying to illustrate how very important Alicia is to me, and how meaningless sex actually is when weighed against all the things that really matter in life. You will know that Sabrina is a good and admirable woman who, I am sad to say, also lost sight of what is right for a while. Because of the letters she still sends me and the messages she occasionally leaves on my phone, I know she continues to find it hard to accept the end of our liaison. I have tried speaking to her once or twice, but to no avail. She seems convinced that I only stayed with Alicia because of the children, and that as soon as Darcie leaves home we will be together. Should she ever repeat this to you, I want you to be very sure that it is not true. If I ever gave her cause to believe that I had plans to abandon my family, either now or at any time in the future, then it was entirely unintentional, because I have never even entertained the idea. I am truly sorry Sabrina is still suffering, and I accept full responsibility for the way my unguarded words and actions could have led her to hope for an outcome that was never going to be. I worry a lot about the threats she makes to end it all, but Alicia and the children are my first concern, and I would like to believe that Sabrina cares far too much for Robert and Annabelle to take such a drastic course of action.

For fear of this turning into one of the longest mea culpas in history, I will now turn away from myself to the two of the brightest stars in your sky, Nathan and Darcie. I know Alicia gives you regular updates on what they are doing and sends you copies of their school reports, so you will be aware of how fast and furiously they are growing up. Darcie is really starting to blossom now, looking more like her mother every day, and frequently behaving like mine! Between us, I adore the way she bosses me around, treating me as though I'm a bit of a delinquent, then comes to me with her woes, certain I'll be able to make everything all right again. That's what we expect of our parents, isn't it? That they can make the world a safe place to be, and chase all the bad things away. It's a hard, but salutary experience when our eyes are finally opened to the fact that they are human too. For the moment I believe I am still safe in my role as Darcie's chief dragon-slayer, but as she herself informed me only yesterday, when I was telling her about my day in court, I mustn't get too big for my boots. So she's still a little madam who effervesces with so much life and affection that she makes it an absolute pleasure to come home every night. Oh, to see that same look of love and trust in Alicia's eyes again, but I think we are making progress, and no matter how long it takes I'm determined to win it back one day.

I know, as soon as I mention Nat, that you'll start to glow, much as Alicia does. I sometimes fear for how popular he's going to be with the opposite sex and hope it doesn't distract him too much from his goals, but at the same time it's my belief that the love and respect he has for his mother will mean that he always treats a girl well. You'll know from his reports how well he's doing at school, both in sports and with his academic studies. He's a lively and popular young lad, with a little too much to say for himself at times, but I probably would say that today after he bested me in a debate on the environment last night. Needless to say he's a member of the debate team at school, and there's a good chance all the victories will soon start going to his head. We'll have to keep that in check, while allowing his confidence to grow.

I am so proud of him, Monica, that it brings tears to my eyes as I write this. Gone are the days when I could sit him on my knee or envelop him in a giant bear hug, so I have to find other ways of showing how much I care. I hope I do that in the time I spend with him, either helping with his homework, discussing and advising on his choices, or simply hanging out as guys. He's great company, always full of opinions, but witty and sharp in a way that can make Alicia and me laugh till we cry. How he enjoys those moments! I can see in his eyes how proud and happy he feels to have made an impression. It's at times like these, when we're together as a family, that I realise how much I could have lost, and how thankful I am that Alicia allowed me to stay.

Like any parent I often wonder what will happen to us all in the future, but I have no doubts that Nat will achieve his ambitions. The road is already set for him to go into the law, and since he remains as determined as ever to do so, I'm already looking forward to (or perhaps dreading) the day I have to stand up against my own son in court. As I keep telling him, there won't be any letting him win then, and he's promised that in spite of the great age I will have achieved by that time (his words!), he won't be cutting me any slack either.

It would be unforgivably boastful for me to run on any more about my children, I simply wanted you to be sure of how much I love them. It is my great hope that things will change before much longer in a way that will make it possible for them to visit you again. Monica, I am truly sorry for the heartache I have caused you. I have often felt closer to you than I ever did to my own mother, and I know it's thanks to you and the influence you've had over Alicia that my children are shaping into such wonderful human beings. Please know, whatever happens, that I will always strive to right my wrongs and to overcome my weaknesses so that your grandchildren will be able to feel as proud of their father as I do of them.

Yours, with great affection,

Craig

Nat's head stayed down as he stopped reading, masking his face, but Alicia could see the slight shaking of his shoulders, and almost felt the cracks starting to open up in his defences. Knowing how close he was to the edge now, she was ready to catch him, and when the first terrible sob was wrenched from his heart her arms closed in fast.

'I want him back, Mum,' he choked. 'I want him back.'

'I know, darling,' she soothed, tears starting down her own cheeks.

'Dad, *Dad*, please come back,' he cried desperately.

Alicia held him tight and kissed his hair as the force of his grief tore through him. It was racking and convulsing him, dragging him to a place of unbearable loss. He dropped to his knees in his anguish. Alicia knelt beside him and stroked his back as one harsh sob followed another.

'Dad!' he shouted again. 'Please, Dad. Come back. Why did he have to die, Mum? It's not right. It's not fair.'

'I know, darling, I know,' she said, still crying herself. 'But what matters now is how much he loved you, and how proud he was of you.'

'He loved you, Mum. He really did.'

'I know, darling.' She knew that now, just as

she knew that it really had been over between him and Sabrina. He hadn't been tearing himself apart, wanting to be with her, becoming so stressed with longing and riddled with guilt that it had ended up killing him. How desperately she wished she could tell him that she finally believed he'd never meant to leave, that she trusted him again and forgave him with all her heart. If only her mother had opened the letter, she'd have known too how truly sorry he was. It would have helped Monica so much to know that. It could have made such a difference to them all, but there was no point dwelling on that now. They couldn't change what had happened, they could only look forward and feel thankful that she'd found the letter when she had, because it was as though Craig himself had stepped in to help his son at a time when Nat couldn't have needed him more.

'I can't let him down, Mum,' Nat gasped, his face ravaged with tears. 'I can't let all this stop me . . .'

'It won't,' she whispered, smoothing back his hair as she kissed him.

'Do you forgive him?' he spluttered brokenly. 'Please say you do. I don't think he meant to hurt you, he just . . . he just . . .'

'It's OK,' she said, as his words ran out. 'Of course I forgive him. This letter has . . . Well, it's told me everything I needed to know too. I think we can start grieving properly now for the man we loved and who we know, without any doubt, loved us.'

* * *

Later in the day, while Alicia went to collect Darcie from school, Nat wandered down The Close towards the river. Though his body ached, and his head still throbbed from all the crying, he didn't seem to feel as heavy as he had before, or as tense. Since reading the letter and breaking down in a way he'd never want anyone to see, apart from his mother, they'd sat talking about his father for a long time, sharing their memories and confiding things they'd never told one another before. They'd cried a lot more and laughed, and for a while they'd sat quietly, saying nothing at all as they read the letter again.

Now, as he reached the riverbank, a fine drizzle replacing the tears on his cheeks, he found himself turning towards the footbridge that led over to the Copse. It was the first time he'd taken, or even looked in this direction, since that terrible night. He wasn't surprised to see that there was no blue and white tape cordoning off the scene now, no police or CSI vehicles cluttering up the road, or crowds straining to get a look at what was happening. It had all moved on long ago, leaving the place leafy and peaceful, the way it always was.

Stepping on to the bridge he crossed halfway and stood staring into the Copse beyond. There was no one else around, and the only sound breaking the silence was of the river trickling over rocks. He wasn't sure why he didn't want to go any further, or why he'd even come this way, he only knew that his footsteps had led him here, almost as though they had a will of their own.

He wondered if his father could see him now, or read his mind, or feel inside his heart. He felt connected to him in a way he hadn't since he'd died, but whether that was because of something beyond him, or deep within, he had no idea. It was a debate he'd like to have with his father, whether there was life after death, or something akin. More tears smarted in his eyes as the future yawned emptily without him. He'd never know his father's opinions on that now, and realising it he felt the terrible loss opening up again and sucking him in.

'I'll always be there for you, son,' Craig said as they walked out of the school gates together. 'An injustice was done, and we've put it right. Never be afraid to stand up and speak if you feel yourself to be right, and be the first to apologise if you find you're wrong.'

The issue his father had come to the school to help him address was irrelevant now, it was the words he'd spoken that mattered, and the way he, Nat, had taken it for granted that day, like every other day, that his father *would* always be there.

He stared down at the water, and seeing the reflection of the sky he wondered if the feeling that his father was close by right now might actually mean that he was. He wanted to believe it, but at the same time he wasn't sure if he had the courage to. What would he say to him, he wondered, if he had the chance to say a final goodbye? He didn't know, he couldn't think, but then Darcie's silly poems came to his mind and he swallowed as he smiled self-consciously. *'I love you very much with all my might, Having you as my dad means I'm getting things right.'*

Hearing a noise behind him he spun round, and seeing Annabelle standing a short way along the bank, he turned cold inside. Afraid it might be a trap, he quickly left the bridge and started to run back the way he'd come. As soon as he got home he picked up the phone to call Jolyon, needing to let him know that he'd just breached his bail.

'I don't know if she followed me, or if it was simply coincidence,' he said. 'I just thought I should report it before she does, because the last thing I need is to be arrested again for something I didn't do.'

Chapter Twenty-Four

It was unusual for Robert to find himself interrupted while working in his study early in the morning, especially by a knock on the door. Generally if someone was looking for him they used the intercom, so it was with a feeling of disgruntlement and dismay that he realised it was probably Sabrina bringing him a breakfast he didn't want, in an attempt to win herself back into favour.

'Robert? Are you in there?'

Surprised to hear Annabelle, he immediately got to his feet and went to open the door. She was standing in the drizzle, a raincoat over her head, masking the top half of her face.

'Are you all right?' he asked, quickly ushering her in. 'I wasn't expecting you to be up yet.'

'It's half past ten,' she told him.

Blinking at the clock he gave an ironic smile, but still concerned about her and what she'd been through the day before, he said, 'How are you feeling this morning?'

She shrugged. 'I'm OK. A bit, you know, down there, but otherwise all right.'

Presuming the missing word was sore, he said, 'Have you taken the painkillers?'

'I did last night, but it's fine now. I just feel a bit tired, I suppose, and fed up and . . .' She shrugged.

Weepy, he thought, by the look of her, but he didn't say it. 'So to what do I owe this pleasure?' he asked kindly, gesturing for her to sit down on one of his visitors' sofas.

After perching on the edge of it and bunching her coat on her lap, she waited for him to sit down too, then said, 'I just thought . . . Well, actually, I wanted to say thank you for taking me yesterday.'

Touched by her gratitude, and the effort she'd made to come here and voice it, he said, 'You were very brave and I was extremely proud of you.'

She shifted a shoulder again, but whether it was to be dismissive or because she was embarrassed, he couldn't quite tell. What he could sense, though, was that she was here for more than a mere thank you, but whatever it was, he'd let her get to it in her own good time.

'If it was up to me I'd have gone back to school today,' she said, gazing around the room, 'but Mum's arranged for Lisa, you know, the woman from SAIT, to come here this morning.'

'Ah, yes,' he said solemnly. 'What time are you expecting her?'

'Eleven.' Tilting her head to one side, she began drawing invisible squirls on the arm of the sofa.

He watched, saying nothing, as he waited for her to summon the words she seemed to be struggling to find.

'I saw Nat yesterday,' she finally managed, her eyes remaining on the sweep of her finger.

'Really?' he said, keeping his tone mild, though his heartbeat had quickened.

She nodded. 'I think . . .' She took a breath that juddered like a sob. 'It looked like he'd been crying,' she said. 'I mean, it was hard to tell from where I was standing, but that's how it looked. I expect, I mean, I wondered if it might have had something to do with him going to court yesterday.'

'I suppose it could have,' Robert agreed.

Her eyes flicked to him, then away again. 'So you haven't heard what happened?'

'If you're asking if I've spoken to Nat or Alicia, the answer's yes, and the next hearing is scheduled to take place on the seventh of October. That's when they'll set the trial date.'

Her eyes stayed down as a flush of colour spread up from her neck over her cheeks. 'Do you think,' she said, after a while, 'I mean . . . What if I said I didn't want to be a part of the trial? Would they just cancel it?'

Treading even more carefully now, he said, 'That would probably depend on why you were saying it. If you want to drop the charge . . . Is that what you're saying?'

Still not looking at him, she continued circling her finger around the arm of the sofa, until in the end she nodded. 'I think so,' she said quietly.

Trying to ignore the leap of hope in his chest, so as not to go too fast, he said, 'You'd have to be sure.'

Her eyes finally came up to his, and it startled and concerned him to see how deeply troubled they were. 'I am sure,' she said, 'but if I do, everyone's going to call me a liar, and I'm not. I told the truth about what happened.'

His mouth turned dry. 'You mean that he raped you?'

'Yes.'

'Then why would you want to drop the charge?'

She shrugged. 'Because.'

He waited.

'It's just making everyone stressed and unhappy, and if it's going to affect the rest of his life, and mine . . . I mean, I know it will, so . . . It's not worth it, is it?'

Sitting back in the chair, he gave himself a moment to think. 'Have you talked to your mother about this?' he asked.

She baulked as though he was crazy. *'Noooo,'* she answered. 'You know what she's like. She'll go ballistic.'

Starting to get a slightly better sense of the picture now, he said, 'So you're hoping I'll do it for you?'

Her eyes turned imploring. 'She'll only try to talk me out of it, or get Lisa Murray to, and I don't want to go on with it any more,' she wailed. 'It's just stupid, the way everyone's getting it all out of proportion and calling people names. It's not like Darcie did anything wrong, is it, so I don't understand why anyone's picking on her.'

'But this isn't about Darcie, or calling people names,' he reminded her gravely.

'I know that, I'm just saying. All the other stuff about court and prison and getting labelled for the rest of his life . . . Well, that's just dumb. It wasn't as though he really hurt me . . . all that much. I mean, I've survived, haven't I?'

Deciding to run the extent of his devil's advocate

role, he said, 'If he forced himself on you, Annabelle . . .'

'I don't want to talk about it any more,' she cut in sharply. 'I just want you to tell Mum what I've decided.'

He regarded her steadily, still not entirely sure which way to go.

'Please,' she added.

He sighed, and pressed his fingers to his eyes. 'OK, I'll speak to her,' he said in the end, 'but you need to be there too.'

Looking decidedly reluctant, she said, 'Only if you promise not to leave me alone with her.'

Having to suppress a smile at that, he said, 'You have my word. So when do you want to do this? Before the SAIT officer arrives, or while she's here?'

She gave it some thought. 'I don't know. What do you think?'

Taking his own time to ponder the options, he said, 'It might be best to give Mum a chance to get used to the idea before the officer turns up.'

Seeing Robert and Annabelle coming across the garden, Sabrina felt a flash of irritation and unease knife through her head. They were conspiring to shut her out, conjuring up a friendship between them that would totally exclude her. She felt suddenly disoriented, helpless even, like an intruder in her own home.

Doing her best to rein in her fears, she quickly returned to her good intentions by emptying the coffee pot to start making fresh, and turning on the oven to . . . She tried to think what she needed to heat up, but couldn't remember. It didn't matter, she told herself, it would come back to her. Meanwhile, she must try looking at Robert and Annabelle's relationship a different way, not as a conspiracy to try and shut her out. Whatever secrets they might have, or closeness they might be pursuing after their shared experience of yesterday, it could surely only be a good thing. The fonder Robert was of Annabelle, the less likely he was to do anything drastic like ending their marriage.

The very thought of that sent so many bolts of dread shooting through her that her hands flew to her mouth as a sob broke in a ragged gasp from her throat.

She had to calm down, she told herself urgently. Everything was going to be fine, she just had to stop letting this ridiculous paranoia get the better of her.

Having bought some of Robert's favourite short-breads yesterday, she laid a rosy paper napkin over a plate, shook three loose from the packet, arranged them decoratively, then put them on the table next to his mail.

'Good morning,' she said brightly as he came in through the door. 'I was hoping you might come over for coffee. How are you feeling this morning?' she asked Annabelle, looking at her with deep motherly concern.

'I'm cool,' Annabelle mumbled, seeming to half hide behind Robert.

Sabrina looked at her, then at Robert, and as more alarm bells began clanging in her head her smile faltered.

'Annabelle's decided she doesn't want to go ahead with the charges,' Robert told her, coming straight to the point.

Sabrina's thoughts hit a brick wall as she registered the words.

'We've talked it over,' he continued, 'and I think . . .'

'Just a minute,' Sabrina interrupted, her voice edged with a harshness that had swept straight past her misgivings: 'What do you mean, you don't want to go ahead?' she said to Annabelle. 'We agreed you were going to talk this over with Lisa.'

'Yeah, but . . .'

'No buts,' Sabrina told her sharply. 'You can't just accuse someone of rape, and then suddenly say they didn't do it.'

'I'm not saying that,' Annabelle cried.

'Then what are you saying?'

'That I don't want to go on with it.'

Sabrina turned to Robert. 'This is your doing, isn't it?' she accused. 'You've talked her out of it to save your nephew. So once again your family comes first and mine doesn't count.'

'That's utter rubbish,' Robert informed her angrily. 'Annabelle took the decision herself, my only involvement was to listen, and then to come and break it to you.'

Turning back to Annabelle, Sabrina struggled to find her next words. 'Tell me honestly,' she finally managed, 'did that boy rape you?'

'Yes, but I don't care. I don't want it taking over my life the way it is. I just want it to stop.'

'So you're going to let him get away with it?'

Annabelle coloured and turned her face away.

'And so are you,' she said to Robert. 'You've decided that a rapist should walk free . . .'

'Stop overdramatising it,' Robert cut in. 'He's a seventeen-year-old boy who might have misunderstood a situation, or overreacted in the heat of the moment . . .'

'You're putting words in her mouth,' Sabrina shouted. 'How do you know what happened when you weren't even there?'

'I'm just trying to help put some perspective on . . .'

'No, you're just trying to help your sister, and somehow you've talked my daughter into aiding and abetting you.'

'He did not,' Annabelle cried. 'I made up my own mind.'

'Really? Then I'd like to have a word with you alone, young lady, to find out exactly what *is* going on in your mind.'

'No way,' Annabelle retorted, shrinking behind Robert. 'I'm not being bullied about by you . . .'

'Sabrina, will you please try to calm down,' Robert said. 'There's someone at the door, and it's probably the SAIT officer turned up early.'

'Good,' Sabrina seethed, heading towards the hall, 'let's hope she can talk some sense into you, Annabelle, because someone obviously needs to.'

After all but pulling a startled Lisa Murray over the threshold, Sabrina took her straight to the kitchen, saying, 'I'm afraid my daughter's having something of a crisis, so I'd be grateful if you could talk to her and make her see sense.'

Lisa Murray looked from Annabelle to Robert and back again.

'Annabelle wants to withdraw the charges,' Robert informed her.

Lisa hid her surprise and returned her gaze to Annabelle. 'OK,' she said carefully.

'OK?' Sabrina repeated scathingly.

Ignoring her, Lisa said, 'Can I ask why, Annabelle?'

'Because she's got bored with it,' Sabrina raged. 'She's had to wait too long for centre stage . . .'

'Mrs Paige,' Lisa interrupted, 'I think it would be a good idea if I spoke to Annabelle alone.'

'You realise everyone's going to call you a liar, don't you?' Sabrina ranted on. 'She's still saying he did it,' she told Lisa, 'but . . .'

'Sabrina, that's enough,' Robert barked. 'Either cool your temper, or leave the room.'

Sabrina's outrage exploded. 'How dare you speak to me like that?' she yelled. *'I'm* not the fifteen-year-old, she is . . .'

'Then stop behaving like one,' he snapped, and, turning to Annabelle, 'Do you want to speak to Lisa alone? No one's going to force you to do anything you don't want to, so it's your decision.'

Annabelle looked uncertainly at Lisa.

Lisa smiled. 'Your stepfather's right,' she said, 'no one's going to force you to do anything.'

Sensing another eruption from Sabrina, Robert took her by the arm and held on to it tightly.

'All right,' Annabelle said. 'But I'm not changing my mind,' she told her mother, 'so don't think I am.'

Once in the drawing room with Annabelle, Lisa waited until they were both seated on the sofas before saying, 'Are you absolutely sure this is what you want?'

Annabelle nodded.

'Your stepfather hasn't influenced you in any way?'

'No! I just want it all to go away so I can get on with my life.'

'But you're still saying Nathan raped you?'

'Because he did.'

'And you're happy for him to go unpunished for this crime?'

'Not happy, no, but it's better than ruining the rest of his life, and knowing I'm to blame.'

'As the victim, you can't be to blame, especially given your age.'

'You know what I mean.'

Lisa regarded her intently. 'On the two previous occasions we met, I stressed to you the importance of telling the truth, and what the consequences could be if you don't. So if you're lying about the fact Nathan raped you . . .'

'I'm not *lying*,' Annabelle shouted, starting to cry. 'I just don't want all this hassle any more.'

'OK,' Lisa said, getting to her feet. 'If you really are sure, then we should go and talk to your parents again.'

Finding Robert and Sabrina still in the kitchen, Lisa kept her hand on Annabelle's shoulder as she said, 'I'm satisfied Annabelle's sincere in her decision to drop the rape charge, so I'm going to contact DS Bevan to let him know. You understand there may be repercussions . . .'

'What does that mean?' Sabrina demanded, clearly still highly agitated.

'I won't know until I've spoken to DS Bevan.'

'Well, when you do, you can tell him that I want that boy prosecuted for unlawful sex at the very least.'

'I'll call from the car on my way back to Bristol,' Lisa told her. 'I've no doubt you'll hear from him by the end of the day.'

'Well, there's an interesting coincidence,' Bevan remarked after hearing Lisa out. 'Annabelle Preston gets cold feet on the very day the CPS gets them too.'

'You mean he's thrown it out anyway?' Lisa said, more shocked than she'd expected to be, given that she'd sensed it coming.

'I got the call about ten minutes ago. Your phone was switched off, so I couldn't let you know.'

'What happened?'

'At a guess, the lawyers' pressure finally paid off. It was always going to be a difficult sell to the jury, but personally I think his lie at the start would have got them on our side. I suppose we'll never know now.'

'She's still adamant he raped her.'

'And she'd better stay that way, or she'll be facing charges herself. Do you believe her?'

'Yes, as a matter of fact. How's Caroline Ash taking the CPS's decision?'

'Hard. The weasel wisely went to ground after breaking it to her by phone, and left the rest of us to catch the flak. She wants the boy for unlawful sex now.'

'So does Mrs Paige. What's your take on that?'

There was a drop-out on the line as he answered.

'What was that?' she said when he came back again.

As he repeated it, she felt herself wincing. 'I'll let you break that one to Mrs Paige,' she told him, 'but please wait until I'm safely back in Bristol before you do.'

'Oh my God,' Alicia said shakily as Jolyon told her the news. 'Are you sure? There can't be any mistake?'

His tone was full of fondness as he said, 'Believe me, I wouldn't be calling if I weren't sure. The CPS has dropped the rape charge.'

As her knees buckled with relief Alicia sank heavily into the chair behind her. 'I have to call Nat. He . . .'

'Just wait on that for now,' Jolyon advised. 'They're still discussing the unlawful sex charge, so let's hang on until we have a full picture.'

'Yes, of course. Oh God, they have to drop that too. Please . . .'

'Leave it to Oliver. He sounded pretty confident when we spoke, so my guess is he's not intending to leave the conference until he has a favourable outcome on that too.'

Detective Inspector Caroline Ash's normally waxen complexion was mottled with fury as she scanned the contents of the letter she was holding. With her in the room was Tom Bradley, aka the weasel, or the CPS lawyer, and the eminent Oliver Mendenhall QC.

'Of course, there will be no need to send this letter to the Director of Public Prosecutions,' Oliver said smoothly, 'if you decided to drop *all* charges against my client.'

'This is blackmail,' Ash growled furiously.

'No, it's justice,' Mendenhall corrected. 'You don't have enough evidence to prove that an actual rape took place, so pursuing this case in any form is, at best, a waste of taxpayers' money, at worst . . .' He gestured to the letter. Since it detailed the ongoing vendetta Detective Inspector Ash was waging against Craig Carlyle QC, deceased, there was no mistaking his meaning. It went on to suggest she was now visiting her grudge on Carlyle's son by attempting to make him pay for what could be termed the sins of his father. The letter concluded with a request for the DPP to instruct the CPS to assess, and ultimately dismiss the case, and was signed by no less than twenty of the most influential barristers in the land.

Ash tossed the letter back across the table. 'I know you silks think you're mightily clever when you band together like this,' she said angrily, 'but it's you who's making it personal, not me. Annabelle Preston is a fifteen-year-old girl. It's time kids out there, like your client, learned that there are consequences to be paid for having underage sex – and it's not just pregnancy or a sexually transmitted disease. They are breaking the law . . .'

'That may be so, Detective Inspector,' Mendenhall interrupted, 'and to a point we all agree with you, but I'm not going to let you use my client to front your crusade, any more than I will allow him to become the victim of your grudge. We now know that the girl herself has dropped the rape charge, which strongly suggests she was lying, and as Nathan Carlyle was uncertain of her age at the time the act took place . . .'

'Oh pull the other one,' Ash cut in scathingly. 'He's her cousin for God's sake, and you don't need me to tell you ignorance of the law is not a defence.'

'And you don't need me to tell you that hanging a teenage boy out to dry because his father once bested you in court is not the kind of impartial behaviour the public expects, and deserves, from someone in your position . . .'

'Listen,' she broke in forcefully, 'I won't deny I'd like to have seen Craig Carlyle fry at some point in his loathsome career, but I'll tell you again, what happened back then has nothing to do with the situation we have here. Nathan Carlyle has broken the law. We have all the evidence we need to prove it, including a confession from the boy himself. He had sex with Annabelle Preston, and I have every intention of seeing he is prosecuted in accordance with the law, which will include his name being added to the Sex Offenders Register.'

Mendenhall sat back in his chair and folded his hands. 'In which case,' he said mildly, 'we will be insisting that the other two boys whose semen was found are also prosecuted and added to the register.'

Ash's face froze.

'Why ruin one young man's life when you can ruin three?' Mendenhall asked, as though she were offering to hand out accolades. 'Or, I'm forgetting,

I believe you've never actually identified one of the boys, have you, so I hope you're prepared to start using some of your valuable police resources to track him down. I also hope it's going to sit easily with you to put the girl herself through the humiliation, and perhaps trauma, of having her promiscuity brandished about in a courtroom. Not to mention the anguish and shame you will cause the families of the other two boys when their beloved sons' names are added to the Sex Offenders Register *for the rest of their lives*, thanks to a casual encounter with an overdeveloped fifteen-year-old at a rave during their formative years.'

Ash looked at the weasel, who shifted uncomfortably in his chair, but apparently the little creep had nothing to say.

Mendenhall knew he'd won, but he waited patiently for her reply.

In the end all he got was a glare of blazing hatred as she rose to her feet and stalked furiously from the room, slamming the door behind her.

Addressing the weasel, Mendenhall said, 'I take it you won't be pressing charges.'

'Correct,' the lawyer replied, and picking up his files he followed Ash from the room.

'At last,' Sabrina barked into the phone. 'I've been waiting for your call, Mr Bevan.'

'That would be Detective Sergeant,' he informed her smoothly. 'I'm sorry it's taken a while to get back to you, but I've only just received confirmation from the CPS that we won't be pursuing a charge of unlawful sex.'

Sabrina's whole frame pumped with indignation. 'May I ask why not?' she said through her teeth.

'Given the circumstances,' he replied, 'it was not considered the right course of action.'

'Given the circumstances,' she repeated scathingly, 'I'd say it was exactly the right course. You know my daughter's age, there's no doubt the sexual act took place . . .'

'Can I stop you there,' Bevan came in. 'Certainly the act took place, but I'm afraid if we charge Nathan Carlyle we'll be forced to charge the other young men who had sex with your daughter that night, and that isn't a course the CPS wants to take.'

Sabrina's mouth sagged as she reeled. 'What other young men?' she demanded faintly.

There was the sound of pages turning before Bevan said, 'One was a local lad called Theo McAllister. Unfortunately, your daughter wasn't able to provide us with the full name of the other.'

Sabrina's face twitched as she tried to reject what he was saying. 'There must be some mistake,' she told him.

'I'm afraid not.'

She opened her mouth, but nothing came out.

'As a parent myself,' Bevan continued, 'I can't imagine you'd want to put your daughter through . . .'

'Thank you, Detective Sergeant,' she cut in suddenly, and without as much as a goodbye she banged down the phone, stormed out to the hall, and up the stairs into Annabelle's room.

'What the hell . . . ?' Annabelle cried.

'I've just been speaking to the police,' Sabrina told her, her eyes glittering with rage, 'and do you know what they told me?'

A dart of fear shot through Annabelle as she drew back against the bed. 'How would I?' she retorted.

'What's going on?' Robert demanded, appearing in the doorway.

'I'll tell you what's going on,' Sabrina shouted. 'I have just been informed by the police that my daughter had sex with no less than *three* boys the night Nathan Carlyle raped her.'

Stunned, Robert looked at Annabelle, who had guilt written all over her.

'One of them was Theo McAllister,' Sabrina ranted on, 'but apparently she doesn't even know the name of the other one.' Her anger turned almost feral as she began advancing on Annabelle. 'What's the matter with you?' she seethed. 'You have everything any girl your age could want. You go to the right school, you come from a decent home, you have more pocket money than some people earn in a . . .'

'Get away from me,' Annabelle shouted, scooting round her and making for the door.

'You are not running away from this,' Sabrina cried. 'You've lied, you've . . .'

'I did not lie!'

'. . . made me look a fool, you've wasted police time, but worse, far, far worse than that, you've turned into a slut.'

Annabelle's eyes blazed. 'Don't you dare call me that,' she screamed. 'It's you who's . . .'

'That's enough!' Robert barked, sensing it was

about to turn physical, and scooping Annabelle round the waist he carried her out to the landing.

'She is such a bitch,' Annabelle sobbed. 'She always blames me for everything and now she's calling me names . . .'

'What do you expect, when you behave the way you do?' Sabrina yelled. 'I can't imagine what . . .'

'Sabrina, go downstairs, or into your own bedroom,' Robert said sharply.

'She's not getting away with this,' Sabrina informed him. 'She's going to be punished . . .'

'Will you please just go?' Robert cut in angrily as Annabelle turned her face into his chest.

'You are grounded until you're *eighteen*,' Sabrina shouted over her shoulder.

'I'll be gone before that,' Annabelle spat back.

'Good. Let me know when you're ready and I'll help you pack.'

Clutching Annabelle tightly in an effort to stop her saying more, Robert bundled her back into her room and closed the door.

'I hate her,' Annabelle sobbed, throwing herself on to the bed. 'She's always picking on me, and saying horrible things . . .'

'Ssh,' Robert tried to soothe, 'she doesn't mean them . . .'

'Yes she does. She hates me and I couldn't care less, because I'm leaving. I'll find somewhere else to live where I'm wanted.'

'You're wanted here, but she's angry at the moment, and you have to admit, she has reason to be.'

'But she's got no right to call me a slut, not

when she behaves the way she does. She's the one who has affairs and . . .'

'She had one affair.'

'How do you know? She could have slept with anyone . . .'

'Annabelle, this isn't getting us anywhere.'

She took a breath, but he put a hand over her mouth.

'That's enough,' he told her. 'I want you to lie here now and try to calm down, because we'll never achieve anything while tempers are running out of control.'

'Tell that to her. She's the one who started it.'

Letting the childish belligerence pass, he said, 'Would you like me to bring you a drink of something?'

She shook her head, then her face crumpled as she started to cry. 'It's not fair,' she sobbed, 'I'm trying to do the right thing so Nat doesn't have to go to court any more, and Darcie doesn't get called names, but no one ever cares about me.'

'That isn't true,' he told her, wrapping her in his arms. 'I care about you very much indeed, and in your heart you know your mother does too.'

'Then she's got a funny way of showing it, coming in here like some crazy freak like she was going to hit me or something.'

'I agree, it's not necessarily the right way of showing it,' he said, 'but try to think of it this way, if she didn't get angry that would mean she really didn't care.'

Swallowing hard, and still looking mutinous, Annabelle turned her face to the wall.

He went on sitting beside her, holding her hand

and wondering how much of what had happened over the last six weeks had been rooted in the truth, and how much was a cry for attention, or rebellion, or a way of punishing her mother. There was no doubt at all she was a very troubled young lady, and something had to be done to try to put her back on the straight and narrow. He wished he knew how to do it, but he wasn't going to flatter himself that he could find the answers alone, particularly when the person she really needed, though he knew she'd hotly deny it if he told her, was her mother. However, he had to accept, whether he wanted to or not, that Sabrina was in no fit state to deal with her right now, so he had to come up with some kind of solution.

'Do you think . . .' Annabelle said croakily. She turned round to look at him. 'Do you think Nat would talk to me?'

Surprised, and completely thrown, and not at all sure Nat would, he said, 'I guess we could always ask him.'

'Would you do it? I mean, I can't go round there, and he probably won't take my call, so . . .' She shrugged, apparently having run out of words.

Still feeling extremely doubtful, Robert said, 'Tell you what, I promised Alicia I'd pop over this evening, so if the opportunity presents itself, I'll put it to him.'

She nodded, and as her eyes slid sadly away he was reminded of how very young she really was. A child in a woman's body, she was no more able to handle her early maturity and raging hormones than she was to change the events that had added such a difficult and damaging mix to the normal turmoil of teenage anguish and confusion.

'I'm going to leave you to have a nap now,' he said, giving her hand a squeeze as he noticed her eyes starting to droop. 'I'll be back up to check on you later.'

'OK,' she said faintly. 'Don't let her come in, will you?'

After closing the door quietly behind him, he crossed the landing to his and Sabrina's room where he found her sitting on a window seat, wringing her hands as she stared out at the garden.

'I feel so humiliated,' she said, when she realised he was there. 'How could she have behaved like that? What's happened to her?'

Though he was able to answer her questions, he wasn't going to now, so all he said was, 'There are some phone calls I have to make, and then I'm going out for a while, but tomorrow, Sabrina, you and I will need to talk.'

Though in many ways Alicia wanted to crack open endless bottles of champagne and celebrate tonight, she knew the past six weeks, not to mention the last twenty-four hours since reading his father's letter, had been far too traumatic for Nat to allow him to feel any real sense of elation yet. So, foreseeing how profoundly the good news was likely to affect him, she waited until they were back in the house after school before telling him that all the charges had been dropped.

For a moment he simply looked at her blankly, then, as Darcie began jumping for joy, the relief came over him so forcefully that he could barely catch his breath as he started to sob.

Taking him in her arms Alicia wept along with

him, and as Darcie wrapped herself around them both they hugged and kissed and laughed as they continued to cry.

'See, I told you it would be all right,' Darcie said tearfully. 'I knew it would be, and now all those horrid people at school are going to look really stupid. *Plus,*' she went on gleefully, 'the whole world will know that Annabelle's a *liar*.'

Having guessed a lot more had gone on at school than they'd told her about, Alicia let the unguarded admission pass, saying, 'Actually, there's something else you should know. Apparently, this morning, before anyone knew the case was being dismissed, Annabelle withdrew the charge.'

Both Nat and Darcie looked at her in amazement.

She smiled, and stroked their faces.

'Why did she do that?' Nat wanted to know.

'Who cares, as long as she did,' Darcie answered.

'Uncle Robert thinks she couldn't face the trial,' Alicia said, repeating what Robert had told her. 'Actually, that might be him now,' she added as the phone started to ring.

Being the closest, Darcie scooped it up. 'Alicia Carlyle's number two slave,' she said into the receiver.

Laughing at the other end, Rachel said, 'I've just picked up Mum's message about Nat. That's fantastic news.'

'Isn't it?' Darcie beamed. *'Rachel,'* she mouthed to her mother. 'We all cried,' she went on, 'and now we're trying to get over the shock of Annabelle withdrawing the charge anyway. So she should, she's such a liar. Do you want to speak to Mum?'

'Please.'

Taking the phone, Alicia said, 'I take it you've been in surgery all day?'

'Correct, and I'm exhausted, but we have to mark the occasion tonight. What are your plans?'

'Actually, Cameron's offered to take us to a place of Nat's choosing, which I haven't got round to telling Nat about yet, but wherever it is, why don't you join us?'

'We'd love to. Todd has football training, but he can always skip it, and whatever's on anyone else's agenda will be dropped the instant I tell them. Call me back when you know where we're going.'

As she rang off Alicia said to Nat, 'So what do you think? Would you like to go out somewhere?'

He shrugged, still seeming shell-shocked and not quite able to take everything in.

'I know,' Darcie cried, 'let's go to that place in Wells, next to the post office. Everyone says it's really cool. I can't remember what it's called.'

Whatever it was called, if it was next to the post office, it was close to the town hall, and since Alicia didn't think Nat needed a reminder of his first day in court, she said, 'We could always just go across the road to the Traveller's.'

Nat turned as someone knocked on the door.

'It could be Uncle Robert,' Alicia told him. 'He said he was going to pop over after you got home from school.'

Colouring as he recalled how abrupt he'd been with his uncle the last time he'd called round, Nat went to answer the door.

'Hello, Nat,' Robert said fondly.

Feeling his colour deepen, Nat said, 'Hi. Come in. Mum's expecting you.'

'I imagine she's told you the good news by now,' Robert said, as he started along the hall. Then he grunted as his niece threw herself at him in jubilation.

'It was you who made her change her mind, wasn't it?' Darcie insisted. 'I knew you would. You're so brilliant.'

'Actually, she came to the decision on her own,' Robert told her, 'but I'm very glad she did.'

'It would have worked out anyway,' Darcie gabbled on, 'because Oliver got the police to throw it out.'

'Hi,' Alicia said, embracing him. 'Thanks for coming over. Would you like a drink?'

'Yes, I think I would,' he replied. 'If you have some wine . . .'

'We have,' Darcie announced, tugging open the fridge, 'unless Mum's drunk it all.'

Rolling her eyes as she pulled out a chair for Robert to sit down, Alicia said to Nat, 'Would you like a glass too?'

'In a minute,' he said. 'I want to go upstairs and send some emails first, if that's OK.'

'Of course,' she said, kissing his cheek.

'So do I,' Darcie cried. 'I have to let everyone know Nat's won, and that Annabelle's a . . .' She stopped just in time, and glanced uneasily at her uncle. 'That Annabelle's changed her mind,' she said, and treating him to another boisterous hug she charged up the stairs after Nat.

'Sorry about that,' Alicia said, starting to pour the wine.

Robert shook his head, as though to dismiss it.

Passing him a glass, she brought her own to the table and sat down too. 'So,' she said, after they'd toasted an end to the nightmare, 'did she really come to the decision on her own, or did you lend a guiding hand?'

'No, it was all her,' he replied. 'I think she started to realise just how deeply it was affecting everyone, and probably what she'd have to go through herself when the time came . . . She has a lot of issues going on that need straightening out.' His eyes met hers as he said, 'That wretched affair has a lot to answer for. The damage it's caused, and the fallout . . .'

Alicia looked down at her wine, but as she started to respond he said, 'She tells me she saw Nat yesterday and thought he'd been crying, though whether that was what clinched her decision is hard to say.'

'Yes, he mentioned seeing her down by the bridge. He was afraid it might be some kind of trap to put him in breach of his bail, so he called his lawyer to report it.'

Robert nodded slowly and took a sip of his drink. 'She's still insisting she was telling the truth,' he said, 'but I'd like to think that's because she's astute enough to realise that if she admits she was lying there's a good chance she'll be prosecuted.'

Alicia kept her feelings about that to herself for now, not wanting anything to spoil today. However, if Annabelle continued to insist she was telling the truth, the ordeal wasn't over yet. 'So how are things at home?' she asked. 'I can't imagine Sabrina's too happy about the decision.'

'No, she isn't,' he admitted, but that was as far as he went.

Steeling herself to confide what was uppermost in her mind now, she said, 'I don't know if I'm doing the right thing in telling you about this, but I've found a letter from Craig to Mum. In it, he's talking about the affair, and what it meant to him. I wouldn't . . . Well, I . . . Would you like to see it?'

After giving it some thought, he shook his head, 'No, I don't think so,' he answered. 'I've come to some decisions of my own lately, and I can't see how going over old ground will serve any purpose.' His eyes came up to hers. 'Did it tell you anything you didn't already know?'

She swallowed as she looked down at her drink. 'Let's say it laid a few ghosts,' she replied. 'It also turned into a cathartic experience for Nat when I gave it to him to read.'

As Robert sipped more wine, Alicia regarded him closely.

'What is it?' she asked. 'I can tell there's more on your mind.'

He waved a dismissive hand. 'Not now,' he said, hearing the thump of footsteps on the stairs. 'Maybe we'll go out for dinner somewhere next week, just the two of us. It's been a while since we did that. I'll probably be able to tell you more by then, anyway.'

Her eyebrows rose. 'I'm intrigued,' she smiled, holding out a hand for Nat's as he came into the kitchen. 'That didn't take long,' she commented.

'I did a round robin,' he told her.

Her heart swelled as she looked up at him. The load seemed to be lifting from him by the minute, allowing her glimpses now of the brighter, livelier, and very handsome young son she'd always known.

'So, do I get a glass?' he asked, rubbing his hands together.

'Of course. Help yourself, then come and sit with us.'

Glancing at his watch, Robert said, 'Actually, I'm afraid I can't stay much longer. I have to meet a colleague at the labs before he flies off to Dubai.'

'Oh, I was hoping you might be able to stay and meet Cameron,' Alicia told him.

'Cameron?' Robert echoed in surprise.

'He's Mum's new mentor,' Nat explained, sinking down in a chair. 'He's mega in the art world and has a fantastic dog.'

Robert gave Alicia a look of encouragement.

'It's not what you're thinking,' she informed him. 'We're just friends.'

'He's going to show some of Mum's work in his gallery on Bond Street,' Nat elaborated. 'When she can find time to go up there. And he's been helping her sort out some local talent to put in the shop.'

'Well, it all sounds mighty friendly to me,' Robert teased, drinking up his wine. 'I'll look forward to meeting him.'

Standing up to embrace him, Alicia said, 'Thanks for coming over.'

Robert touched her cheek fondly. 'There's one other thing before I go,' he said, looking from her to Nat. 'I don't know how you're going to feel about this, and she's likely to change her mind by tomorrow, but Annabelle wanted me to ask you if you'll see her.'

Nat's glass stopped in mid-air as his face started to drain.

Alicia's eyes darted from him to Robert. 'I don't think that's a very good idea,' she answered for him.

'Don't worry, I told her it probably wouldn't happen,' Robert assured her.

Nat put his glass down. 'I'm sorry,' he said, 'but after everything, I just can't trust her.'

'I was sure that's how you'd feel,' Robert replied, 'and I can't say I blame you,' and after giving him a hug he allowed Alicia to link his arm as they walked to the door.

'Actually,' Nat said, coming into the hall behind them, 'tell her as long as someone else is there, like you, then I'll think about it.'

Chapter Twenty-Five

After a near sleepless night, still deeply distressed by Annabelle's behaviour, and worrying herself sick over whether she still had a future with Robert, Sabrina could hardly bear to look at herself when she got up in the morning. One glance in the mirror caused her insides to shrink. Her eyes were bloodshot and heavy, and her skin was as puckered and puffy as an old sponge.

Splashing cold water on her face, she dabbed it with a towel and began trying to repair the damage wrought by so much angst. She must do her best to remind Robert, when she saw him, of how attractive he'd always found her, or she wouldn't be able to stop this runaway train she could sense heading towards her.

She knew he was already up, because she'd heard the guest shower running about twenty minutes ago. She'd also heard him return home from his meeting last night, but when she'd got up to ask him if he was coming to bed, he'd told her he still had a lot of work to do, so he'd sleep in the guest room in order not to wake her.

She'd known it was an excuse, just as she knew that something vital had shifted in their marriage, but no matter what decisions he might have reached, she wasn't going to allow herself to believe that she couldn't change his mind. She needed to talk to him and explain how foolish she'd been not to have realised before how very fortunate she was to have him for a husband. More than that, *much, much more*, she loved him in a way that made anything she'd ever felt for anyone else pale to insignificance (with the possible exception of Craig, but of course she wouldn't be so insensitive, or stupid, as to tell him that, and anyway she was no longer sure it was true).

She would make it clear that she was prepared to do anything he asked to try to make up for all the heartache and pain she'd caused him, and Annabelle. They could start afresh, she'd tell him, draw a line under everything that had happened, including all this dreadful rape business. She might even consider apologising to Alicia for the remark she'd made about Nathan and Darcie at the Roswells' party, if it was what he wanted. Anything, just as long as he didn't say he could take no more.

Dressed in plain black jeans and a tight-fitting polo neck, and with her hair clipped in a tasteful tortoiseshell slide at the nape of her neck, she let herself out of the bedroom and went to listen at Annabelle's door. Hearing nothing, she pushed it open. The curtains were still drawn, and she could make out Annabelle's shape beneath the covers. Apparently she was still asleep, so she closed the door quietly and started down the stairs. She needed to straighten things out with Robert first, then she'd be ready to confront her daughter.

Tomorrow, Sabrina, you and I will need to talk, he'd said yesterday. As she recalled the words now, they were resonating so ominously through her head, like dark prophecies of doom, that she almost stopped and ran back to her room. She wanted to hide, the way she had after Craig, to bury herself under the covers to try and escape a world that was turning into a place she was afraid to be. But there was no need to be afraid, she told herself firmly. It was only Robert she was dealing with, her husband, the man who loved her, *adored* her, and would forgive her anything.

Finding the kitchen empty, she set about brewing a fresh cafetière of coffee, which she placed on a tray together with two cups and a selection of biscuits, and a single rose that she plucked from an arrangement on the table and popped into a dainty vase. Then, steeling herself bravely, she carried it over to his office.

'Can I come in?' she called out, unable to knock.

When he opened the door her heart immediately tripped with unease. His expression was too grim to be welcoming, but she smiled anyway, saying, 'I hope I'm not interrupting. I heard you get up and thought you might like some coffee.'

Noticing two cups as he stood aside for her to come in, he said, 'Are you intending to join me?'

'Only if it's OK,' she assured him. 'If not, I can always . . .'

'It's fine,' he told her. 'We need to talk, and I guess now is as good a time as any. Where's Annabelle?'

'Still asleep.'

He nodded, and closing the door, he waited for

her to pour the coffee, then sat down on the sofa facing the one on which she was perching nervously. Yesterday Annabelle, today Sabrina.

'How was your meeting last night?' she asked chattily as she offered him a biscuit.

Declining, he said, 'Much as I expected.' He took a sip of his coffee, then putting the cup down again he gazed steadily into her eyes. 'I hope you agree,' he began, 'that we can't go on like this, so . . .'

'I know,' she came in hastily, 'and I'm . . .'

'Please listen to what I have to say.'

'No, you need to hear . . .'

'Sabrina!'

The sharpness of his tone brought her to a stop.

'I think we have to accept that our marriage is no longer working,' he said gravely.

'But it can . . .'

His hand went up. 'I've tried hard, since it started breaking down,' he continued, 'to hold it together, but we've reached a point now where there's no more I can do. I'm sorry it's come to this, but . . .'

'No, no, wait,' she gasped. 'You don't understand. I love you, Robert, I want us to be together . . .'

'Whether or not that's true . . .'

'It is. I swear it. You're angry now, and upset, after everything that's happened. We all are, but it would be silly, and wrong, to do anything drastic. We can make things all right again.'

'All this time, since Craig,' he went on, almost as though she hadn't spoken, 'I've believed we could somehow get past the difficulties, but your obsession with him, and the way you still can't let go, even after all this time, makes it impossible for us to stay together.'

'No! Please don't say that,' she cried, trying to stifle the panic. 'What happened with Craig, I had it all wrong. I thought he was the great love of my life, but he could never be that, because it's you. I know that now, more surely than I've ever known anything. I got carried away during the affair. I couldn't see straight . . .'

'It wasn't just during the affair,' he reminded her. 'It's the way you were after, refusing to come near me for months, going to pieces in front of Annabelle . . . You took to your bed and wouldn't get up for weeks. You kept threatening to kill yourself because there was no point carrying on. And the saddest part of it all is that you still don't seem to realise, or at least accept, how much damage you caused your daughter during that time. You have no relationship with her, Sabrina. You've become so wrapped up in yourself and your own world that you might just as well have walked out of the door and abandoned her two years ago, for how much good you've been to her since.'

Sabrina's eyes were bewildered and defensive.

'She has no respect for you, and who can blame her? She's utterly devastated by the way you turned your back on her, and angry and frustrated and almost completely rudderless. She hardly knows right from wrong any more, and one of the most tragic things I've come to find out over this summer is how little respect she has for herself. That's why she's sleeping with anyone who wants her. She doesn't care about herself. She thinks she's worthless, because that's what you've indicated in your treatment of her.'

Sabrina's face was ashen. 'I love my daughter,' she said shakily, 'and don't ever try to say I don't.'

'I wouldn't, because I know that deep down you do, but you never show it in the right ways. You don't even seem to realise that this cry of rape has very probably been a cry for your attention. She's trying to get through to you in any way she can, and you're still not hearing her. Something happened out there in those woods back in July, and you've never really sat down to discuss it with her. Just two days ago she had an abortion, and I'm not sure you've even asked her how she is.'

'Of course I have . . .'

'Your relationship with your daughter is the most important in both your lives. I'm aware that on some level you know that, but lately you've come to set so much store by being invited to the right parties, or book clubs, or God knows what else fills up your diary, that it's really not surprising that everything between you and Annabelle is breaking down. She looks to you for guidance, as a role model, and all she sees is you attaching more importance to the trivia of your life than to her – or going to pieces over an affair that she didn't even know about at the time. Imagine how confusing and frightening it was for her when you started to reject her. Try to think about how unprepared her survival instincts were when they kicked in, so is it any wonder they've got it so wrong?'

Sabrina's eyes were heavy with confusion. 'I couldn't help the way I was,' she said plaintively.

'When Craig and I . . . At the time we were forced to part . . .'

'You weren't forced,' he pointed out. 'Craig chose to stay with Alicia, and in my opinion that's what triggered the hysteria that came after. You simply couldn't take the rejection. You thought you were better, or more deserving than my sister – actually I don't know what was going on in your head, but the way you've fixated on trying to get rid of her since she came back to Holly Wood only proves my point. You're jealous of her, and I think you always have been. For all I know it's why you seduced her husband, to try to prove to yourself, or to her, maybe both, that she can't always win, or that someone's noticing you even if she isn't – which she wasn't when Darcie was a baby. Does it all stem from that? I don't know, but I do know that you seem almost as obsessed with her as you were with Craig. You've tried to stop her earning a living, you've even gone so far as to try to use the situation between Nathan and Annabelle to force her out of the village. Well, Sabrina, you're right in thinking that you can't both go on living here, but you're wrong in believing she's the one who has to leave. This is her home, it's where she belongs . . .'

Leaping to her feet in panic, Sabrina cried, 'This is *my* home! You and I have lived in this house for over ten years, which makes me every bit as much a part of this village as she is. More so, because I'm the one who's been here, on the ground, fighting all their battles, giving to their charities, organising their . . .'

'No one's trying to take any of that away from

you. You've done a lot of good while you've been here, but it's perfectly clear to me that you and Alicia cannot live in the same vicinity, and if you and I are no longer married . . .'

'You can't just throw me out like I'm yesterday's rubbish,' she raged wildly. 'I'm your wife. Annabelle's your stepdaughter. You have responsibilities . . .'

'Which I have no intention of shirking. I shall make sure you have enough money to get started again, and I will continue to pay for Annabelle's education until she finishes university. I will also pay for some kind of mother–daughter counselling if you'll agree to it, because more than anything I'd like to see Annabelle back on the right tracks and starting to become who she really is, beneath all the damage that's been done.'

Sabrina's face was stricken with fear and frustration. Sweat was beading on her forehead, her hands were clenching and shaking. The picture he was painting was all wrong. It didn't fit together in her head, nor would she let it. She must smash it apart before it became a reality. 'What she needs is to be at the same school,' she protested angrily, 'and living in the same house she's known since she was five. It would really damage her if you threw her out on the street . . .'

'I'm doing no such thing,' he interrupted. 'I'll always be here for her, and I'll make sure she knows that, but nothing matters more than her relationship with you. You have to get some help with it, Sabrina, please, for your own sake, as well as hers.'

She started to pace back and forth, wringing

her hands as a jumble of terrified thoughts charged through her head. She knew she wasn't handling this properly, was even in danger of losing, so she had to come at it another way. 'OK,' she said finally, 'I'll do as you say, and take Annabelle to therapy . . .'

'Not just Annabelle, you too.'

'Yes, me too,' she agreed, 'on the condition that we work on trying to repair things between us.'

He sighed wearily, and for a long time he only looked at her, his expression, behind the sadness, as inscrutable as the projects around him. After a while she actually dared to hope that he was going to give her another chance. But then he said, 'I'm sorry, Sabrina. I've already told you . . .'

'You don't have to make a decision now,' she cut in hastily. 'Just give us a chance. Please. Annabelle's . . . She trusts you, she needs you. You can't turn your back on her now.'

'I'm not suggesting you move out today,' he told her, his expression finally showing how torn apart he was inside. 'We can do it in stages, and hopefully, by the end of the year . . .'

'Everything will be sorted out by then,' she promised, assuming a brightness that sparked like a light at the end of the tunnel. 'We'll have pulled ourselves together and put this behind us . . .'

'Sabrina,' he came in gently, 'are you giving any thought to whether Annabelle should continue associating with the friends who led her into bad ways, or at least encouraged them? Or whether she should remain around the boys who took advantage of her? Wouldn't it be better for her, and for you, if you made a fresh start?'

She looked at him desperately. She couldn't deny that, but she wasn't going to admit it either. Then her eyes flickered with hope as she said, 'I know, why don't we all make one? We could move away from here . . .'

'You're not listening to me,' he told her. 'I've already said, we can't go on the way we were.'

'I know, I know, but I'm prepared to change. I'll do anything . . .'

'I'm sure you will, but I'm afraid it's already gone too far. My feelings for you aren't what they used to be. I still care for you, naturally, but I . . .'

'No, don't say it,' she cried, covering her ears. 'You don't mean it. I know you think you do, but you're angry and upset, and I admit I've got things wrong . . . *Terribly* wrong. Let me make amends, Robert, please. We can find some help together, someone who specialises in families. We can all go.'

Sighing heavily, he said, 'I'm not going to argue with you now. I want you to go away and think about what I've said, and try to start coming to terms with the fact that at some point in the not too distant future we will be taking steps to go our separate ways.'

'No! No!' she cried. 'I love you, Robert. I swear it.'

'I know,' he said, 'that's what's making this so hard.'

Much later in the day Annabelle wandered over to Robert's office looking pale and shaky, and very much as though she'd been crying.

'What is it?' he asked, his eyes darkening with concern, as she came in.

'Mum told me that you want us to leave,' she sniffed, wiping her cheeks with the back of her hand. 'It's my fault, isn't it?'

Wanting to shake Sabrina for such a stupid and selfish attempt to get to him, he said, 'Absolutely not. It has nothing to do with you, apart from how sorry I am that it has to happen now, when we're just starting to become close again.'

'I thought we were too,' she said woefully, 'so why do you want us to go?'

'It's not going to happen right away,' he assured her, 'and you can come whenever you like. I'll always be here.'

She was shaking her head. 'I understand why you want her to go,' she wept. 'I would too, if I were you, after what she's put you through, but can't I stay with you? I don't want to live with *her*. She hates me and we'll just be rowing all the time.'

'Believe me, if I thought it was for the best, and I was able to make it happen, I'd let you stay, but a girl your age can't live in a house with a single man who isn't her real father. And besides, you don't really want to be parted from your mother . . .'

'Yes I do.'

Smiling sadly, he said, 'This is a chance for the two of you to start making things right between you, and given the proper help there's no reason why you can't become as close as you ever were.'

'I don't want to.'

'Yes you do. And any time you feel the need to

talk, or to get away for a while, you only have to pick up the phone. I'll be here.'

'It won't be the same as being able to walk across the garden though, or finding you in the kitchen.'

'No, it won't,' he admitted, starting to feel the dreadful void of her no longer being here, even though it was probably still months away.

Her head went down as more tears welled in her eyes. 'No one ever cares about me,' she said brokenly.

'That isn't true,' he said, coming to wrap her in his arms, 'and in your heart you know it. You just have to do your best to be patient with Mum as she tries to work things out between the two of you.' Tilting her chin up, he smiled into her eyes. 'It could be quite an adventure, finding a new home and setting it up together,' he said, hating the words as much as the false cheerfulness he was putting behind them.

'It might if you were there,' she replied, and as her head went down again he wrapped her tightly back in his arms. This was proving far, far more difficult than he'd expected, and he still wasn't entirely sure he could go through with it, but for the moment at least, he was determined to hold firm.

'Where's Mum?' he asked.

'She's gone to see June. I expect they'll be discussing tactics on how to get you to change your mind.'

Not having much doubt of it, he pulled a face that brought the hint of a smile to her lips.

'You'll never guess what June said to her on the phone,' she confided, a mischievous little glimmer showing behind her distress. 'She told Mum we should buy somewhere in Holly Wood, and when Mum said there was nothing for sale, June said there was a really nice detached place on the new estate. Bet you can imagine how Mum reacted to that?'

'Indeed I can,' he said with a laugh.

She laughed too, then the moment of humour faded and she said, 'I don't want to leave here, but actually, I wouldn't mind going to a different school. I don't really have any friends where I am now.'

'I'm sure that's not true,' he responded, 'but after everything you've been through, it probably would be for the best if you made a fresh start.'

She didn't argue, nor did she look up, and he could only imagine the pain and confusion in her young heart. She'd been through too much already, and here he was putting her through even more.

In the end she said, 'So did you ask Nat if he'd see me?'

'Yes, I did. He's thinking about it, but he says if he does, he wants someone else to be there.'

At last she brought her head up, and his heart ached with guilt to see the anguish in her eyes. 'That's OK,' she said. 'I don't mind that, as long as it's you.'

Two days later Nat walked along The Close towards the high street, knowing his mother's and Darcie's eyes were following him. His anxiety about this meeting with Annabelle, together with his suspicions of her motives, were increasing with each step he took.

'Just make sure you're not left alone with her,' Darcie had cautioned darkly before he'd left. 'We know what she's capable of now, and we don't want the police coming down on us again.'

'Don't worry,' he'd replied, ruffling her hair, 'Uncle Robert's promised to be there the whole time, so I shall be as safely chaperoned as one of your Jane Austen heroines.'

He was wondering now if he really wanted his uncle to hear everything Annabelle might have to say, but then reminding himself that he had nothing to hide, or to fear – apart from her lies, of course – he pushed himself on.

There was no sign of anyone as he approached the house at the end of Holly Way, but the gates were open and to his relief there was no sign of Sabrina's car. She was someone he really didn't want to see, ever again if he could help it.

He knocked twice and turned in the porch to stare back towards the street. He guessed the Holly Wood grapevine would be buzzing by now, because someone was sure to have seen him coming here. How were those who'd taken sides feeling now? Did it matter? Not really, but he knew it would be a while before he could forgive those who'd cold-shouldered his mother over the past seven weeks.

Hearing footsteps in the hall, he turned around and gave a small smile as his uncle opened the door.

'Nat,' Robert said warmly, standing aside. 'Come in. Sorry if I smell a bit smoky, Annabelle's been helping me with a fire in the garden. She's still out there, actually.'

'Thanks,' Nat said, as he stepped into the marble-tiled hall. The smell of the place immediately wrapped itself around him, bringing images from the past that filled him with a sense of nostalgia, and a much more uneasy mix of emotions as the stolen times with Annabelle seemed to waft down from her room. 'Where's Sabrina?' he asked, as Robert directed him through to the kitchen.

'She's shopping in Bath. Would you like a drink of something?'

'No, I don't think so, thanks. Do you know what Annabelle wants to talk about?'

Robert shook his head. 'I'm guessing it'll be about what happened,' he said, 'but she hasn't specifically told me that, so I'm as much in the dark as you are.'

'You're going to be there though, aren't you?' Nat said, needing confirmation.

'I am, but she says she'd like to talk with you privately at first. Don't worry, she's suggested you go and join her in the garden, and I'll be right here in the kitchen where I can see everything that's going on.'

Nat glanced outside to where Annabelle was hunched inside a black anorak, throwing hedge clippings and dry leaves on to a smouldering pile. 'You understand, don't you?' he said. 'I just don't want her pulling any more stunts.'

'I don't think you need to worry about that,' Robert assured him.

Nat cast him an anxious look. 'I'll go out there then, shall I?' he said.

Robert nodded. 'I'll make some hot chocolate

in case you feel like some when you come in. There's a bit of a nip in the air today, don't you think?'

As Nat wandered across the lawn to the edge of the vegetable garden where Annabelle had started to poke the fire with a stick, he picked up a stray stump of wood and threw it into the struggling flames as he joined her.

'Hi,' she said, colouring slightly as she glanced at him. Her hair was pulled back from her face by a curly black scrunchy, and her eyes seemed different, he thought, kind of lighter and less full on. Then he realised she wasn't wearing any make-up. It made her look younger, more like the Annabelle he used to know.

'Hi,' he said. 'So what do you want to see me about?'

She shrugged. 'I just thought, you know, that you might want to apologise for what you did.'

He stood very still. 'What are you *on*?' he asked her angrily. 'I've got nothing to apologise for . . .'

'Yes you have, you raped me . . .'

'The hell I did. You were begging for it . . .'

'Yeah, until you started trying to kill me.'

'No way was I trying to kill you. You'd just really wound me up and then you were laughing and telling me to come on . . . You got what you wanted, Annabelle.'

'I told you to stop and when a girl says stop that's what you have to do.'

'It's what I did.'

'Not straight away, and you were really hurting me *and* scaring me. I really thought you wanted to kill me.'

'And as soon as I realised it I stopped. Jesus Christ, you go around with no underwear on, you follow me into the woods, you even offer to teach me how to do it . . .'

'You didn't need teaching though, did you?' she broke in cheekily. 'Except on how not to be violent.'

'OK, I admit I was a bit rough . . .'

'A bit! I was covered in bruises.'

'But I didn't rape you.'

'Yes you did, and then you had to go and say all those horrible things to me, calling me a slut and saying you hoped you hadn't caught anything after going with the biggest whore in Holly Wood.' Her eyes were suddenly shining with tears. 'If you hadn't been so mean to me I might have been able to forgive you, but you just kept on saying I was a slag and I should keep away from decent people because all I was good for was spreading disease around.'

'I'm sorry about that,' he said, dashing a hand through his hair. 'You're right, I shouldn't have said those things, but I was angry and you'd just told me about your mother and the affair she had with my dad. I wasn't thinking straight, and you got me so riled up . . . But that still doesn't mean I raped you.'

'Except you did.'

'Damn it,' he growled. 'You're not . . .'

'And what's more,' she cut in, 'you shouldn't only be apologising, you should be thanking me too, for dropping the charge, otherwise you could have ended up in prison.'

'No way. My lawyers got the charge thrown

out, because it was never going to stand up in front of a jury.'

Annabelle looked puzzled. 'No one told me that,' she said. 'You mean it didn't all stop because I said I wanted it to?'

Realising this could be a bit of an issue for her, he said, 'It might have done, if you'd got in first, but by then my dad's colleagues had drafted a letter to the Director of Public Prosecutions telling him why it shouldn't even have gone into the system, never mind as far as it had. Once the police saw that, they knew they had to back down.'

Annabelle's face seemed pinched and uncertain. 'So actually, no one was really on my side,' she said, her eyes starting to fill.

'Yes, they were. There was the police, for a start, and your mum, and Uncle Robert and half the village . . .'

'Robert tried to stay neutral.'

'Well, that's just him.'

'I don't actually know if my mum ever believed me,' she confided sombrely. 'She says she did, but you can never tell with her.'

'There was still the police,' he said awkwardly.

'It's not like having the whole world weighing in for you though, is it, the way you did?'

'It was just a few lawyers, and anyway, it's not the point.'

'No, I suppose not,' she said, and stared down at the fire again. 'The point is,' she went on, 'everyone thinks I'm a liar now, and I haven't really got any friends any more – I mean Georgie and Catrina say they are, but they don't invite me to anything now. Not that I care, because I don't want to go anyway, but you've still got everything. All your friends, your mum, Darcie . . . I expect they hate me now, the same as everyone else. Robert's the only one who likes me really, but even he doesn't want me here. He says it's because a girl my age can't live in the same house as a single man who isn't her real dad, but I know that's just an excuse.'

'Actually, he's probably right,' Nat told her seriously. 'It would seem a bit odd if it happened, but why are you saying that? Your mum's here . . .'

'He's talking about divorcing her.'

Though surprised, and thrown, he couldn't bring himself to say he was sorry, so he let the difficult silence run.

'Do you think Robert doesn't want me here because I've got such a bad reputation?' she asked in the end.

'No, it'll be because people think the way they do about stepfathers.'

'I do have a bad reputation though, don't I? It's why no one wants to have anything to do with me. I mean girls my own age. Some of them haven't even had a boyfriend yet.'

Not knowing what to say to that, Nat stared down at the flames, feeling their heat on his face and the smoke stinging his eyes. He thought back to when they were younger, and how close they'd been, not only because of the secret games, but because of how well they'd actually got on. They were different people now, though, their innocence had well and truly gone, and he felt shocked and sorry all over again about the way things had turned out between them.

'It's weird, isn't it, that I feel you're the only

one I can talk to,' she said after a while. 'Bet you're not very pleased about that though, because you probably hate me the most of all.'

'I don't hate you.'

She gave him a quick look and started to prod the fire again. 'Are you going to tell your mum what we've talked about?' she asked.

'I don't know.'

She shrugged. 'You're lucky having a mum like her. I don't think mine will ever change. Robert says she will if she gets the right therapy.' She giggled. 'God does she need therapy! She's pretty mental, if you ask me.'

Nat's smile was weak. 'I guess what really matters,' he said, 'is that you put all this behind you and get some decent friends.'

She nodded vaguely. 'Robert's right, it's probably the best thing if I move to a different school, somewhere no one knows anything about me.' She took a breath, then quite suddenly she was sobbing so hard that before he'd even thought about it he'd put an arm around her.

'It'll be all right,' he told her, as she turned her face into his chest.

'No it won't,' she wailed. 'Everyone hates me. They're all talking about me . . .'

'That'll stop,' he assured her. 'Everyone's way more interested in their own lives really. They'll forget all about this before very much longer, and if you're going to move away . . .'

'I know,' she choked, 'but I don't want to be on my own all the time. I don't have anyone to talk to, or anywhere to go, and I know it's all my own fault, but . . .'

'Sssh,' he said, patting her back. 'It'll change, honestly, things always do. Look at us now. A month ago, a week ago, no one would ever have thought we'd be talking together like this, and you're the one who made it happen.'

She gave a shaky sort of smile. 'Because I thought you might want to apologise,' she reminded him. 'I still think you should.'

'I will, for scaring you that night, and saying so many hurtful things, but I swear, when I . . . Well, you know, when we did it . . . I swear on my father's grave I thought it was what you wanted, and when I realised it wasn't, that's when I stopped.'

She nodded. 'And I swear that when I told the police it was because I truly believed you'd raped me – and I suppose I wanted to punish you for everything you said after.'

'Well, you've definitely done that.'

'Sorry,' she said softly.

'Me too,' he said.

Standing at the window, Robert could only smile with relief as he watched a second embrace that seemed to end in an eruption of giggles on Annabelle's part, and a bemused sort of grin on Nat's. It filled him with such pleasure to see them like that, he almost felt light-headed. He could only wish their mothers might follow the example. However, all things considered, he guessed he'd be waiting a very long time for that.

Sabrina and June were sitting in Sabrina's car, parked outside the colourful garages adjacent to the Coach House, close enough to see, but shielded by another car so unable to be seen. They watched in silence as Alicia came out of her front door and went to drop something into the dustbin at the gate.

June cast Sabrina an anxious glance. 'Are you sure you want to go through with this?' she asked doubtfully.

Sabrina continued to stare across the street, glassy-eyed and frighteningly pale.

June wasn't at all sure they should be here. She felt certain if Robert knew, he'd forbid Sabrina to go over there, but on the other hand, considering Sabrina's intentions, it might actually be what he wanted.

As the front door closed behind Alicia June's eyes flickered towards Sabrina again, but she was still fixated on the Coach House, as though seeing through its walls to the woman inside.

A few more minutes ticked by, then suddenly pushing open the driver's door, Sabrina got out. She didn't utter a word to June, nor did she hesitate as she started across the street. She merely kept her eyes trained on the front door she was approaching.

Watching her, June was becoming more concerned than ever by how unstable she'd seemed during this past twenty-four hours. It was reminding her of the early days after she'd broken up with Craig, when everything on the surface had still seemed to be functioning, while underneath it all she was already in pieces. She wondered if she should run after her and try to persuade her to go home. If she felt she had any chance of succeeding she probably would, but she knew she didn't, so the best she could do was sit here and wait, letting Sabrina feel safe in the knowledge that she was close by if she needed her.

Alicia frowned as the sound of someone knocking on the door penetrated through the blare of Darcie's iPod speakers. 'Didn't Nat take his keys?' she said, glancing at the clock.

'Dunno,' Darcie answered, engrossed in the chocolate sponge she was making.

Quickly rinsing her hands, Alicia wiped them on her apron as she went to find out who it was.

The instant she saw Sabrina, her insides froze in shock. 'What the . . . ?'

'Please, listen,' Sabrina interrupted, putting a hand on the door to stop Alicia slamming it. 'I have something to say. Can I . . . Could I . . . come in?'

Alicia's eyes were cold. 'I'm not interested in anything you . . .'

'Please,' Sabrina said. 'It won't take long.'

Alicia stared at her hard, not trusting her an inch.

'I need to talk to you,' Sabrina said shakily, and her eyes filled with tears.

Though unmoved, Alicia stepped outside, pulling the door to behind her. 'Darcie's in there,' she said. 'I don't want her hearing whatever it is you have to say, especially if it concerns her father.'

Sabrina visibly flinched. Then her fractured gaze seemed to fix on Alicia's, as she said, 'I want . . . I'd like to apologise for what I said at the Roswells' party.'

Alicia blinked in disbelief. A moment later her suspicions kicked in. 'Why?' she demanded.

Sabrina appeared confounded by that. 'I just . . . It was . . . I shouldn't have said it,' she finally managed.

'You're damned right you shouldn't, but there's no way I'm accepting your apology, because frankly, I don't trust your motives.'

Sabrina seemed thrown, as though the possibility of being rejected had never occurred to her. Then quite suddenly, as though something inside her shifted, her eyes flashed with temper. 'Perhaps you'd like me to get down on the ground and grovel,' she suggested bitterly.

'If you like, but it won't make a difference. Either Robert's put you up to this, or you've got some other reason for coming here that serves only you.'

Sabrina was about to snap a denial when she seemed to think better of it. 'OK,' she said, pushing a stray strand of hair from her face, 'I've come here because I was hoping that we could put our differences behind us and start again. We both love Robert, and feeling torn between us the way he has, especially with all the dreadful business with Annabelle and Nathan, has been very difficult for him. I think he's unwell, and I'm afraid if we continue this . . . feud, we'll only make him worse.'

Alicia was watching her closely. She was putting on a good show, she'd hand her that, but she still wasn't buying it. 'My brother was here only yesterday,' she told her. 'There's nothing wrong with his health, or nothing that getting you out of his life wouldn't put right.'

Sabrina recoiled as though she'd been slapped. 'How would you know how he is?' she seethed. 'You don't live with him.'

'I don't need to, to know you're lying. So what's this really about, Sabrina? Don't tell me he's finally come to his senses and decided to throw you out? Is that why you're trying to apologise? To impress him? Oh my God, I'm right. He has.' She almost felt like laughing.

Sabrina's eyes turned deadly, but as she started a scathing retort Alicia put up a hand.

'You've had this coming, Sabrina,' she told her bitingly. 'I can only wonder why it's taken him so long.'

'It wouldn't be happening at all if you weren't here,' Sabrina hissed. 'Everything that's gone wrong in my life is because of *you*, first Craig, then Annab—'

'Don't ever speak my husband's name to me again,' Alicia growled furiously. 'You pushed your way into my marriage, you did your best to destroy it, and you broke my brother's heart trying. So go somewhere else with your lies and false apologies, Sabrina, because they won't wash here.'

'No, wait, wait,' Sabrina cried, grabbing Alicia's arm as she started to turn away. 'Please. Think of Annabelle. I know this has been a difficult summer . . .'

Alicia gave an incredulous laugh.

'. . . but if Robert makes us leave,' Sabrina pressed on, 'she won't only be losing her home and her friends, she'll be losing him and neither of them really wants that.'

Not entirely unmoved, though amazed that Sabrina would try to use Annabelle to soften her after all that had happened, Alicia said, 'You should have thought about all this a long time ago, and besides, if I know my brother, he'll never give up on Annabelle even if she's not living under the same roof as him.'

Sabrina's hands suddenly clutched at her head in frustration. 'Look, I understand why you hate me,' she cried, 'but to try and punish me for something I had no control over . . . I didn't ask to fall in love with Craig, any more than he asked to fall in love with me.'

Alicia's expression hardened with anger. 'It's time to stop fooling yourself, Sabrina,' she snapped. 'He didn't love you . . .'

'Those were the last words he said to me,' Sabrina shouted desperately. 'What were . . .'

'You've asked me that before,' Alicia cut in sharply, 'and it's none of your damned business, but I'll tell you what his last words *about* you were, shall I? He wondered how he could have risked so much for so little. You were a madness, a compulsion, he said, but sex with you was *meaningless*.'

Sabrina took a step back, as though she'd been struck. 'You can tell yourself whatever you like, but I know the truth . . .'

'No, Sabrina, all you know is what you've told yourself. In that pathetically sick head of yours you've twisted and changed things to suit your self-delusions and fantasies, when all the time he was here, loving me and his children and doing his level best to try and get rid of you . . .'

'It's you who's the fantasist,' Sabrina cried wretchedly. 'He came back to me, remember? He couldn't give me up . . .'

'But he did in the end, and the only part of it that was difficult then was dealing with the guilt he felt at having hurt me so much. While you, to quote him, were nothing more than an aberration. In other words, you were the biggest mistake of his life and one he regretted till the day he died.'

Sabrina's face twitched and blanched with denial. 'He would tell you that . . .'

'Actually, it was my mother he told. He wrote her a letter, over a year ago, telling her what your affair had meant to him, and how his family always had and always would come first. I could show you the letter, but I won't, because it belongs to me and my children, as did he. You had no right to him, Sabrina, either when he was alive, or now he's dead. So go away. We don't want you in our lives any more.'

As Alicia turned round something inside Sabrina suddenly snapped, and launching herself forward, she slammed her fists into Alicia's back, sending her crashing into the door.

Stunned from the blow, Alicia barely registered Sabrina grabbing a rock; she only saw it at the last moment and managed to spin away before it smashed into her head.

'Noooo!' June yelled, leaping out of the car.

Sabrina spun round as June came racing towards her. 'Stay back, June,' she warned. 'She's had this coming.'

'No, no,' June begged, tripping as she dashed in through the gate.

Darcie flung open the door. 'Mum!' she cried, seeing Alicia picking herself up from the ground. 'What is it?'

'Go back inside,' Alicia gasped, pushing her in.

Darcie screamed as Sabrina threw herself at Alicia again.

Just in time Alicia ducked out of the way, then she was on her feet, dragging Darcie into the hall and slamming the door behind them.

'You bitch!' Sabrina shrieked. 'You're taking everything that's mine and I won't let you.' She stood back and hefted the rock straight through the sitting-room window.

'Robert,' June panicked into her mobile. 'You have to come. We're at Alicia's and Sabrina's . . . Oh my God, she's lost it.'

Inside, Alicia was huddled with Darcie in the kitchen. They both gasped and flinched as another window was broken at the front. They could hear Sabrina screaming and ranting, but Alicia's hands were over Darcie's ears, trying to block out the madness.

'What's the matter with her?' Darcie cried. 'Why's she doing this?'

'She's . . . I don't know,' Alicia answered shakily. 'I'm going to call Uncle Robert.'

As she grabbed the phone she jumped as another rock smashed through a window.

'You don't belong here!' Sabrina was screeching. 'This is my and Robert's house . . .'

June was trying to grab her. 'Sabrina, please stop,' she begged.

'I want to kill her,' Sabrina hissed savagely. 'She's the reason I'm losing everything. She's to blame . . .'

'Sabrina, Darcie's in there. She's just a child . . .'

'I don't care,' and shoving June out of the way she scooped up another rock.

'Sabrina, you have to get a grip,' June begged, trying to snatch it away. 'People are watching . . .'

'Let them. I want everyone to know how much she's taken from me,' and with all her might she flung the rock at the playroom window.

'Oh my God,' June muttered as the glass smashed into a thousand pieces.

'Sabrina!' Robert shouted as he ran into The Close.

She spun round, and when she saw him she yelled, sneeringly, 'Here he comes, riding to his sister's rescue. I'm starting to have my suspicions, you know, always putting her first . . . What the . . . ?' she growled as June wrenched both her arms behind her.

'For God's sake, pull yourself together,' June muttered as Robert ran in through the gate.

'What's happening?' he demanded, looking at June. 'What's she doing here?'

With helpless eyes June said, 'She came to apologise . . .'

'What?'

'I'm sorry, I thought it might be all right.'

Catching hold of Sabrina as she broke free of June, he turned her towards him and was about to demand an explanation when Nat and Annabelle came running down the street. 'Mum rang,' he shouted. 'What's happening?'

Sabrina recoiled. 'Keep that boy away from me,' she spat. 'He's evil. He's a rapist . . .'

Clapping a hand over her mouth, Robert said to June, 'We have to get her home.'

'I'll get her car,' June said.

'Mum, what's the matter?' Annabelle cried, looking terrified as Sabrina started to scream and scream as though unable to stop.

'Nat, go inside and make sure your mother's all right,' Robert barked.

Digging out his keys, Nat threw a look over his shoulder to Sabrina and Annabelle, then opened the door.

'I've always hated you too,' Sabrina yelled as he disappeared inside. 'I hate him,' she told Annabelle. 'He's no good. He raped you . . .'

'Mum, stop, please,' Annabelle begged.

Robert had hold of Sabrina, but she was struggling ferociously to try and get free. Her hair was like a torn nest and her cheeks were streaked with tears and mascara. 'This is your fault,' she raged at Robert. 'You're throwing me out. You don't want us any more . . .'

'Sssh, stop this, please. Now!' Robert commanded, giving her a shake.

'I can't,' she gulped. 'I'm . . . Oh God, Robert, I can't stand it. I can't take any more . . .'

Pulling her against him he held on to her tightly, and as she shuddered and gasped with despair, he felt himself filling up with guilt and dismay. She was right, this was his fault. He should have realised how close she was to the edge, how hard their talk would be for her to take.

'Please don't make me leave,' she begged, clinging to him. 'You're all I've got. I won't be able to survive on my own.'

'What about me?' Annabelle said. 'You've still got me.'

Sabrina looked at her blankly. Then, seeming to realise who she was, she started to sob. 'Annabelle, my baby,' she gasped, covering her face with her hands. 'What have I done to you? Why do you hate me?'

'I don't,' Annabelle cried, going to her. 'You just . . .'

'Sssh,' Robert said, gently cutting her off. 'Let's get her home. There'll be time later for everything else.'

'Yes, I want to go home,' Sabrina wailed. 'Please take me home.'

'June's here with the car,' he said soothingly, and guiding her towards it he nodded for Annabelle to open the gate.

'Is Annabelle coming?' Sabrina choked.

'Yes, I'm here,' Annabelle said, slipping an arm cautiously around her.

'I'm going to call the doctor and ask him to prescribe something to help calm you down,' Robert told her quietly.

'Yes, yes,' she agreed. 'I need to calm down. I shouldn't have lost control like that, but I couldn't help it.' She looked at him anxiously, her head and shoulders still jerking with sobs. 'She tried . . . She tried to say Craig didn't love me,' she said haltingly, 'but I know he did. It doesn't matter now though, does it?'

'No,' he answered, and opening the back door of the car he waited for Annabelle to get in first, then eased her mother in beside her. 'Take her back to the house,' he said to June. 'I'm going to make sure my sister's all right, then I'll follow you over.'

'No!' Sabrina shouted. 'I'm the one who needs you now.'

'I'll be there,' he told her, 'now please try to pull yourself together for Annabelle's sake, as well as your own,' and leaning past June through the driver's window, he hit the button to child-lock the doors.

June looked up at him, and after giving him a small smile of sympathy and encouragement she drove off. They'd been here before, and she felt as saddened and worried as he did that they were here again.

'Are you all right?' Robert said to Alicia as he followed Nat into the kitchen.

'I'm fine,' she answered, turning from dabbing away Darcie's tears. 'A bit shaken up, but we'll survive.'

Darcie's eyes were dark with confusion as she looked at her uncle. 'What's the matter with her?' she wailed. 'Why did she shout at Mum and break our windows like that?'

Both Nat's and Alicia's eyes went to Robert, anxious that he would realise that Darcie was too young to have her illusions about her father shattered yet.

Pulling up a chair to lower himself to Darcie's height, Robert said, 'She's not well, sweetheart. She couldn't help herself, so we're going to get her some help. Now, I don't want you to worry that she might do it again, because I'll make sure she doesn't.'

'But what's wrong with her?'

He sighed and stroked her hair. 'She has a lot

of problems going back a long way,' he told her, 'maybe as far back as when she was a child and her mother ran off and left her.'

Darcie looked troubled. 'Why did her mother do that?' she asked, seeming unable to comprehend such a thing.

'She met another man and so she left Sabrina with her father, who went on to have lots of different girlfriends. This meant that Sabrina was brought up never really knowing who her mother was, and not being very well cared for either.'

Darcie glanced at Alicia. 'You'd never leave us, would you?' she said worriedly.

Alicia smiled. 'Of course not,' she assured her, while hiding her surprise. She hadn't known that about Sabrina's past.

'Actually, I feel sad for Sabrina now,' Darcie decided.

Nat turned away, and Alicia put a hand on his shoulder. When he looked at her she gave a brief shake of her head. Now wasn't the time to be condemning Sabrina further, especially not while Darcie was around.

Getting to his feet, Robert said, 'I should go and see how she is. Oh, and I'll find someone to come and take care of the windows.'

'Don't worry,' Alicia said, walking him to the door. 'I'll give Rachel's Uncle Pete a call. He'll know what to do.'

As they stepped outside he said, 'Are you sure you're all right?'

'Honestly,' she promised. Then, after giving him a hug, 'So you've asked her to leave?'

He sighed and drew a hand over his face. 'I

don't know if it can happen while she's in this sort of state,' he said, sounding doubtful about everything. His eyes came to hers. 'I blame myself for today,' he confessed. 'I should have realised how fragile she was. Apparently, asking her to go was the final straw.'

Hugging him again, she said, 'You weren't to know she'd react the way she did.'

'I should have,' he argued. 'I saw the way she was before . . . I think it's worse this time. I have to get her some help.'

'It'll be for the best,' Alicia assured him.

He nodded soberly. Then, seeming to brighten a little, he said, 'Things seemed to go well between Nat and Annabelle, so with any luck that little nightmare's in its dying throes.'

Alicia smiled weakly, knowing it would be a long time before anyone forgot this terrible summer. 'I'm sorry you've still got so much to deal with,' she said. 'You know, if there's anything I can do . . .'

He gave her a look of gratitude. 'I have a lot of thinking to do over the next few days,' he said wearily. 'It'll help having you here to talk things through with, if that's OK.'

'Of course,' she told him warmly. 'I'll always be here for you, you know that.'

After touching her face with an affectionate hand, he turned to go, the heaviness of his footsteps seeming to reflect the growing burden in his heart.

Alicia stood watching him, feeling his sadness and confusion pulling through her as though they were hers. Knowing him as she did, she had no doubt he'd do his best by everyone before he considered himself. However, she was going to do her utmost to make sure he wasn't forgotten.

Chapter Twenty-Six

A week later Cameron's car was parked outside the Coach House, piled high with luggage and a dog bed and all the various bric-a-brac and brochures he'd collected during his forays into the county over the summer.

The first signs of autumn were showing themselves now, with the darker nights drawing in and the edge of a chill crisping the air. For the past hour the sun had been dodging between clouds, and there was a welcome lull in the wind that had turned quite blustery and loud during the night.

'Let's hope the rain keeps off until you get back to London,' Alicia was saying as they finished their tea.

'The forecast isn't too bad,' he replied. 'I should make it before the storms start again. Is Robert coming over later?'

'He said he might.'

'I enjoyed meeting him. He's a very interesting man.'

She smiled. 'It did him good to spend some time with you,' she told him. 'It took his mind off things for a while.'

Picking up their cups, he carried them to the

sink. 'He's under a lot of strain,' he said, 'but I think he's come to some good decisions.'

'They'll work for the time being,' she agreed, 'but I'll miss him while he's in London.'

After much soul-searching, and several discussions with a London psychiatrist, Robert had decided to move himself, Sabrina and Annabelle into a rented house in Chelsea for the next few months so that Sabrina could be close to the doctor who was treating her. Annabelle would go to a local school that they were now in the process of sorting, and since Robert had agreed to reschedule his work so that he could be at home more, at least some of the pressure had seemed to lift from them all. There had been no more talk of him and Sabrina separating, and Alicia knew that in his heart he was relieved that this was not happening, at least for now. The road ahead was going to be difficult enough without putting themselves through the strain of a divorce, and besides, it wasn't in him to turn his back on the people he loved, particularly when they needed him so much.

'A part of me doesn't think Sabrina deserves such loyalty,' she remarked, as she and Cameron started towards the front door, 'but at the same time I keep finding myself feeling sorry for her.'

He seemed surprised as he glanced at her.

She shrugged. 'Knowing something about her background now,' she said, 'I can see why she finds it so hard letting go. Anyway, I don't want to go on detesting her. It won't get either of us anywhere, and if you'd seen her when she came here . . . Well, let's just say she's clearly suffered for that affair, and maybe it would be in everyone's best interests now if we all tried to put it behind us.'

There was a look of admiration in his eyes as he said, 'Do you think you'll ever be able to get together as a family again?'

She shook her head. 'I don't know,' she answered truthfully. 'It's still very early days, and pretty hard to imagine, but maybe one day we'll be able to. I'd like to think so, anyway, for Robert's sake if no one else's. That's presuming they stay together, and provided she gets through this, I think they probably will.'

He gave a sigh as he said, 'I guess no one ever considers what the repercussions might be when they go into illicit relationships, or who might end up paying the hardest price. The worst is when it's the children who do, and Nat and Annabelle certainly picked up their share of the flak over this one.'

'As did Sabrina when her mother took off with another man.'

He was about to reply when, behind them, Jasper gave a woof, and turning round he chuckled to see the dog politely tolerating Darcie's clinging embrace in the sitting room, while hoping he hadn't been forgotten by his master.

'Please let him stay,' Darcie begged.

'If I thought he would, he could,' he told her, 'because then I'd have an excuse to come back.'

Surprised, Alicia said, 'You don't need excuses, you're always welcome. I'm just sorry we didn't have much luck finding you a house. Then I'd know for certain you'd be around more.'

'You can count on it,' he said. 'In fact, I've been thinking of sounding Robert out about renting his house while he's in London, so I could come for the odd weekend.'

She smiled with pleasure at the idea. 'That would be lovely,' she replied. 'I'm sure Robert would be keen to take you up on it. It's always better to have a house lived in, and as he knows you . . .'

'I'll wait until he's got the London move out of the way before broaching it,' he said. Then, turning back to Jasper, 'OK, you. Time to go.'

Needing no second command, Jasper bounded into the hall and crashed straight into Cameron's legs.

'He still hasn't quite got the hang of stop yet,' Cameron informed them, with a roll of his eyes.

'Bye,' Darcie said, coming to join them. 'Thanks so much for everything.'

'You're very welcome,' he replied, giving her a hug. 'And thank you for letting me share some of your mother's time these last few weeks.'

'Oh, that's OK, I think she liked it.'

'I hope so,' he said, with an ironic glance Alicia's way. 'Now remember your promise,' he said to Darcie, 'you're going to make sure she starts creating again on Monday, and if she doesn't, you're going to . . .'

'. . . get straight on the phone to you to report her,' she finished. 'No problem. Nat's on the case too, and she can't argue with him because he's bigger than she is.'

'And don't you forget it,' Nat told his mother as he came down the stairs two at a time. 'Sorry, that was Jolyon on the phone. I'm going to spend half-term with him, if that's OK, doing more work experience. He's even offered to pay me this time.'

Alicia looked delighted.

'Oh, and a couple of my friends have been in touch to find out when I'll be in London again. So would it be all right if I see them when we go next weekend to put your sculptures on display?'

'Of course,' she assured him. She was tempted to ask if he'd heard any more from Summer, but decided not to go there in the end. It was time to move on, and though she knew he still minded about the break-up, like everything else he'd been through, he'd get over it, eventually. It was just a pity he hadn't been officially declared innocent of the rape charge. However, things didn't work that way, as she well knew, and what really mattered was that he was no longer facing the harrowing ordeal of a trial – or being subjected to any more unpleasant verbal abuse in the village and at school.

Turning to Cameron, Nat shook him warmly by the hand. 'It's been great meeting you,' he told him. 'Thanks for everything, especially what you've done for Mum, and I don't just mean her work.'

'It was my pleasure,' Cameron assured him.

'She was really down when we came . . .'

'Hello, I'm still here,' Alicia interrupted, feeling herself starting to colour. 'Now make yourselves scarce, you two, while I say goodbye to my friend.'

Holding Jasper back as Nat and Darcie obediently disappeared into the sitting room, Cameron pulled open the front door, saying, 'Go and wait by the car.'

Always happy to oblige, Jasper trotted down the path and settled in a flump next to the gate.

'Good boy,' Cameron murmured, and turning back to Alicia he smiled into her eyes. 'I might not have stumbled upon the right house yet,' he said, 'but I'd like to think I've found a new friend.'

'I'd like to think so too,' she replied softly. 'You've made this summer much more bearable than it would otherwise have been. Actually, more than that, you managed to make me feel happy and optimistic at times when I thought the world might have given up on me.'

'I'm glad,' he said. 'You've made quite a difference to my summer too, and I'm more determined than ever to make this area my second home now,' and pulling her into his arms he hugged her tightly.

'Don't forget, you're starting work on Monday,' he told her, 'and by Christmas you should be clear to open the shop.'

'The children were thinking we should have a party to celebrate, with mulled wine and chestnuts.' It was going to be their first without Craig, and she was already deeply dreading it, but at least the shop was something they could look forward to, having put so much effort into it.

'An excellent idea,' he agreed. 'We can invite our contributing artists, as well as the neighbours and local press. It should get the season off to a very merry start.'

Feeling pleased by the 'we', and hoping his daughters might be around too, she smiled. 'Call to let me know you've arrived back safely,' she said.

'Of course,' he murmured, and after giving her hand an affectionate squeeze he went towards the car.

She stayed at the door watching him until he drove away, and as he turned the corner at the pub she felt a familiar sense of loss coming over her. The need for Craig was always with her, but she was going to miss Cameron too, she realised, and maybe more than she'd expected.

Turning back inside, she closed the door behind her, and felt buoyed by the fact that they'd be seeing him again in a couple of weeks. She wasn't sure yet about Nat's suggestion that they invite Annabelle to come and help set up the display – she'd make a decision about that after discussing it with Robert. However, with the way things were at home, it would probably do the poor girl the power of good to get away for a while.

'So, did you kiss him?' Darcie demanded as Alicia came into the sitting room.

Alicia gave a laugh of surprise. 'No, of course not,' she answered, feeling herself starting to blush.

Nat was regarding her closely.

'I didn't,' she cried, throwing out her hands.

'In that case,' he said, swinging her into his arms, 'here's one to keep you going,' and he planted a resounding smackeroo full on her cheek.

'And here's another,' Darcie cried, leaping up to join in.

Laughing as they tumbled into a heap on the sofa, Alicia clasped her arms around them and held them tight.

'You know, there's something I keep meaning to ask you,' Nat said, following the direction of her eyes to his father's photograph on the mantel, 'what did Dad say to make you laugh so much in that wedding photo?'

'Oh, yeah, I know the one,' Darcie cried excitedly. 'Dad has that typical look of his going on, you know, when he's said something outrageous and he's trying not to laugh.'

'So come on,' Nat urged. 'Spill.'

Alicia was shaking her head. 'I couldn't repeat it,' she told them, feeling herself bubbling with laughter at the memory.

'He told me once what it was,' Nat said, 'I've just forgotten.'

'Then he gave you the clean version,' she informed him.

'Oh, I know,' he exclaimed. 'It was that he'd just gone through the entire ceremony with his flies undone.'

Darcie shrieked with laughter.

Alicia laughed too. 'That was it,' she confirmed.

Nat eyed her suspiciously. 'No it wasn't,' he said. 'I mean it's what he told me, but it was something else, wasn't it?'

She started to get up, but he pulled her back. 'Talk, or we'll tickle it out of you,' he warned.

'OK, OK,' she gasped as they began their attack, 'what he said was, one day we'll have children and when we do, please don't ever tell them what I just said.'

ALSO AVAILABLE IN ARROW

Out of the Shadows

Susan Lewis

Since Susannah Cates' husband was sent to prison three years ago, life has been a constant struggle to provide for herself and their teenage daughter. Nothing ever seems to go right and the most she hopes for now is that nothing more will go wrong.

Worried by her mother's unhappiness, thirteen-year-old Neve decides to take matters into her own hands. And when Susannah's closest friend Patsy discovers what Neve is up to, she immediately lends her support. As their plans start to unfold they have no way of knowing what kind of fates they are stirring, all they can see is Susannah's excitement, because at last a way seems to be opening up for her to escape her bad luck.

However, the spectre of horror is all the time pacing behind the scenes and never, in all Susannah's worst nightmares, could she have imagined her happiness causing so much pain to someone she loves . . .

'Spellbinding!' *Daily Mail*

'Sad, happy, sensual and intriguing' *Woman's Own*

arrow books

ALSO AVAILABLE IN ARROW

Missing

Susan Lewis

It's an early autumn day like any other as Miles Avery drives his wife, Jacqueline, to the station. Nothing remarkable crops up in conversation, nor do either of them appear anything other than their normal selves. At the station, Jacqueline gets out, takes an overnight bag from the back seat, then turns towards the platforms. This is the last anyone sees of her.

Three weeks later, Miles calls the police. Enquiries are made, but there is no evidence of her boarding a train, or even entering the station. Very soon the finger of suspicion starts to turn towards Miles, and as dark secrets from the past begin to merge with those of the present, the great love he has been trying to protect is not only revealed but thrown into terrible jeopardy . . .

'A multi-faceted tear jerker' *heat*

'An irresistible blend of intrigue and passion, and the consequences of secrets and betrayal' *Woman*

arrow books

ALSO AVAILABLE IN ARROW

A French Affair

Susan Lewis

When Natalie Moore is killed in a freak accident in France her mother – the very poised and elegant Jessica – knows instinctively there is more to it. However, Natalie's father – the glamorous, high-flying Charlie – is so paralysed by the horror of losing his daughter, that he refuses even to discuss his wife's suspicions.

In the end, when their marriage is rocked by yet another terrible shock, Jessica decides to go back to France alone in search of some answers. When she gets to the idyllic vineyard in the heart of Burgundy she soon finds a great deal more than she was expecting in a love that is totally forbidden and a truth that will almost certainly devastate her life . . .

'One of the best around' *Independent on Sunday*

'Spellbinding! . . . you just keep turning the pages, with the atmosphere growing more and more intense as the story leads to its dramatic climax' *Daily Mail*

arrow books